The Highland Heart

By

Bobbie M. Pell

Bobbie M. Pell

Imaginary Lands
Mars Hill, NC

May Celtic blessings follow you!

Cover Photo: Bobbie M. Pell

Cover Design: Glenda Owens

Text © 2015

ISBN 13: 987-1514816998
ISBN 10: 1514816997

DEDICATIONS

This book is a story about fathers and daughters, so I dedicate this novel to the one man who taught me how precious that relationship can be through his constant faith in me, supportive love when life pathways disappeared, and safe haven he created in his warm embrace where all the worries of the world disappear.

For my daddy, Jim Moffitt.

ACKNOWLEDGEMENTS

The seeds of this novel were brought to life at Goddard College. So, I thank my two advisors and mentors, Rachel Pollack and Jeanne Mackin for their invaluable insights along with Paul Selick and the Goddard family of 2004-2006. To Celeste Mergens and Shawn Kerivan, for their uncanny assistance in revisions. To Saundra G. Kelley who proved a task master at line editing. This final draft, undergoing many changes, was reviewed by Dawn Dailey and Nancy Napier whose eagle eyes kept me on target in bringing this book into fruition. To each of you I give my thanks, friendship, and appreciation.

Last, to my husband Ron, for your consistent faith in my abilities when I doubted them, I give you my love.

TABLE OF CONTENTS

CHAPTER ONE
Feshiebridge, Scottish Highlands

The sickle moon, an orange scythe over the farmlands of Feshiebridge, sliced the starry sky as the lovers below quarreled. The pair sat beneath the rowan tree on a knoll above the MacLaren farm overlooking the Feshiebridge valley. These patchwork farms and furrowed fields met river and stones, bordered by stands of ancient Caledonia pine forests.

"Lukas, you know your parents will never let you marry me, no matter how much we love each other. Loving you just isn't enough," said Hannah, her broad, straight shoulders now curling inward.

Lukas MacLaren's woolen plaid wrap, created for keeping out the rains, could not bear the weight of her sadness. His long, russet curls dampened in her wake. He hated to agree with Hannah's doubts, but according to his family, marriage meant only one thing: prosperity and position over true love. Being part of the landed gentry families in the sixteenth-century Highlands, Lukas's mother Eglantyne dedicated herself to protecting these privileges for her three sons, regardless of the price. But Lukas cared for none of these.

He held Hannah close, whispering tender words to assuage her fears, yet he did not succeed.

"I don't understand why you're with me at all," Hannah pleaded, her freckled cheeks flush. She pushed him away and began circling the tree beneath the maze of red-berried boughs. Normally its branches offered Hannah sanctuary, but not today. Her thick, auburn braid swung back and forth like a pendulum. "By the flames of Saint Brighid, you're landed gentry! You could be with any of those fine girls up in Ruthven or even Inverness, but I'm only the weaver's daughter. No title, no money, not even a father, of good repute or ill." She dropped suddenly to ground beside Lukas, ripping the tall autumn grasses. Hannah leaned against the rowan's sturdy trunk, its gray rooted web-work forming a cradle of safety. But could she tell Lukas the depth of her doubts, ugly fears of never being loved by anyone?

"Sure enough there've been tongues a-waggin' in the village as to fair catches amongst the other landowners, but none compare to you," said Lukas, "not my Hannah. Eh, you remember Sallie Murchison from Ruthven? Now there's one that will soon be a plump pumpkin by any man's fire soon enough after sayin' 'I do.' And what about Maire Stewart? I know the lass can bake an apple tart that will sweeten even an angel's tongue but that temper! Why she could put cold fear into a highland warrior with some of her looks."

The smile began to emerge before Hannah knew of its existence, smoothing the lines of her worried face into the vibrant woman Lukas loved.

"Ah, but Hannah," said Lukas, taking her hands in his, "don't you know lass, you're after my very soul," he said. "Your eyes are as green as Caledonia white pines while your laughter," he released his grip then reared back with arms outstretched, "your laughter rings like the silver bells announcing the faeries themselves, so how could I not love you?"

She felt foolish now. Her shoulders relaxed as she smiled coyly at him, inviting him into her heart.

He saw the surrender, so he lifted her chin close to his own, his brown eyes searching the eyes he knew so well. "You shall be my wife," he whispered, his lips gently caressing her cheek. "I swear it." He kissed her deeply now, sealing his resolve.

The two meandered down the hill, arm in arm, cocooned from the world, if just for one night.

The lovers did not see the rowan branches quiver in farewell. Slender golden fingers emerged from the tree, followed by a lithe greenish-gold form, draped in pastel spider silks which flowed between the tunneled bark. Lavender eyes framed by wisps of white hair watched the pair until they disappeared from view. "Later, little one. Later."

"Ma, don't go. Not again," begged Hannah. She sat on the brown woolen blanket that covered her sleeping pallet in the small white-washed crofter's cottage she still shared with her mother, Rosamond.

"But Hannah, you know the Highland Weaver's Guild only meets once a year," said Rosamond, packing the last of her belongings for the trip. "It's a time for me to see old friends, let them know I'm still working." She glanced at the trappings of the weaver's trade along her back wall. Two vertical looms stood in the back right corner with a tiny spinning wheel between them. A high wooden bench with deep pockets on either end for weaving tools sat before each loom. Multi-colored yarns tumbled over the side of the river willow baskets which lined the floor beside the looms for easy access during weaving time. As she finished packing, Rosamond added, "I hope someday you'll join them, too."

"I know," said Hannah, her pout belonging more to a four-year-old than a girl on the brink of womanhood at seventeen. "It's barely been two weeks since you've returned from the Lammas Fair at Perth, and I, I," the young woman hesitated, releasing a longstanding sigh. She jerked the blanket and began straightening invisible wrinkles.

Rosamond stopped, remembering such rifts between Grann and herself so many years ago. The two women had mirrored each other in their tall, slender frames, but the similarities ended there. Grann lived a quiet life of a farmer's wife then widow, happy and content with weaving for the local villagers. She passed this trade on to her daughter, yet never understood the wilder nature of this girl-woman. Rosamond's brown eyes were wide-set crowned with heavy eyebrows (much like her father's); her small straight nose

8

and generous lips framed by long, mahogany brown hair had twisted the heart of many a young lad in Feshiebridge.

Now it was her time to play the mother role. "Hannah, what's really wrong? Why, by the look on that lovely face, I'd say you were a lost sheep among the heather and gorse. Out with it, girl."

Being a plain spoken lass, Hannah finally told her. "Well, it's just that every time you leave, I hate it. I could stand it a bit when Grann was still alive, but it's been years now since she died. I just feel so . . ." Finally the truth blurted itself aloud: "alone."

The last word fell between them, echoing the emptiness in both their hearts.

Rosamond had been forced to live with the loss of her best love, yet she'd been so wrapped up in her grief that she could not see the effects on her only child. She sat on the bed next to Hannah, pulling her close and stroking her daughter's long hair. "Hannah, you're never alone. Not really. You know that Grann is always watching over you, and I'm not gone for long."

As a child, during Rosamond's long absences at market, Hannah wondered if her mother would ever return. Once, after a longer stay than usual, Hannah met her mother as the weary woman came up their path, crying, "I knew you'd come back! I just knew it!" Even now, the darkness of those empty nights swallowed her whole, winding its way around the edges of her heart.

Hannah had never shared this hurt with Rosamond, but now that it was exposed, she had to finish this. "But Ma, when I was little, you left me with Grann for weeks. It felt like forever."

"But you knew I'd come back. I had to go to the fairs to sell my cloth."

"Not always. Not that time when Grann started yelling at you, about my father."

Rosamond's eyes widened. How could Hannah have remembered that dreadful fight? She had been only five back then, and both women thought the child was asleep. Rosamond well remembered the burn from her mother's angry words, yet a smoldering fire of her own had lashed back at the old woman, resulting in Rosamond's hasty flight to Perth. "Hannah that was a long time ago. But I did come back, didn't I?"

Hannah pulled away, looking at the new lines now creasing her mother's brow. "Yes, you did," Hannah replied softly. "But what did Grann mean, about my father? Whenever I've asked you about him, you look so sad, so I just quit asking."

"I've told you before, child. We were living in Perth. Your father died soon after you were born, and since my father had recently died as well, I came home to help my mother. We moved in with Grann and that was that." The lie had a life of its own, and breathed once more, leaving truth in the shadows.

"But don't you miss loving someone, other than me, I mean?" said Hannah.

Hearing this question brought Rosamond's longings for the man she had loved for so many years to the surface, too quickly for retreat. Had not this question of living full-time with Michael, a handsome traveling harper, plagued her since the first time they met in Perth? She fancied them living together on some grand estate where the halls would ring with his musical performances or the playful notes of beginners under his tutelage. Scores of admirers would grace their dinners. But she knew him all too well, and though he drew her deepest love, she would not be the reason for regrets of a life unlived.

Her voice trembled. "Yes, I do, but I really can't talk about that now, or else I'll be walking in the moonlight." She kissed Hannah's forehead, whispering, "You have to trust me, Hannah. It's all for the best."

Rosamond picked up her belongings, then turning to Hannah said, "Lally should be here soon. And her parents will keep an eye on you two. Why don't you girls try to finish balling up those woolen skeins in the basket? That will help me when we go to Ruthven for the Market. I'll be back in five days." Leaving all in order, she traipsed into the afternoon sun, her form silhouetted against the small barn as she descended the humble path to the main road.

As the southbound carriage rocked and swayed, Rosamond sat bewitched by her daughter's many questions. How long before the truth would be known? Silenced by lies and deceit. She recounted the men that she had loved, the men who said they loved her, and yet none had ever asked her that magical question. Even Hannah's father, oblivious to his own daughter's existence, initially sought this highlander for only a night's pleasure. But that all changed.

Her heart ached for the love of her handsome harper, absent now these past five years from the Perth market, with no news of him at all. Oh, she had queried, from bar maid to music master, but Michael had simply disappeared. For all her dalliances with matters of the heart, Michael had won her simply, and she feared forever.

She stared into the starry night, fingering the golden pendant underneath her shift, and wondered, "Oh Michael, why have you left me so alone?"

Isle of Iona, Caledonia

The solitary seal sat motionless in the moonlight, facing the stone walls of the Abbey while the cry of the curlew welcomed the night.

Inside the cloister, the monks were preparing for a good night's rest. Most of the monks, that is, except for Brother Aidan and his charge. "Is that enough light for you, friend?" This man, who rose like a giant over the other brethren, stood in the shadows behind his companion peering down at the parchment. He watched his friend create bold black lines then scrutinize minute details on the pale surface. Michael was one of the more talented scripture transcribers on Iona.

"Yes, Aidan. I believe there is just enough ink left to finish. If you'd like to help, the fire is getting thin. Perhaps a bit more peat?" said Michael. He never lifted his eyes from the manuscript before him.

Aidan left quietly through the heavy cell door, descending the upper cloister floors as a cold draft entered the quarters from the open courtyard below. The wind almost extinguished the ivory candle, almost. The red and grey stone walls held the cold close.

Michael completed his task, satisfied with his work. He leaned back in his wooden seat, stretching and lengthening the tired back muscles, strained from their daily chore of holding him upright while he wrote. He wondered if St. Columba himself ever wearied from his solitary scholarly pursuits after arriving from Eireann to establish this monastery. Columba's cell, separate from the Abbey and now grossly overgrown, was singular in its construction, one of the dry-stacked stone bee-hive huts that provided comforting darkness for solitude of the soul. But Michael knew no such comfort, for when darkness fell, it brought him nothing but pain.

His black-tipped fingers ran through his tonsured auburn hair, revealing a bowl-shaped balding dome in the brethren's tradition. He sighed, remembering days when it fell past his shoulders in thick waves. "Other days, other times," he whispered. As he rose unsteadily, a golden pendant, shaped in a Celtic triad knot, swayed inside his cloak. He ached at the remembrance of the gentleness of the one who had placed it around his neck. Her face still lingered in his memories, times spent with his highland lass. Where was she now, he wondered. It had been five years since their last meeting at the market in Perth. Did she come for him at Lammastide when the harvest was aching in the fields? He rounded his shoulders inward like a porcupine curling in defense, laying his face in his open palms. He could not cry anymore. He hated himself for causing the grief that must have carried her back to her home in the hills in Feshiebridge, alone. She would have searched for him, for days or weeks probably. But he had not been able to return to her.

He reached for the walnut cane with the wizard's face impressed into the staff. His thumb caressed the face like always, a silent reminder of people and places now very far away.

Brother Aidan returned with enough peat to last the night. He sat opposite Michael on the small bed, a simple goose-down pallet supported by rope inter-lacings. These sank beneath this monk's large frame. He began to speak, but hesitated, remembering Father Callum's strict instructions at Michael's arrival that none should question the man, so fragile was his state of mind; but that was five years ago, and Brother Aidan only hoped to ease the pain he saw daily plaguing his friend. So he ventured now with boldness and asked, "So, Michael, I wonder if you'd like to tell me what brought you to our humble sanctuary?"

Michael had never spoken of those horrific events, but lately they came without mercy in his dreams. Perhaps by sharing them in the light of day, it might loosen their hold. So he began.

"I'd been commissioned to play before the Grand Duke and his family in celebration of the youngest daughter's wedding on the Isle of Mull at Duart Castle. The Duke trusted my extensive training with master harpers for over ten years to make this celebration a success. As I journeyed from the mainland to the island, I overheard gossip about the couple by the ferry passengers, saying the young woman truly loved another, a stable lad. This gave me pause."

"But surely you did not voice any concerns," said Brother Aidan.

"No, for it was not my place," continued Michael. "After the ceremony, I played as I'd be instructed to the delight of the guests, filling the hall with beloved tunes such as the song concerning a clever young woman outstripping the Devil in

"Riddles Wisely Expounded." I watched the young bride, hoping to see a glimmer of joy in her eyes, yet there was none. The dark-headed groom by her side scowled.

"But what could you do?" asked Brother Aidan, leaning forward now so as not to let a word slip by him.

"I did the only thing I could do. I sang. For my last song, I chose one to match her melancholy. All the women sighed as I finished the tale of the dead lovers rejoining in the afterlife as the brier entwined the birch in "Lord Thomas and Fair Annet." As I plucked the final string, the note hovered in the air, like a vaporous shape, then vanished. Through that song, I attempted to supply hope, for a future love. So when I rose, accepting the applause which soon followed, I glanced sideways at the young girl. Tears glistened her noble eyes, yet they did not fall, knew they could not fall. I saw that pain, and without any consideration for myself, but rather needing to ease her pain, I stole a single white rose from a nearby vase and handed it to her, bowing slightly. She nodded in thanksgiving, yet no smile appeared on her lovely face. The song and this simple act of kindness were to be my undoing."

"But how could offering a flower to a new bride be misconstrued?"

"I did not count on the groom's pride. After I packed my harp, covering it for a walk in the evening air, I proceeded to a nearby inn where the family had provided lodgings since the wedding guests filled the halls of Duart Castle. As I rounded a dark curve, a small band of men attacked me. The velvet night hid their identities at first, yet their curses rang around my head like angry bees. They came from behind, the cowards, and struck me first on the head with something blunt. I reeled, dropping my harp. A fist met my stomach deep in my gut, while another fist, clad with a silver ornamented ring, raked my face, leaving this deep gash across my cheek and my jaw bone hanging limp." The harper's eyes widened as the fears of that night rose deep in his throat.

His hand instinctively touched the scar, as if to hold back the pain. Tentative fingertips outlined the unnatural furrow that now crossed his cheek over the misshapen jaw line, once fancied by many women. But now he held back the tears, determined to tell this story to its near-fatal conclusion.

"Then he screamed, 'You'll never play again, harper! I'll teach you to embarrass me, especially in front of my new bride!!' So now I knew my assailants. A blinding heat seared my hip, wrenching cartilage apart. I fell at the sound of splintering wood and slipped into a world of darkness . . ." Michael leaned forward heavily, the weight of grief assailing him.

Brother Aidan sat still, dumbfounded at this telling, as tears streaked his own cheeks. He crouched beside Michael, towering over his friend who now let the familiar darkness wash over him, his whole body trembling. With arms as big as his heart, Brother Aidan held Michael and made a silent vow to protect him for the rest of his days. Brother Aidan reached for the prayer book then began reciting aloud the prayer for healing: "Healer of Galilee, you come to take upon yourself all our hurts. You hold us when our bodies are racked with pain, our minds confused, self-belief lost, failures overwhelm, and faith falters. Aid us in our loneliness to move beyond tears."

He picked up Michael, helping the weakened man lie onto his bed next to the fire. Brother Aidan pulled the navy woolen blanket over his friend's shoulders then repeated a silent blessing. He slipped silently down the hall to bed.

The comforting words washed over Michael like the waves below his window then he allowed the sea to lull him into slumber . . . until the next time.

Lally MacPherson arrived soon after Rosamond's departure. The two girls, appearing as twins with their matching frames and long braids, sat opposite each other with Lally's upraised palms parallel as the woolen loop skirted around her hands.

"Hannah, you certainly are good at this," said Lally to her friend who moved rhythmically, swiftly, twining the threads into manageable balls for market.

"Well, I should be," said Hannah, "Ma's had me helping her since I was five. I can roll woolly balls faster than you can pray to Saint Brighid. I'm also good at gathering just the right roots and leaves for the dye pots."

Both girls surveyed the colorful skeins of dyed wool lining the back wall with heather yellows, blackberry purples, acorn browns, henna oranges, cedar reds, and St. John's Wort golds: a weaver's rainbow. Underneath these lay multiple iron pots with heavy stains of past dye lots. Two long-handled wooden paddles, used for dipping the wool into boiling colors, hung from a black hook crammed into the grey stone walls along with carders and spiked metal combs.

"Does your mother want you to be a Master Weaver, like herself?" asked Lally, tying off one ball and beginning another.

"Aye, she does, passing down the traditions from her mother to me, then on to my children someday. But . . ." Hannah's voice softened.

"But what? Isn't that you what you want to do?"

Hannah leaned in close to her best friend and whispered, "I really want to be a singer."

Lally laughed out loud, a generous smile gracing her face. "Well, that goes without saying, silly. You've the best voice in the village, not counting your mother. But could you make a living at it?"

"I'd like to try, maybe someday," said Hannah, considering a traveling life. But she knew from her own mother's weaving ventures that life on the road could be difficult for a family, especially those left behind. Hannah reflected on her recent conversation with Rosamond. "Lally, what's it like to have a father?" asked Hannah.

"A father?" asked her best friend. "Well, my father works hard, shouts out commands like a bellowing bull, and always takes my brother's side in an argument. Why do you ask?"

"I miss having one some days, that's all."

"But didn't your father die when you were a baby?" asked Lally.

"That's what Ma has always told me. She never talks about him. But one night, when I was little, Ma and Grann had a terrible row. Often harsh words passed between them, but not like that night, not ever. Grann started scolding Ma, talking about how Ma should find a good man to marry and settle down. But then she said mean things about my father."

"Oh Hannah, that must have been awful," said Lally. Of course Lally had heard the village gossip for years, saying Rosamond had become pregnant before ever leaving Feshiebridge, but the young girl never put stock in the vile insinuations. But now, for some reason, she wondered how Hannah felt about it all. "So, do you believe her, your mother I mean, about your father living in Perth and him dying so suddenly after you were born?"

Hannah closed her eyes, recalling the whispers of villagers as she walked past or the old women pointing at her, shaking their heads. Even if her mother's story were true, the shame of the possibility that her parentage lay here, in Feshiebridge, accompanied her every day. Could he have been a married farmer, or lad too young for such responsibilities? She opened her eyes and shook herself as if from a dream saying, "Believe her? Of course, I do. My mother might lie to others, even to Grann, but she would never lie to me, especially about something this important." Yet deeper still, a part of Hannah wondered, reflecting on those endless nights during her mother's absences, filled with dark dreams. She faced her friend, "Lally, I miss not having a father's love. How does it feel?"

"Hmmm. Well, my father breaks more peace than makes it," said Lally, laughing aloud. Then she quieted, "But there's nowhere in the world I'd rather be when I'm hurt or scared than in my father's arms. It could be storming all about, but I feel safe with him."

"I feel that way about Lukas," said Hannah. "When he holds me, it's like the highlands themselves curling about me, protecting me."

Lally scooted closer to her friend. "Oh Hannah, tell me what it feels like to be in love, really in love?" asked Lally, giggling then almost dropping the wool onto the floor.

"I feel him before I see him," said Hannah with a dreamy lilt in her voice. She cut the thread then tossed the ball into a large basket. "It's like tiny silver pins pricking my skin, but from the inside-out. Sometimes, when I see him, I shiver."

"Ooooh," whispered Lally. "Go on."

"Why, my Lukas," she smiled, standing up then lifting her hands high, twirling like a blown oak leaf in the afternoon breeze, " he's such a fool sometimes, but I love how his laughter rolls across the fields. It startles his sheep from their lunch, and they bleat loudly, scolding him. Then Lukas, that silly goose, bleats back as if he's actually talking to them." She gazed across the hills, suddenly somber. "But Lukas could have any of those finer Ruthven girls, the ones with lace gloves and fancy cauls for their bouncy curls." She palmed invisible curls with a false air of superiority. "But even though I can read and write a bit, I'm still from common stock. I know I'm just not good enough for him," she continued, "at least according to his family."

"Then you'll have to let them see what a fine match he'd make by marrying you!" She stood up, strutting her shoulders and hips about like the finest hen in the farmyard. Lally squared off to Hannah so her point would be clear. "Hannah, you love him. He loves you. Give Lukas time to prove it to you."

"You're just saying that because you're my best friend," sulked Hannah.

"You're right! I am, but you forget it yourself sometimes. I just wonder where you'd be without me to remind you!" She reached out, hugging Hannah fiercely.

"But what have I to give him?" Hannah searched her friend's face for answers she could not find alone.

Lally beamed confident rays through Hannah's despair. "Give to him? I'll tell you why that boy should be grateful you even look his way. You're the smartest girl I know, able to weave and add up sums at the market without flinching. You've the loveliest hair, outshining even the golden oak leaves in the fall. Everyone knows your singing is matched only by the birds you practice with, and I don't know a kinder person in all of Feshiebridge!"

Hannah pulled Lally close and whispered, "My soul aches to be with him. When he looks at me, the world melts."

Lally clutched Hannah's hand, gave it an encouraging squeeze then asked quietly, "Hannah, the Samhain fires will be burning soon." She imagined the act of ritual coupling for those over fifteen, symbolizing the union of earth and spirit on All Soul's Night. "Will you . . .," her voice faltered, "Will you take him into the woods?"

Hannah considered the question carefully, and leaning forward so not a drop of conversation could be lost, she whispered, "I will.

CHAPTER TWO

The harvest moon cast a tangerine glow over the wooden pilings which dotted the hilltops as the farm folk of Feshiebridge prepared for the annual Samhain bonfires. On All Soul's Night, the sacred festival beginning on the eve of October 31st, revered souls gone from this earth may revisit while traditions keep evil spirits from mischief. Father Logan, the local priest who believed in merging the Old Ways and the New Religion, joined in this festival marking the beginning of a new year.

Hannah and her mother Rosamond crossed the dark pine lines of the Caledonia forest to the open hillside above the MacLarens' property. Their tall and slender shadows danced with the evening shades of Samhain darkness as they wove through dense bracken ferns. Each woman carried a carved turnip lantern, its otherworldly face illuminated by pale golden flames. Discordant drum beats from the goat-skinned bodhrans summoned villagers to the hilltops ablaze with flickering flames, spitting oaken scents into the evening air while connecting the rhythms of earth with mortals. The pulsating beat mirrored Hannah's uncertain heart as she followed Rosamond to the clearing. Tonight she would choose Lukas, but would he accept her?

Darkness cloaked the night as a blue-black velvet canvas for lanterns, flames, and stars. All sacred. All glowing. All welcoming the night.

For this special night, Hannah selected her clothing with the greatest of care: a golden kirtle with ivy embroidery, a hunter green ribbon to grace the tip of her long auburn braid, and her brown cloak.

After placing her lantern in the ring of others encircling the fire, Hannah parted company with her mother then stood next to

Lally in the circle. She noted Nell Robertson squatting between two neighboring girls, giggling, then pointing towards a tall boy who stood across the fire. It was Lukas. Hannah glared at Nell, unwilling to believe that Lukas would ever couple with anyone but herself. Yet the evening rituals were clear, and if Hannah remained shy without revealing direct intentions, then Lukas would have no choice.

She watched the shadows flit across Lukas's squared jaw and subtle cheek bones then flee to their next prey. Memories of caressing those lines, fingertip tracings etched with Love's pen, enveloped her. His eyes were hidden, but she knew them all too well. She must act quickly once the ritual storytelling ends.

The drumming increased as songs of the past bonded neighbors and friends. They danced freely around the flames with arms swaying in primal joy. Lukas winked across the fire at his love while Hannah sang with a fevered fullness as night-veiled voices united into lusty choruses, corn stalk warriors at the ready. Rory, the youngest MacLaren, posed as the Green Knight, clad in greenery, spiraling amidst the merrymakers holding high the holly bush to mark the old year's passing.

Without signal, the drums ceased. The dancers took their seats upon the ground, awaiting the seanachaidh, the storyteller. Tonight it fell to Rosamond. Her silhouetted form rose from the gathering, solitary in her purpose.

Hannah so admired her mother's tellings, full of pathos, incident, and passion. If the tale sprouted its origins from one of the ancient ballads, Rosamond often sang the refrain, encouraging the listeners to actively engage in the story by singing aloud. Once Hannah found herself so deep within that story that she shook at its completion, as if resurrecting from a trance. The power of the word, whether spoken or sung, was one she hoped to master someday as well. Tonight she would simply enjoy her mother's gift.

Rosamond began the ancient love story with an old nurse's voice, cautionary and strict in the retelling of "Tam Lin."

"O I forbid you, maidens a'

That wear gold on your hair,

To come or gae by Carterhaugh

For young Tam Lin is there."

She wove narration with verse in such a seamless rendition that all who heard were astonished. She told the legend of Janet MacKenzie who sought to reclaim her family's land from the sidhe, the Shining Ones, the faeries. Janet pulls a rose, the only piece of beauty left in the ruins of her clan seat, when Tam Lin appears, demanding a ransom. Rosamond now changed her voice to seducer, roving the edges of the crowd and grazing her fingertips across the shoulders of aging men.

"There's nane that gaes by Carterhaugh

But they leave him a wad,

Either their rings, or green mantles

Or else their maidenhead."

She moved quickly so as not to entice too long then shifted to the impassioned sweetness of Janet as she discovers Tam Lin's captivity by the Faerie Queen. Glances darted across the fire for the listeners knew that Janet softens towards this handsome man, and she soon would carry his child. The riddle portion of the ballad occurred when Tam Lin tells Janet that he will be sacrificed on All Hallow's Eve and how she may save the father of her unborn child. Then Rosamond sang the internal refrain so others could join in.

"Janet had kilted her green kirtle

A little aboon her knee,

And she had snooded her yellow hair

A little aboon her bree,

And she's awa' to Carterhaugh

As fast as she can hie."

Rosamond pulled a silver bell from her pocket, jingling it softly at first then more insistently as Janet, at the well by Miles Crossing at midnight, listens for the fairy bells tinkling the arrival of the fairy host. As instructed, Janet allows riders upon the black and brown steeds to pass then pulls Tam Lin from the milky-white horse.

As Hannah listened, she harkened her own thoughts towards what she might do for love, true love. What would be required of her to finally win Lukas? Would he have to choose between herself and his family? Would she need unyielding courage like Janet displayed to release Tam Lin from the faerie spell? The story continued.

Rosamond extended her arms, fingers taut, then screamed in anger as the Faerie Queen berated the couple for their deception. Tam Lin is transformed into a lidless adder then a raging lion, but Janet holds firm. Rosamond became Janet as she embraces the phantom lover. She drops him into the well when the beloved becomes a fiery brand, sprinkling him with holy water. Soon Tam Lin climbs from the well, fully mortal once more. Rosamond returned to her neutral narrator's voice as the queen rides away in fury, leaving the lovers in a wake of anger.

Rosamond concluded with a final chorus, revering the courage of Janet and all young women willing to risk all for love's sake. A rousing cheer for a story well done echoed through the woods then the crowd sifted into the melting darkness around them.

Hannah knew then that she, too would risk everything for the lover of her heart.

With a renewed sense of direction, Hannah strode like a champion towards Lukas, pushing past the stocky frame of Nell Robertson heading in his direction.

"Well, who would dare to push . . ." said Nell, but before she finished her remark, the answer stood next to the prize. Nell glared as Hannah gently pulled Lukas away from the flickering embers, lacing her fingers through his own. This night surrendered to the woman's leading. He gave her hand a conspiratorial squeeze, assuring her of his own intentions. The wait was over.

In silence, the two plunged into the woods, maid and lover, as the laughter of other couples grew faint with only the resounding yet steady POM POM POM of the drums offering audible paths for the night's events. Lukas threw his black woolen cloak beneath a sturdy oak where the fallen leaves cushioned them as they lay together, side by side, curling into each other.

Despite the couple's desire for each other, an initial shyness opened between them, both taking notice and care with the other. Their lips danced across tender cheeks, outlining the lover's features while fingers fumbled with bodice lacings and trouser ties. Both the kirtle and white shift fell from Hannah's shoulders, exposing her birthmark, the four-pointed star. Her flesh, shimmering gloriously in the moonlight with an iridescent luster, connected with its birthright to be free among its starry brethren.

"Are you real or fey?" he asked, mirroring Janet's earlier request of Tam Lin.

"I am only a woman," whispered Hannah. She leaned forward, never once leaving his stare as Lukas pulled the ribbon from her braid. He sighed, sinking beneath the auburn waves. Despite the chill, Hannah did not shiver.

He kissed her now, hungry for the passion he knew lay within and pulled her close. She matched his intensity, kisses and caresses swirling into one delicious feast.

"Tonight, sweet Hannah, I take only what is given freely," he said.

"Then know well what I want of you, Lukas," she replied, running her fingers in arcs across his back.

"And what more can I give you this night, Hannah darling, than myself?"

She leaned into his ear, her lips lingering, "I want your soul."

She fell back onto the cloak then wrapped her trim thighs around him, instinctively pulling him towards her. She lifted his shirt over his shoulders then tossed it on the ground next to her kirtle.

Innate rhythms matched the drums . . . POM POM POM. They rocked like first waves upon the depths of an endless sea.

Hannah swooned as his lips found the hollow of her hips, trembling beneath his touch. Muscles contracted then released with ecstasy replacing the initial pain of first promise. POM   POM POM. Orange flames fused. She laughed aloud as flesh connected with flesh, their spirits merged in sheer joy.

Passion's fire consumed them both as two bodies eclipsed one another.

"I'm yours," he gasped, "all yours."

Labors spent and limbs in pleasured exhaustion, they redressed then wrapped Lukas's cloak about them, encircling their love.

The drums ceased their play, for the burning embers had released their heat into the night's embrace, and the couple found themselves now chilled but at peace.

The morning sun overslept, leaving a cold wind to wake the lovers. They snuggled close, their breath misted through low over-hanging boughs. They kissed then departed quickly since Hannah would be needed early to assist her mother with dying the wool, for market days were coming.

Hannah scrambled through the forest undergrowth heading towards home down Feshiebridge lane. Recent cart tracks cut parallel ruts down the center while bits of rock littered the edges near the golden bracken. Hannah stepped carefully when she noticed two girls on the path ahead of her, dressed in white smocks covered with autumn colored kirtles and heavy cloaks. By their disheveled appearance, Hannah knew the Samhain drums had led them also to nighttime lovers. Their morning voices were loud and excited, unaware of the traveler in their wake.

"Well, that was certainly fun!" said Maire Stewart, her hips matching the blonde curls heavy with dew that swayed back and forth. "Douglas Finlayson can be fine when he wishes!"

Her companion giggled, then hooked her arm in Maire's as they strolled on. "I went with William, just to see, mind you."

"Did you take the herb, Nell, so no surprises?" asked Maire.

"Of course, silly. My mother wouldn't abide a child born out of marriage," said Nell Robertson. "But you see, I've never lain with a lad, and I wanted to get it right before . . ." Nell poked her pudgy fingers into Maire's ribs.

"Before what?" asked Maire.

"You know, before I marry Lukas MacLaren," stated Nell, as if this news were a well-known fact.

Hannah's steps faltered. Marry Lukas?

"Oh, really," asked Maire, craning her head down to her shorter companion, "and what makes you think one of the finest looking lads in the county is going to ask you to marry him?" She unlaced her arm from Nell's embrace, slowing their pace.

"Why," said Nell, "just two days ago did I not hear Ma telling Pa that Lukas MacLaren was needing to take a wife soon? He'd have to choose between gentry families here or in Ruthven. Also, Ma has been talking with his mother. And you know what happens to couples when mothers begin planning." Nell giggled. "Ma said she knew for a fact that Lukas was not promised."

Maire considered this news, but quickly interjected, "What about Hannah, Hannah MacFey?"

"That freckled girl?" asked Nell with a lofty lilt, gazing at her left hand where she hoped a wedding ring would soon be seen. "What about her?" Nell took advantage of a fallen oak by the wayside, sitting on the bright green moss and spreading her green cloak around her in regal fashion as if she were holding court.

Hannah, still unseen by the pair, ducked into the low brush nearby, concealing herself within hearing distance.

It took Maire a moment to absorb Nell's sentiments. She knew that in spite of the fact that the MacLarens owned one of the largest holdings in the county, they never put on airs. She'd also grown up with Hannah, being only a hedge or so away from the MacFeys. Besides, Hannah's love for Lukas was no secret. Suddenly Maire responded like a feral defender of true love. "But he loves her!"

"Love?" said Nell, raising a smug satisfaction despite Maire's rising fury. "What's love got to do with anything? He's gentry, you fool. Landed gentry! He can't marry any milking-maid-goose-chasing-singer just because he's tricked himself into believing he loves her! Why, I'm sure he's had his good times with her, but honestly, to marry? Ha, the MacLarens would never allow it." With that pronouncement, Nell straightened her shoulders then smoothed a few blonde stragglers back into place.

Hannah's knees buckled beneath her. The autumn leaves rustled as she fell. She was still too shocked to speak.

"What was that?" asked Maire, quickly turning in Hannah's direction. The bracken was so dense, however, that Hannah, wrapping her brown cloak around herself, remained unseen.

"Probably just a squirrel, or maybe a red deer passing through," said Nell. "Besides, what do we know about that girl's parentage? Nobody really knows where she comes from, do they?" The question erupted like a dueling glove tossed in challenge.

"Well, now you're just being silly," said Maire. "She's the daughter of Rosamond MacFey, the weaver." Thinking she had won this point, Maire prepared to walk away, dodging the dimpled tracks.

"Hold on, now. Of course, I know she's the weaver's daughter. I'm not daft," said Nell, lowering her voice now. She stood up and grabbed Maire's arm, pulling the girl down to her face. "But who's the girl's father? Some say Hannah resembles the Goins family in Ruthven more than her own kin! Why, there's lots of stories floating around about why Mistress MacFey really traveled to Perth so many years ago. And then returning here, with no husband, and a baby to boot!"

Hannah clamped her hand over her mouth to keep from shouting.

Maire jumped back as if she'd been slapped. "What a cruel thing to say, Nell Robertson!" said Maire. "What makes you believe that horrible gossip?"

"I heard my Ma and Pa discussing it," said Nell, rising to her full stature. It would have looked comical had it not been so serious with Nell a full head shorter than Maire and both looking like ruffians ready to fight. "My parents say the weaver would take up with whomever she pleased, and might have even gotten herself in a child-bearing way from some gypsy or traveling man. Or even worse, one of the Fair Folk!"

"Well, I can't listen to any more of this rot," said Maire. "I'm going home." She spun on her heels, quickly taking a turn at the right footpath when she heard Nell calling after her.

"You mark my words," cried Nell. "Lukas MacLaren will be married before next spring, and it won't be to Hannah MacFey!"

That was it. Hannah roared from her seclusion like a bristling wild boar. As Nell stood there, Hannah barreled into her, knocking the girl over her royal log into the ferns. Hannah stood over the surprised young woman, shaking with anger.

Nell pulled the decaying fiddleheads from her curls then looked up to determine her mysterious attacker. "Hannah MacFey! What in damnation are you doing? Are you crazy?" yelled Nell. She wobbled as she stood, dusting debris from her cloak.

"How dare you say such things about my mother, you cow!" screamed Hannah, not caring if all of Feshiebridge heard them. The two young women faced each other.

"I can say whatever I please," scoffed Nell, jutting out her chin.

"Not in front of me," said Hannah, and she slapped Nell firmly across the left cheek.

Nell raised her hand to fend off another blow, but Hannah stepped back. "You're not fit to lace my mother's shoes. And as for Lukas, he'll never marry you. I've won his heart, and nobody else shall have it!" She flipped her cloak as she stalked away, leaving a stunned Nell Robertson alone in the road.

"Oh, Hannah MacFey," she said in a low growl, "what a mistake you've made. We'll just see who marries Lukas MacLaren now, won't we?"

The next morning, eager to see Hannah possibly about running errands, Lukas wandered onto the main road where he sat on a fallen log, pulled out a small piece of wood, and began whittling. He soon noticed someone with a small, girlish figure bumping down the road towards him. Even though the hooded cloak was wrapped tightly around the young woman, concealing her face, he knew this was not his beloved, so he continued whittling.

"Why there you are, Lukas MacLaren," said Nell, flipping her hood back and running her fingers through her short brown curls. She sat down next to Lukas, a little too close for his liking who immediately moved further down. Despite his silent protest, she edged closer while he continued whittling.

"Good morning to you, Nell," he said. "And what brings you out so early on such a crisp day as this?"

"Why you do, of course. I've just come from your house after a lovely chat with your mother," said Nell triumphantly. "And she was only too glad to see me."

"Really now," said Lukas. "And what were the two of you magpies sorting out?"

"Why, our wedding, silly!" said Nell.

"Our what?"

"Our wedding Lukas, or rather our marriage. I took over a mulberry cake, so she'd have no worries about me feeding her boy once he's out of the house." She tried to crook her arm through his, but he jerked suddenly, cutting his left palm with the blade.

"Damn it all, Nell! Now look what you've made me do!" He pulled a rag from his trouser pocket to stop the bleeding, but soon the white cloth turned vermillion red.

Nell whitened, worried that Lukas was truly hurt. "Hold your finger up, Lukas! I saw my father do that once after nicking his thumb while carving the beef. Quickly now!" She grabbed his hand, lifting it high above her head. Her cloak opened and flecks of blood spotted the fine taffeta cloth. "Oh no!" she screamed, "Look what you've done! It's ruined, it is!" She rose in a flurry like a ruffled grouse after its prey, hitching up her gown to avoid further mishap.

Lukas noticed the blood flow slowing, so with his hand remaining high in the air, he said with resolution, "Nell, you've got to get this marriage notion out of your head. I'm marrying Hannah, Hannah MacFey. And there's nothing your parents or mine can say to change that. Do you understand that, woman?" By the end of his tirade, he was shouting.

"Well, we'll see about that," she said, huffing under her breath. She turned so quickly that she ran right into Hannah.

"Nell," said Hannah in a low tone. Her indomitable figure towered over Nell.

"Hannah," Nell retorted. She lifted her nose as if to avoid some nasty smell, then waddled down the road, barely escaping the ruts. Soon she was gone.

Hannah now turned her attention to Lukas. "And what have you done to yourself?" asked Hannah, looking at the queer sight of Lukas with his bloody hand raised over his head. She sat down next to him on the log.

"Oh, nothing that matters now you're here," he said, kissing her cheek. Hannah tore a strip from the hem of her white linen shift, took his left hand firmly in hers then bandaged it properly. The bleeding ceased completely as the two sat on the fallen timber. "Now tell me what happened?"

"It's that crazy Nell," said Lukas. "She's been around to see my mother, talking about marrying me, and spreading silly gossip like it's true." He leaned into Hannah, kissing her neck then whispered, "But you know, woman, you're the only one for me."

"Truly?" she asked. "But what about Nell?"

He stood up, stomped his foot, and said, "I've had enough of this foolishness. I'm going to stop her lying tongue before she does any more damage." With steadfast determination, he marched in a measured pace down the road towards the MacLaren farm while Hannah continued down the lane towards the village, each lost in their own thoughts.

As Lukas rounded the barn, practically running into his father, Gerald MacLaren greeted his son. "Good morning, Lukas," said his father, closing the barn doors. The two were headed for the house when Lukas tugged on his father's bloused sleeve, just as he'd done as a younger lad.

"Father, I've something to ask you," said Lukas, "in private."

The older man's curiosity aroused, he led his son under the birch trees where they sat, man to man. Lukas seemed taller to Gerald, now able to squarely look his father in the face. The elder MacLaren stroked his red beard in thought then leaned back on the black-speckled birch, pulling a palm-sized piece of wood and a small carving blade from his pocket. "Well, son, what's this all about?" he asked, whittling the beginnings of a small figurine.

Lukas could think of no proper way to say it, so he just blurted out, "Father, I want to marry Hannah. And even though I would not be pleased to go against your wishes, for I love you and Mother both, my love for Hannah is stronger still." Lukas watched for some reaction, yet his father simply continued whittling.

"Well now, boy, marrying is a serious thing. But what makes you think we would not approve of the match?"

"Oh Father, you know she is not gentry born, like you and Mother," said Lukas. "But I was thinking, with Malcolm being the oldest, and the one to inherit this place someday, that I would prefer to remain a farmer with land of my own, looking after the crops and tending sheep rather than be sent off to cleric's schooling." The boy pulled out his own small blade and wood, mirroring his father, and continued on the piece he had begun before being interrupted by Nell.

The two sat in silence, the elder and the younger, while the weight of experience passed between them. "Remember when I first taught you how to carve, boy?" asked Gerald.

"Aye," said Lukas, "I cut my thumb ever so deep." He looked at Hannah's mending of the morning's incident.

"But not deep enough to wound you forever, right?"

"That's right. Why, there's barely a scar from it now," said Lukas.

"So, if you were to marry a woman, Lukas, say one of your Mother's choosing, would the loss of young Hannah wound you forever?" The old man stopped now, regarding his middle son. He recalled such a conversation with his own father years ago, remembering the blush of true love.

Lukas took a moment before answering. He'd known Hannah all of his life: played in the fields together as children, watched the stars converging in wondrous patterns at night, and grown up in this community of farmers in Feshiebridge. He had taught her to read, and her love for language braided their hearts. Her fiery spirit paired with her nurturing nature made her unpredictable. As a man, he loved her spontaneity. The women he'd met through landed gentry gatherings were simple, polite, and pasty. He needed a strong woman who enjoyed roaming the hillsides, tending the animals. One that loved him for himself, flaws and all. He did not need the fineries of lace tablecloths, high teas, or protocol. He would leave that to Malcolm.

"Father, I crave her very being," he said, releasing a lover's sigh. His simple statement surprised him. It was indeed a fact, not a romantic notion that lay between his lines of poetry.

Gerald MacLaren laughed out loud. "My dear boy, you are done for," he said, slapping Lukas on the back. "I know well how such a burning can last a lifetime."

"You? Do you mean Mother?"

"Aye, son. Do you not recall that most of my kin live in the south of Perthshire, in Balquidder? My parents rallied me about like a cock in a hen house during those damnable dances when I came of the marrying age. They would have me marry one of 'the ladies' befitting a gentleman. But like you, I wanted the open hillsides of the highlands with a good woman by my side. I ventured north, visiting our relatives in Ruthven, when I met your mother at a ceilidh one evening. Lovely she was, with a silvery singing voice. I fell in love before I knew her name." He closed his eyes then smiled broadly.

"She came from gentry herself, yet not so fancy as those in the south. But my parents had an agreement with the Balquidder Campbells that I was to marry Megan. So, against my family's wishes, I married my Eglantyne. My uncle told me he owned property just five miles south in Feshiebridge that he'd be willing to part with for a fair price, so I worked with him for two years then we settled here. So, even though your mother has learned some of the finer ways from my family, you cannot blame her for wanting the very best for her own darlings." He took up his blade again, placing the finishing touches on the shaggy highland cow.

Lukas stood up, his shoulders shivering as an early winter breeze. He replaced the wood and blade in his pocket. "So, do I have your blessing?"

"You do, son. What do farmers need with the ways of proper society anyhow?" He placed the cow and blade back into his trousers then reached for the boy, embracing him. A silent knowing passed between them, father to son, that all would be well. "Besides, you're a young man of one and twenty years now. T's time to put the other girls out of their misery of wanting you," he said, grinning. "You'll get no hindrance from me, but the final say will have to come from your mother."

"Will you talk to her? Please, Father," asked Lukas. He suddenly looked like a young boy caught snatching a cooling pie. "I've courage enough for facing animals in the wild but not a mother protecting her bairns."

"Aye, lad, I'll tell her your mind," said Gerald, "then we'll see what she has to say about it. She cares for Hannah, that I know. But I'm not sure if that opinion will hold in light of calling her 'daughter.' And I know she's got her sight set on either the Murchison girl in Ruthven or a daughter from one of the gentry families here in Feshiebridge, even as we speak!" The two men walked towards the MacLaren homestead, their appetites whetted by good conversation, yet Lukas felt uneasy.

CHAPTER THREE

Rosamond was bagging some woolen scarves for the Ruthven Market when Hannah returned from feeding the animals, the heavy oak door groaning as it scraped the stony floor. "We shall need some roof repairs before the winter comes," said Rosamond. "Come, child, have some tea by the fire and rest, for I have a favor to ask of you."

Hannah took her seat in one of the two wooden chairs angled toward the hearth which was centered on the short wall opposite the sleeping pallets, filled with horsehair and goose down, covered with hand-woven blankets. A heavy coarse curtain running from front to back walls separated the sleeping area from the rest of the cottage. The fuel varied, either peat or wood, depending on availability. Many evenings the two women would sit together carding, spinning, or rolling wooly balls from which Rosamond would then weave her wares.

This cozy cottage was the only home Hannah knew. Soon she would be leaving it to build a new family with Lukas. She glanced around at these all too familiar surroundings, wondering how it would differ from her new home. The kitchen area, to the left of the door, was comprised of two shelves filled with pottery bowls, wooden trenchers, and earthen mugs along with a corner filled with bunches of dried rosemary, sage, mint, and fennel balanced like step-dancers on point. Bins of dried meats, fruit, and bread loaves were stacked neatly in the corner. A short planked table surrounded by two wooden benches filled the left side of the cottage while various iron spatulas and spoons hung in descending patterns on the wall. A sense of safety pervaded the walls - this would be difficult to duplicate.

Handing her daughter some chamomile tea, Rosamond said, "Now, Hannah, it's a clear day, and I'm in need of a helper to walk these scarves up to Ruthven. You and I'll be tending the stall tomorrow, but Mistress Faegin has requested this batch early. I thought you could drop them by her house near Loch an Eilein then stroll around it on the way back. I know how fond you are of the Shaw's woods."

After drinking her tea, Hannah took the cloth bag from her mother, wrapped the green cloak about her shoulders as she headed north. She followed the low stone wall lining the dirt path. It ribboned the oak and Scots pine forest with graceful turns determining family boundaries. Browning thistle stalks that earlier held petalled pin-cushions now bowed their heads to the upcoming winter. Serrated wintergreen and creeping lady's tresses still poked their foliage through the dense bracken ferns of the Cairngorm peaks and valleys while an occasional red deer darted through the undergrowth.

After walking several miles, Hannah located the small crofter's cottage just off the path before Ruthven. Mistress Faegin, busy herself with goods for tomorrow's market, opened the door, grabbed the sack, and escorted Hannah to the door. She closed the wooden door without even a "Thank you."

Hannah, feeling a bit rebuffed, decided to take her mother's advice and walk around Loch an Eilein. A lovely footpath wound through the surrounding copse full of purple-tipped grasses, waist-high ferns and brilliant mosses. Her favorite spot was a birch grove, now bare of its golden leaves, but majestic with ermine white trunks speckled with dark splotches against the pine evergreens. She sat down on the mossy riverbank, staring across the grey waters of the loch, which shimmered as the winds whipped over the surface like dragon scales rippling in moonlight. A pair of ospreys broke the water's surface, fishing for an afternoon treat. In the branches above her, she heard the flurry of autumnal birds such as the Crested Tits and Capercaillies, but saw only a red squirrel hoarding its winter feasts.

Lost in her musings, suddenly a popping noise, like that of hot soup spurting in the kettle, startled her. She looked up to see a strange being standing beside the river bank. He was about waist high with blue-green skin. He had knobby knees and fingertips.

His webbed feet sprouted from beneath a large tunic made of water grasses.

"I'm Newt," he said, sprinkling a shower of river drops on Hannah as he danced about.

"You're not a newt," said Hannah, brushing the drops off her cloak. She tried to stay calm, yet her heart was throbbing. She'd never been visited by the Fey before.

"But I am Newt," he said, stomping his slimy foot. "Been Newt for as long as I can remember." He looked her over, frowning a bit. "But you're the tallest nymph I've ever seen. And wearing human clothes!" He did a backwards somersault as if to please her with his agility.

She knew him to be a faerie, but was he a pleasant one or a mischievous one? She wanted no tricks, so she decided to be courteous.

"But you are mistaken, kind sir. For I am not of faerie. I'm mortal."

"A human child, you say? What name go you by?" asked Newt.

"Hannah," she said, "Hannah MacFey."

"Ah, then you are mistaken, for you are one of us!" he said. "Newt is never wrong. See, fey, faerie. Most mortals pass by without a notion we exist, but you must have a bit of faerie in you to see me so clearly." He waggled his fingers at her, moving closer.

"But, I . . ." stammered Hannah, shaking her head furiously.

"Why 'tis nothing to deny, human child," he said. "Either your mother or your father must have the faerie blood in their veins. Which is it?"

"Why, not my mother, of course," said Hannah.

"Ah, then it must needs be the father, usually is. Those rascally fellows, always finding some sweet mortal to impress with their faerie tricks! Your mother must have liked his tricks very much!" Newt leered towards Hannah with a devilish grin, spreading his thin lips to the outskirts of his face.

"She did nothing of the kind! And I'll thank you to leave her out of this!" Hannah stood up, not realizing that Newt was stroking the hem of her cloak. When he stretched his sticky fingertips across the hunter green wool, he'd stuck fast. And her swift rising caused the cloak to flip over the water, flinging Newt promptly into the gray mirrored waters. Hannah laughed aloud, but cut herself off quickly, not wanting to appear rude for fear of his cursing her. "I'm so sorry, Newt! I'd not seen you there," she giggled.

Two large eyes popped above the water's surface. "What a ride, Hannah MacFey! You must come back again, for you never know when we might be of service to one another, now do you? But I cannot fiddle-faddle any longer." Before she could say another word, he disappeared.

"Well, never have I seen anybody so ridiculous in all my days, even if he was a fey," started Hannah, as if conversing with the trees, or the wind, or the water. "And he thinks my father is faerie! Ha, such a silly notion." Yet it haunted her, causing her to wonder more than ever about the man who had loved her mother then died suddenly, leaving Rosamond alone, with a baby girl. Too much to wonder about some days.

Hannah stretched her arms overhead then lay down on the carpet of moss and variegated grasses, suddenly recalling Nell's caustic face. Neither could forget the morning after Samhain, and Nell chose every opportunity to prick Hannah's love for Lukas with darting jibes. Losing Lukas to the likes of Nell Robertson was unthinkable, yet Hannah was certain that Nell'fs societal connections meant more to Mistress MacLaren than Hannah's love.

Still, lose Lukas?

She succumbed to the drowsiness of the afternoon, and drifted into the wandering world of dreams.

The maze snaked through the Perth market stalls. The small figure wandered aimlessly while a tall woman with a long cinnamon braid, gingered with light greys, walked through the stalls ahead of the child. The little girl followed the enticing scent of spicy meat pies and bubbling hot cheese. Sometimes she would smile at a vendor who offered her sugary horses and sheep made from marzipan, tickling her tongue. They all knew her: Hannah, the weaver's daughter.

But soon she tired and wanted to go home. The brown braid swung carelessly around a corner, unnoticed, leaving the child alone. The girl's head barely crested the table edges, but she knew her mother's weavings. She looked for scarves of rubied scarlets, emerald greens, and slate blues hanging over the table rim like woolen garlands. She spotted them and ran to them, plunging her face into their fuzzy softness. Yet her mother was nowhere to be found.

But then she saw the familiar braid, swinging down the aisle once more. "Ma!" she cried. "Ma, I'm here!"

Suddenly the scarves turned into vicious vines, twisting and slithering over her body, pinning her arms to her side and entangling her legs. "MA!" But the leaves curled into her mouth, gagging her. She fell to the ground, kicking her feet together like a mermaid's tail, for now they were woven together as one. The ground, once firm, transformed into powdery sand and began to swallow her whole. She tried to scream once more but found her mouth filling with tiny grains of grit.

Hannah woke up to find her fingers ripping invisible cords about her neck. Her cloak had wormed its way around her slender frame like a shroud. "Not again," she wailed, "O God, not again."

Straightening her cloak, the young highlander meandered once more along the inviting path. As her nightmarish gloom passed, she considered her life's direction. A weaver? A singer, perhaps? She fancied herself beyond the walled pubs performing for the wealthy lairds who would pay handsomely for her fine voice.

She curtsied to the invisible audience, imagining the surrounding woodland transformed into the grand halls with well-trimmed tapestries hanging from gilded finials where her clear notes could soar and bounce to the high ceilings above as ornate cherubs smiled down at her from every corner. For Rosamond had taught her daughter many of the old songs popular with traveling minstrels and harpers, and Hannah learned them all as well as most of the singers even at the grand "sang skule" (song school) in Dunkeld.

With a full heart and a deep breath, the singer began.

"Come by the hills to the land

where fancy is free.

And stand where the peaks meet the sky

and the rocks reach the sea."

Regaling the woods with verse after verse, Hannah heard the scurrying scratching of pine martens and feral minks seeking cover beneath sprays of saffron bracken, but for Hannah, she imagined these sounds as thunderous applause. Nearing the final refrain, Hannah sustained the ending notes, her soprano tones rang clear, their misty majesty of ancient times hovering over the waters.

"And cares of tomorrow must wait

till this day is done."

She bowed, flourishing her cloak, then sat on a large fallen log, much to the surprise of a water vole who sloshed quickly into hidden realms.

As she hiked through the final stretch of overgrown path, Hannah rounded the last corner then stepped lightly onto the southern path leading back to Feshiebridge. The restorative tune reminded her of those things dear to her, including a certain shepherd. With her confidence well intact, Hannah decided that all the schemes Nell might conjure would never succeed against true love.

A light snow began to fall, early for November, like flour flakes from a heavenly bread board. Hannah quickened her pace, knowing it would be at least an hour's time before reaching the MacFey cottage. Her hair tumbled down her back, the braid swinging from side to side, but her neck felt the warmth of her mother's love, for the woven scarf held back the cold. Thoughts of marrying Lukas logically led Hannah to consider a time when she might walk through the woods with a daughter of her own. In the winter, she would teach the child to embrace the cold, to listen to the faerie whispers on the wind. In spring, her daughter would learn the flowers by name, reciting their healing properties. The summertime would be spent in playful eddies and pools along the riverbank, cooling away the heat while the fall would bring long days of harvesting, ending with spiced apple tarts.

And what would the girl learn from her father? Why, she'd ride on his back through golden barley fields shouting commands to the bearded soldiers, bowing their heads before her, or have a hand at herding the sheep with Alpin, the family Border Collie. Learning her letters would be of utmost importance, for she would still be of the gentry class. Songs and poetry would fill their home throughout the day, but especially at night when both parents would sing lullabies to their dearest one. Yes, Hannah and Lukas would have a fine daughter indeed!

The snow enveloped Hannah's reverie. She sidled methodically over the rooted path, gliding over possible hazards to a less familiar walker then soon saw neighboring rooftops chimneyed with smoke. The twinned oak by the main road signaled Hannah's departure to the ferned footpath leading to her home. Her reddened fingers would welcome the fiery warmth of their hearth.

Hannah pressed her shoulder against the stubborn oak door, heaving all her weight against splintered timbers. Suddenly the door gave way, and she fell into welcoming arms rather than onto the river-rock floor.

"By all that's holy, what the . . ." but her confusion melted faster than the snow on her shawl, for it was Lukas.

He held her tightly, almost too much so, but he dared not release her, for he had a question and would not leave until he knew her mind.

"Lukas, bring her over to the fire," said Rosamond, laying her woolen aside. "I'm sure she's had her fill of the cold. Quite a sudden storm from the North that was. Why Hannah, I'd never have sent you had I seen it coming." The mother separated the pair and ushered her girl to a seat by the fire.

Hannah allowed herself to be led, like the child she remained in her mother's eyes. Warm blankets soon draped her shoulders while wet boots and stockings were replaced with blue and grey striped wool socks. While Rosamond poured tea for all three, Lukas knelt in front of Hannah and began rubbing her hands, blocking her mother from view.

"Would you like something to eat?" asked Rosamond, pulling tea cakes from the tin and humming a tune to herself.

"Thanks, Ma. I am a bit hungry," said Hannah. She smiled then rolled her eyes at Lukas, who more than warming her hands had progressed to kissing the fingertips.

"You, too, Lukas?"

"Aye, Mistress MacFey, I am half starved for sure," he said. "Perhaps you have some cheese and bread as well?" He continued his kisses, moving to the backs of her hands. "Hannah," he whispered, "Marry me. Marry me before my soul bursts out my skin. I love you, darlin', and can wait no longer."

Hannah was shocked that Lukas chose this time to propose with Rosamond only several feet away.

"Please answer me, Hannah. Will you marry me, girl?" He clutched her hands together with his, leaning close to her now.

Hannah's heart could hold no more love than it did at that very moment. "Are you daft, Lukas?" she said.

Crestfallen, Lukas sat back on his haunches, about to let go.

But Hannah quickly continued. "Could I marry any other man than yourself? Why, of course, I'll marry you." She leaned forward and kissed him with such delight that he leapt to his feet. Gathering Hannah in his arms, he twirled her about as if they were dancing in a royal ballroom. Their laughter pealed like the morning bells of Christmas mass.

"What's all this?" asked Rosamond, placing the cheese and bread on the planked table and reaching for the ale.

"She said 'Yes' Mistress MacFey! My darling Hannah said 'Yes,'" grinned Lukas.

Rosamond almost dropped the pewter pitcher of ale. "What?"

Lukas sat down, pulling Hannah onto his lap. Securing his arms about her small waist, Lukas stilled.

"Ma, he's asked me to marry him!"

"Why, that's excellent news! Surely God in his heaven couldn't have created a finer match. Let's have a toast, shall we?" Rosamond passed round the crimson tea mugs. The threesome hoisted their mugs: "To the new couple!"

"Well, when shall we celebrate this coupling?" asked Rosamond, passing out slices of her best barley bread slathered with butter and hunks of orange cheese.

As the two ate their fill, the lovers looked at one another. "What do you think, Hannah? When would you like to be my bride?" asked Lukas, savoring the simple feast.

"I think at Imbolc, on February first," she replied.

"Ah, St. Brighid's Feast Day," exclaimed Rosamond, taking a seat opposite the two sweethearts, "an excellent choice. What better time to say good-bye to wintry patterns of the past and welcome new bonds with the Lady of Spring?"

"That's settled then," said Lukas. "Now, will that give you women folk time to make the necessary preparations for the ceremony? We've got Christmas close at hand followed by Hogmany, the New Year. That will give you only about a month."

The two women looked at each other and just burst out laughing. Had they not talked over this very occasion by late night fires for so many years that they saw it all, down to the bride's dress? "What silly notions men do have," said Rosamond, smiling now at Hannah. "So Hannah, do you think you'll be ready by then?"

"Aye, Ma, for certain Lally and Caitlin have been planning this for months."

"Lally and Caitlin?" asked Lukas. "But how . . ."

"We've known for quite a while, boy," said Rosamond. "We've all been waiting for you to gather your courage to ask the girl!" She laughed such a hearty laugh that Lukas could not complain, but merely joined her.

"My father said I was a goner," he said, his cheeks red now but not from the nearby flames. "I guess it wasn't much of a secret how much you mean to me, lass."

Hannah curled her arm around his head as Lukas rested on her shoulder. "No love, but I wanted you to come to me when you were ready, not because others expected it of us."

The three chatted till the snows abated while Lukas donned his black cloak.

"Here, lad," said Rosamond, wrapping a black and green striped scarf around his neck. "I've just finished this one, and it looks mighty fine on you." She stood on tiptoe and kissed him on the cheek.

Lukas blushed once again, but he did not mind. These MacFey women were special, and he knew it. He would enjoy being a member of this family. With one last kiss upon his Hannah's sweet lips, he practically flew out the door, careful to not allow the freezing winds inside. The women cleared the food away then with tea in hand, seated themselves by the fire.

"Ma, I can't believe it! I'm actually going to marry Lukas," said Hannah, her voice trembling at the incredulity of it all.

Rosamond knew her daughter's doubts well, despite the growing love between Hannah and Lukas. "Here, daughter, roll up this blue wool for me while we talk," she said, handing the spun woolen strands to Hannah.

Hannah wound the strands so fast that her fingers became entangled in a spidery web. "Oh, Ma," placing the blue mess in her lap, "I still can't believe Lukas would really choose me, over all the other girls in this county. Compared to them, I always come up short. Why Lally always looks so lovely, even after working in the fields, and Caitlin knows how to organize household affairs just right. Why me?"

"Because you're a kind, loving, clever girl, that's why," said Rosamond, who didn't miss a beat as she carded some brown-speckled white wool. She knew Lukas was, indeed, a perfect match for her girl because he knew how to reassure Hannah when her ungrounded fears crept upon her. With a familiar gentility, Rosamond continued, "You have something no other lass in the county has to offer young MacLaren. Don't you know what that is?"

For her whole life, only Rosamond had loved Hannah completely, until now. "I love him, Ma. Is that it?"

"Yes, and he loves you. I've rarely seen such a couple so set upon another." She stood up, "Now, it's been a long day. I'll smoor the fire tonight. You get yourself some rest." She kissed Hannah on the cheek and began covering the burning embers with cold ones.

Hannah dropped the swirl of blue into a basket on the floor, changed into her nightshirt, then climbed onto her pallet, pulling the dark brown wool blanket close to her neck. Could it finally happen, just like he said it would? She smiled to herself, snuggled deep beneath her covers, and releasing a long-awaited sigh, fell into a peaceful slumber.

But this was not to be a peaceful night as Rosamond sat by the fire, bewitched by the evening's events.

"HO! Way to me, now, boy!" Alpin nipped the heels of rambling sheep still eating thistle blooms as he flanked the flock to the right down the last leg of the pass towards the MacLarens' lowest field next to the River Feshie. Lukas nodded his approval. He remembered bringing home the black and white collie when Alpin was six weeks old. The pup was a natural at herding. They moved the flock closer to the small stone wall which acted as a barricade barring any slippage into the river's cold depths, for the sheep liked it best where the sweet grasses lay amidst the pointed hillocks and pine peaks.

Gerald MacLaren and his two other sons had left early for the upper barley fields, inspecting the winter grass.

After putting the luncheon provisions aside, the young man sat on the low stone wall, watching both the herd and rushing current as the vigilant dog settled at his feet, safeguarding the herd.

"I'm going to marry my girl, boy," said Lukas, pitching a small stone into the river, skipping it across the southerly ripples.

The dog looked up at hearing his master's voice, ears pricked to attention.

The young farmer sighed, then smiled, lost in reflections of his lovely Hannah. He knew the flock was safe with Alpin's constant vigilance. His mind meandered in his love of words, for often Lukas would write verses for his Hannah, practicing recitations aloud on Alpin. "Listen to this one, boy."

She pulls me into her dancing place

. . . we sway together

in the sun gone orange,

flowing into a fire-fly evening.

"What do you think?"

The dog remained silent, but watchful.

"Too much? Aye, probably, but Hannah loves it when I whisper such words to her," he said, stroking Alpin's ears.

Lukas and Alpin remained in the lower fields all morning, ate a quick lunch then led their charges back towards the barn on the MacLaren farm. They reached the higher pastures soon enough where the sheep were allowed to browse while Alpin followed his master into the gentry home.

Eglantyne MacLaren, matriarch of the MacLaren household, sat next to the fire knitting a winter cap for her youngest son, Rory. Ringlets of grey tinged with an earlier auburn escaped the edges of her caul, framing her round face and penetrating blue eyes. Above all, Eglantyne MacLaren was a practical woman when speaking of marriage. "You shall marry gentry, Lukas, and a wife of my choosing," she said in a quiet yet firm manner.

"I won't do it!" shouted Lukas. The frustrated young Highlander paced circles around his 12-year-old sister Muriel who sat cross-legged on the floor, pretending to read. Her small frame, hidden beneath the white shift and green kirtle, appeared restless, more listening than reading. "How can you even ask me to do such a thing, Ma? Marry Nell Robertson? Why, wouldn't it be choosing between money and true love? I don't want to end up living with a, with a . . ."

" 'A fat fadge by the fire'?" piped Muriel, quoting the sisterly advice from the old ballad of "Lord Thomas and Fair Annet." She buried her head in the book again.

"Aye." He gave his sister a wink. She offered a conspiratorial smile. "Ma. I won't do it. Nell's a mean-spirited woman with a devil's heart." He plopped down in one of the floral-covered chairs.

"Now Lukas," Eglantyne started in a calm voice, "is that any way to talk about a young lady? Besides, she's a bright girl with a determination for a sophisticated life. Why, just think of it, Lukas. The Robertson family owns the second largest farming tract in Feshiebridge. When you marry Nell, there's sure to be plenty for generations to come." Her confidence in the match lit up the room.

"But I don't want to marry Nell!" cried Lukas, slapping the overstuffed chair arms.

Eglantyne continued, ignoring her son's protests. "Then, after you two start having bairns, we can set you up with a proper farm, maybe with holdings from both families!" The mother brightened at the thought of such prosperity for her middle son.

"But I have all I need from the sheep and the barley fields right here," said Lukas. "Besides, I've begun building a cottage up in the north meadow already. A quiet place to live with . . ."

"Nell has birthing hips," interrupted Eglantyne, "for lots of grandchildren."

Lukas slumped, wondering how best to tame his mother to his way of thinking.

As she continued knitting, she said, without missing a stitch, "Well, perhaps you need some time to adjust to the idea, get to know Nell better. In fact, the Robertsons have invited us over for dinner this evening which would be a grand time to begin this courtship. Woo her; show her what a good match this could be." As if the matter were settled, she looked back at her handiwork.

"Woo Nell?" asked Lukas. "Mother, you make it sound more like a horse bargain rather than my life. Malcolm is the eldest, and he could marry her. But I won't be dictated to like some schoolboy about such a matter as this!" He jumped to his feet, shoving his hands in the brown trouser pockets.

"You could choose Sallie Murchison from Ruthven if you wish, but you will do as you're told, boy" said Eglantyne slowly and evenly. The death knell sounded with her final words.

Yet for once, Lukas would not yield to his mother's wishes. He knelt in front of her, then softly replied, "But Mother, I've just asked Hannah MacFey to marry me."

His mother put down her knitting, looked him straight in the face, and without hesitation said, "You'll have to undo what is newly done, for you cannot marry the weaver's daughter." And before he could protest, she said in a low voice, "And don't be late this evening for dinner at the Robertsons." Without looking at her son, she resumed her handiwork.

Muriel remained quiet yet her eyes were wide with fear. She'd never heard her favorite brother so angry, or so disrespectful.

Lukas jerked his cloak from the peg near the door, slammed the door behind him, and marched towards the fields to be with the animals. Women! At least he understood sheep.

The next morning, Rosamond continued preparing for market. "Hannah, run over to the Stewarts' and borrow their horse and wagon. They've already agreed, so they'll be waiting for you. And don't you dally about, girl, for we've much work to finish, so we can be on the road before evening!" Rosamond cranked the plaid cloth around the upper warp beam once more, nearing the end of the cloth web. The MacLarens' tartan design shared four colors: dark green and blue as primaries followed by narrow strips of yellow and red. Mistress MacLaren had requested it for Rory to wear for the approaching winter weather.

Hannah reached for her green cloak hanging on the wooden pegs near the door and sweeping it around her shoulders, met the day. Unseasonably balmy October weather had retreated as nippy November days marched on. Hannah followed the path which led through the MacLaren property along the river, over the bridge then south two farms over. Her footsteps sure, Hannah stepped lightly over entanglements of roots along the rocky walkway towards the River Feshie. She sat on the low stone wall that held swollen waters at bay from fields heavy with harvest then swung her legs over to walk along the riverbank. She watched as the black-blue water ran swiftly over stones of reds, cream, and grey. She noted jagged branches jutting into the air, their fallen host buried in the watery grave. All the valley children were told that water kelpies lived beneath these waters as well, waiting to snatch lonely swimmers beyond the shallow eddies. Hannah smiled, wondering if she would ever tell such cautionary tales to her daughter someday.

As she came into view of the MacLaren farm, Lukas hailed her from his chilly perch overlooking the grazing bottomland. With the sheep stabled in the barn and Alpin off chasing unknown prey, this shepherd was left with nothing to herd but his thoughts. "Hannah darlin', come up here and keep me warm!" he called, waving her to sit by him.

"Not now, you silly lad," she yelled back, "I'm off to borrow the Stewarts' wagon. The Ruthven Market is tomorrow, you know, and Ma and I must be off soon to set up the weaver stall." But despite her protests, she clambered over the low stone wall, gained the knoll then planted a kiss on her sweetheart's lips. "But I've always got a kiss for you, Lukas," she whispered, running her fingers through his thick curls. She laughed then turned away, sprinting quickly through the fields to the Stewarts' farm.

"But Hannah, wait! I've got to talk to you!"

"After market, Lukas. I'll be back at week's end," she cried, her voice trailing in her wake.

He rose to follow then reconsidered. What would he say to her? His mother insisted he recant his marriage proposal, and instead make Nell an offer. But he was not going back on his promise to Hannah, no matter what his mother said.

CHAPTER FOUR

Market Day in Ruthven appeared like a cornucopia, teeming with variety. Craft guild members from all over the highlands displayed their goods on long plank tables sheltered by canvas tents of reds, blues, and greens topped with yellow banners and Cairngorm Guild embroidered flags. The guilds insured quality goods by regulating the number of artisans per craft, setting prices, and forbidding advertising. Customers could wander down the aisles, tasting samples of the delectable pastries from the bakers while perusing woven wearables, iron hooks, metal pots, dyed woolen skeins, leather belts, canvas paintings, practical earthenware, exquisite jewelry (in both silver and gold), sturdy shoes, and embroidered bedding. Metalwork displays included knives, swords, scabbards, and cutlery which gleamed in the morning sunlight. Members of the architectural guilds such as stone masons, builders, and carpenters set up miniature displays while food vendors tempted customers with fruit tarts, cheese wheels, fresh breads, shepherd's pies, cinnamon scones, and sculptured candies. Wandering dogs panted near the butcher's stall hung with prime cuts of viands heavily salted, but ladies swooned at the luscious rainbows of ribbons available to adorn their braids. The market would last three days.

The first two days passed with great success for Rosamond and Hannah. Not only did yards of woven fabric leave with satisfied customers, but the new shawls in various lengths proved quite popular. Since most highlander men created a plaid or feilidh-mor for themselves out of yards of fabric belted at the waist, it was best to offer them a variety of earth-toned weaves to blend in with the hill surroundings. But the women preferred ready-made goods such as cloaks and shawls, often in brighter colors.

On the second afternoon, Hannah noticed her mother dealing with a couple who were examining a woman's cloak, turning it this way and that to check the workmanship. The wife coughed, a wheezing cough that shook her tiny shoulders so much that her towering husband gathered her up in his arms until the episode subsided. He whispered in her ear, but she shook her head, saying she was all right. Hannah surmised the couple was married by the gold band visible on the woman's ring finger and their close affection. The husband, a bit older than his wife, produced the fee then waved the lovely cloak over his wife's shoulders, kissing her cheek. She twirled, ever so slowly causing the cloak to float on the air, casting an angelic quality to the young wife. Her husband watched, yet Hannah noted his heavy sigh, signaling some sadness here as he opened his arms once more. The young woman slipped her hand into his welcoming embrace as they proceeded down the line for their next possible purchase.

"Ma, did you know them?" asked Hannah.

Rosamond palmed her money, securing it away, then answered, "I've seen them here many times, but I cannot seem to remember their names. I believe they come from Kingussie. Why?"

Hannah leaned her head to one side and sighed. "Oh, I was just thinking how lovely it is to have a man so in love with you, that's all."

On the last day, while Rosamond was saying good-bye to other vendors, Hannah manned the stall alone. Men lingered about, fingering the fabric yet with a closer eye on the weaver's daughter. Hannah remained courteous but not eager.

As the morning wore on towards noontime meals, customers rallied about the food vendor stalls, leaving Hannah to some much needed solitude. As she folded some opened yardage, she heard a familiar voice. She shuddered as if someone just walked on her grave.

"Oh Mother, why look who's here," said Nell, her voice rising and falling like a chorister. "It's Hannah MacFey selling her mother's cloth. Isn't that sweet?" Nell grabbed her mother by the elbow, pulling her to the weaver's stall. "But we usually buy our fine cloth, the linens and the velvets, at the Perth Market, don't we, Mother?"

"Yes, dear, but you do need a new shawl," said Mistress Robertson, unhooking herself from her daughter. "Good morning to you, Hannah." The older woman began flipping through the remaining fabrics.

"Good morning," said Hannah. She stood at attention, rigid, awaiting enemy fire.

"Well," said Nell, "I was hoping for a new silk dress for Christmas. We shouldn't waste our time with these," she quipped, flipping the woolens carelessly about.

Her mother ignored her daughter's petulant musings and continued rummaging through colors at the farthest end of the table.

"Oh, Ma," continued Nell, "you'll have to be teaching me to cook the way you did the other night for the MacLaren family. I'm such a fool when it comes to such things. Why baking breads and cakes to perfection is not enough to fill a young man's belly, now is it? Don't you agree, Hannah?"

Hannah gave no reply though she had much to say. She did not want to embarrass her mother with ill behavior at the market.

"And the way that Lukas MacLaren was courting me. Shameless he was. Did you see the way he looked at me after dinner, Ma?" Nell continued.

"He's a very amiable young man," said Mistress Robertson, "and I'm sure he'll make you a fine husband." She began pulling a red and yellow plaid from the bottom of one stack.

"Yes, I think he'll do quite well," sneered Nell, "for me, that is. But Hannah dear, I'm sure with you here selling at the market, you won't have heard the good news. Come spring, Lukas and I are to be married!" She leaned across the table then pressed her face close to Hannah.

Hannah was about to give a sharp retort when Rosamond, having returned in time to hear this declaration of war, placed her arm about her daughter's waist and interceded. "Why Nell, Mistress Robertson, good to see you both." Turning to Mistress Robertson, she said, "Ah, now that plaid is six yards in length. Good size for that young man of yours, though I doubt not big enough for a kirtle for sturdy Nell here."

Nell straightened, realizing she'd just been slighted. As she opened her mouth to respond, Rosamond continued.

"And about marriage in the spring," she said, "why Nell, I'm sure you must be mistaken, for I heard Lukas MacLaren with my own ears ask my girl to be his wife just the other day, didn't he, Hannah?"

"Yes, he most certainly did. And I accepted him," said Hannah. The two MacFey women towered over Nell in a column of strength.

"So Nell, he could not have asked you, now could he? That t'would be wrong to ask two girls at once." Rosamond placed her hands on her hips, waiting for a reply.

"Well," stammered Nell, "he didn't exactly say it in those words." She began to retreat behind her mother who, oblivious to the verbal sparring, was marveling at the expertise in the cloth she was examining rather than listening to the conversation.

"No, I'm quite sure he didn't," replied Rosamond, lowering her voice in tones that could chill a running stream.

"Why Mistress MacFey, you have such a delicate hand with wools," said Mistress Robertson. "Most I find at these smaller markets are coarse, best suited only for outer coverings. But yours are so fine, with such even edges. I'll take two blue shawls and this roll of cloth for young Freddie." She began reaching in her purse for the appropriate coinage while Rosamond wrapped them in brown paper.

Nell smoldered behind her mother, unable to think of anything else to say. The transaction completed, Mistress Robertson said, "Come along, Nell," handing her daughter the goods. "We must be heading home soon. Good-bye Mistress

MacFey, Hannah," she waved, pulling Nell after her. Nell turned, mouthing to Hannah, "He's mine!" then lifting her head, trotted alongside her mother like an obedient bitch.

Rosamond sat down on the bench, wrapping her arms around her daughter. She knew there had been a rivalry on Nell's part from town gossip, but never imagined it would go this far. "Hannah, let me get you some cider and a hot cheese bridie. That will fill your belly on the ride home," she said, then kissing Hannah lightly on the forehead, she hurried away.

Marry Nell Robertson, thought Hannah. Is that what Lukas had wanted to discuss with her three days ago? Surely his heart could not have changed so quickly. Yet, here was Nell, describing a dinner with him while wedding proposals floated in the air. What if his parents objected to Hannah as his wife? Would they stop the wedding? Nell's venomous lies fed Hannah's insecurities. It was too much for tears, too shocking to be true.

While lost in this nightmare, Lally careened around the lower corner stall looking for her best friend. Her smile dissipated into concern as she approached the weaver's stall, staring at Hannah. "What on God's holy ground has happened to you, Hannah?" She sat down next to Hannah and waited.

"I can't believe he could do this. Surely not," said Hannah, her voice quivering.

"Who? Do what?" asked Lally. "Is it Lukas?"

Tears brimmed like water on the ledge of a waterfall then slipped down Hannah's cheeks. "It's Nell, Nell Robertson."

"What did she do?"

"She was just here with her mother. Nell said Lukas is to be her husband. That he came over for dinner, courtin' her last night. Lally, he might marry her!"

"Oh Hannah, now that's just silly old Nell trying to upset you," said Lally, cradling Hannah around the shoulders. "You know what a spiteful girl she can be. And I'm sure Lukas would never even consider it. I mean, he's already asked you, hasn't he?"

"Yes, he did. But it was before he'd had time to talk with his family. And you know how his mother goes on about being 'gentry folk' and living the rich way of life. What if they don't think I'm good enough for their son? What if they stop the wedding?" Hannah stood up and began pacing.

"Even if they tried, Hannah, nothing would keep Lukas from marrying you. Look at me." Lally blocked Hannah's path, placing her hands upon Hannah's shoulders then stared straight into those swollen eyes. "He loves you," she said slowly, deliberately. "And there is nobody, especially obnoxious little Nell Robertson, that can ever separate the two of you. You do believe that, don't you, Hannah?"

"I do believe he loves me," she said, "but what if they convince him otherwise?"

Before Lally could answer, Rosamond walked up. "Hello, Lally. Good to see you," she said, hugging Lally. "Hannah dear, sorry I took so long. Maire Peters started telling me one of her stories, and I could not get away. But here, drink this cider and taste this cheese bridie; let the cheese warm your insides." Rosamond handed the food to the girls then began folding the leftover fabric and loading the cart. She was glad there were few goods remaining for that meant more coins in her purse.

Hannah shared her bridie with Lally and both finished quickly.

"Lally, will you be riding home with us? There's room in the cart now, and you girls can chatter away while I walk in front. Up with you now, for darkness will be upon us soon." The two young women hopped in the back, settling the woolens around them as their conversation continued.

"You must be strong, Hannah," said Lally, "for you don't want Lukas to have to choose between you and his family. Win them over. Let them see the wonderful lass we all know you to be."

Hannah cringed, considering how to impress the MacLarens.

But Lally intervened before the fears of insecurity clouded Hannah's mind, "And most of all, you must trust Lukas to do what's best for you both. He's a stout lad when it comes to speaking his mind, and he'll not be bullied into marrying that chit of girl Nell Roberston!"

Hannah tried to smile, but simply hugged her best friend as they rode back to Feshiebridge in silence.

"Hannah, he's coming! Hurry up!" Lally released the maroon curtain, a stiff broadcloth good for keeping out the sunlight but rough work for a lookout. The three girls flitted about the small room like a brood of mad hens, placing finishing touches on the simple floral decorations while Rosamond placed the scrumptious foods on the table.

The two months of engagement had evaporated on the northern winds with Christmas gifts, Yule festivities, and New Year's Eve Hogmanay tidings. Despite all Mistress MacLaren's efforts to delay this wedding, attempting to persuade the MacLaren men that this match was doomed, Lukas's mother was glad of one thing: Lukas was happy. She honestly couldn't deny it, but there would be terrible times ahead, for she'd seen it too many times marrying outside one's station. She would bide her time and come to her son's rescue when he was ready, even if it meant stopping the wedding.

The celebration of Imbolc, the early burgeoning of spring, was finally upon them. It was time. Hannah sat by the fire, gathering the pleats of her hunter green kirtle in her sweaty fingertips. Only two days until the ceremony to wed Lukas - ah, Lukas. All the preparations, all the planning would now come together in a mixed package of nervous moments, of love ever-after. Lukas, Lukas MacLaren, would finally be hers.

"What's this?" cried a husky voice as rowdy lads entered the small stone cottage.

"Patrick Chisolm, you know very well what's here," said Rosamond. "Now you boys come on inside before the early spring wind has a taste of my spiced apple pudding." She shooed the boys inside, unbundling them as they passed by. She gave Patrick, the round-faced lad, a peck on the cheek. Lally and Caitlin hung the boys' cloaks on the wooden pegs.

"Why, Lally MacPherson, is it a feast you're having here?" asked Patrick, swaggering around the room as if he were a king. "If I'd known that I'd have brought my mother's finest mince pie. Ah well, at least I brought some stout lads with an ache in their belly and a heart for the dance!" Patrick whisked Lally off her feet, twirling her about while her long brown braid flew behind her. Caitlin giggled, dusting wispy rouge red curls from her face as Gavin and Seamus quickly slid the table and chairs next to the wall, opening a small dancing space. Being the only fiddler present, Seamus placed a chair for himself in the corner. The lad almost disappeared in the shadows due to his dark complexion and straight, black hair.

Lukas knelt on the floor beside his beloved and asked, "Hannah, will you dance with me this night? There won't be many more nights when we can dance as light-hearted single folk. Why, we'll be an old married couple with babes around your feet before you can say 'Saint Brighid!' " He held his hand out to her, waiting for her response.

"Of course, I'll dance with you, silly lad."

He reached for her then, reached for his only relief in life, and encircled her tiny waist with his arms, full of strength. He ran his fingers through her long, wavy hair, filled with all the colors of evening twilight, then he kissed her. Hannah softened, allowing him to take her into a port of safety, the only one aside from her mother's arms where she knew she was loved.

After signaling Seamus, Lukas began dancing with Hannah, holding her close as music swelled in the cozy cottage. The dancers picked up the hint, and couples took turns circling the cottage. The evening was off to a grand start. But there was serious business to be done before the night's end.

While resting from his playing, Seamus cornered Lukas. "So, I know it's a silly tradition, being this close to the wedding and all, but you still must have parental consent. Granted, asking for a girl's hand in marriage is not a simple thing, especially with them riddles. So, who's speaking for you tonight to Mistress MacFey?"

"Patrick said he'd do it," replied Lukas.

"And you trust him to do it right?" said Seamus. "The reitach? You know the lad's got hay for brains, although tossed about with a good sense of humor, but he can't ask for the girl outright. I heard Colin MacDonald say his father asked for a boat. Tim Fraser asked for a sheep. What do you suppose Patrick will ask for?"

"I reckon I don't rightly know, Seamus," said Lukas. "He's my best friend and my best man at the wedding. Since Hannah has no father, the job will go to Mistress MacFey to make the final approval."

"Well, the night's almost spent, so I hope he comes up with something soon." Seamus took out his pipes for the last dance, playing a slow air.

Patrick had been wondering all night how to approach Rosamond. Well enough he'd seen it played out, but never been one of the actors. He ran through choices in his head: cow, goose, pig, dog. None of these seemed to come easily into conversation. While he finished his last spoonful of pudding, he got an idea. He drank a swig of ale, cleared his throat, then loud enough for all to hear said, "So, Mistress MacFey, I've a notion to take home some of your spiced apple pudding."

The dancers all stopped; the music died. Hannah grabbed Lukas by the arm and sat down with him by the fire. All eyes were on Patrick.

Rosamond took off her apron, and laid it aside. Her maple brown kirtle with a golden-leaved bodice revealed that she had taken good care of herself over the years. She moved to the center of the room where all could watch. She was ready now. "Patrick, say again?"

"I said that I've a notion to take home some of your spiced apple pudding."

"Is that so, Patrick?" asked Rosamond.

"Aye, 'tis so." Patrick stood only a foot away, looking her straight in the eye.

"And what makes you think I'll be letting you take off with my pudding?" Her lips curled into a smile like that of a cat tasting its first mouse.

"Well, you know that I can take better care of your pudding than anyone in all of Inverness-shire," he said, pushing his broad shoulders back. "I know that it's the sweetest pudding I've ever laid eyes on, and to preserve that ah, sweetness, I'd uh, uhh . . . ."

"Yes?"

"Well, I guess I'd put her in a cooling shed to keep her from spoiling," said Patrick, fumbling with a few farthings in his pocket.

Laughter spilled from all corners of the room at his brave attempt. Patrick's face flushed as he looked at Lukas, silently pleading like a sentenced man to his executioner. Lukas only shook his head and grinned, knowing his role in this play was to remain still.

"Keep her in a cooling shed, eh? Now, that would be a chilly way to spend an evening," replied Rosamond, circling him now.

"Well, I've got to keep her fresh," said Patrick, jamming his hands in his pockets.

"Fresh? Are you saying you'll be 'fresh' with my pudding?"

Seamus howled while the others tried to contain themselves. He leaned over to Lukas, "How's Patrick's ever going to get out of this one? Nothing graceful about it, that's for sure!"

Lukas never faltered though in his decision about using Patrick. Things always worked out for the boy, somehow.

Patrick knew this was going to be tough, but he didn't fancy Rosamond at being such a bandy-about of it either. He needed a finishing touch- a clincher. Aha, he thought! "But if you were to keep that pudding all to yourself, how could others ever know how pleasurable a thing it is? Why, I will take it 'round to all the neighbors, letting others sample its goodness while I save the best for myself. For indeed, Mistress MacFey, I love it best in all the world."

With that, a hush fell over the room. He had done it, with style and grace. Hannah squeezed Lukas' hand, her green eyes now twinkling.

Rosamond sighed. This was her only child. Letting her go was the second most difficult decision in her life. She placed her hands on her hips, leaning towards Patrick. "Very well, then, you may have the spiced apple pudding. But mind you, if I ever hear of you treating it poorly, you'll be having to deal with me, understand?"

"Aye that I do, Mistress MacFey. Aye that I do." Patrick looked towards Seamus and asked, "Are we ready to go now?

"Let us go now and leave these lovely ladies to their gossip."

The girls fetched the cloaks, dispersing them to appropriate owners. Lukas grabbed

Hannah, whirling her about then placed a tender kiss lightly upon her lips.

"Meet me tomorrow at noon on top of Rowan Hill," he whispered, twirling his fingers around an errant ringlet. "I've a surprise that just can't wait."

"I've so much still to do, but just for a little while. I'll bring a sampling of the feast food with me. That be fine enough for you?" asked Hannah.

"More than fine. Why, that would be perfect." He bowed, with a flourish of his arm like an actor at the end of a play. And so, with fond farewells, the boys disappeared into the winter night. Giggles rippled through the night air while the ladies set in motion final bridal preparations for the next evening. The hour was late when Lally and Caitlin made for home.

As Hannah was preparing for bed, she looked over at her mother, still bustling about the hearth to secure the embers for the night. As lovely as the evening had been, a singular sadness dampened her spirit. Rosamond noticed.

"Hannah, are you not pleased with the results of the reitach?"

Hannah hesitated, not wanting to hurt her mother's feelings, but still blurted out, "The reitach is supposed to be for the father. The father," she said more softly. "Where is mine, Ma? Is he truly dead in the grave or did he just leave you when he knew you were with child?" Remembering her grandmother's accusations, Hannah trembled, both needing yet not wanting the answer.

After all these years, Rosamond had hoped her lies were secure. Silence had seemed the best choice, yet now her daughter's fears and frustrations over not having a father grieved Rosamond's heart.

Rosamond stared at her only daughter, lying under the soft wool blanket with more stars in her eyes than present in the sky. What good would the truth do now, so many years later?

Rosamond needed Hannah to believe that she was loved not by one parent alone, so she kept her secret.

"Darlin', your father did not leave you, if that's what you're thinking," she started, hoping to distract Hannah. "But I want you to know that he loved me, of that I'm sure. And I'm certain he would love you, as well, for what's not to love, child? But now, let's think about your new family, the one you'll start with Lukas. We've a wedding in two days!"

Hannah, following Rosamond's lead to think on happier topics, focused on weddings. "Ma, did you make such a fuss for your wedding?" asked Hannah. "You've told me so little about it. Was it fine?"

Rosamond did the only thing she could do - she lied. "Well, it was nothing, really," said Rosamond, who finished smooring the embers, put on her dressing gown, and sat beside Hannah. "Nothing quite so grand as yours will be. We needed to make it official, so we borrowed the sexton from St. John's Kirk in Perth, and made our pledges along the River Tay. The window boxes along the river were filled with such flowers, more colors than I could tell you. But I had no friends nor family to stand with me. That was my only regret."

"But Ma, I thought you had a cousin in Perth. Is he not the one you visit every year at Beltane in May and again during Lammas Fair?" Hannah sat up now, alert, for the lateness of the hour no longer betrayed her. "You always bring back such lovely things, special things. Your box is quite full of them, you know."

Rosamond straightened. Beltane . . . Lammas Fair. A sudden glimmer of memories filled her mind. Strolling down the avenues on the arm of the most handsome harper. Glowing with pride as she listened to him play. His eyes by candlelight during a night of loving. Would she ever find him there again? No word would ever be sent to her if he were ill, for nobody knew of their love. She had taken great risk to give her heart to a traveling man, yet his love remained. "A cousin in Perth? Yes, of course, Hannah. But he was busy with his own bairns that day and unable to come down to the village." Rosamond held her breath to see if the lie would hold.

"Oh, that's too bad," yawned Hannah, stretching herself back down on the horsehair mattress. "I'm sure his wife would have made . . . a lovely . . . bridesmaid," then sleep fell heavily upon her. She yawned one final time, then whispered, "I love you best, Ma."

Rosamond smoothed the stray hairs from her daughter's face then whispered, "I love you, too, daughter." She rested her head on the goose down pillow, caressing the Celtic triad knot which hung so delicately between her breasts. "Where are you, my love?"

Isle of Iona, Caledonia

The sunlight glinted through the chapel's large arched window above the altar, creating shadowed patterns of triads on the floor during morning song at the Iona Abbey. The sea, midnight blues swirled with turquoise, made little offerings today. The playful waves gently slapped the rocks just behind the Abbey while the sea's briny smell rode the soft breezes through the open side windows.

Father Callum, a tall, lean man with clear blue eyes like the sea, closed the Bible, lifted his arms and with a strong voice blessed the brethren:

"May the raindrops renew your brow,

May the winds freshen your spirit,

May the sunshine enlighten your heart,

May the burdens rest lightly upon you,

And may God hold you

in the shield of his love. Amen."

With the prayers completed, the brothers silently filed up the sanctuary steps past the ornately carved stone arches of the Choir, exiting through the heavy oak door at the east Cloister alley. They always met in the chapter house immediately following matins for the morning reading from the Rule of St. Benedictine, where afterwards they would confess their sins and conduct business of the day. Careful strains of liturgical songs played softly upon a harp while each footfall echoed on the blue-gray stones.

The musician outside the sacristy, just left of the altar, continued plucking the harp strings until all the brethren exited. Normally he would stop now and join the others. But today, his fingers continued moving, flitting like butterflies in figure-eight mating patterns back and forth upon the strings. He closed his eyes, surrendering to ballad scores of other days, other times. Michael leaned into the harp, like a lover into the shoulder of a beloved. Delicate notes spoke more than the man ever had the courage to say. He did not see Father Callum sitting silently beneath the stained glass windows of Columba, Brighid, and Patrick, waiting for this matin concert to close.

The Abbey bell rang clear, a tolling that brought Michael back from his past to the cold stone abbey walls. He quickly covered the harp, and rose, mantled by sadness. He picked up his cane from its usual resting place in the corner and slowly walked down the aisle.

"Michael, I've not heard that tune from you before," said the monk, standing to meet his friend. "It brings out a greatness in you, allowing you to fill every nook in this sanctuary. Quite pleasing it was, yet not of the style we traditionally hear."

"Father Callum, I did not see you there. Forgive me for playing something so worldly," said Michael, bowing his head.

"There is no need to ask for forgiveness, Michael. Why, listening to you just then, it was as if I were seeing your soul. No man should have to excuse himself for that. Here, sit with me a moment." The monk placed a hand on Michael's shoulder, allowing the harper to lift his head now and take a seat.

"I've found myself to be restless as of late," said Michael. "I hear the old tunes in my head now, ever present. This is the first time they spilled from my fingers in so many years. It took me back to a place inside myself that I thought never to see again." He carelessly let a finger graze his cheek, running the length of the old wound.

The monk watched the subtle movement. He had assigned brothers to care for Michael when he first arrived on their doorstep. Before that broken incident, Michael was a renowned harper, traveling for many years throughout Caledonia and Brittainia. Father Callum allowed Michael to be called a "brother" when, in fact, Michael never underwent training nor took vows. The monk seemed so impressed with Michael's reading and writing skills that Father Callum would have done anything to keep Michael at the Abbey, so Michael was given leave to attend only Abbey services and work during other Iona rituals.

"Michael, tell me then, what is it you miss about the outside world? Our simple life here must pale in comparison to your old ways, harping for royalty and feasting year 'round."

Michael sighed. "Well, there was a woman, a lovely fiery lass from the Highlands that I only saw twice a year, but of all the women I'd known, (and that list is long) this one captured my heart. I should have married her, despite the many protests of my parents, her only being a weaver. But regardless of my family's displeasure, I'd have married the woman anyway. I was on my way to do that very thing, after the Duart wedding, but now . . ." He stared down at his less than perfect leg. "I imagine that I hear her laughter on the wind as I walk the shores, drilling an ache into my heart as real as the pain in this leg. She knew me to be bold, even arrogant she used to tell me, yet she loved me all the same. But for her to see me now, so much less of man than my earlier self, in this broken state," Michael choked on his words, honoring the loss of one so dear.

But then it happened - a subtle darkness shrouded his face, bringing tremors in its wake. Then suddenly he was back at Duart Castle . . .the wedding . . . the unfortunate bride . . . then darkness. He remembered only fragments of his journey to this blessed isle, as if carried on the backs of angels.

Father Callum watched as Michael closed his eyes; his head began rocking slowly back and forth then his shoulder jerked as if an invisible hand pulled him upwards. His eyes flew opened wide, like a doe sensing its death. Michael screamed, a silent scream.

"Michael! Michael! Are you all right?" said Father Callum. "I had no idea, man." The priest put his arms around the harper's shoulders, supporting him as Michael slumped backwards against the cold stone wall. The priest quickly whispered Psalm 42: "Your song pierces even my darkest days . . . ."

Michael knew where he was, and what was happening, and wailed aloud at this monstrous presence still in his life. The nightmares at least had the decency to happen in private. But a public episode? He didn't know how to stop it. His hip and leg had never healed properly, leaving him with a permanent limp while the scar remained a constant reminder. But this - revels of the horrors within – was unspeakable.

The two men now walked towards the chapter house together, one steadily, one slightly limping while their early morning shadows bumped into each other. Father Callum helped Michael back to his cell, requesting a cup of warm ginger tea from a passing monk. While Michael sat on his pallet, leaning against the wall, he watched the priest. Neither mentioned the outburst in the Abbey, for there were no words.

Trying to turn their focus, Father Callum approached Michael with a new opportunity. "Michael, we here at the Abbey have been immensely pleased with your transcription work," started the elder. "It surpasses the work of our own in many instances. Ever since the finishing of The Book of Kells hundreds of years ago, we still have many requests for illuminated manuscripts. If you wish, I'd like to ask you to create some of the colored illuminated psalms requested by other monasteries."

Michael held Father Callum in high regard, remembering his previous kindnesses. The darkness had passed, and Michael wanted to please the priest, so he could remain in this secluded community. "That would be quite an honor, Father. When would you like me to begin?"

"How about tomorrow, my son? You should rest awhile today, perhaps take a walk in the late afternoon sunshine. I'll have the new parchments and colored inks brought to your cell by Brother Aidan. He so enjoys your company. Begin with the Twenty-Third Psalm, then have Brother Aidan find me to review the work."

"Yes, Father. Thank you," Michael said. He laid back on the pallet and closed his eyes, hoping for some relief. Father Callum closed the door quietly. He could not forget the sadness in his friend's eyes after playing the music earlier today, nor the wildness later. He pondered how much longer Michael would be with them.

CHAPTER FIVE

"Ma, it's still so early that I must not be thinking straight at all, "said Hannah, throwing the blanket off herself. "Where is Grann's embroidered sheet, Ma?

Rosamond continued stirring the oat brose, adding milk and honey, just the way her daughter loved it. She would miss Hannah's grumblings as much as her soft laughter. "Darlin', you washed it out and left it on the line, it being such an unseasonably warm day yesterday. Look to the line."

Hannah dashed outside, wrapping her green wool shawl tightly around her shoulders. The sheet flapped in the cool wind, like a sail ready to embark on a voyage into unchartered waters. Hannah glanced at the fields and laughed as she saw the MacGillvray's collie running the sheep to a new pasture. She closed her eyes then took a deep breath, listening for ripples along the River Feshie from recent rains. The moors were still purple with heather, but the tall evergreen ferns were beginning to dominate the landscape. Her heart was so full that she began to sing,

"I sow the seeds of love,

For to blossom all in the spring. "

She took the sheet down, careful not to let it touch the winter grass, then ran back inside. "Well, it isn't a bit warm out there today. It's a miracle it is that the sheet isn't frozen like a sickle." She shook it out, as if releasing the cold, then continued singing as she began folding it:

"O the violet I did not like

because it would fade so soon . . ."

Rosamond, hearing the familiar clarity, remarked, "You've a fine voice just like your father." She continued with her work, not realizing her slip.

But Hannah heard it, and hid this in her heart.

The young woman relished this time, realizing that after tomorrow it would never be the same. It was her mother that taught Hannah the value of song, whether lullabies to soothe Hannah's recurring nightmares or simple ones accompanying any task. Rosamond showed Hannah how to imitate the birds of the fields to pitch her notes just right. Yes, there would always be singing in Hannah's home.

She brought her mind back to the task at hand, placing the sheet in the top of the chest. "I still love this sheet the best. You did such a lovely job working the flowers into the corners. The purples are my favorites." Hannah closed the wool curtain separating their pallets from the room then sat down for breakfast.

"I'm pleased, Hannah," said Rosamond. She spooned out the steaming oat concoction into two cups, then sat down to eat with her daughter.

"You don't think I made the wedding too fancy?" asked Hannah.

"Why, no, not at all. That hunter green gown with maroon bodice was a fine choice, especially the matching ribbons. I'm sorry I hadn't any lace to give you for the bodice, but the sleeve caps make you look like one of the good folk themselves, a queen even." She smiled at Hannah, easing her daughter's mind. "Now, I've been up early baking today for the wedding party, even added three eggs to the honey-oat bridal cake batter for leavening's sake, baking it first off. Let's see how it goes." Rosamond grabbed a cloth then pulled the iron skillet from the burning logs, using wood rather than peat to create a fire extra hot for baking. She brought out a large, yellow cake. She carefully placed the cloth over the top, then flipped the cake out onto a large wooden trencher. She beamed.

"Oh Ma, it's beautiful it is," said Hannah. "We'll decorate it with nuts, wild berries, and fresh cream. Won't you be the envy of all the ladies for cooking such a wonder?"

As the two women stood there admiring it, the cake shifted. Both held their breath. The cake's edges seemed a bit heavy, drawing the middle tight. Suddenly, the cake cracked right in half. All smiles vanished.

"Ma, it cracked!" shouted Hannah.

"Now, you know as well as I that a cracked cake doesn't mean a thing," said Rosamond.

"But Ma, it means unhappiness for the couple if the wedding cake cracks." Hannah sat down, sobbing into her hands.

"Gather your wits, child, and calm down. There's nothing a little butter and fresh cream can't fix. And as for unhappiness or bad luck even, why would you believe such a thing? You love the boy, and he loves you. Everything will be all right."

She snuggled her daughter tightly, pressing out the silly fears. Rosamond's faith washed over Hannah, who let herself be calmed once again by her mother's steadfast, sustaining love. "There, there now. Dry those tears. Too much to be done today. I have time to bake a second cake, which we'll probably be needing anyway with so many coming to the wedding. Now, you go finish up your packing. It should have been over at the MacLarens' house a week ago. Be off with you." Rosamond took the large baking bowl to the wash tub, rinsed it out then began gathering ingredients for the second cake.

When asked about her own wedding, Rosamond had told her daughter what Hannah needed to hear -dreams - not the truth. There had been no wedding.

Soon footsteps could be heard on the broad gray flagstones leading to their house. Lally came up the walk and knocked on the door. "Any bride-to-be about this morning, or is she sleeping in after last night?"

"She's finishing up her providan," said Rosamond. "The girl has been folding and folding the same clothing all morning. You would think she was moving to the Orkneys up north as many times as she has packed that trunk. Would you like a cup of tea?"

71

"Aye, that would be lovely," said Lally. Turning to the bride she said, "Hannah, you best get on since we've still got the flowers to deal with today." Then sneaking up behind Rosamond, Lally whispered, "And then there's the jumping the chanty tonight! Are you ready?"

"Absolutely, my girl. I'll have a lovely little feast a-waiting once you've taken her around." The two women chuckled. "Hannah, I'm stepping over to the Chisholms' to borrow some eggs. You girls finish up, now" said Rosamond, wrapping her purple shawl about herself then disappearing into the day.

Hannah was just closing the oaken chest lid as Lally sat opposite her. "I can't believe it's taken me so long to get this done," said Hannah.

Lally sat on the smaller pallet with the brown blanket then picked up a heart-shaped mahogany box with mother-of-pearl inlay on its top sitting on the floor, nestled between the pallet and the wall. "Will you be taking this lovely box?" asked Lally. "I don't believe I've ever seen it before." She turned the box carefully in her palm, noticing the delicate engravings.

"Oh no, Lally, that belongs to my mother. She keeps private things in there, mostly from her travels down to Perth during festival times. Funny though, she rarely looks at them now. But I know better than to steal a peek. Why, she caught me about three years ago when my curiosity was pulling at me worse than a goat freeing a shirt from the line. Ma had never smacked me before, but she raised her hand as if she might when she saw me sifting through her treasures. Best put it back."

Lally quickly replaced the box, not wanting to ever see the wrath of Rosamond MacFey.

"As for my clothes and personal things," said Hannah, "we'll store this box in his parents' house for now. Someday soon we will have our home, in the south pasture. Lukas and his brothers need to wait till spring to build it." Hannah looked out the window at nothing in particular. "Our home, Lally. Can you believe it? Tomorrow I'll be living with the man whose soul I know better than my own." She wrapped her arms around her shoulders, squeezing herself as if he were holding her.

"So tell me, Hannah, how did you know your husband would be Lukas?" asked Lally, playing with the edge of the blanket. "Tell me the truth. Time's up."

"Promise you won't tell a soul?" asked Hannah, sitting down beside Lally, her eyes growing wide.

"I'm your best friend," said Lally, straightening her shoulders like a warrior at attention. "Of course, I won't tell. Why, did you do one of the old divination tricks?"

"Well," started Hannah, "once when I was maybe eight or nine even, I heard about the lint-seed sowing to see the face of your true love."

"I've heard that rare it is for a girl to see her love that way because it only works for those with second sight, and that's not you," said Lally, sipping her tea.

"Well," said Hannah, rolling her eyes towards the ceiling, "I decided to try it anyway, once I was older, of course. So, when I was twelve, I waited until just before Beltane at planting time, and went walking on the ridge with a handful of lint seeds. I let them slip to the ground, one at a time, then covered them up with my shoe. I sang the song:

> "Lint-seed I saw ye,
>
> Lint-seed I saw ye,
>
> Let him it's to be my lad
>
> Come after me and pull me."

"No, you didn't!" Lally sat on the edge of the pallet.

"Yes, I did," said Hannah, gathering the folds of her skirt.

"Did you see Lukas coming after you? They say the lad's spirit comes and pulls the flax behind you." Lally craned her neck closer to her friend's face.

"Well, yes, and no. I didn't exactly *see* Lukas, but I did see what looked like Lukas, more like a ghost ye know, than actually him," said Hannah. "The lad was tall, with hair like Lukas, but the face was bit fuzzy." She leaned back onto the goose down pillow. "But you never know for certain. It's just a possibility, that's all."

"'That's all?' 'That's all', she says. Holding out on your dearest friend all these years that you've the gift. Why ever didn't you tell me?" asked Lally, setting down her cup.

"I didn't want you to think me daft, that's all," whispered Hannah. "I know how some folks are treated once the news gets out, and it's not always a lovely sight." Hannah told Lally how years ago a group of young lads had jeered at an older woman with second sight, calling her crazy. Hannah had vowed then never to let on that she had the gift. She had not even told her mother, yet today, Lally was so insistent. Maybe just this once.

"But Hannah, you must have known that I'd never mistreat you." Lally put one hand on Hannah's shoulder, facing her friend. "I think it's just wonderful!" Her smile dispersed all doubts.

"Really?" Hannah searched Lally's face for reassurance.

"Really!" said Lally. "Now tell me, did you know before the lint-seed, I mean did you ever see things or know things before?" Lally held her friend's eyes steadily.

"Well, once in a great while I might have a dream that came true or sensed someone in pain without their telling me. Most folks with second sight will only see death a-comin', but I'm not like that, predicting who'll die. But Grann, I knew she died before they told me." Hannah stood up, thinking of the sheet she just packed that held the loving care of her grandmother.

"Really? Did you dream her death?"

"No. She came to me that night, kissed me on the cheek the way she always did to say good-night. They told me the next morning that she'd died after supper over at the Stewarts, but Ma wanted me to sleep, knowing how upset I'd be."

"Oh Hannah, that must have been so sad," said Lally.

"I miss her, but I don't miss the cold words she'd speak to Ma sometimes. I'm still not sure what they were always on about, but peaceful those two weren't."

Lally saw how uncomfortable Hannah looked, and the last thing she wanted today was for Hannah to feel anything but sheer joy. She jumped up, grabbed Hannah around the waist, and said, "Now, we've got some posies and garlands to finish over at Caitlin's. I know that rascal Lukas asked you to meet him today at noon, so we best be off."

"Thank you," said Hannah "for everything." The two girls hugged each other like only best friends can. Hannah grabbed some muffins, cheese, dried apples, and a flask of wine for her lunch with Lukas. The two women practically skipped like girls all the way to the MacDonalds' house.

Caitlin would not wait for them. She sat on the floor near the hearth, surrounded with green ribbons and dried flowers: purple heather, gilded marigolds, and white rose buds. The girls walked in, saw the floor strewn with flowers, and immediately sat down, twining colored ribbons around the stalks into posies.

"Hannah," said Caitlin. "I was saving the best for your bridal bouquet. I've got extra rose buds that will dangle ever so delicately around your wrist, tied with green ribbons to match your dress. We can mix the heather and marigolds into a bunch if you'd like. I've even got three love knots that have been blessed by the priest, for good luck!" She raised the love knots in her right hand then smiled brightly enough to make the rose buds bloom.

"Looks like you've thought of everything. That all sounds wonderful, just too wonderful," sighed Hannah. She tied her hair back with a green ribbon then stood up with a hand full of rose buds, twirling around the room with an unseen dancing partner.

"Caitlin, have you the boxwood and the ivy for the garlands? They're supposed to be at the church today by two o'clock for hanging," asked Lally.

"All ready to go!" said Caitlin. "But I still need some help with these posies. And just whose idea was it for every guest to get one, I'd like to know? I'll bet you it was someone who never had to make them." She set a determined face to the task at hand. Lally grinned at Hannah, each grateful for their friend's care in details, regardless of her complaints. They knew she was loving every minute of it.

The next two hours passed quickly, and under Caitlin's careful supervision, the task was soon completed. Both girls knew that Lukas had asked Hannah to meet him around noon, just one last time today before the boys took him off to Ruthven for a night of frivolity.

Lukas sat under the rowan tree, watching Hannah's easy gait, the sway of her hips as she headed towards him. It reminded him of a similar time when he'd noticed her, rather heard her. The sun hung low in the sky, mellowing gold on midsummer's eve, as he walked home from visiting cousins in Ruthven. That's when he heard it - a solitary voice so haunting he feared it could be the Good Folk, the fey themselves out reveling on such a feast night.

He had quickened his pace when he saw her, standing on a knoll above a small stone house, swaying back and forth, with her hands on her hips then arms raised high in supplication. Her body moved with the lilting notes she sang, as if dancing with an invisible lover. At first, he thought her crazy and decided to walk on. But something stayed him. He closed his eyes, listening, then upon opening them again, found himself drawn into her dance with the wind. He'd never seen grace so inexplicably real, nor felt such a stirring deep in his heart.

Although he'd known Hannah for years, this was the first time he saw the woman in her. He spoke with her after church, and she received his advances readily, both sensing a quickening of hearts and spirits. Their first kiss was at Beltane, yet their love-making began only months ago in the shadows of the forest while the hillsides blazed with bonfires at Samhain. Their heat matched that fire, and they had burned together.

He would recite lines of verse to her while he watched his father's sheep or lie in pastures of winter grasses. They would sit near shallow pools by the river's edge and share their dreams, share them all. He loved her completely, and tomorrow she would be his, for always.

He hummed "Raglan Road," an old favorite, then inserted his own words, singing for his love as she mounted the hill.

> "Though I've gained not gold,
>
> I have wealth untold
>
> For my heart is bold and free.
>
> Come live with me and be my love,
>
> He whispered tenderly.
>
>
> My lines of verse though unrehearsed
>
> Tell of love beyond our years,
>
> Under stars of light, play my shepherd's pipe
>
> Like the music of the spheres."

Hannah appeared from the brush, elusive as a faerie.

"Well, it's about time you got here, woman! I was beginning to think you'd stood me up." Lukas grinned then rose from the soft plaid he'd placed over the coarse January grasses to meet his bride.

"And who would argue with her husband-to-be, on the very day before their wedding, I ask you? Certainly not I, Lukas

MacLaren," laughed Hannah, placing her food basket on the plaid then opening her arms wide to meet her lover. Hannah closed her eyes as Lukas held her, breathing deeply. She smelled the fresh hay woven into his sweater. She loved his earthy scent, imagining him at times more of a wood spirit than mere mortal. She sighed then rested her head on the delicate curve of his shoulder.

"Come now, woman, I've a powerful hunger inside me. What feast did you bring for us today?" He kissed her hair lightly then pulled himself from her arms. "Come, sit close by me, my lass of the white pine eyes, and tell me all the news."

Hannah chittered like a magpie in summer as she opened the basket, decisively spreading out the large cloth. The muffins tumbled out while Lukas sliced the cheese. Hannah poured wine for them into the two cups, careful not to spill any. The dried apples proved a sweet treat.

She told Lukas all about her morning then laid back on the soft woolen plaid. "Lukas, do you ever wonder what we'll be like as an old couple? You know, like Jack and Sarah in the village. They've been married nearly fifty years, and I still see him wink at her in church, as if they was courtin'. He's always holding her hand whenever they're out walking."

She faced him now, her eyes more serious than befitting a happy bride-to-be. "Will you still love me then, Lukas, when I'm old and hunched over with a mop of hair to frame my face? Will you?"

"Will I still love you? Is that what you're asking me? A day before our wedding, and you still doubt me?" His fingertips gently tilted her head up, allowing their eyes to meet. "Any other man would be angry at your fears, Hannah. It's enough to test God himself. But I know your tender heart, with all its silly notions, and I love you in spite of them all. So yes, Hannah, I will love you when your breasts hang to your waistline, your arms swing like a sheet in the breeze, and you've not but one tooth in your whole head. How's that?" He smiled with such warmth that even snow would have melted on those glistening lips.

"Now you're making fun of me," she said, pursing her lips together as she sat back a bit.

"I'll admit I'm having fun, lassie, but I would never hurt you, Hannah. Not for the world."

"But Lukas," she whispered, "even if I got sick, and you had to take care of me for a long time, would you love me still?" She was leaning in towards him now, close enough that Lukas could see her furrowed brow.

Before she knew it, Lukas reached across the plaid, grabbed her around the waist, and began rolling down the short hill with her till they reached the bottom. They lay sprawled about like a four-legged, four-armed starfish adrift on the sand. "Love you still, you ask?" he laughed, holding her tight. "I'd rather love you moving, girl!" Hannah smiled, then Lukas kissed her, long and deep before she could reply. "C'mon now, I've got a surprise for you, but it'll not be found at the bottom of this hill." He helped Hannah to her feet, and the couple walked back up the hill, hand in hand. They snuggled together on the plaid, drinking the wine and finishing their noonday feast.

"Now, you just sit right here," said Lukas, "I'll be back before you can say 'God keep the Good Folks at bay.' " He reached behind the rowan tree, its winter limbs stretched taut against the grey sky, and pulled out a small leather pouch.

"For my little wood nymph," he whispered, offering her the bag. "Open it."

"But what is it, Lukas?"

"You won't know, girl, until you look inside. Go ahead, now." He nudged her shoulder.

Hannah knew that sometimes the bride and groom gave each other gifts at the wedding, but they had not really discussed it. She had nothing for Lukas. She glanced at him again.

"Go ahead," he said. "Everything will be all right now." He put his arm around her, cradling her in the protection of his love.

Hannah opened the small pouch and could not believe her eyes. There sat a ring, a ring more beautiful than anything she'd ever seen. It was a pointed oval amethyst, set in silver with a triad on either side. The triads were joined by a silver band of ribboned knot work etched delicately into the precious metal. She held it up, and the sun sparkled through the lavender facets. "Oh Lukas, but how . . .?"

"Don't you worry about the how, just know that it's done."

Hannah started to place the ring on her finger, to admire it when Lukas stopped her.

"Here, wait a minute. Don't you be putting that on your own self. If I don't do anything else right in my life, this will be it. Give me the ribbon from your hair, Hannah."

She untied the slender green ribbon then offered it to Lukas.

"Now, give me your left hand."

She switched the ring to her right hand, clasping it tightly, then presented her left to him. Lukas held it with his left, then looped the green around their hands, over and over again until its end. "Now, I know this is not a proper handfasting, seeing as how we don't have any witnesses around, and we're actually marrying tomorrow. But I want to tell you, just you and not a whole crowd of folks, that I love you, Hannah McFey." He placed the ring on her third finger. "I will love you more than my own life, placing you above all others, as first and forever in my heart." He leaned in now, hungrily touching his lips to hers. He noticed that she quivered, and mistaking it for trembling held her close.

"Take me, take me now," she whispered.

He quickened his kisses, hungry now for all of her. They swooned together and when satiated, they lay together, limbs entwined like a Celtic knot.

"Lukas, forgive me for being so foolish at times," she said. "But one thing I will never doubt." She pulled her head back just enough to see his loving face. "Lukas," she said softly, "you are the twin to my soul. I know that no person can possess another, but I hunger for all that you are, be it shepherd, poet, or simply husband. I breathe in; you breathe out."

He kissed her again, holding her close. He buried his head in her neck, breathing her very essence into himself with a sigh. "You always smell like purple," he whispered, then untying their hands, he picked her up, and whirled her around in an innocent swirl. "I love you, Hannah McFey," he yelled, loud enough for the nearby crofters to hear him. "Let's be married tomorrow, shall we?"

"We shall," she giggled, trying to catch her breath. "But as lovely as this ring looks on my finger this minute, I can't go about wearing it till you give it to me in the kirk tomorrow."

"Here," he said, placing the green ribbon through the ring and tying the ends off. He placed it around her neck. "Wear it next to your heart tonight, hidden from view. I can get it back just before the service in the morning. I want you to keep it close by, to chase away any last minute fears." Hannah tucked it inside her dress, looking more radiant than the full moon on the waves of Loch Lynne.

"We'd best get going, now," said Hannah, packing up the last of the food. "I've still got a few last things to tend to before the girls come over this evening. Will you be out with the lads tonight?"

"Of course. A man's got to celebrate his last night being single."

"Mind you that they don't blacken you up like they did Grey McCrady," said Hannah. "His wife Lucy told me it was days before that black soot came off him, and that he smelled like a smoldering fire on their wedding night!"

"I've already warned both Patrick and Seamus. None of those shenanigans for me. I'll see you in the morning." He kissed her once more, then they both set off with much on their minds. A gathering of pale grey clouds slipped surreptitiously over the hills as the afternoon faded into early evening.

CHAPTER SIX

"Come lads, we're away to Ruthven for an evening of ... well, to celebrate Lukas's last evening as a free man!" said Patrick. "Step lively, now, for though it be only five miles north sure it will take us at least an hour for us to walk there." He slapped Seamus on the shoulder while Lukas and Gavin came out the front door of the MacLaren home. The sharp sound created a ripple through the woods, alerting the russet red deer to take cover in the dark winter greens. Red squirrels scampered higher through the protective branches of the larches surrounding the MacLaren farm while low rumbles of thunder rippled through the winter night air.

"Rory!" shouted Malcolm, Lukas's older brother. He was standing beneath the Scots pine, pacing back and forth. "Get yourself out here, so we can send our brother off in true MacLaren style. Rory!" The youngest MacLaren came running from the barn, his shirttail flapping behind him like the tail feathers of a Capercaillie while his red, unkempt hair appeared as if had not been brushed for days. He waved at his parents standing in the doorway then made a silly face at Malcolm. "Boy, you look a mess! How do you expect us to . . . ."

Before Malcolm could finish his reprimand, Lukas cut him off, "Rory, hurry lad. We'll never make it if Malcolm starts on you. Tonight's my last night as a single man, and I don't want to miss it." He grinned at Rory, spotting the stray bits of hay around his shirt collar. Lukas knew that Rory had a leaning towards a certain maid from the neighboring croft who was probably fastening her clothing in the upper loft of the barn at that very moment.

Rory grabbed Lukas by the arm and started down the dirt path shouting, "Come away, lads! We're off to the Lion's Head Inn! To Ruthven!!" The young men returned the challenge: "To Ruthven!" they yelled and slipped into the night.

The MacLarens now hugged one another, reminiscing about this same night before their own wedding. "Do you think he knows they're up to no good?" asked Eglantyne.

"Well, they wouldn't be his friends if they weren't!" laughed Gerald. "Besides, the blackening doesn't hurt. Foot-washin' the bride and groom is customary, now ain't it? At least, if you don't fight it. I sprained my ankle trying to get away from my group. Perhaps Lukas will have better sense and just enjoy it. But have you seen your other sons lately? Malcolm and Rory have been secreting away soot for the past week in readiness. They'll get him on the way home."

"Did they blacken just your feet?" asked Eglantyne, raising an eyebrow ever so slightly.

"Clear up the legs they went once I was on the ground. Stripped me of my breeches then slathered me clear up my backside. Don't tell me you don't remember what I looked like on our wedding night?"

"All I remember is the loving that night, Mr. MacLaren," she answered, tilting her head upwards with clear intention.

"Why Mistress MacLaren, you still make me quiver," he said, taking her in his arms and kissing her slowly. She slid her arms over his sleek lean back then pulled him close. They held each other for a few moments, savoring the fire between them that still lingered, seemingly doused at times by daily routines. The couple smiled at one another as they closed the front door. Muriel sat beside the fire finishing her wedding present of embroidered napkins. The family settled in for a comfortable evening. They did not notice the tiny droplets of rain beginning to click clack on the window sill.

As the five young men made their way north, Lally, Caitlin, and Hannah were enjoying a lovely dinner in the MacDonald home. The apple tart aroma from dessert still lingered, filling the room with cinnamon. After dinner, Mr. MacDonald and his two sons parted quickly for the Stewart farm, leaving the women to their business.

The women spent a full hour in bridal rituals, from the bridal foot-washing to the "finding of the ring," a tradition where a wedding ring, along with other objects, is placed in a basin of soapy, ashen water. Supposedly the girl to find the ring first will be the next to wed, so when Caitlin herself found the ring balancing delicately on her pinky, shouts and hurrahs rang to the rafters.

"Well, have you ever seen anything like that?" said Mistress MacDonald. "I've never seen anyone retrieve the wedding ring that way!"

Caitlin stood up, whirling and twirling around the small living room with her hand swathing imaginary arcs through the air, admiring the ring. "I'll be next, Hannah. My turn to play the bride." She plopped herself down at Hannah's feet, still gazing at the ring.

"Well, now that we've finished here, we're off for one last adventure," said Lally, rising from the floor. She gathered the winter woolen cloaks for each girl from the iron hooks by the door and escorted her friends across the MacDonald fields.

The girls wandered down the main road, dodging the raindrops that fell gently from the sky now deepening to a midnight blue when they came upon the fork to Lally's house. Lally stooped under the twin larches that marked her family roadway then handed the lantern to Caitlin. "Here, Caitlin. Hold the lantern if you would, please."

Lally stood up with a milk pail, apparently filled with dried flowers while several colored ribbons flowed over the lip and handle. She giggled, holding out the pail in the gleaming lantern light. Both Caitlin and Hannah smiled in disbelief. "Now, what we'll do is visit a few houses. At each one, you'll jump the chanty, or bucket as it were, so they can leave you a surprise in the pail or even money to help the new couple get started. Now, come on ladies, folks are waiting for us."

The two girls knew that when Lally set her mind to something, you best not quarrel with her. Hannah accepted her fate.

"All you have to do is jump, Hannah," said Lally. "C'mon girls. It's tradition."

So off they went down the road, arms linked like when they were schoolgirls, loaded with lantern, milk pail, and a bewildered bride. There were only about fifteen families along the River Feshie with a few outlying hermits in the upper regions. The girls visited many of the neighboring homes and left with generous surprises hidden in the pail for the happy couple. Each time Hannah jumped over the pail, she felt the ring bouncing between her breasts as if Lukas himself were knocking at her heart. He had gained entry years ago, his place certain now like no other person in her life. She smiled to herself, longing for tomorrow to come quickly.

They were rounding the lane toward the MacFeys when a small figure, lantern in hand, approached. The fur-lined cloak covered the face, but all three knew that frilly dress which sported just below the cloak's hemline.

"Why, it's Hannah MacFey," said Nell, pausing in the lane before them, "with her two faithful watchdogs. Scared to walk the night alone, are we?" She tossed her head to one side, her blonde curls bouncing in the night air.

With Caitlin and Lally present, Hannah tried to hold her tongue, yet civility was simply lost. "I walk with my friends, Nell, because I have them."

Nell held the lantern up towards Hannah's face, just a little too close. "I'll have you know I have pedigreed friends from the best of families, not that you'd know anything about that!"

"Why you little," Caitlin began, reaching for Nell, but Hannah pulled her back.

"What? Can't even make a proper sentence, can you!" she said, a satisfied sneer belying her thin lips. Then she noticed the ribboned pail. "And what is that hideous thing? Don't tell me you're out looking for hand-outs already?"

"We're following tradition, you daft turkey!" said Lally, straightening the pail and adjusting ribbons while trying to keep her lip from trembling.

Hannah would stand for no more. She grabbed Nell's left arm then forced Nell's lantern in her right hand too close to her head, singeing a stray curl.

"Ouch! You're hurting me!"

Hannah ignored Nell's plea. "Listen, you little tart, you tried to win Lukas, but you lost. He's mine, and you'll never find a husband because you'll die a sour old woman, alone in her big house with only simpering servants surrounding you. But I'll not listen to any more of your poisonous ideas, about me, Lukas, or my friends, do you hear! You best stay out of my way, Nell Robertson." She shoved the lantern back in Nell's face, laced her arms through Caitlin and Lally's, and began walking away as the gentle rain changed to snow.

Nell quickly recovered, screaming at the threesome. "Or what, weaver girl, what will you do? You don't scare me, you bastard!"

Caitlin and Lally froze.

Hannah turned, slowly. "What did you call me?"

Nell, pleased with the attention, lifted her nose in the air and said, "You heard me right well. I'll bet you don't even know who your father is because your mother would mate with anything that moved!"

Hannah lunged towards Nell, but her two friends grabbed Hannah about the waist.

Nell just laughed. "You'll never marry Lukas MacLaren as long as I've got breath in this body to tell the world what a little whore you are, just like your mother!" She trotted down the lane, hurriedly, for a strong wind now blew, mingled with icy barbs.

Hannah stood in shock, too embarrassed to move. She recalled the cruel things children had said to her about growing up without a father, but none had been this blatantly cruel. Caitlin held back tears while Lally took control.

"Now, come on," she said, ushering the small group forward. "We're not going to let Nasty Nell spoil this evening. After all, Hannah, your mother's waiting for us." Lally continued to usher the girls down the lane where they finished the evening at the MacFeys with Rosamond, sipping on hot cider by the fire and relishing the special cinnamon cakes fixed just for this occasion.

Horrific winds shook the small cottage. Rosamond opened the door to a swirling mass of snow. "Girls, you best hurry home. This storm will do nothing but get worse. Be off with you, now." Rosamond shooed Lally and Caitlin out the door like a hen sending her chicks out into the yard. "Hannah, make sure the barn is closed tightly. I wouldn't want any sheep getting lost in this tonight. Looks like a powerful storm."

"Yes, Ma," said Hannah, following her friends outside. Hannah ran down to the barn to secure the latch. She was relieved to see the geese waddling inside amidst the eight to ten sheep already clustering inside. All was well.

The rain sharpened to icy swords prickling her face as Hannah fled back to the warmth of the cottage. She watched from the window, for through the trees she could barely make out Lally's lantern, swinging back and forth through the low branches of Scots pine. Hannah shivered, then stepped inside, hoping her beloved was safe.

Meanwhile, the lads, now full of local ale, had enjoyed their time at the Lion's Head Inn. Lusty songs or tunes filled with buffoonery about marital bliss such as "The Farmer's Curst Wife" or "Our Goodman" reverberated through the oak beams. After many rounds, the glasses were raised for a parting toast, then off they went, wobbling down the road. The trip back from Ruthven turned into a brisk walk as the wind kicked up, dotted with snow as the icy darts fell from the winter sky, accompanied by razor winds.

Malcolm sobered first. "Run, fellas, run!" cried Malcolm.

They sped down the dirt path, transformed into a ribbon of slick slime like newly made soap. Prior arrangements for all to spend the night were now a blessing as neither Patrick, Gavin, nor Seamus wanted to venture farther in such a storm.

Within thirty minutes they rounded the curve leading to the MacLaren farm, sobering with each footstep. Lukas heard his father shouting, as did Malcolm and Rory, attempting to herd the sheep into the barn when Lukas ran up beside him.

"Hurry, son," said his father. "Jed's gotten loose! When it started thundering earlier, he took off towards the river. Never seen such a thing like this. One minute as soft as a spring rain then icy spears coming from the sky, whirling and swirling about. Go and bring back Jed. You're the only one he'll listen to if he's scared."

Jed was their only work horse, so protecting his life was crucial. Lukas himself had picked out Jed at the horse fair in Pitlochry over two years ago, so as the pair had worked side by side, a special bond was created. With little thought for his own safety, Lukas plunged into the falling snow as he headed towards the river. The other boys helped Mr. MacLaren gather the other animals into safety.

Lukas leapt over a low stone wall dividing the fields, but when he landed, the slippery snow caused him to tumble down a shallow ravine. He jumped up, but a sharp pain in his right foot told him he had sprained his ankle, causing him to stumble against the wall. He sat there, crying out for Jed, when he saw the horse fifty yards away on the river's edge. He tried calling again, but the howling winds were his only reply.

The horse appeared frozen with fear.

If I can only get to him, thought Lukas, then Jed will let me ride him home. Lukas stood again, shifting most of his weight onto his left side leaning against the stone wall. If he could just use the wall as a crutch, he could get within hearing distance of Jed. Lukas carefully slid one hand over the other, heaving his right leg behind him. "Jed, come here, boy. Jed!!"

But the horse stood still. Snow swirled so heavily around him that he appeared caught inside a spider's web.

"Damn that horse!" cried Lukas, slipping once again. The river, already swollen due to rains two days prior, was bound to be near flood stage, possibly overflowing into the MacLaren barley fields. His decision was made. He inched out from the wall, slowly, carefully, cringing with the pain. A burning sensation shot up his leg. He was within ten yards of the frightened animal when Jed turned around and saw his master. He whinnied a soft whimper, heard only by the falling flakes, then began moving slowly towards Lukas.

Soon Lukas reached Jed's nose, pulling on the frozen lead saying, "Good boy, Jed. It's all right, boy. Let's go home."

Jed nuzzled his master, sensing some comfort despite the horrendous storm. But a sudden cry in the nearby wild startled Jed. The horse reared, causing Lukas to lose his balance. He fell to his right, begging his body for support, but the ankle was too weak and buckled again. "Damn it all!" screamed Lukas. He rolled through a gap in the wall, sliding down a hidden slope to the crunch of fractured bone and torn ligaments then slipped right into the River Feshie. As he hit his forehead on a submerged log, his head lolled to one side, the river slapping his face. In the darkness, he remembered her. *Hannah . . .*

CHAPTER SEVEN

Hannah snuggled under the dark woolen blankets trying to sleep, leaving the curtain partition open to heat her side of the room. Rosamond let the fire blaze a bit longer rather than smooring it for the night. Such a cold evening. She dozed in the chair, sitting close by the fire's edge. This last night, of all nights, she wanted to provide protection for her daughter. Tomorrow the duty would fall to Lukas, and Rosamond would be alone.

Hannah tossed and turned, barely able to discern between waking and sleeping while her sleeping shift twisted about her legs. The smell of peat lingered from the smoored coals while Rosamond's rhythmic breathing ebbed and flowed around Hannah, cocooning her. Focusing on Lukas and their life together would keep her warm. Clutching the ring on the ribbon about her neck, she fell into a deep sleep, imagining herself warm beneath a blanket of snow.

She drifted into dreams, but then heard her name, as if someone were calling to her from a distant place. First a whisper, tentative yet entreating. She dared to open her eyes, and beheld a dark figure at her bedside, his features shadowed by an ivory luminescence which haloed his face. "Come here, Hannah," said a familiar voice, his tone unyielding. But then he softened, whispering, "I've come to say good-bye, love. Let me hold you."

She rubbed her eyes then realized it was Lukas, covered with snow. She wondered if she was still dreaming, but as she looked around the cottage all seemed in order, for Rosamond slept peacefully by the glowing embers of the late fire. She grabbed her shawl then leapt into his arms, confused at this presence, the lateness of the hour, the eerie way he spoke to her now. "What do you mean, good-bye?"

"Hush, Hannah. Just hold me, lass." He held her close, as he had so many times before, sliding his wet arm around her back.

She cradled her head in the nape of his neck, longing for that familiar scent of hay and sheep, of heather and hillside

He whispered lines he'd longed to say to her softly as they swayed in small circles:

> "I'll live with thee and be thy love
>
> for as long as Time allows.
>
> Though the flesh may fail,
>
> the soul prevails
>
> throughout all eternity."

Then he tilted back her head, and kissed her, long and deep. "Always, Hannah, I am with you always." She stared at him, pulling back just far enough to see the face she adored.

A smile tugged at his lips, then he closed his eyes and sighed, tilting his head heavenward. "Look for me in the moonlight," he said, as his image melted in her arms, waning slowly until nothing remained but the scent of snow.

Hannah stood in the center of the room, her arms empty, limp by her side. She wrapped her arms around herself, but the woolen fibers provided no comfort, for the back of the shawl was wet.

A quiet trembling created small tingles, like tremors of thought, moving throughout her whole body. Understanding gripped her heart like a white hare hearing the snap of a trap.

She knew.

He was gone - forever.

She did not know how, but she knew her beloved was dead. He had come to say farewell before leaving this earth.

Hannah flung open wide the cottage door, running into the blackness. The moon hid its face now behind darkening clouds. No more snow, but wild winds slashed her long hair, whipping her face. She flung her grief into the universe, and it responded. Staffs of lightning coursed the sky. "Lukas! Come back!" she screamed. "Don't make me live without you!" She screamed again, but the pain was so great that no words emerged. She raised her fists towards the clouds, pounding the sky. She fell to her knees then slumped onto the hoary ground, white with cold.

Strong arms lifted Hannah up as Rosamond led the shivering girl inside the cottage, embraced in loving arms once more. But this time it was her mother, not her lover who held her close. "Child, what in heaven's name were you doing out there? Are you trying to kill yourself with a fever? What's wrong?" Rosamond settled Hannah in the chair by the fire and added a few more logs. She blew on the embers until they blazed like the eyes of a fearsome highland wildcat.

Rosamond filled the kettle with water for mint tea and hung it over the fire. Tiny droplets of water hissed on the logs below. Rosamond sat on the floor on a large blue pillow, facing her daughter, and waited.

Hannah suddenly stopped crying, muted by the horror. Slight clouds of breath encircled Hannah's head. She gasped, having forgotten to breathe. Her eyes froze in a silent stare, as if no soul resided within.

After two cups of the healing tea, life reappeared on Hannah's face. She seemed to now recognize her surroundings, looking at Rosamond as if her mother had just entered the room. "He's dead, Ma. Lukas is dead," she whispered.

"Now child, it must have been a bad dream. So many thoughts on the night before a wedding. It's natural for a young girl to have nightmares when the happiest day of her life is just brimming on the morn." She rubbed her daughter's hands, warming the still cold fingers.

"No, Ma," she said, looking past her mother. "It wasn't a dream. He was here. He held me, told me he loved me. Told me he would always be with me. Then he disappeared." Looking straight into Rosamond's eyes, "He just . . . sort of . . . faded away."

"Well, then, for sure it was a dream if he just up and vanished," said Rosamond. "Don't you think I'd have awakened if he'd come visiting this time of night?"

"Well, yes," said Hannah slowly, wanting to believe. Although a part of her heart held this dreadful truth, her mind could not wrap itself around losing Lukas. Still, her past experiences told her differently. "But it was just like when Grann visited me just after she had passed. You didn't believe me then, but it was just like that. She talked to me, told me she loved me and not to worry. Then we found out she had died that very night."

Rosamond did not know what to say. She knew her daughter had strong intuitions, a version of the sight, but she had rarely spoken to the girl about it. She never told Hannah that Grann saw visions, too. Perhaps Hannah was right this time. "Well, even if you're right, there's nothing to be done till the sun rises. You know that Patrick is supposed to be here early to take you to the kirk. Why don't we just wait till then?"

Hannah wrapped her arms around her shoulders and began slowly rocking back and forth. Her head nodded forward, like a fading snowdrop

She sighed - deep and long.

"You've worn yourself out now," said Rosamond. "You go back to bed and try to get a little sleep. You'll see that all is well in the morning." She helped her daughter onto the pallet, pulling the woolen blanket around Hannah's shoulders. The tea soon worked its magic, relaxing strained thoughts into strands of solitude. The soon-to-be bride lay exhausted, white, like a corpse in repose.

Rosamond smoored the fire, stacking peat bricks atop the slow burning embers, and took her seat once more. What would the morning hold?

Hannah awoke later than usual, her eyes crusted shut from tears during the night. She lay quietly on her pallet, not wishing to disturb Rosamond whose rhythmic snores echoed off the cottage stone walls.

What should she do? It was inconceivable that Lukas should leave her in this world alone, for their future seemed so certain. She rationalized his leaving, that ghostly visitation, concluding it was merely a dream.

On this day, her wedding day, she should be dressing now, awaiting the arrival of Patrick, the best man, to lead her to the kirk where the rest of the bridal party would be watching for her entrance. Was it simply jittery nerves, before the wedding? She shook herself, as if casting off a sorrow-filled cloak, then glanced at her wedding dress, lovely in the morning sun, looking like the forest floor in May. Although there was nothing normal about dressing in a wedding gown, it held some comfort, so she began.

As she was about to slip one arm through the sleeve openings, she paused, spotting her shawl draped over the chair next to the hearth. Could it still be wet, she thought, where Lukas had embraced her? She dropped the wedding gown and took three tentative steps then with trembling fingers, caressed the soft woolen fibers.

Damp, still damp - any thoughts of hope evaporated.

He was dead, and he would never return.

Then she slumped to the floor, her sleeping shift spread about her as if she were a water lily floating in water, or drowning.

A stillness spread over her body. The sudden sound of an inner door, slammed with intention, reverberated through the hallways of her heart. Locked. She rose, moving slowly with a glazed expression.

She remembered the dried flowers, so carefully placed by Caitlin throughout the church, delicate reminders of love, purity, and steadfastness.

She wondered now if they would be used to cover the coffin.

A soft knock at the door woke Rosamond, who stretched out her tired muscles, yawning freely. "Hannah, are you up so soon, lass? Did I hear the door?"

Hannah looked at her mother, but said nothing. The young woman draped her green wool shawl about her shoulders, floating like a wraith towards the door. Hannah struggled with the door's weight as it scraped against the stone threshold, barely opening.

"Hannah, can I give you a hand with that?" asked Patrick quietly, peering around the edges of the door. He stood there, not in his full highland regalia for a wedding, but rather in his rambling clothes from the night before. His haggard eyes and ashen face told Hannah that he'd known little sleep after the reveling in Ruthven.

She wanted to speak, knowing the dolorous news he must deliver, yet no words came. So she simply moved aside, inviting him in where they pulled the kitchen bench by the hearth. The pair sat down together, a numbing silence passed between them.

"Will you have a cup of tea, Patrick?" asked Rosamond, fully awake now and throwing her blue kirtle over her sleeping shift then setting the water kettle over the hearth. She blew on the ashes, bringing them to a gentle glow that quickly warmed their little cottage. "Come lad, sit. You look like you've seen a ghost."

Patrick sighed. "Aye, Mistress MacFey, "that would be a welcomed sight for me this morning." He glanced at Hannah, but turned away when their eyes met.

"But Patrick, what a strange thing to say," said Rosamond. "When would anybody be glad of a haunted visitation?"

"When the living are in need of knowing where a soul has traveled, Mistress MacFey. At least the ghosts would know who was roaming about on their side, now wouldn't they?" Patrick stared at the woman, wishing for some kernel of hope, for his own thoughts betrayed him.

"Well," started Rosamond, "I don't know for sure, mind you, but I'd be betting they would. But why, lad, would you be asking such a queer thing of the dead?"

The moment had come. Hannah knew it. A rumbling began, deep inside that caused her whole body to quake. She did not want to hear this.

"NO!" she screamed, jumping up from the bench with such force that she knocked it into the hearth, overturning the kettle of water into the fire.

The pair stared at Hannah, her eyes wild like that of a winter white hare standing before a hungry red fox, its teeth ready for death.

Rosamond and Patrick both hurried to the hearth, shoving the bench out of harm's way. Rosamond wiped up the spilt water then added kindling and several logs to the remaining embers. Her hands trembled as she passed the empty kettle to the grief-stricken lad.

"Patrick, please get us some water from the well," said Rosamond, her quavering voice betraying her resolve to remain strong. "It's out back behind the goat pen. Be quick about it now, lad."

He grabbed the kettle then left the little cottage, muttering "O holy mother of God . . . ."

Hannah paced the tiny room, her slender fingers covering her eyes, as if by not seeing she could not hear. Her mother tried to console her, to hold her, but Hannah would not accept any comfort. Patrick soon returned with the water, and new tea water began to boil. He stood, not knowing how to tell Hannah his dreadful news.

"Tell us, lad, now what has happened? Is it Lukas?" asked Rosamond. She believed that her daughter's anxieties about marriage had caused her to dream the nighttime visitor.

"He's dead," Hannah said flatly. She sat again by the fire, staring at it like a seer seeing his own mischance. She curled her shoulders inward, a protective wall from the hurtful world, yet nothing could stop this pain.

"But how? How could you know?" asked Patrick. He dropped to his knees, deflated yet somehow relieved that as incredulous as it seemed, Hannah already knew.

Could she tell him about last night? She could say, "Why Patrick, he came by last evening for a farewell embrace then disappeared right before my eyes." No, she didn't welcome others knowing about her second sight. So she did the next best thing - she lied. "I had a most dreadful nightmare last night about Lukas, you see. Ma had the worst time calming me down, didn't you Ma?" She gave her mother a conspiratorial look.

"Sure enough, daughter," said Rosamond. She gave Hannah and Patrick both some tea then sat in one of the hearth chairs. "Worried about the wedding and all, I guess. I found her kneeling on the ground outside, door flung wide open, sobbing that Lukas was dead." She wanted to hold her, so Hannah would not feel so alone, but instead Hannah crossed her hands over her chest and waited, waited for whatever was to come next.

"Well, we don't know exactly what's happened to him, God's honest truth," said Patrick. "Last night when we came back from Ruthven, the storm was scaring the animals. We lads helped Mr. MacLaren with the livestock while Lukas went searching for Jed. Dumb old horse - wouldn't let nobody touch him but Lukas. Anyway, Lukas took off down towards the river, just barely able to make out Jed's tracks in the snow. It came falling hard then, winds howling, ice hard bullets coming from every direction. I've never seen such a storm!"

"Did Lukas find Jed?" asked Rosamond.

"That's just it," said Patrick, slapping his knee roughly. "Jed came back to the barn about an hour later, but he was alone. We knew it was rough going, walking in that January wind. But Lukas knows this land better than any of us, so we weren't worried. Well, since the MacLarens had invited me and the lads to stay over, we got the animals settled then headed indoors for some much needed rest, and maybe a nip of whiskey."

"But Lukas, didn't he come home? Is he all right?" asked Rosamond.

Patrick sighed. "Mistress MacFey, I wish I could tell you yes, but I can't. We fell asleep in the main room by the fire, so tired we were. But I woke up a little later and noticed that Lukas was not among our number. I woke up the lads, worried I was then. We checked his bed, but it was empty. By now, the whole household was awake. We grabbed our coats, lanterns, and started a search party since the snow had stopped. Malcolm and Rory headed towards the barns while the rest of us took the back hills, thinking Lukas got lost in all that blinding snow. We looked all night, but the snow covered any tracks he would have made."

The young man took a sip of his tea then continued. "Mr. MacLaren is rounding up some neighbors now to continue looking, but Mistress MacLaren thought I best come tell you, Hannah. We just don't know where he is." Patrick finished his tea. "Many thanks, Mistress MacFey, for your hospitality this morning. But I best be going back now. Don't worry, Hannah. We'll find him. There'll be a wedding yet." He tried to sound hopeful, but too much had happened. He walked out quietly, leaving the two women alone.

It was out now. Lukas was missing, more than missing according to Hannah.

"Hannah, I'm sure the men will find him. The boy is probably holed up somewhere for the night. He knows that farm, every knoll and hillock, so there's no way that boy could ever get lost - even in a snow storm. Now, why don't we put away these somber notions and start getting you ready. How about a nice warm bath? I'll heat up the water and fill the basin for you, right by the fire."

"Ma, there will be no wedding," said Hannah.

"Then maybe we should be praying for the menfolk as they look for the boy," said Rosamond. She knelt by her pallet and began, "Our Father . . ."

"There's no need for prayer now, Ma" whispered Hannah. "It's too late."

"But child, you don't know. . ."

"But I do know, Ma," she said, with such finality that it gave Rosamond pause. She looked out the window and noticed that the branches of the pines were still. "I'm going for a walk." She quickly changed into her russet day shift, pulled the ivory wool sweater over her mass of tangles, and with cloak in tow headed outside.

Hannah's steps were measured and slow on the slippery path. The morning sun, having melted the upper layer of snow, left a river of ice in its wake. Hannah reached for stray limbs and fell onto more than one gray boulder on her journey. She saw no villagers, but heard faint callings of "LUKAS!" from the search party. They must be down by Stewart's farm now, she thought, looking in the direction of the River Feshie. But why would he have gone that far south?

Hannah wandered towards the MacLaren farm on the path she'd walked for years, yet now it was masked by a slender shroud of winter white. She passed the road leading to the main house and followed the footpath to the back acreage up to Rowan Hill.

She remembered a tune Lukas sang to her under their tree about a young woman being visited in a dream by a fairy lover on just such a hill. Without realizing it, she hummed the tune, the silent words winding their way through the pines. It lifted her spirit to remember Lukas singing to her, even if it was a ghostly song. She meandered through the spindly shrubs, now covered with snow. This white world, once comforting, now felt as if she walked in the Otherworld.

She reached the top, crowned by a single rowan tree, its shape rounded by nature. She stood before it, flooded with memories of times spent with Lukas. She brushed the snow from the roots and sat down, leaning into the supportive trunk. She wrapped her arms around herself, closed her eyes, and imagined

Lukas holding her. She did not see the red deer, silent guests to this winter lament, as they foraged for food.

She leaned forward, cradling her head with frozen fingers, not caring about the wind, or the cold, or anything at all. Here he said he loved her. Here they shared their first kiss. Here they sealed their future. She cried until the tears abated, leaving her face streaked with tiny veins of sorrow.

The song, sung only within her heart, made her gasp as she remembered that the lover vanishes from the sight of the woman, just like Lukas. She whispered the last line, barely audible in the green world around her:

"I am the haunted woman of the hill."

She believed that now. Finally, the master of dreams came to Hannah, opening the doorway to the Otherworld, filling her world with visions of veils over long white hair and lavender eyes.

She sat on a well-known hill, and yet it seemed dissimilar, for the ground felt spongy, and the red berried-limbs waved in welcome. There was no chill, yet Hannah shivered as she spoke aloud, "O Spirit of the Grove, will you not comfort me this day?"

"But where is your man?" asked a voice from within the tree. "Has he not come with you, daughter, like always?" The voice echoed in hollow reverberations like those heard inside the River Feshie caves. Slowly, a lithe greenish-gold female form, draped in pastel spider silks, emerged from the tree. Lavender eyes framed by wisps of white hair stared now silently at Hannah while her long, white hair cascaded over the hooded collar, swirling behind her broad shoulders in arcs like fairy wings.

Hannah stood up quickly, wrapping her shawl about her shoulders in defense, her highland woolen armor. She had never seen a woman in this grove, yet there she stood, beside the tree. She gazed at Hannah through lavender eyes which to Hannah seemed gentle, yet cautious. Hannah marveled that the woman's skin bore a tint of golden green.

"Who are you? And what do you mean, 'like always'?" asked Hannah. *"I have never seen you here."*

"Ah, but I have seen you many times, you and your man beneath my tree. Surely you are not surprised by my presence now." She faced Hannah squarely, inquiring, *"Did you not call for me?"*

"But you can't be. I mean, I was just . . . ." Hannah found herself speechless. She reached out to touch the cape, thinking it would disappear like the faerie lover in the song. But it was soft to the touch, and the woman remained. *"Are you the Spirit of the Grove?"*

A gentle laughter, like the sound of tinkling bells, erupted around Hannah, leaving a shimmer of radiant purples dancing through the tree branches like fireflies waltzing in the maroon sky. A parade of snowflakes drifted now towards the young woman, driving the sadness of Hannah's lament from the circle of trees while icicles formed, tinkling like silver bells. *"The Spirit of the Grove, you ask? Why Daughter of Earth, you should know better than that. I am merely one of its keepers. No, my name is Oonagh. I am from the Land of Ever Faire, and make my abode in this grove."*

"But how do you know about me, and Lukas?"

"O gentle girl, do not think that I have wandered far during your trysting visits here. He is quite a good singer, as are you, little deer. Though I wonder at the sadness you bring today. Is he unwell?" Oonagh caressed a near-by rowan branch.

Hannah could not answer. Yet, she wondered at Patrick's question earlier about spirits knowing each other. Even though Oonagh was not a ghost, perhaps she had knowledge about Lukas after all. *"Do you know where he is? Has he passed into your world now?"* She stood in the snow before the faerie.

"Darling child, I know not the affairs of man, save what I witness. I know he is not here. But sit by me, little deer, and I will tell you what I know."

Hannah practically fell down beside Oonagh, worn from worry. Hannah knew you could not rush the faerie folk, so she sat in silence.

After several minutes, Oonagh broke the stillness. "I cannot say that I have seen your man. But I do recall the river sprite commenting that her waters were imbalanced. You might search for him there." Oonagh ended her statement with the finality of a judge.

In a timid voice she asked, "Has he drowned?"

Oonagh rose then stretched her arms, reaching east and west. Her fingertips, tinged with silver, sparkled as the moon began its journey over the crested mountains. She paused before answering, then said, "This I do not know, little one. I can tell you nothing more."

Before seeming ungrateful, Hannah bowed to Oonagh saying, "Thank you. I will tell them where to search now." And as Hannah watched, the woman began dissolving, like a snowflake on a warm tongue.

As Hannah awoke, the dream stayed with her. She heard the skirl of a red vixen's cry nearby, so she knew herself to be awake. Was this second sight a curse or a blessing? She did not know, yet somehow she felt comforted, for despite the dreamy origin, the girl knew truth when it was spoken. She hurried down the hill towards the MacLaren farm to see if there was any news, wondering along the way how she would tell the searchers why they should focus their efforts on the river.

CHAPTER EIGHT

By the end of the second day, there was still no word. No sightings of any kind.

A lonely wildcat could be heard crying, like a newborn babe, in the hills behind the MacFey cottage as the dawn receded. The clouds spiraled on wintry drafts over the snow-covered hills. Hannah sat by the warming embers, rubbing her swollen eyes. She stared at her providan, her dowry, waiting to be taken to her new home. Now there it sat. And there it will stay, she thought.

The day passed into night. Nightmares pounded through Hannah's dreams till she woke to find her mother sitting on the pallet, stroking her daughter's hair. No amount of chamomile or mint tea could console her. Rosamond sang softly, a favorite lullaby in soothing Gaelic strains which vanquished the recurring nightmares of Hannah's childhood:

"Seothin, Seo ho lu lu lo lo.

Seothin, Seo ho lu lu lo lo."

The next morning, Mr. MacLaren sent word for Hannah to stay home, should Lukas come in search of her, so she remained at her post. Rosamond was silent, respecting her daughter's grief, but gave Hannah brown bread with oat brose for breakfast. Hannah sat by the fire, facing her mother's chair, too distracted to twine purple skeins into balls, resulting in a web of madness.

Soon after breakfast, a sudden knock on the door caused Hannah to straighten, dropping the purple wool onto the floor. Rosamond opened the door wide - but it was only Lally and Caitlin. They had wanted to see Hannah the day before, but they were just too upset to visit. More tears were not what their friend needed, so rather than upset her they'd joined the search parties. This morning, their pale faces betrayed their grief.

"Oh, Hannah," said Lally, embracing her friend. Lally buried her face in Hannah's woolen shawl, forcing the tears away.

Caitlin said nothing, but stood by the fire, warming her hands. Her unusual silence broke through Hannah's quiet demeanor.

"Caitlin, I'm sorry about all your plans . . . the flowers," said Hannah.

Caitlin stared at the flames, unable to respond. Then, as if shaken by invisible hands, she roused from her reverie, "The flowers? Oh, the flowers, at the church you mean?"

"Yes," said Hannah. "I know how hard you worked on making everything just right. It would have been a beautiful . . . wedding." She choked on the word "wedding" but sipped her tea to recover.

"Well, Lally and I stopped by to speak with Father Logan on our way over here," said Caitlin, still rubbing her hands even though she was wandering around the small room like a penned goat, and no longer near the fire. "Since we still do not exactly know what has happened, we've left the church just as we prepared it yesterday, if that's all right with you, Hannah."

Hannah considered it. "Save the flowers for the funeral," she said. "For I'll not be needing them."

Both girls protested at once. "But Hannah, we don't know whether Lukas is alive or . . ." Neither could say the word, but Lally continued, "Surely he must just be hurt and retreated somewhere to get out of that dreadful storm. It's only been one day, and . . ."

But Hannah cut off their hopes quickly. "Two days now, and two full nights in the winter winds," corrected Hannah. "No man could survive that. He is gone, dead and gone." She stared again at the fire, not willing to meet the eyes of either girl. The fortress around Hannah's heart, now as impenetrable as the cold river rock beneath her feet, became visible to her friends through her stony gaze.

"Oh no, Hannah," pleaded Caitlin. "You must be wrong." She knelt down in front of her friend and clasped her cold fingers around Hannah's hands. "You will marry him; I just know you will. You two were meant to be together, and when souls such as you and Lukas meet, it will be forever." She tried to smile, but her lips curled into a grimace.

Then whispering low enough for only Hannah to hear, Lally asked, "Have you seen him, his spirit that is?"

Hannah nodded, then stared again at the fire.

Lally choked back her tears, not wanting to betray Hannah's secret. She glanced at Rosamond whose face could not conceal the fact that she, too, felt all hope was gone.

Lally and Caitlin moved towards the door, ready to aid the search parties. "They're searching mostly the woods," said Lally, "thinking the horse would have originally sought shelter from the storm. But his brothers are checking some of the shallow caves where Lukas used to hide out. We'll let you know as soon as we hear any news, all right?" She kissed her friend's cheek then quickly turned away, ushering Caitlin out the door. The two girls hurried down the road towards the MacLarens' farm.

Later that afternoon, with still no word, Father Logan knocked on the MacFeys' door.

"Welcome to you, Father," said Rosamond, opening the door wide, for he was a short, portly man. "Come in and warm yourself by the fire a bit. I'll make you a cup of mint tea. I might have an extra biscuit or two around here as well." She ushered him to her chair and bustled around the hearth area for a few moments before producing two cheese biscuits to go with the mint tea.

Father Logan sat opposite Hannah, who nodded politely at him but said nothing. His pencil-thin moustache twitched nervously as he took the tea and biscuits saying, "Now Mistress MacFey, what a veritable feast you've given me here. And I thought I was the one bringing comfort to you both." He smiled a thin smile, showing his corn kernel teeth.

"We welcome anything you might have to share with us, Father," said Rosamond, sitting on the bench next to Hannah's chair. "Isn't that right, Hannah?" She placed a protective arm around Hannah's shoulders and gave them a maternal squeeze. Hannah remained silent.

The MacFey women spoke little of spiritual matters, but Rosamond had attended meetings regularly, with Hannah by her side. Mistress MacFey could easily lay aside the vicious village gossip concerning Hannah's father, for she knew the truth of it, ignoring the whispers and sideways glances often cast at the pair as they sat down for services. But her daughter, without such knowledge, cursed the lips filled with lies.

Hannah stared at this man of God, this emissary for the One who had torn her heart apart.

"Well," began the well-wishing priest, "since we have no definitive news yet, we can still hope that Lukas will be returned to us soon, safe and well. In the meantime, let us pray that God's angels will guide the search parties to the lad and bring him back whole. Shall we pray?"

Rosamond bowed her head and joined him, saying, "Our Father, who art in heaven . . ."

Suddenly Hannah's grief transformed into fury. She shook off her mother's embrace and glared at the priest, her soft, white pine eyes now cold as iron. "If God be in His heaven, and wants nothing but my happiness, then why did He take Lukas from me, eh? What use has God of my sweet Lukas in heaven that could be better than him being my husband? Answer me that, priest!"

Rosamond was shocked by Hannah's retort, yet she knew how grief wounded a loving heart, leaving ugly scars. She lived with Michael's loss daily, but for Hannah, this wound was fresh.

Father Logan was ill-prepared for such a response. He thought Hannah to be independent but never disrespectful. He took a moment to consider his counsel. "The ways of God are a mystery to the common man, my dear. And we do not know that Lukas is with God, not yet."

"He's dead," she replied.

"Well, if that's what you choose to believe, my girl. But I will still hope, until a body is discovered, that you are mistaken." He stood up, bracing his shoulders back against an invisible chill in the room. "Mistress MacFey, I thank you for your warm hospitality on such a cold spring morning, but now I must be off. God's speed to the search parties. And may His grace comfort you both."

With those parting words, he left, much to Hannah's relief. She could take no more "comfort" and focused on twining the wool once more. Although she believed the ghostly visitation, a part of her heart hoped she was mistaken - that Lukas was still alive.

Golden orange lantern lights filled the MacLaren household. Mistress MacLaren and Muriel served drinks and tea cakes to neighbors who had labored throughout the day searching the woods for Lukas. When Hannah entered the room, all became still.

"Well, have you found him?" she asked, staring into Rory's face. She knew he would not lie to her, for although he was mischievous, Hannah trusted his true heart.

"No, Hannah. Not a sign," said Rory, hanging his head as if he were to blame. "We've searched every farm along this valley, but found nothing. We thought perhaps he'd gotten himself hurt, and crawled off somewhere to get out of the cold. We searched barns, goat pens, forest glades, even small rock caves twisted among the roots of the Scots pines. But the snow has proven to hide any tracks he might have made. It fell so hard that night that even Jed's big footprints were invisible."

Hannah rose abruptly, asking, "Have you searched the river?"

"Not really," said Mr. MacLaren, coming from the corner shadows of the room. "We knew Jed didn't like the river, so we felt certain Lukas would not find the horse there. Why do you ask?"

Not wanting to reveal the dream source, she simply said, "Well, he's not to be found in barn, glen, or cave. What if Jed himself got lost that night, wandering around in the snow till he just stopped for fear? Could the horse not have made his way down to the river without knowing it?"

Hushed whispers broke out in little conversations around the room discussing the possibility. The hum grew louder, until Mr. Stewart said, "Why, you know, the girl may be right. We could drag a net from your farm, Gerald, and move south along the banks. We could wade where the river shallows and prod loose rocks that may be holding . . . ."

His words trailed off into a silent pause. If Hannah was right, if the river held Lukas now he would be dead. As that revelation struck the household, all movement stopped. The grief would be too much to bear.

But Hannah's voice of reason broke the invisible walls of mounting sorrow. She charged all who would listen, saying "We must search the river, tomorrow, at first light. If we went now, even with lights the river is too dark to reveal anything. If Lukas is dead, we need to know." She picked up her lantern, lit it quickly from the hearth embers, and left the house.

As she walked home, she saw other lantern lights bobbing through the trees as the villagers slowly made their way home. She knew her words struck true, and tomorrow she would be with the search parties by the river.

The next morning, the snow lay two feet deep in low areas, but that did not stop the purposeful neighbors of Feshiebridge. By sunrise, the riverbank was abundant with chatter, netting, poles, and extra woolens (for the sodden ones who waded). Hannah and Rosamond joined the ranks as Gerald MacLaren gave the orders. "Let's start up by Fisher's Bridge then work our way south, passing the Stewarts, the Campbells, then onto The MacInnes and Fraser farms. You ladies stay along the riverbanks while the men do the wading. Look for anything amiss, and yell like the devil if you see anything."

The solemn group dispersed, following Mr. MacLaren's lead. He was taken by surprise when he felt his cloak being pulled to one side. He looked down into the face of his youngest child, Muriel, whose innocence seemed out of place here by a possible watery grave. "Sweetheart, what are you doing out here in the cold? You should be inside keeping your mother company."

Muriel's tears glittered her pink cheeks in the morning sunlight. "But Pa, I want to find Lukas, too. Here, I brought something that may help." She handed him a loaf of brown bread.

"Daughter, I'm not hungry right now," he said, handing the loaf back to the child.

"But Pa, it's not for eating. Grann Scott told me once about a cousin who drowned. They couldn't find him for days. But on the ninth day, she put a loaf of bread in the river and waited for it to start swirling."

"Now why on earth would it start swirling?"

"Because that told them where the cousin's body lay. The loaf began whirling about in the water and sure enough, there rested the boy directly under it. So, I was thinking, that if Lukas is in the river, the bread might help you find him." She offered the bread again, like an alm for the poor that could not be refused. "Please, Father?"

Gerald took his daughter by the hand and led her to a shallow spot by the river. "Here, sweetheart," he said, "you put it in the water. We'll watch together." The river was flowing steadily over the rocks, no longer swollen from the heavy snows. The brown bread did float, snaking its way to the river's center then right down the middle southward. They watched for several moments until the loaf went around a bend in the river.

"Father, I can't see it anymore!" cried Muriel. She started to run after it, but Gerald held her fast.

"Now girl, I don't want two children claimed by this river. You go on back to the house now, and I'll watch the bread. I'll send a message along the river to all those here to keep an eye for it swirling."

The child beamed up her at her father, who then bent down and held her, long and hard. She ran back through the snow to the main house while Gerald MacLaren turned towards the river. The sorrowful face reflected in the blue-black water could have turned a man to stone.

Progress was slow. The men spread out on both sides of the river, some wading in shallow areas while others dragged the net. Women poked with long poles and prodded at reeds and tall grasses by the river's edge, hoping yet fearing to find the body. Hannah and Rosamond split up, hoping to find some evidence of any kind. But it was Malcolm who saw it first.

"Pa, come over here," he shouted, walking up the riverbank out of the cold water. Mr. MacLaren ran to where his eldest son stood. Malcolm pointed to the stone wall that ran the length of the river on their land. "Pa, look at this break in the wall. See these stones tumbled out towards the river, as if someone fell over it? I don't remember it being this way at all."

Gerald MacLaren examined the break. Surely if an animal had done such a thing he'd have lost them to the river as well, but no sheep or goats were missing. Then he saw two tracks where the snow had melted over the past two days, two mud skids leading straight into the water. He knelt down on the cold hard ground and sobbed.

Soon the others crowded around him, looking at the broken wall and muddy tracks. All hope faded. The women broke into wails while the men tried to hold back their sorrow. The group took on a grim demeanor now as they searched not for the man, but for his body.

As Hannah looked at her mother, a knowing passed between them. Hannah continued down the riverbank. Somewhere downstream a badger feasted on a loaf of brown bread.

"He's found!" The cry rang out, pealing along the riverbank in ripples three mornings after the search began. The neighbors looked downstream while their anxious hearts rose as one. He's found, but is he alive or dead? As they slipped and slid over the wintry snows, the group of neighbors soon had their answer. For there was Lukas, eyes opened heavenward in a solid stare with a frosting of snow on his face, his body pinned in the fallen pine that crossed the river from the Stewarts' property. Children came running, saying it was the water kelpie that grabbed poor Lukas from the bank while women sighed, cradling each other about the shoulders as if to keep the bad news at bay. But the men seemed more reassured in that tragic evening's events after hearing Mr. Stewart claim that he noticed a considerable knot on Lukas's forehead.

"It's tough to swim when your brain's been knocked about a bit," said Mr. Stewart to Father Logan, as the two men heaved the swollen body over the pine trunk and onto the frozen ground.

Rory and Malcolm came splashing through the water, with no care for their own safety. Rory bent over the body of his brother then grabbed Lukas by the shoulders, shaking him as if his brother were simply frozen, not dead. But Malcolm pulled Rory away, saying, "He's gone, Rory. All the shaking in the world won't bring him back to you now. Leave him be." Rory shook with anger, sobbing so hard that Malcolm held him.

Now it was Hannah's turn. The crowd moved aside, making room for Hannah and her mother to pass as a heavy mist like swirling wraiths rose from the river, surrounding the pair. Rosamond held Hannah's hand securely, saying quiet prayers. With a nod, Hannah released the maternal grasp and knelt down by the frozen body, stroking the white flakes from his face. No tears fell. An unearthly silence encompassed her, shielding her from the onlookers. She searched his eyes for that vibrant soul, yet only a vacant gaze met her stare. Quickly closing the eyelids shut, she whispered, "Take him home. It's time this was over."

Hannah and Rosamond returned to their cottage that morning while Rory and Malcolm carried their brother's body to the MacLaren home. As they walked through the shrouding mist, Rosamond glanced at her daughter, wanting to hold her, but instead Rosamond simply placed her hand around the frozen fingers of the one she loved and led her home.

The maternal instincts to comfort and soothe manifested themselves in chamomile tea laced with valerian and St. John's Wort along with some honey nut bread. Although Hannah insisted she could not eat, Rosamond's will proved stronger, knowing her daughter would need her strength for the upcoming wake and funeral. The cottage fire warmed their bodies as the orange embers sparked to life, phantom flames caressing the earth brown fibers of the dewy cloaks hung nearby, hissing in cackling undertones.

Grief comes in many forms, none right or wrong. Everyone must find their own way with it. For once, the MacFey household was silent.

That afternoon, Hannah knew the MacLaren family was preparing the body, so she stayed at home, helping Rosamond. The daughter sat on the floor next to the hearth, staring at everything and nothing, with her upraised palms facing each other, holding the dyed skeins. The mother rolled them into balls, tossing the finished wooly eggs into the basket. The afternoon slipped by without mentioning Lukas.

Rosamond plopped another blue ball in with the others, thinking she would be ready to warp the loom soon, for spring festivals were quickly approaching. "Hannah, dear," said Rosamond, "I think you've worked enough for now. Rest and see if you can sleep a bit."

Hannah nodded, shuffled over to the pallet and crawled under the blanket. Overcome with exhaustion, she slept, relinquishing her thoughts to the darkness.

Two hours later, a tolling bell shocked Hannah back into the world of the living, saying, "Ma, do you hear that?"

"Aye that I do, child," said Rosamond, unpacking the providan stuffed with Hannah's clothing: a sleeping smock, two wool sweaters, a linen shift handed down from Grann, a crisp white smock along with her favorite russet one, three pairs of leggings, a green wool shawl, two pleated kirtles, a handful of rainbow-colored ribbons, and a red surcoat. The providan was meant to carry the bride's belongings to her new home, but not now.

"It's the bell, Ma, telling everyone about Lukas."

Father Logan had begun ringing the church bells that afternoon while Mr. Robertson, the sexton and Nell's father, tolled the hand bell throughout the small community, announcing the news. The sad bell sang its death knell while mournful shouts of "Lukas MacLaren is dead; Lukas MacLaren is drowned" filtered through the green boughs like a soughing wind. There would be a three-day kistin before the burial where people could pay their respects to the family.

"Shall we go over tonight, Hannah?" asked her mother. Rosamond sat beside her daughter, brushing the stray hairs away from her daughter's pale face. "We could wait till tomorrow if it's too soon for you, dear."

Hannah laid back down, turning her face towards the wall. Could she go tonight? Could she face that clay cold resemblance of her lover? The villagers would expect to see her, but she just wasn't sure she was ready.

Rosamond ached for her daughter's pain, and remembered a tune her mother sang after her own father's death. It seemed right to bring memories of Gran into the cottage now, so Rosamond sang "Deep in Love" in a soft, slow voice. As she sang the second verse telling of love's blooming, she hoped it would comfort her grieving girl. She paused, lingering for a moment as the notes hovered over Hannah like an angel's crown.

But Hannah looked at her mother, her mind reeling with too many words to say what lay deep in her heart; so she let the last verse say it for her, spoken barely above whisper:

"But now he's dead and in his grave,

Poor boy I hope his heart's at rest.

We will wrap him up in some linen strong,

And think of him

now he's dead and gone."

Death hung in the air between them like a shadowy veil.

"Tonight, Ma," she said, taking a deep breath. "I think we'll go tonight," said Hannah, breaking the spell.

"Well, if you're sure. I'll let you wear my black kirtle, maybe over your dark maroon smock. You're too young a girl yet to be wearing all black." Rosamond kissed Hannah on the forehead then began rummaging through her own clothing until she located the needed items. "Here, now you go ahead and put these on. I told the MacPhersons that if we went out tonight we'd come by their house first. Lally wanted to be with you."

"As you say, Ma," said Hannah, rising from the bed as if in a trance. A glassy countenance slipped over her face as she began to undress.

CHAPTER NINE

The wake started that evening in the MacLaren home around ten o'clock. The walls were covered with ivory wool sheets while a black cloth veiled the looking glass. Lukas's body was laid out in the main room, away from the fire, in a white pine coffin made by the local joiner. He was dressed in a white linen shroud with a penny over each eye. Muriel helped her mother dress Lukas, cocooning the winding sheet around his body, clipping a corner for Hannah. His pallid skin appeared bluish-gray, looking more fey than mortal with swollen, distorted features. Normally salt would be placed on his chest to prevent swelling, but three days in the river had engorged the body beyond help.

The small room buzzed with quiet laments.

Relatives from Ruthven would be arriving over the next few days, but tonight mostly Feshiebridge neighbors appeared. Mistress MacLaren served ale to her guests, saving tea and honey brown bread for the midnight callers.

Nell Robertson, sitting in the corner with her mother, kept weeping, "But we had a plan! He was going to marry me, not her!" Mistress Robertson cradled her daughter, speaking in hushed tones while the Sutherland sisters, two spinsters known as gossip lovers, were the first to pay their respects. The hovered over the body like two buzzards over a fresh kill.

"Sister, can you believe that poor Lukas is dead?" asked Aulaire Sutherland, shaking her head so fervently that her caul almost slipped off, giving way to a waterfall of silvery gray locks.

"Nay, not at all, Sister dear," said Claire Sutherland. "But after all, Death is not particular who he takes away." She took her sister's hand, patting it gently.

"Why, a truer word weren't never said, Sister," replied Aulaire. The two women, like woodland red squirrels perched on tree limb discussing the weather or their next meal, chattered away then turned to find Eglantyne to extend their condolences.

A steady stream of well-wishers came and went throughout the evening. Little ones, particularly the boys, would dare younger siblings to touch the body. "Iffin you don't," said Danny, a twelve-year-old himself, "why you'll have nightmares for weeks!" he exclaimed, putting more than the fear of God in the intended victim. Tiny fingers would creep over the edge of the coffin, pause then scramble away with shrieks trailing like a mighty wind behind them while the older boys would double-over with laughter.

"Danny Finlayson!" roared Malcolm. "Quit scaring the little ones like that! If you don't, I'll give you what for!" He raised a menacing fist in the boy's direction. Danny shot through the door into the back bedroom faster than a rabid hare. Malcolm gathered the young ones close to the fire, giving them each extra ale and a cookie to quiet their nerves.

Patrick and Seamus came in together, eyes weary red with bright noses to match. Seamus was expected to play for the dancers, if any were willing. Some villages celebrated a death by dancing in the same room with the dearly departed, if lodgings were small, in order to celebrate a life well lived. Seamus did not appear up to the occasion, but even blind drunk the fellow could play better than anyone else in the county. Not a word of reprimand was handed down, for who could know the sorrow that mantled their hearts. They would wait for Hannah to begin.

The MacFeys entered soon after, followed by Lally and her family. Hannah knew all eyes would be on her, so she greeted Mistress MacLaren first with a warm embrace. She hugged Muriel next and nodded to the gentlemen.

"Here, Hannah," said Muriel, handing the young woman a snippet of white cloth. "It's from the winding sheet. You know, something to remember him by." Muriel lowered her head then backed away, not knowing what else to say.

"Thank you, Muriel," said Hannah, hugging the small slip of a girl that would never be her sister-in-law.

Before Hannah turned towards the coffin, Nell strode quickly across the room, swells of indignation in her wake, and with a firm swat, slapped Hannah squarely across the jaw.

Hannah stood, statue still.

The onlookers were speechless.

Rosamond rose to her daughter's defense, but Hannah shook her head, requesting this duel be resolved.

"It's all your fault, you stupid cow!" screamed Nell, her voice rising in higher decibels with each word. "He was mine! It was all settled so that he would be MY husband, not yours! MacLaren will never be your name, you fatherless bitch!"

Mrs. Robertson moved slowly to her daughter's side, trying to calm the young woman, but Nell pushed the elder aside. Like a cornered wildcat, Nell stared at the shocked mourners, then stated in illogical progression, "You all know it's true! He'd never have been out in that storm had his friends not taken him to Ruthven, as lads will do the eve before a wedding. No wedding, no Ruthven! No storm, no dead body now!"

As Nell prepared to strike another blow, Hannah grabbed Nell's shoulders, pinning the girl's arms by her waist in a strong embrace, as if containing an outrageous child for its own protection. Nell shook with rage, but as the anger dissolved, tears plopped down her plump cheeks as she surrendered to Hannah's unsaid forgiveness. The two stood, mirroring each other as one who truly loved Lukas and one who loved his social standing.

As the wake quelled, Nell stilled. "Hannah, I . . .," sobbed Nell, her words faltering as she pulled away.

"Nell, it's done," said Hannah. "You will find another, of that I'm sure." And without reproach, Hannah offered her nemesis a grim nod, thus ending their combative roles.

Glancing at the pine box in the corner, Hannah took a deep breath, straightened her shoulders then tread steadily towards the coffin. She shuddered.

She looked squarely at Lukas's body, a cold form now unrecognizable as the man she loved. No laughter came from those blue lips. No warmth came from the brown eyes tightly closed beneath those pennies. No strength would be found in those muscular arms to embrace her and chase away her insecurities. This was not her love.

She knew that her parting had occurred in private three nights before. She closed her eyes for a moment, sighed then quietly moved away. Her body trembled as she placed her hand in Patrick's and gave him a nod. Seamus, even in his brewed haze, knew it was time, so he picked up his fiddle and began a slow air. Patrick gathered Hannah in his arms while the crowd moved to the edges of the room. They'd been waiting for her lead, not knowing if the girl was able. She proved them wrong. To honor Lukas, she bit back the watershed of tears and with head held high, let the music swirl about her. Other pairs soon followed her lead, dancing in small circles to celebrate the lost life of one so dear. An odd way to honor the dead, she thought.

Meanwhile, Danny had roused a small group of listeners in the back room, telling them stories of the body-snatchers and other ghostly legends. "Ah, one of my favorites," he began, settling back on Lukas's pallet, "is the one about the jealous sister and a ghost."

"Tell it! Tell it, Danny!" cried the youngsters.

"Well, it all began with Helen getting married. See, Princess Helen was going to marry Sir William. But when he got a gander at Helens younger sister, oohh! He changed his mind ever so quickly, thinking she weren't only more lovely but also more kind-hearted."

"Aaawwwhhhh!" the boys chorused.

"You just wait! Anyway," Danny continued, "when Sir William called off the marriage, saying he wanted to marry the other girl, Helen got mad. She got so mad that she planned to kill her sister."

"NO!" said the girls, covering their mouths.

"Yes!" said Danny. "Not only that, but she was sneaky about it, too. She told the sister to follow her down to the river, the Binnorie River, and watch for the King's ships to come in laden down with all kinds of treasure. When they got there, poor thing, she stood on top of a large flat stone overlooking the waters. Before she knew what was about her, Helen grabbed the girl around the waist and flung her into the raging waters below, knowing that her sister could not swim."

"That was mean!" said little Mary.

"Mean? Do you want to hear so mean that it's cruel?" asked Danny. "Well, when the sister began flailing about, screaming for help, Helen said she'd not touch a hair on that head till the sister lay beneath the waters completely dead."

"Did she drown?" asked Mary, her lips quivering beneath her watery green eyes.

"O' course, she drowned!" said Mary's older brother Stan. "How can there be a ghost story without somebody a-dyin'? Go on, Danny, what happened next?"

"Well, as I was saying, Helen leaves the sister in the river to drown . . . "

"You mean like Lukas?" whispered Seline, Danny's eight-year-old sister cutting in.

"No, silly," said Danny. "Lukas fell in the river during a storm. Nobody pushed him in. May I get on with my story?" He shot his sister an evil glare.

"Yes, do!" squealed the children. Seline looked down and remained silent.

"Okay," Danny continues, "so the girl drowns. Her body is carried downstream near the miller's dam. But the miller's daughter sees the body floating closer and tells her father to stop the giant wheel. Well, he does. Then when the young princess's body comes close to the shallow edge, he pulls her from the water and lays her on the ground. She was wearing a long white dress with a golden lace about her waist and pearls in her long yellow hair. But you see, they didn't know her, so they didn't bury her."

"But what did they do?" asked Stan.

"Before they did anything, a harper fellow came by. He looked at the girl and thought she was the most beautiful girl he'd ever seen."

"But wasn't she dead?" asked Mary. "How could he think she was so pretty when she's dead?"

"She was dead," said Danny. "How do I know why he liked her looks? Anyway, he left the miller and went on his way, yet every night the face of the dead young girl would haunt his dreams. He traveled for many months, far away, until he circled back to the very spot where he'd last seen her. The miller had not buried her, thinking he might be accused of foul play, so he'd left her there for someone else to find. But now all that was left were her bones, bleached white by the sun, and her long golden hair. For some reason, the harper took her bones and made them into a harp."

"Oicht!" said all the girls, screwing up their faces as if they'd just eaten a rotten egg.

Malcolm approached the group quietly and stood unseen by the doorway.

"Wait," says Danny, "then he takes her hair, braids it, and strings the harp. He puts it under his arm and marches up to the King's palace. There was a wedding feast at the palace, so everyone asked the harper to play in celebration. Now, you won't believe what he does with that harp. First he plays songs on his old harp, making everybody happy, but then he puts the bony harp on a flat stone in the middle of the floor so all can see." Danny leans forward, lowering his voice, "Then the harp began to sing."

"Ooohhhh!" whispered the children.

Malcolm knew this old ballad, "The Twa Sisters," and wondered if the teller knew the song. But he decided to let the boy play it out to the end.

Danny stood up and began circling the small group, leaning into the face of each listener. "The voice of the drowned princess sang about her father, her mother, and her brother Hugh. She calls to her William, sweet and true. But then, she accuses Helen of drowning her saying, 'Who drowned me for the sake of a man.' Then the harp broke into a thousand pieces (Danny spreads his arms wide), and Helen stands up. She looks afraid, like she's seen a ghost. She begins clutching at her throat as if icy fingers are taking the very life from her. And before her family could reach her, she fell to the floor . . .cold, stone dead."

With the final word, Danny smacked his palms together loudly, causing raucous squeals and screams while children backed into walls trying to scurry away. Danny just laughed, and laughed, and laughed. The sorrows of that day refused to touch their innocence.

Two days passed as many mourners visited the MacLaren household even though relatives from Balquidder, the clan home for the MacLarens, would not be told of Lukas's death until after the winter thaw. Sending the news south now could be a treacherous crossing through the drover's pass towards Perth for even a skilled traveler.

Rosamond busied herself, along with other parish women, preparing foods that would be eaten after the funeral. The warmth of the fire could not thaw the chill now coursing through Hannah's veins. She chopped the stew potatoes with mechanized precision, but each downstroke hit the wooden cutting board with a heavy thud. A vacant haze settled over her.

The service was brief, held in the MacLaren home with the coffin lid closed. A few of the wedding garlands draped the pine box. Father Logan read scriptures pertaining to the dead being raised again, a virtuous life, and everlasting love then served mass.

Hannah held herself in tight reserve while others cried freely.

At the resounding final "Amen," Seamus stood at the doorway, no blushing red on his face this day, with his fiddle at the ready. He slowly led the procession down the kirk road playing a death dirge from generations past while the MacLaren men carried their son, their brother, to his grave. Father Logan followed the coffin with Mr. Robertson next in line, ringing the sonorous bell. The women walked in pairs behind the coffin, consoling and weeping as spilled tears froze on the crusty ground.

Mistress Stewart cradled the sobbing Eglantyne while Caitlin held Muriel's little hand. Hannah walked arm in arm with Rosamond, supported by her mother's strength, as Lally followed, at the ready should her dear friend need assistance. The cold morning mirrored the emptiness of these sojourners. After the coffin was lowered, Father Logan said a final prayer of thanksgiving and remembrance.

The group made their way back in hushed conversations to the MacLaren home where whiskey was passed around freely amongst the men, and the women laid the table high with meat pies, cheeses, dried fruits, apple muffins, and pitchers of ale. The ale flowed well into the day and on into the night as various neighbors offered their condolences and stories about Lukas.

Rosamond and Hannah left early. As they made their way along the forest footpath, icy spikes on the rooted trail belying winter's touch, a light snow began to fall, producing a thin veil which mantled the somber pair.

It was over.

CHAPTER TEN
Isle of Iona, Caledonia

Snow fell in sheets on the Caledonia pines of the Scottish Highlands as well as on the blessed isle of Iona, a fitting farewell to winter since the first of February, the beginning of spring, had now passed. Ever since his episode before Father Callum, nothing but sleepless nights visited the harper. Michael tried once more, turning on his side, feeling the rope lacings beneath the thin mat while his long-tailed shirt twisted around his legs. He kicked off the blue wool blanket, in spite of the cold, and began pacing his small room while muttering curses unknown to such holy walls. He sat at his desk again, cradling his lolling head as if to keep it from rolling off his shoulders. His head ached after these instances, leaving him woozy and unsettled.

"Damn it!"" he said, with as much violence as a whisper could muster. He still couldn't believe that the horrors came upon him so quickly, with such a vengeance and no regard for his privacy.

The throbbing beat inside his head reminded him of the drums at Samhain, dancing with a ferocity that challenged life. Many a maid he'd made happy on those nights, rolling in lustful pursuits.

Yet despite his vagabond behavior, he still held one lass separate from the others - Rosamond. Did she understand why he had never proposed marriage to her? Surely she could see that his braggadacio ways were best with an audience present, and that in his secret moments he wondered if anyone would wish to love him beyond his grand accomplishments. He could not face her refusal, so he had left the question unsaid.

But more than that, he would need to tell her about his aristocratic heritage and how his parents disapproved of him trading the position as first-born son, eminent lord of the family estate, for a harper's casual life of traveling. From their viewpoint, all of his education and training were now wasted for sheer crowd entertainment! He had left after a heated argument, not seeing them now for almost twenty years. He also knew they would stop the marriage since Rosamond was not of noble birth. Yet marriage invites family, and although he could have married Rosamond secretly, he wished no ill repute to fall on her shoulders.

He'd often wondered if highland farmers pursued her, wishing to expand their personal flock with bairns. But the two had resolved never to speak of their "other life" apart from one another, the better to focus on their love for the few days each year they had together. He lamented that decision now, for it made their love seem temporal.

Now, all destroyed: the handsome face, the easy gait, the lilting voice full of sentiment and sensuality. He would not go to her now, for to see the pity on her face would break what little heart remained within him.

The visions came daily, at first. But once his days of healing at Iona began, with brothers prayerfully kneeling at his bedside, the harpies had fled. But now they were back, not daily, yet often enough to keep Michael disturbed. Writing in his private journal would ease the ache of rampaging thoughts, letting the warrior words create havoc on the page instead of in his spirit. He took up his quill and began to write, blackness darker than the ink spilling onto the unsoiled page in ragged lines.

> *Blackness smacks me.*
>
> *Bones crunch like broken shells*
>
> *on the littered shore.*

He wrote feverishly.

> *Banshee wails on silent winds*
>
> *remain locked inside my hidden world*
>
> *Throbbing pulses, like waves*

pounding the innocent shore,

batter my sanity.

Tears mingled with the parchment, blurring the words.

Invisible harpies rip my soul,

leaving shreds to gather dust.

His desperation reached new depths as he cried aloud, "Oh God, I wish I were dead!"

Michael dropped his quill, and fell into a deep sleep. The antidote of words worked again, a soothing balm for a fevered mind. He drifted off to the greens of Scottish pines, a small cottage he imagined where the woman he loved lay dozing by the hearth while a young couple danced in the background.

When Michael awoke two hours later, he still felt drained but considered a walk along the seashore just before evensong. Putting on his worn smock and leather shoes, he wrapped his earth-brown cloak around his shoulders and headed into the cold. Despite the February chill, he loved this quiet time of day, not quite nighttime yet the day no longer lingering - twilight, the gloaming. He left the solitude of his room, pressing firmly on his cane down the narrow stone stairwell. Most of the brothers were either in prayers this time of day or preparing the evening meal in the kitchen.

For Michael, everyday held such a staggering sense of loss. He could not voice it, not yet. His life here at the Abbey had been safe, hidden away from the hideous acts of the world, hidden away from her. He lost himself in parchments and inks, no longer composing love songs. When not needed in daily chores such as gathering vegetables from the community garden or etching out transcriptions, he spent hours walking along the shoreline, gazing mindlessly out to sea. The solitude was a salve for his soul. On days when relentless winds drove in the cold, he would be found in the small secluded chapel with a single window opening seaward behind the main Abbey. Ironically, it was named Michael's Chapel.

He wandered slowly down the cobbled pathway known as The Street of the Dead but islanders called it Said Nam March, wondering how the kings felt traveling down this lane.

He limped slowly forward, carefully choosing each footfall. Although it was difficult for him to manage the uneven surfaces, Michael had created his own tradition of following this ancient pathway leading through the graveyard of kings and chiefs, a touchstone of his former days regaling tales to regents.

Today he rested at St. Oran's Chapel, as was his habit for these shoreline ventures. The brother tending the candles lit in prayer requests simply nodded at Michael then left as he sat down on the small wooden bench facing the simple altar. He was alone. The oil brazier hung only a few feet above him, casting a soft amber glow on the whitewashed walls while creating an unearthly luster in the small chapel. "Now this is more like faerie light," said Michael aloud, knowing that the stone pavers beneath his feet were the only ones listening. "Did I ever tell you the tale of 'How Cormac Mac Art Went to Faerie?' " Without hesitation, old habits revived. Like a consummate teller, he began retelling the story, savoring the words as they slid over his tongue then passed through his lips.

His earlier weariness began to slip from his shoulders like a mantle no longer needed. He stood; the performer in him awakening as he walked, bowed, and gestured with his hands to the imaginary audience. He elaborated this magical tale with flourish. Caught up in his own performing, he did not notice that his limp had momentarily vanished. The mastery of the language was still intact, for somewhere inside Michael still remained a man able to be anything he chose to be: a harper, a singer, a storyteller, or a victim on an isolated island.

He bowed to a remembered audience, and upon rising, realized that his life as a harper and performer may not be over, despite his perceived physical limitations. He stood in amazement. For the past several years his future seemed to never venture beyond the haven of Iona; but realizing he could perform again, even enjoy the act, presented both exhilarating and frightening possibilities. Yet paired with this recognition came the vision once more of the last time out in the world - that dreadful night.

He fought back the darkness once more. He crouched forward, holding the dizziness at bay. Slowly he recovered then reached for his cane, sensing the frailty in his limbs once more.

He left the chapel and following the dirt path past St. Ronan's Chapel (the island parish for the villagers), rounded the Nunnery then slowly walked along the seashore. He ventured along the coast road, past monastic grounds, towards the village where a few farms dotted the coastline. Bitter sea breezes buffeted his unprotected head, forcing Michael to pull his worn brown cloak tightly around his shoulders, while the angry screech of a lone white-tailed eagle reeling above the waves sliced through the wind like a siren. The sea slapped against the red rounded rocks, battering the shore with determined might.

Michael noticed the shell-encrusted boulders which formed a solid line of defense from a tempestuous sea, but not the silent grey figure sitting on the opposite boulders. Even though his writing had helped to release some of the blackness, the anger and the frustration at his public display in front of Father Callum taunted him.

He raged aloud . . . at his Maker. "How could you let this happen to me? Why? What's to become of me now, all broken and useless? My harping 'tis but a shadow of older glories while my body reminds me daily of my ugliness!" He raised his fists, as if pummeling an invisible opponent. "What good is it for me to simply exist, here, on this island, placing words on paper when my heart grieves daily for my Rosie?"

He sank down into the soft sand, kneeling in the presence of his Master. "My Rosamond," he whispered, "Oh, I'm so scared to have you see me like this. You loved the proud harper, embracing me as a lover. But that man is gone. I would only be burden to you now. Oh my God, what is to become of me?"

With great difficulty, he pulled himself atop a small rock outcrop facing the sea. The sea shimmered with iridescent greens and blues in flecks of starlight, glittering the ocean's gown with gold. The waves calmed as if spent like Michael himself. He settled himself in a dimpled crevice and breathed in the newness of the night.

Then SPLASH! He looked around, but saw nothing. He craned his neck to the left where he saw a large grey shape waddling between two boulders, its body close to the sand. This natural gateway welcomed the visitor, its royal robe of amber and brown seaweed trailing behind. Michael knew there were common seals in the area, but he'd never seen one in all his years on Iona. The seal lumbered up the rocks again to his watchtower, then stared, grey-eyed, directly at Michael.

This encounter with one so wild was foreign to the harper. He found himself entranced, staring back at this feral creature. He was shocked by the seal's steady demeanor, not frightened of a human being.

"Are you here to bring me solace, my watery friend?" said Michael. "f only you could speak, what wondrous tales of the deep would you tell to me?"

The seal turned his head slightly to the right then sighed, as if in response.

As a child, living by the sea where seals were plentiful, Michael's early days had been spent with nurses who told him tales of faeries, of magical creatures in the depths of the sea, but the stories that drew his interest most were those about the selkies, the seal people. Though none knew their origin, it was believed that during the full moon, these creatures were allowed to shed their seal skins and stand, as humans, from moon rise to sunrise. For those few hours, they could delight in their humanity, yet as the sun rose, they were destined to become seals again, returning to their watery home. Older ballads spoke of selkies taking human form at will, remaining that way indefinitely until the song of the sea pulled them back.

Remembering that, Michael laughed then broke into song, reminded of an old favorite of his called "The Great Silkie of Sule Skerry,"

"I am a man, upon the land,

I am a silkie in the sea;

And when I'm far and far frae land,

My dwelling is Sule Skerrie."

"Is that your secret then, my great grey companion?" asked Michael. "Are you selkie, like the old tales say? Right well that would be a blessing for me to see." Extending his palm across the water, he said, "Well, pleased I am to meet such a fellow of few words."

The seal only stared for a second longer then dove back into the sea.

"Fare thee well on your return journey back to Sule Skerrie," Michael shouted. He slowly slid down the rocks, landing on his good leg where he eased himself from the uneven shore. Evensong would begin soon, and he did not want to worry Father Callum with his absence.

As he rounded the Nunnery heading back towards the Abbey, he noticed the villagers filing out of their parish door at St. Ronan's Chapel. "Ronan," he said aloud to himself, "aren't seals known as 'The Ron'?"

Swish! Swish! Swish! The working sounds of shuttles, weaving boats wound in woolen rainbows, raced back and forth across the looms of the MacFey cottage for several weeks following Lukas's death. The serenity of late March snowflakes falling outside provided an insular atmosphere for weaving.

"Hannah, pass me that dark purple skein, would you?" asked Rosamond.

Hannah moved like a white swan through the water, placid yet focused on her task. Locked within the silence of her sorrows, she wore grief to keep away intruders. Some nights Rosamond would hear her girl weeping, but Hannah never shared her grief. She felt a jagged rip in the very fabric of her being, a rending that no weaver could ever mend. She guarded it, for it was her way of keeping Lukas alive. She would see him in her dreams, and for now, that would suffice. To the world, she would hold her tongue, frightened of lashing out on some unsuspecting soul with the rage that daily built inside her. Even Nell knew to keep her distance while both Caitlin and Lally proved unsuccessful in waking Hannah from this grey reverie. Long-lasting snows prohibiting visits offered Hannah privacy.

"I'm trying to finish up this plaid for Mistress Finlayson for her son Danny, that rascal of hers," said her mother. "He'll soon be coming of age where he can work with the men, and needs himself something to keep warm up in the shieling when he takes the sheep to the high hills overnight. Hannah, do you know the boy I'm talking about?" asked Rosamond, patting the selvages.

"Aye, Mother," said Hannah, returning to her seat by the fire where she was crocheting a green shawl.

"I'm told he's got quite a gift for the telling of tales. Mind you he's got no singing voice, though." Rosamond liked to chat while she was weaving; it made the work go faster.

"Have you ever heard him tell a story, Hannah?"

"No, but I believe Malcolm said Danny was telling one of the old ballads at the. . . "

her voice trembled.

Rosamond looked up, beholding her precious girl. The wave of grief came suddenly sometimes, without warning. Hannah froze, crochet hook at the ready while the green wool thread trailed into her lap. She just stared ahead, eyes moist with misty memories.

"Yes, love," said Rosamond, letting the pain pass in Hannah's own timing. "I believe I heard Claire Sutherland saying after the kirk service last week that she'd heard about Danny trying to scare the little ones with ghostly tales that night." She changed the purple shuttle for the brown, to create the common tartan weave. "I'm almost finished with this piece, Hannah."

Hannah took a sip of tea and resumed her crocheting project.

"Darlin', it does seem to be clearing a bit today. Would you like to come with me this afternoon to deliver this plaid?" she asked. "You've hardly been out of the house, and the walk would do you good." Rosamond wove steadily, holding back her own wall of tears. It crushed her heart to see her daughter in such daily pain, reminding her of her own loss.

Glancing at the table, Rosamond saw her dearest possession, "the parting box" as Michael had so named it, a heart-shaped box topped with mother of pearl inlay filled with tokens to create memories of their times together or adventurous places where Michael's harping had led him.

Not relinquishing the task at hand, her mind's eye reviewed the box's contents, liberating a bittersweet sigh. Inside lay bands of colored ribbons from numerous county fairs, an amethyst torque from the Isle of Mull, and an abalone necklace from the waters of Loch Linne near Ballachulish. But underneath these vestiges of market days gone by was the prize: a pearl- embedded caul for Rosamond's long brown hair.

She remembered his tender kisses after beholding her wear it. Yes, she knew the pain of such heartache would come less frequently with time.

"No thank you, Mother. You go without me. I'll finish this shawl for Mistress Stewart," said Hannah. The hook no longer swooped and dipped like the seagulls spotting fish but rather serpentined lazily through the green chain.

"Very well," said Rosamond. "I'll finish up then make us lunch. How about a savory fennel soup today, with shallots and dried peas? I've got a bit of apple tart for dessert." The shuttles fairly flew as the weaver neared the end of her project. Before long, she tied off the ends creating the fringe, clipped the loom waste from the frame, and hand-stitched a line of black along the open selvage to keep it from unraveling.

Lunch finished quickly, and before Hannah knew it, her mother was gone.

Hannah continued crocheting for another two hours. Mistress Stewart commissioned many shawls from Hannah because of her creative stitch work. The finishing shell stitch blended with the herring bone pattern. Besides, severe arthritis prevented the elderly woman from creating her own woolens now.

As Hannah let her fingers mindlessly work, a lilt of a tune tugged at her heart. She'd rarely sung since Lukas's death, but some tunes eased her pain. She whispered the words, recognizing a woman's loss for her true love in the song "Lament for Red-Haired John."

> "You took away from me the sun
>
> in the heavens.
>
> You tore from out of me
>
> the joy of my heart.
>
> Cold is his body . . . "

Her voice trembled, unable to continue. Her body convulsed. She laid down the shawl and buried her face in her palms, sobbing over and over. She needed such private releases in order to maintain her public resolve. As the tide of grief swept over her, she calmed, knowing with certainty it would rise again. But for now, it was spent.

Laying the shawl aside, she rose slowly, stretching her arms above her head as she opened the door, allowing the soft winds to paint her face. Yet no refreshment came, rather only bitter winds embraced her. As Hannah allowed the cold to seep into the cool shades of her heart, she looked up in surprise to see her mother returning so quickly from the errand. Rosamond almost floated like a specter as she walked past her daughter into the warmth of their cottage. She slipped off her cloak, hung it on the iron hook by the door and sat down next to the fire. She gazed into the amber flames with an eerie glazed countenance.

"Mother! What's happened? What's wrong?" asked Hannah, kneeling beside her mother.

"Oh, what darlin'? Wrong, why it's . . . " then she collapsed. Hannah eased Rosamond away from the fire to her sleeping pallet, frightened by her mother's cheeks like red rowan berries. "You just rest now," said Hannah, helping Rosamond into her sleeping shift.

"I'm all right, Hannah," she said softly. "I must have walked home too quickly. I'm fine, really, dear." She patted Hannah on the shoulder, "But I do think some tea will do me good. Put a pinch of feverfew in mine if you would, please."

Hannah kissed Rosamond on the cheek and quickly made the tea, holding the cup to her mother's dry lips. "Mother, you feel a bit hot to me," said Hannah. "You're not coming down with a fever, are you?"

"If I am, let's hope that feverfew will do its work," said Rosamond. Hannah propped up several pillows, cushioning her mother's shoulders. Rosamond leaned back, cupping the hot tea in her trembling hands. Several minutes later, Hannah grabbed the cup just before it fell to the floor as her mother closed her eyes and drifted off. She covered Rosamond with warm blankets, checked the fire then remained vigilant by her mother's side throughout the night.

By the next morning, Rosamond was not better. Her back ached dreadfully while a persistent fever flushed her face. Hannah tucked the brown wool blanket securely into place beneath the pallet and rushed to the well to fetch cold water for compresses. She made a poultice out of sage and ginger then placed it across Rosamond's forehead. She supplied Rosamond with chamomile tea laced with feverfew and toasted brown bread tips dipped in light beef broth to give her strength. This routine lasted for almost a week. She'd never known her mother to be so ill, and no visitors were seen due to another snowstorm.

Hannah took on the nursing with a vengeance, laying aside her grief, yet the March winds blew so fiercely that Hannah barely made it daily to the well. She tended the fire, cooked simple meals, looked after their sheep and goats, and still wove in the evenings. Sitting by the bed, Hannah often spoke in gossamer tones, reading aloud in hopes of assuaging her mother's delirious outbursts as the fever played havoc with her body. Rosamond, who dozed in and out of her fevered state, rested little while moans of "Michael!" woke Hannah several times during the night. Hannah recalled hearing about a "Michael" from the Perth markets, a harper who seemed special to her mother, but wondered why Rosamond should be calling upon him now. It had been many years since her mother even mentioned his name. Curious, thought Hannah.

Sleep wandered into other cottages, but not the MacFeys.

The caretaker role began to wear on Hannah. She took little thought for herself, focusing only on Rosamond. The previous weeks of grief now layered with despair, leaving her with sallow cheeks and despondent gazes.

By the end of the week, Hannah noticed a rash of flat, red spots on her mother's neck and cheeks. "Holy Mother and Saint Brighid!" cried Hannah. "Not the pox!" She sat down by the pallet and just cried.

Fortunately, the storm abated, and it was visiting day for Father Logan. He'd been more than concerned about Hannah's well-being since Lukas's untimely death, despite her initial need for consolation from God's words, and stopped by once a week to visit the MacFeys. Hannah heard the knock on the door, whispered gratitude to Saint Brighid, and opened the door ever so slightly.

"Good morning to you, Hannah," beamed the minister. "And how are we today?"

"Oh, Father Logan, not well, not well at all," said Hannah, shying away. "I'm so glad to see you, but I'm not sure you'll be wanting to come in."

"But why ever not? Is something the matter?" His jovial expression changed to one of deep concern.

"It's my mother. I think she's got the pox. And if she does, you know how easily it spreads to folks."

"Hannah, open the door," he said, lowering his voice to that commanding tone when he admonished sinners.

She did as he bid. The minister knelt by the bedside of his dear friend Rosamond, fearful at the deathly pallor of her face. He examined the rash then felt her fevered forehead. He said a quiet prayer, crossed himself and Rosamond then rose quickly. "Hannah, I'll be back. I'm going to fetch Mistress Stewart. You're right, I'm sorry to say, that indeed your mother is taken with smallpox. There have been several outbreaks in Ruthven, but this is the first for some time in Feshiebridge. I do know that Mistress Stewart nursed folks years ago with no harm to herself. She's the best healer in these parts."

Hannah's face whitened. She knew that many folks died from this disease, often within two weeks of illness. She could not bear the thought of losing both Lukas and her mother - it was too much.

"Hurry then, Father Logan," said Hannah. "I'll try to keep her cool."

Father Logan wrapped his scarf tightly about his throat, kissed Hannah on the forehead then scurried quickly down the snowy path.

It wasn't until after the sun dropped below the River Feshie that Mistress Stewart arrived, alone. As Hannah opened the door, she heard the sexton tolling the bell, shouting, "Smallpox at the MacFeys. Smallpox - stay away." Hannah winced, knowing how deadly this disease could be to a small community such as theirs.

Mistress Stewart bustled by Hannah carrying a small bundle. She laid it open on the table then quickly began organizing its contents. There were large cloves of garlic, dried red clover and marigold blooms, dark green nettle leaves, and camphor. "Now Hannah, I'll need a small bowl and a pitcher of water that shall never run dry. We need to keep lots of fluids in her. Also, I'll need you to leave me to her. I'd ask you to leave the cottage, but I need someone to fetch the water and prepare the food while I'm tending to her." She looked at Hannah who was staring at the fever-soaked form of her mother.

"Hannah, do you hear what I'm saying to you, girl?"

"Aye, Mistress Stewart, I hear you," said Hannah, with a small child-like obedience.

"Very well, we've much to do here," said the healer. Then she took a closer look at the young woman. "By Brighid's flame, you don't look much better yourself. But I'll wager it's lack of sleep and nursing your Ma here rather than any pox."

"I am a bit tired," confessed Hannah.

"Well, you can rest now that I'm here," said Mistress Stewart, patting Hannah's shoulders, releasing this burden she'd taken on alone. "And don't you worry, lass. Your mother is a strong woman. It would take more than a fever to get the better of Rosamond MacFey."

I pray you're right, thought Hannah, and she set herself to working by the healer's side.

The first few days passed slowly, with Hannah making sorrel soups and brown breads for the three women. The rash blossomed into pus-filled sores, covering not only Rosamond's lovely face but her arms and hands as well. Her face became swollen while her eyes transformed into doughy slits. She continually passed in and out of fevered deliriums, still calling out for Michael. Once, when Hannah was changing the cool rag on her face, Rosamond grabbed Hannah by the shoulders and began shaking her saying, "Find him, Hannah. Michael, he's . . ."

"Where, Ma? Where is Michael?" urged her daughter. But Rosamond fainted again, lost in the madness of the fiery dreams.

CHAPTER ELEVEN

As the March winds blasted the Highlands with sudden storms, so fevered outbursts and heavy tears disrupted the MacFey household. Rosamond often wailed in deliriums for Michael. Once when Hannah drew near to calm the disheartened woman, her mother clutched Hannah's shoulders, clenching her fingers into the stiff russet kirtle and said, "I'll not have you alone, my girl. Michael will know, must know. You must find him." She breathed heavily, pausing between each phrase while breaking Hannah's heart with her pleas, for the daughter could not leave the mother.

Despite the irrefutable healing reputation of Mistress Stewart, Rosamond's health continued to decline, her strength ebbing from her body like a noon-day wavelet upon the sandy river's edge. Hannah feared if this death came, so soon following Lukas's tragedy, she would break. Since his death, nightmares ravaged her sleep with incidents of drowning, freezing in snow-filled caverns, or wandering lost in the woods. Hannah's youthful appearance dissolved in grief's wake.

Despite her wearied body, Hannah remained the dutiful daughter, keeping to herself except for the daily pilgrimage to Rowan Hill. Lally and Caitlin were forbidden to visit, as were other neighbors due to the small pox contagion. So, without any confidants, she held her grief in silent restraint in the cottage, not wanting to add to her mother's desperate situation. Mistress Stewart informed Hannah of village news while the pair kept a vigilant watch over Rosamond. Hannah was not surprised when she heard Nell was already engaged to a gentry lad in Ruthven.

The cottage air often proved hot with stifling illness, so one afternoon, while Rosamond lay sleeping, Hannah left her mother in Mistress Stewart's care and headed towards the village for supplies. The weight of her grief moved into her chest, causing a severe bronchial cough, so violent at times that her shoulders and stomach muscles ached.

She simply needed to breathe.

She could not face Rowan Hill today, so she meandered down the rutted lane, dodging deep puddles. She glanced towards the river on her right, through the woods to the farmlands trimming the banks. Layers of life appeared as one-room crofter cottages dotted the towering pine bark woods like the markings of a young doe amidst the first flowers of spring. Finer gentry homes lined both sides of the road as Hannah neared the village square; their two-leveled thatched roofs were covered with ivy racing over stone facades. Hannah had often mused that these homes practically smiled at visitors, their clear glass panes filled with welcoming light. Yet they never readily opened their doors to her, even now, for if they pitied her recent loss, to them she was still only the weaver's daughter, the offspring of an illicit affair.

She walked on, alone.

Thinking to place some fresh flowers on Lukas's grave, she began picking some purple saxifrage, the herald of spring, along with serrated wintergreen. As she held the simple blooms, so tender in the harsh winds, she pulled out her light blue hair ribbon then wound it around these tokens of her love. She fingered the ring, his ring, still dangling in her cleavage beneath the dress, keeping their vows a secret. Yet by all the gossiping tongues in Feshiebridge she was tagged the "poor lass whose lad died too soon" since their marriage contract was never consummated.

But for Hannah, she would never forget that time on Rowan Hill where vows were spoken, a ring exchanged, and love made whole.

She wandered through the small village, gazing up and down at windows filled with goods. The village contained the normal fare of mercantile needs with nothing outstanding except the iron spire of the local kirk which stabbed the grey sky, pointing its parishioners heavenward. As Hannah regarded the metal stake, she considered that Father Logan's sermons expounded on restraints of the human spirit and virtuous acts rather than recounting the tender mercies of a loving God.

The false smiles and condolences of gossiping neighbors since Lukas's death were more than Hannah could bear, so she declined attending. Moreover, since the funeral, she could not bring herself to honor the God who had robbed her, taking her most beloved possession. She tolerated Father Logan's visits, remaining civil yet inviolate to his spiritual offerings.

Today, she passed the church doorway, making her way around to the back where the gravestones stood in quiet rows. She gingerly stepped around the older stones, the ground soft beneath her feet due to heavy rains. She spied a small section where the name MACLAREN appeared emblazoned on several headstones then dropped to the ground, kneeling on her cape beside the newest grave, LUKAS MACLAREN. His mother had insisted on placing an etched lamb centered above his name, an image of purity often used for children under the age of twelve, but she could not be dissuaded.

Hannah cleared away some decaying boughs of remembrance, replacing them with her fresh bundle. This brought little comfort to her grieving, yet she felt it still appropriate, not wishing to sully his memory by her lack of funereal decorum.

Her fingers trembled across the etching of his name as she whispered, "Lukas, no more verses from you, love, to tell me how much I mean to you. No more silly laughter as you talk with your sheep, nor scowling looks when I tell you that you're daft." The tears came once more, gently, slowly, directed. She looked at the dove-gray clouds skirting over the highland hills and sighed, "I always knew I would be your wife, but you've left me widowed instead. So what is left for me here, with Ma so sick that she could die at any moment as well? I don't think I could stay here with you and Ma both gone. Nothing here for me but folks who'd stare, with either pity or contempt."

The grievous maid was startled when a solitary blackbird whooshed close by, dipping and swooping around her then perching atop Lukas's headstone. Hannah knew that spotting blackbirds served as omens of an inner calling, forging your heart's purpose with passion while some villagers, who knew the older tales, would say the blackbird revealed gateways to the Otherworld. Either way, to see one earlier than twilight was a rarity.

She stared at it, lost in the oddity of its timely appearance, for her life's direction had become a mystery. The songbird cocked its little beak heavenward then trilled a lovely tune, just for Hannah. It paused after the concluding note, looked her directly in the eye then flew away, just as suddenly as it appeared.

Hannah tried to watch its flight, but the winged messenger cloaked itself with the coming nighttime shadows.

She rose, pondering this grave-side visitor, and grabbing her soaked cloak, headed home.

Isle of Iona, Caledonia

Channelled wrack seaweed lay over Iona's rocky coastline like discarded gloves, with tubular fingers caressing the stones. Orange sea squirts freckled the grey boulders creating a polka-dotted seascape. Mixtures of grey, yellow and black lichens topped the natural painting with splashes of color.

Michael wandered along the coastline behind the Abbey, past the Bishop's House, after matins before attempting his day's work of illumination of the Twenty-Third Psalm. Father Callum had closed the service this morning with a traditional prayer dealing with healing. The words, like a constant companion, walked with Michael now. He whispered them to the waves: "Lord Christ, help me place my trust in you, to live in present moments. Forgive me when I forget that you long for my peace, healing in both my mind and heart. Your hands are everywhere in the brethren who surround me. Be the source of my journey back to wholeness, Jesus, the Risen One."

Michael was struck by the prayer's simplicity, the call to wholeness. As he walked, he reflected on the tear in his soul, cavernous at times, a bottomless pool with swirling dark waters that never receded. Yet the prayer suggested an end to such torment. When would Michael know wholeness again? Indeed it would take a miracle.

A sudden barking, like that of a dog, broke his meditation. There were a few farm dogs on the island, yet they rarely wandered down to this point. Perhaps one is injured or lost, thought Michael. His stiffened limbs disabled him from moving quickly this morning, but he urged his body forward towards the sound. Just around the tip of the western shoreline was an inland dip surrounded by boulders. The sound seemed to emanate from behind the boulders.

At first he saw nothing. Then subtle movements, like shadows, made the rocks appear as if they were alive. I must be seeing things, thought Michael, rubbing his eyes. But in reality, the "moving rocks" were seals, more seals than he'd ever seen, lounging and sleeping amidst the foundations of the rocky shoreline. Great grey seals with Roman noses and golden fur stood out while the common seals, in coats of white and grey, remained camouflaged amidst the stone outcrops. He did not wish to disturb their repose, so he respectively stayed a safe distance away. He knew little about seal customs, but he remembered seeing large groups like this during the summer breeding months when visitors came to Iona on pilgrimage. There must be at least fifteen to twenty seals, thought Michael. But in March? Why would they be here now?

While attempting to sit and watch the seals for a few moments, Michael lowered himself onto the rocks too quickly, causing him to slip into the sand on his bad leg. "Damn it," he said, much too loudly.

Many of the seals turned towards him at once. They slid swiftly like raindrops down a stained-glass pane into the safety of the sea. Within seconds, they were gone.

"Sorry," yelled Michael, as if his apology could be understood, leaning on his staff for support as he rose. His crippled leg slightly twisted in the fall, and his knee now ached in spasms. "What good am I, Lord, when I scare even the seals away?" His deepest doubts rushed at him like the gales that crossed the island. He walked around a bit, knowing that sometimes stretching his contorted muscles healed the soreness of his limbs, so he decided to walk to the village to clear his mind.

He followed the dirt track, stretching his leg before him from time to time, leading toward St. Ronan's Port where the ferry arrived daily with supplies and visitors. Since Michael was not an ordained monk, he sometimes worshiped with the villagers at Teampull Ronain, the local parish which stood on the corner next to the Nunnery. The nuns followed a life of simplicity and meditation much like the brothers of the Abbey. Noblemen's daughters studied within the red stone arches where Michael was treated as a welcomed visitor by the Abbess. She often invited him to sit in their cloister garden and discuss choir music over herbal teas from plants grown in the cloister gardens. But not today, thought Michael, for nothing grew in the wild winters of Iona.

A sudden wind sent a shiver down his back, driving him within the protective shelter of Teampull Ronain. It was a small chapel, much like the one behind the Abbey that bore his own name. No chairs were present, and only tiny shafts of light entered through the arrow slit windows near the structure's corners. It did appear, however, that a wooden bench had been placed inside to assist in some ceiling repairs, so Michael took advantage of this welcomed blessing and rested. He massaged his knee while stretching the heel of his foot outward, creating a taut line with his muscles. He pointed his toes then stretched, back and forth for several minutes until the pain began to subside. Years of walking over endless tracks of hills and valleys taught his body how to relieve such aches.

The smell of peat from the fire in the small hearth meant the villagers would be arriving soon for service. Not wanting to make conversation, he decided simply to warm himself then return to the

Abbey. The sudden opening of the oak door banging against the grey and white stones broke his solitude as a stranger entered the chapel.

He was tall with long, black curls cascading down the nape of his neck. His blue eyes shone like calcite crystals on dark velvet. "Pardon me for disturbing your prayers," he said, "but I fear the winds have given me no break this morning. May I stay a moment to warm myself?" he asked.

"Surely you are welcomed, as are all visitors to the island," replied Michael.

"Ah, but you see, I am no visitor to this isle." He sat on the floor at Michael's feet, warming himself by the fire.

"But I've lived here for over five years, sir," said Michael, "and I've never seen you."

"Perhaps, or perhaps not." The man stared into the hearth, ignoring Michael's perplexing gaze.

"Well then, my name is Michael. I live at the Abbey with the brothers transcribing manuscripts and playing the harp for services. Who might you be?"

"Some call me Ronan," he said softly, now looking directly at Michael.

"Like the saint this chapel is named for? Why, what a coincidence," said Michael.

"If you say so," said Ronan, a slow smile spreading across his thin lips.

"But tell me, why have I never seen you before if you're no stranger to the island?" asked Michael, leaning forward towards his guest.

Without answering the question, Ronan glanced around the chapel then sighed. "I find buildings interesting. They shelter man, like the body shelters the soul."

"I suppose so," said Michael, frowning at not having his question answered.

"I have a question for you now, if you don't mind."

"Very well," said Michael.

"Tell me," said Ronan, glancing towards Michael, "when the body changes its form, does the soul change as well?"

Michael fell back against the stone wall, stunned. Every day he felt his own soul completely incongruent with his injured form. "What? Why, I don't know really. I would think the soul retains its natural qualities, regardless of the shape it inhabits." Yet as the words passed over his lips, he believed it untrue.

"So it would seem," said Ronan.

The two men sat in silence while the question remained, floating in the air like a faerie's song - - - haunting.

"I must go," said Ronan. "The winds have calmed."

"Peace be with you," said Michael, in rote response.

"And with you, my friend. Till we meet again." Ronan quickly opened the door just wide enough to allow him safe passage back into the world without allowing the winter cold entrance.

Michael wondered at this strange conversation. But more than that, he could swear that a salty fragrance, like the sea, lingered in Ronan's wake.

During the next week, the lesions began healing, creating cavernous scabs. Mistress Stewart continued plying her patient with healing teas and poultices, changing the dressings every few hours to prevent further infection. The healer would return home in the evening, leaving the night duty to Hannah. Rosamond still suffered from severe headaches, sleeping for long stretches. The ordeal had been only three weeks long, yet it felt like three years to Hannah.

The snows melted into sprouting green grasses as Spring strode upon the earth. Song birds tentatively made their presence known. Rosamond fell in and out of sleep with little conversation or coherency. The scabs began to dry, falling off unceremoniously after such devastation, leaving pitted scars in their wake. The fever finally dissipated, and with its departure came the healer's analysis.

"Well, Hannah dear," said Mistress Stuart, "even though the fever is gone, it's wracked your mother for so long that her strength is nearly gone. She can barely see through the swelling."

Hannah wept by her mother's side, unable to face the impending truth. "What shall we do?"

"I can continue to give her something for the headaches, but she'll need her strong will to stay with us. At times, I feel she's given up. I fear this illness may do her in." The older woman stroked Hannah's hair outlining the MacFey cheekbones, shook her head then set about to make some tea.

For the first time in her life, Hannah felt completely alone.

The next morning, while Mistress Stewart was napping, and Hannah was finishing a shawl, Rosamond wailed, "Hannah, my box!" She spoke with such clarity that Hannah quickly obeyed.

Rosamond tried to sit up, bracing herself on her elbows, but she was too weak. "Help me up." Hannah quickly stuffed the pillows behind her mother's shoulders, supporting her head. Rosamond leaned back, heavy with the duty she knew could wait no longer. If she did not survive this illness, Hannah must know that she will still be loved.

After searching for several minutes, Hannah found the box where it had fallen between the pallet and the wall. She handed it to Rosamond who, with unseeing eyes, fingered the ornate edges until she said, "Hannah, open this for me."

With great reverence, Hannah slowly lifted the lid, remembering still the scolding from her childhood. Now she would be her mother's eyes. Everything was there - her treasures from days long gone: colored ribbons, a small farthing, an amethyst torque, and an abalone necklace. But still highly prized was the pearl- embedded caul. The only necklace Hannah knew her mother wore was a simple Celtic triad knot, but Hannah never saw Rosamond wear any of these beautiful gifts, so she gasped, fingering the delicate craftsmanship of each one, entranced by their intricate lines and never-ending spirals. Rosamond, barely able to discern the features of her daughter's face, said, "They are elegant, aren't they?"

"Ma, they're all so lovely," gasped Hannah. "But why do you never wear them?"

"A bit much for a highland weaver, don't you think?" She settled her hands in her lap to keep them from trembling. "Imagine the villagers' gossip about me putting on airs, wondering where I came by such expensive tokens when they know we barely scrape by. No, I'd not open the door to such gossip."

"I know you're right, but t's a shame they see only darkness when the sunlight would make them sparkle!" For a few golden moments, Hannah seemed lost in the wonder of it all, imagining her mother's features clad in such finery strolling through the markets at Perth. The netted caul looked more like a treasure for a mermaid than a mountain farm girl, yet Hannah kept fingering it, feeling the smooth pearls.

"Take the box, take them all," said Rosamond.

"But Ma, I couldn't. These are your most precious things," said the young woman,   placing the box in her mother's lap.

But Rosamond cast it aside. "I can't do this anymore," she sighed. "You must find him," gasped Rosamond, betraying the weariness quickly consuming her strength.

"Who, Mother?" asked Hannah,

"Michael. He's the one who's brought such beauty into my life. But it's been over five years now since I've laid eyes upon him," then she sobbed, tears barely escaping their solid prison.

"But who is this Michael you cry out for in the middle of the night?"

Talking proved difficult as her conversation broke into ragged phrases. The sadness choked her words, "Perth . . . at the market . . . festivals . . . Beltane coming soon."

"But why should I find him, Mother? What good can he do here?" Hannah, now more intrigued with this missing man than the lovely jewelry dripping through her fingers, looked into her mother's haggard face.

"Just promise me you'll go. Promise me, now."

"I'll do what you ask," said Hannah, not realizing the impenetrable pact she just created.

"I love him, deeper than I knew possible. If I die . . . can't bear you not knowing . . .," she moaned then Rosamond suddenly swooned, her head lolling from side to side.

"Mistress Stewart, come quick!" cried Hannah. She held her mother's face, reddened now and swollen, barely recognizable as the lovely Rosamond MacFey.

The healer woke suddenly. She pushed past Hannah, removing extra pillows so Rosamond could lie flat. Hannah, careful not to spill the box, replaced its contents then set it on the kitchen table. The young woman stared at the almost lifeless form of her mother, wondering what finding this Michael would accomplish. If she did find him, then what? Bring him back to Feshiebridge? But what if he was the lifeline her mother needed? And without him, would Rosamond still fight for her life?

Hannah knew she could not go through another funeral, not this funeral. She shivered, shuddering deep within.

No more words were spoken as Mistress Steward plied her patient with a special tea and hot beef broth. Hannah moved by the fire, poking the embers till they blazed once more, sputtering in chaotic patterns, mirroring her distracted thoughts. Fragments of truth spiraled in her memory, snatches of conversations between Grann and Rosamond. Still they conspired to confuse, not clarify.

Sorrow-filled years had been her mother's constant companion, and now Hannah finally understood. Both women were living without the men they loved.

For the second time in her life, the path was clear. She'd known she loved Lukas, and surged ahead to become his wife. With that option now gone, this second one presented itself. She must find Michael, no matter the cost. For her mother, for herself. So Hannah devised a plan.

The next day she made several extra loaves of bread then washed all the dirty bedding. While both Mistress Stewart and her mother slept, Hannah packed a few clothes into a small brown sack, stuffing the parting box beneath her sweater for safe keeping. She added some cheese, tarts, dried apples, a mug, and wooden bowl. Water would be plentiful as she walked along the river, so she filled a wineskin with brown ale. She draped the abalone necklace about her slender neck beside Lukas's ring. She would keep these tokens of her dearest ones nearby.

She tended the fire by the snoring Mistress Stewart, knowing this woman would still tend to Rosamond in Hannah's absence. Should Rosamond die, Hannah's heart could not withstand the blow, so she would leave, with just a drop of hope to sustain her.

Hannah decided to first locate Rosamond's relatives in Perth, for surely they knew about Michael and could assist her. It was only a week's walk to Perth by way of the drover's pass, so being mid-April, she could be back within three weeks' time with this man Michael. He might be at Perth, for the Beltane festival was only two weeks away.

"I'll find him," Hannah whispered, caressing her mother's cheeks now riddled with scars, "and I'll bring him back to you, to both of us." She picked up her belongings and walked quietly out the door into the dark grey morning. She gently closed the door, leaving her childhood in the safety of the cottage. She looked down at the Feshie River, for she'd not walked its banks since Lukas had been found. As she breathed in the newly ploughed earth from the fields below, she felt a heaviness in the air beside her. "Travel with me, my love," she said softly.

"Always," he murmured on the passing wind. With shoulders high, Hannah headed south.

CHAPTER TWELVE
Isle of Iona, Caledonia

Early spring fogs settled over Iona like a faerie mantle. Father Callum offered Michael total freedom to work as much as he requested; however, mistakes slowly but steadily marched across the pale parchments, filled with illuminated colored plates and embellished Celtic knot work.

"Father, I'm sorry," Michael apologized again one morning as the priest scrutinized Michael's daily work. "I can't seem to keep my mind on the work, yet the work keeps my mind off other things." He dodged the priest's glances, not wanting to see pity. His days of healing in this sacred shelter called Iona seemed to be ending. The darkness, ever present, rarely yielded.

"Michael, what can I do to help you?" asked Father Callum, sitting on the pallet next to Michael's desk. "It tears at my heart to see you hurting like this. I've seen many a broken man venture to these shores, but they often leave with a renewed sense of hope and wholeness. Yet for you, the longer you stay, the worse your condition."

"I've been noticing that recently myself, Father." He placed the color-tipped quill in the well and leaned back in his chair, exhaling a heavy sigh.

"Michael, I know it may seem trite to you, but perhaps you need to face your demons instead of letting them wreak havoc at will." He began pacing the cold, stone cell in thought.

"But how, Father? Find the man who beat me and confront him?"

"Maybe," said Father Callum. He paused in his circling, "Do you know the man's name?"

"No," replied Michael. "But t'would be easy enough to discover by visiting the girl's family at Duart Castle. I do recall that she and her new husband were going to live with his family somewhere on the Isle of Skye after the wedding rather than remaining on the Isle of Mull." Just thinking about that wedding initiated a slight trembling in his fingertips.

"Visiting Duart Castle and the Inn where you were beaten might be enough. Mind you, I'm no doctor concerning illnesses of the mind, but I've heard stories about miraculous healings after returning to the place of your undoing."

Michael began to consider this possibility. Did he have the courage to return? It could be no worse than what he faced now. He needed a reprieve from this life sentence. Moreover, he'd even fancied playing his harp again, for the old tunes took flight through his fingers, trying to ease his troubled spirit. But could he ever play in public again? The gash across his left cheek could heal no more, nor could the lowered jaw. Would he not horrify his listeners by his ill-favored appearance?

While Michael contemplated these questions, the priest brightened. "Michael, I've an idea. But let me talk it over with a few of the brethren first."

"As you wish," replied Michael, rising from his chair. His shoulders tightened into a broad brace as if facing invisible foes.

Father Callum patted Michael's shoulders, assuaging the defenses. "Not to worry, now. I'll see that your secret is safe. But I will need to get approval. You just rest now. Let the work wait a bit. I'll speak with you again soon." The priest whispered a silent prayer as he retreated down the cloister steps.

Go back? Into the world of men? Of late, Michael had begun to think he'd risk it all just to see his sweet Rosamond. He sorely missed being by her side.

Michael found his nightmares becoming day mares, riding him unmercifully into dark valleys he'd never known. Yet putting these brackish images on parchment seemed to bring him comfort. He took up the quill, dipped it in the black ink, and wrote:

Bestial pounding shattering,

splattering both tissue and blood.

The words and images battered him like the fists that had pummeled his face:

My brain reels on relentless tides.

They filled the page in jagged lines, so unlike his skillful transcriptions. Slants and curves now echoed his fears:

Silent screams pierce

the morning reverie

while night predators

devour my sanity.

The quill fell to the floor.

Exhausted by his efforts but too restless still to sleep, Michael wrapped himself in his cloak and headed for the shore. He often walked along the shore, regardless of the hour or the cold. He had to create some sense of normalcy. He wandered along the western shore again where he'd seen the seals the month before. The full moon breasted the sky with an ivory fullness, shining on the waves and boulders below. Michael filled his lungs with the sharp, salty air as he limped through the short sea grasses among the boulders.

Then he heard it: a haunting tune emanating from the waves with bell-like harmonies. Their voices rose and fell like the waves around them, voluminous base and soprano timbres shocking the night with their shimmering clarity like starlight. Michael recalled the sacred music of Iona, and knew there was none to compare with this magical melody. He listened intently, peering around the boulders, completely mesmerized by the music.

There they were, splashing about in the waves like children at play. Their bodies glistened in both the water and the moonlight, silk upon satin. They cavorted in the marbled waves, lifting their arms in outrageous joy. Unlike the villagers who swam in the summers, he sensed a marked difference in their movements, fluid, as if one with the sea.

A childhood memory crossed his mind when he saw what he dared not believe. There on the sand were the seal skins, piled one on top of the other, shining in the moonlight as beads of water covered them, shimmering like precious jewels. Their colors were easily discernible in the evening glow: sable browns as lush as molasses, greys with white spots like barnacles on sea stones, and gold, honey gold. Selkies - seal people.

During his travels though, Michael knew that families living near the ocean often spoke of selkie blood in their lines, "a dark one" every generation whose mysterious absences and undeniable longing for the sea could not be explained. Yet until now, he believed them to be nothing more than children's tales.

His curiosity aroused, Michael went over to the pile and placed his hand on the uppermost skin - the grey one. Its weight reminded him of rain-soaked sweaters. He noticed eye holes in the head piece as he ran his hand along the short fur, expecting it to be rough, but it was smooth, like polished stones. He steadily made his way to an outcropping then sat in wonder. He remained this way all night, mesmerized by their ethereal songs.

As the morning sun began its daily course, the selkies returned to the shore. Their laughter rode on the waves as the swimmers approached the beach. Michael noticed dark hair framing the swarthy complexions of these mysterious men and women. Each person reached for their seal skin from the pile, placing it around their shoulders like a mantle. One man stood apart from the rest, holding himself back as if to relish this form a little longer.

Michael recognized the sharp, angular face at once. Ronan. "Holy Mother of God!" he exclaimed.

The laughter ceased. The selkies turned, saw Michael then quickly finished their transformations. Suddenly the beach was filled with seals. They moved slowly into the water; heavy limbs on land now swam gracefully through the waves, diving into the shallows and out to sea in a moment's time before Michael could say a word to them.

But Ronan remained, glistening in his human form, apparently undisturbed by the cold. He draped the remaining grey skin around his waist then navigated himself through invisible channels of small rocks to the boulders where Michael sat in shock.

"Good morning, Michael," said Ronan, sitting beside the stricken man.

"And good morning to you," replied Michael, staring at Ronan in disbelief.

"So, I see you've come out for a walk, is it? Couldn't sleep?"

"Ah, no," stammered Michael.

"So, I guess you've a few questions for me," Ronan said quietly.

"I don't know where to begin, man," said Michael, "or should I say seal? How in God's name could such a legend be true?" His fingers crested his brow then ran over the remnants of the balding tonsured haircut. "Yet here you are, and there they swim - people one minute then seals the next. By all that's holy, I'd never have believed it had I not seen it with my own eyes."

Ronan smiled, nodding his head in agreement. "Aye, t's strange indeed. I cannot tell you how it is possible, only that it is. I do know that we are free to live as humans should we choose to, yet the sea tugs at our souls, her waves cradling us like no house or building can."

"Here, take my cloak man," said Michael. "There's no telling what news might get about if anybody saw me here talking to a naked man."

Ronan wrapped the cloak around his shoulders, mantling his humanity. He laid his seal's skin over the wall as salty drips cascaded down his dark features, barely discernible in the morning dusk.

"But are you happier in one place more than the other?" asked Michael.

"We belong to both worlds, and that duality allows us choice," replied Ronan. "While one world appears a refuge, we deny our truest sense of being by not partaking of both."

As Ronan spoke, a sudden tingling sensation, like a quickening, ran up Michael's spine then rippled down his arms. The tolling of these words reflected his current situation. Should he stay in the haven of Iona or venture again back into the world where his music and Rosamond remained? He rubbed his hands over his forearms, mollifying the prickling hairs beneath his cloak. "Do any of you stray far from these waters?"

"I travel, in both forms, with family in the north on Skye and the Hebrides. Do you know these places?"

"I was born on Skye, at Dunvegan Castle," said Michael.

"Are you a MacLeod, then?"

"You know my family?"

"I do. One introduction often leads to another. I'm sure in your previous line of work you knew this to be true," said Ronan.

Michael nodded.

"So, I see then I am not the only one acquainted with strange family heritage," continued Ronan, a slight smile now crossing his face.

"Aye, I'll grant you that," said Michael, shifting his weight a bit. "As a boy, there were always folks trying to sneak in to take a look at that damnable "faerie flag," supposedly left by a fey woman who married an ancestor, but to me, it just looked like a large, fancy napkin. Finest linen you'll ever see, I'll grant you that, but nothing Otherwordly."

Ronan simply nodded, but not in agreement. "Then answer me this, Michael. Why are you not with your family?"

"I've not seen them for many years," Michael said, looking westerly as if he could see over the hills to Dunvegan Castle itself. "I left under difficult terms. I'm uncertain if I will ever be welcomed home again. But what of you, man?"

"I, too, live a solitary life," said Ronan, "born to aging parents with two daughters. They could not reconcile my condition with their beliefs, so believing me to be cursed, they left me with relatives on Skye. As I grew to manhood, I met these few others here. But I must go now." Ronan stood, handing Michael his cloak. "Our transformation is private, but I sense a need in you. Shall you watch?"

"If you allow it," said Michael. The two men stood, facing one another.

"Well enough by me. You have choices to make soon, Michael. You will make the right one when the time comes." He walked towards the water's edge, then turned one last time. "Until the next time," he said.

Ronan draped the grey skin over his back, like a cape, pulling the head piece over his dark hair. He then crouched forward, placing his palms upon the sand. His feet stretched out behind the bent knees, while the skin covered his toes. His arms changed, thickening from slender limbs into the short fins of a seal, as if invisible fingers swiftly stitched the skin together. Skin incorporated limbs and bones and flesh. Michael was transfixed, watching as the seal edged his way into the water. When the seal reached the waterline, he dipped his nose into the water, allowing it to rush over his head. The transformation was complete. He disappeared beneath the foam-flecked lines of the sea.

Michael thought he was imagining this revelation, but this had been no dream. The morning found his stomach aching like a grunting sow while his right leg, now stiff from the night's excursion, trembled under his weight beneath the woolen black habit. He stretched his arms high over his head then down to his toes in one fluid movement, bringing life back into his tired body.

As he limped back towards the Abbey, he marveled that such a mystery be opened to him, a simple harper.

Michael spoke to no one but moved silently into the morning matins. His place near the sacristy door provided him concealment, so the brethren would focus only on his music and not the maker of the tunes. So many thoughts swirled through his mind.

As the brothers filed out after the closing prayer, Father Callum motioned Michael towards the Choir area to the left of the elaborate grey arches. Brother Aidan took a seat in the Choir next to Michael, grinning broadly.

"Ah, I see you are both here," said Father Callum. "Good. Now Michael, after several days of work I have gained approval from the ruling Benedictine brothers. We feel that your time here at Iona must come to an end."

Michael started to object but knew there was no point. The priest spoke the truth.

"We have been exceedingly pleased with your work," continued Father Callum, "and I shall craft a letter of recommendation should you ever wish to house yourself in another monastery. You may find the Ardchattan Priory a convenient respite along your journey."

"That's most generous of you, Father."

"Well, possibly. But more to the point, we here at the Abbey wish to show you our support of your talents, both in music and transcription, so we wish to send you into the world with a humble beginning." The priest reached beneath his black habit, past the knotted belt, and pulled out a small purse.

"Father, no," protested Michael. "I couldn't . . ."

"No, you wouldn't, but you shall, Michael. Both the nuns and the brethren have designated our monthly collection to support you as you leave us. Mind you, it is no king's ransom, so you will need to begin working in a few months. But I believe you will know what to do when the time comes." He winked at the harper and shot him a brief smile.

Michael took the purse handed to him, shaking his head in disbelief.

"Now, there's one more thing," said Father Callum. At this Brother Aidan brightened. "We know that in times past you often wandered on foot, traveling the countryside with ease. But as your comfort is somewhat limited now in such a mode of travel, we offer help. We want you to take Molly, one of the Fraser family's work horses, while Brother Aidan accompanies you as friend and guide, attending to whatever needs you may have. He has concluded his studies here, so as his first act of service as an official priest, he has requested this. The Church will support you both in your travels through prayer and shelter, when necessary."

Michael turned thoughtfully to Brother Aidan, "Are you sure, Aidan? Do you really want to travel with me?

"Aye, Michael," said Brother Aidan. "T'would give me more pleasure than you know. I've never seen much of the world, and I value your friendship above all others. This will be my means of service, and if you'll have me, I'd be happy to go with you." He stuck out his right hand, as if sealing a bargain. "You never know when you might be needing a priest!"

Michael took his friend's hand, and rather than shaking it like in a market deal, lowered his head and kissed it. "T's my honor, my friend, to travel with such a man as yourself. I know not exactly what you'll be gaining in this venture, but I welcome your company." The two friends smiled then looked up at their benefactor.

"Good," said Father Callum. "It's settled. Now, as to your leaving - you'll have two days' time to say farewells then be on your way."

The two men followed Father Callum to breakfast where they shared a simple meal of oat cakes, brown bread, and black tea with cream and sugar. Michael hurried to his cell to finish the psalm he was illuminating. The colored inks and quills would remain behind. Completely astounded by the generosity of the brethren, he felt a new life calling. He personalized the Iona Pilgrim's Prayer that night as he lay down to sleep:

"Lord, take my pilgrim heart

and walk beside me and

before me as I leave.

May your Spirit bring

surprises along the path.

Give me eyes to see

your presence,

O Lord of the unexpected."

He drifted into dreams filled with seals and the slapping of fins on the sea.

CHAPTER THIRTEEN

The riverside path leading south from Feshiebridge appeared as a chocolate sash thrown carelessly on the ground. Spring thaws were slow to come to the highlands, yet with Imbolc well passed and April rains impending, the ground welcomed the warming. Red squirrels scurried rampant through new canopy growth while the sweet melody of the Crested Tits fell silent on the dispassionate young woman as she began her search for Michael.

Hannah walked swiftly, not wanting to answer questions from well-intentioned neighbors. Rosamond would have said much about such a venture for a young woman, alone, when the weather for safe travel still hid its face. But Hannah cared little for herself these days. Even songs no longer graced her lips.

The grey morning mist lifted within an hour's time, allowing the sun's rays to filter through the pines lining the riverbank. Time lacked in preparing the sturdy leather boots for such a journey; however, the seams held the slippery mud from seeping into the homespun hose.

The path transformed in the early light, taking on the new greens of spring as long grasses covered the way. As Hannah followed the river path beyond Auchlean, the ground trembled. Believing the sound emanated from a cartload of travelers yet wishing to remain alone, she dashed into the tree line, hiding amongst the scabrous trunks of the birch grove. She sighed with relief as she watched a herd of roe deer crossing. Velvet-antlered bucks, doting does, and precocious yearlings pawed the ground, running in circles yet moving steadily towards the water. She observed one doe grooming the face of her fawn while others, lying in the fresh heather, jerked their heads, chewing their cud.

Family, even in the wild, proved a sore reminder to Hannah. She did not know what family meant any longer. Without Lukas, the family she'd wished for would never be. She wept now, missing when she might have walked through the woods with a daughter of her own. She recalled the hopes she once painted on her heart when considering a child, a daughter, and all the wonders they would share as a family. Learning flower names, singing songs, herding sheep with Alpin at the shieling while Lukas looked on - all gone now. Respectability for their girl would surround her, not a girl shunned as Hannah in her childhood days, for the girl's father would be landed gentry.

"LUKAS!" she cried aloud, not caring if she disturbed the surrounding wilderness and its inhabitants as the deer scattered. "How could you rob me of such a life? You fool! Chasing after a damned horse in the middle of snowstorm rather than warming yourself by your family's hearth fire? What were you thinking?" She fell to the ground, mud splattering her cloak as her limbs plopped down on the spongy terrain. A solitary bitterness wrapped her heart.

At times like these she also missed never knowing her father, especially with her mother's life so precarious. So why would this man Michael be certain Hannah was never alone, as her mother protested? These questions bore their way into her vast pit of loneliness.

She picked up her things, apologized to the remaining deer for her outburst then picked up her pace. The river now veered west, connecting the path to the drover's pass taken to Blair Atholl. Even in the best of conditions, shepherds avoided this treacherous pass until late April, knowing that sudden snow storms were often created by low-lying clouds trapped in the ridged terrain.

The snow-capped peak of Allt Garbhalch rising on her right comforted her. She was not ready for the gaiety of a new season but rather connected more with the cold. She stared at the peak towering over similar pinnacles nearby, the sunlight glinting over the snowy remnants. Stone, standing, stone, frozen, stone dead. She moved on.

She was surprised to come upon a stone circle. Although the dolmens creating the circle were not as tall as other standing stones, the circle's construction was undeniable. But by noon, hunger reminded her body that she needed nourishment. Seating herself inside the circle, Hannah opened her bag and tore off a chunk of bread, lacing it with a sliver of orange cheddar. She munched on dried apples then retied the sack. She sipped some ale from the wineskin but before leaving this space, she paused.

Hannah knew these places to be powerful, sacred in the Old Ways. How this one had remained hidden was a mystery. A soft whisper, as if emanating from the stones themselves, invited her inside the perimeter, encouraging her to walk the circle's fullness. She closed her eyes as she walked, sure of the way as if she'd followed this dance before. The stones created a wall of voices singing around her, comforting strains of dulcet tones. With each footstep her fears assuaged, bolstering her to continue. She walked the circumference three times.

For the first time since the death of her beloved, she sang, matching her voice in harmony to the invisible singers. Her arms swayed as her body twirled in a spiral design. A wave of warm tingles spread from her head down her shoulders throughout her entire body, connecting Hannah to the Divine Inspiration of Creation.

She did not see him emerge from the rock. His tall grey form, similar to his stony abode, rose solid against the morning sky. His square head sat atop a mass of muscular shoulders with a handsome face, despite his granite coloring. Legs, like ironwood, sprouted downward into two slabs of large feet. Oddly enough, his eyes were blue, scintillating sapphires set like jewels in a royal diadem. He lumbered towards her, moving slowly.

"Who are you?" asked Hannah, more curious than afraid.

"One who knows much after many turnings of the years," said the stone fey, sitting near her, causing the ground to quake. "I see the circle lightens your spirit as it does for those with ears to hear its melody."

"I am feeling a bit better, now that you mention it," said Hannah.

He moved closer to this child of earth, and she allowed him to take her hand. His touch was like coarse russet fabric rubbing her skin. She did not pull away. Despite his massive form, he wore an air of gentle seduction.

"I see a deep sadness," he said. "Stone knows no hurt, so I can take away your pain."

"But how?"

"Stay with me," he whispered, kissing her palm. He began pulling her to him.

Although the ground remained firm, Hannah felt like she was falling in time, as though motion slowed beyond its normal coursing. She'd heard tales of how maidens would fall in love with such gentle fey then be useless amongst mortals. She closed her eyes and saw Lukas's face. She felt she would never love another man, fey or mortal. The bond with Lukas remained true in her heart, and their love dispelled the stone fey's enchantment. She shook herself as if waking from a dream then leaned away, standing to leave.

"You have much wisdom for one so young," he said, acknowledging her rejection. He rose, walking over to one of the dolmens. "Never forget. You are strong, inside."

"But how do I find that strength?" she asked.

"By standing," he said, leaning against the rock, "like the stones."

She watched the stone fey melt into the standing stone until only his face remained visible. He smiled, bowed his head to her then vanished.

"Well, it seems the Fair Folk keep wandering onto my path. I wonder who will be next?" she asked aloud to nobody. She grabbed her belongings then slinging both sack and skin over her shoulder, journeyed on.

With each footfall, the miles accumulated - five. . . ten . . . fifteen. By late afternoon she found herself maneuvering through a narrow gorge at the foot of Allt Coire Bhlair. The steep hillsides were laden with thick heather, dense pines, and rippling stone scree which cascaded like a stone fountain, making the way unstable. Several times she stumbled, once tearing her hose at the knee, but still she persevered. Late snows like freshly whipped cream dotted the landscape. Hannah knew this portion slowed the drover's pace, yet without the animal faction, she reached the summit just before sunset.

Sleeping on a peak was less than wise, but Hannah found refuge under a rowan tree jutting perilously out of its rocky womb, providing slim shelter from nightly winds. She perched herself beneath its spreading limbs, recalling the dream of Oonagh from the rowan on the MacLarens' farm then laying her belongings aside, made camp.

She gathered some kindling and a few large branches to make a nighttime fire to ward off wild beasts then stretched her legs in front of her like a feline after a nap. Although she was tired, her muscles ached little. Years of activity among the woods of Feshiebridge had toned her trim frame. The sudden screeching of a golden eagle startled her as she watched the winged creature aiming straight for her. Hannah had never heard of these birds attacking humans, but she rolled herself into a ball, covering her head with her cloak. She heard the beating of wings above her pass by then all was still.

She slowly unfurled, looking through the maze of branches overhead. Nothing. Then she looked below her, down the rocky crag.

Ah, she thought, settling back against the tree. The nest. Large tufts of heather outlined the shallow cup with bits of moss and dried grasses holding the eggs. Of course, she thought, a perfect spot for an eagle aerie. The bird ruffled its feathers a bit as it resettled into the nesting position. Hannah knew it took almost two months before the eggs hatched followed by several weeks of care by the maternal eagle. Would this eagle bring her courage for a journey, like the Old Ways taught? Or perhaps lead her heart to a place of rejuvenation? A cavernous echo deep within resounded, "No."

She brought the slender kindling to a glowing blaze, laying three large fallen limbs in a triangular shape on top. She considered the possibility of wildcats this time of year, and rose to gather more wood to last the night. Soon she returned, her arms heavy with an assortment of pine and rowan branches. She stacked them next to the fire, cleared a spot for her to lie down then using her sack as a pillow, tried to sleep. Several times during the night she replenished the blaze, its hunger constant for more fuel.

Her thoughts rambled down hallways of her history with Rosamond, remembering with clarity the argument between Grann and Rosamond concerning Hannah's father.

"Please, God," whispered Hannah, "make them stop!" The five-year-old child cupped her hands over her mouth as she bridled the whimper that demanded release. Hannah perched on the edge of a small pallet behind the partitioning curtain in the small crofter's cottage, her little legs trembling, as her mother and Grann continued arguing.

"It shames me, it does, Rosamond MacFey, for you to make such a fool of yourself," said Grann, knitting by the peat fire. The steady rhythm of her wooden rocking chair against the river rock floor accelerated, betraying its traditional lullaby gait. "Running down to Perth, year after year, for that traveling man. He has no decency, I tell you." The old woman practically poked herself with one of the needles, an infrequent occurrence in the MacFey household. She shifted the green shawl over her square shoulders, not stooped with age like her peers, and adjusted her hair combs, catching a loosened straggling iron-grey strand. The old woman's nimble fingers fairly flew, ignoring the antics of arthritis. "What's the man's name again?"

"You know his name, Mother," said Rosamond, trying to remain calm. "It's Michael." Ignoring Grann's rants, Rosamond packed a few

simple belongings in her travel bag then placed a small heart-shaped box with mother-of-pearl inlay at the bottom for safety's sake. "Why do you detest him so?" asked Rosamond.

"Why, you ask, girl? Why don't I sing his praises as you do? For years that man has tied your heart to him without the slightest attempts at binding himself to you properly." Grann's voice rose in sharp tones. "And does he even know you have a daughter? And what about Hannah? You leave the child with me, for weeks on end, thinking of nothing but yourself." With expertise dexterity, she knotted the line's end with a loud snap while changing colors from maroon to navy then continued creating the scarf. "You know, the two of you deserve each other!"

Hannah was supposed to be sleeping on the pallet behind the curtain partitioning the sleeping area from the rest of the small crofter's cottage. With knees drawn into her chest, Hannah wrapped her small arms about them. She closed her eyes, willing the harsh words away, yet they wove themselves into her very being. Hannah cringed, pulling the woolen blanket over her head.

"But he's a well-renowned harper who makes his living traveling," said Rosamond, as she continued her packing. "What kind of life is that for a wife?" Rosamond breathed deeply. Had not this question of living full-time with Michael plagued her since the first time she saw the handsome harper?

Grann surveyed her daughter carefully then said, "Why to think my only daughter would run about so wild. You need to settle down, Rosie. Marry a good farmer. The child needs a father."

The child had a father, thought Rosamond, but what good would the truth do now? It would not change her situation. Still, Rosamond loved Hannah, almost best of all.

"Answer me this, then, who is the child's father?" The old woman had waited five years for a solid answer to this simple question. She surveyed her daughter with a scrutinizing glare. How could her only child bring such shame to their family name? "You know what folks around here say, don't you?"

Rosamond ignored this standard line as she completed her packing by placing the white sleeping shift on top. She pulled the leather strands together then hoisted the bag onto her back. "Ma, I'm in a hurry if I'm to reach Ruthven in time to catch the morning Perth carriage south."

But Grann continued, for she had waited too long for this conversation, and she would have the truth. "Folks say you were pregnant before you went away, some farmer lad with no sense of honor or even a married farmer. Why, your story about some mysterious man in Perth, you marrying him then suddenly he dies at the child's birthing is absolute rubbish! Tell me his name!" scowled the elder MacFey.

But Rosamond could take no more. "Leave me be, old woman! You're nothing but a bitter old harpie with nothing better to do than try to run my life. Well, I won't have it! I'll take Hannah away, if you want us out, but I'll not stand for you talking to me that way anymore!" She stalked out, leaving a wake of clamoring wood as the door slammed shut.

Hannah shuddered.

Grann trembled. She'd never seen such rage in Rosamond before. Would her daughter return?

No one saw the small, auburn head poke around the edge of the curtain. No one saw the pair of green eyes peeking around the edge of the sleeping curtain.

Hannah looked to the stars, as if trying to pattern her beloved's face among the shining lights. Oh Lukas, I miss you, darlin'. I should be lying in your arms right now, loving you, not stuck on a stony ledge, alone and cold. I hardly know myself these days. I'm sure you'd wonder at how your light-hearted Hannah has disappeared." She paused, allowing a few tears to soften her heart. "I'll tell you where she's gone, my love. She lies in the grave with you." Hannah wrapped both arms around herself and cried herself to sleep.

She awoke just before sunrise, stiff with cold. She rubbed her eyes, wishing for some water to splash her face, but settled for a sip of ale. The night air had worked its way deep into her lungs, causing several coughing fits. Her fiery protector, successful at fending off nighttime enemies, was reduced now to black ashes scattered about. She wrapped her shawl closely about her shoulders then fastened the brown cloak over it. It warmed her body, for the weather had turned overnight from balmy breezes to bitter cold once more. The sun remained elusive. She ate a cold apple tart and stared at her surroundings before beginning her descent. A waterfall, unnoticed last night, sparkled like silver rain threading its way down the mountainside. Soon it would run headlong into the valley, heavy with spring rains.

Her task loomed before her like the holy grail, an unquenchable quest, to bring peace to her mother, for surely Michael would ease the sorrows of Rosamond's heart. "I must get to Perth before Beltane," she said, making her descent.

Careful not to slip, she slid on her backside down the plunging slope without incident. As she neared the gap between Glen Feshie and Glen Geldie, the path broached a bog with no bridge in sight. Staying close to the mucky outer edges, Hannah navigated the verdurous channel like a seasoned sea captain, the vegetative vines greening the murky waters. Yet once her boot plunged too deeply into the mountainous quicksand and was sucked off, despite the lacings. It was completely sodden when she returned it to her foot. Hannah cursed aloud as the cold water iced her foot, but no one heard.

The bog continued for several miles with Allt Dhaid Mor now looming to her left, shading the chilly pass. Before the path returned to solid track, several large grey stepping stones had been laid for the drover's safe passage. Hannah determined not to fall again, so she carefully placed her weight on one foot before stepping to the next stone. She had two more stones to traverse when her wet boot betrayed her, slipping over the right edge and catching on smaller stones below. Hannah screamed.

She fell sideways, landing on her shoulder while her sack flew forward, fortunately onto the well-trodden path. She crawled over the last stone, her right leg lagging awkwardly behind her. Pulling herself into a seated position on the dirt track, she flung the dripping muck from her cloak and shook debris from her hair. Her kirtle and shift were soaked at the hem.

Her reserve shattered. The pain in her ankle did not rival her anger. Her ribald screams echoed, surrounding her with a wall of rage. "Damn it all!" she yelled, pounding her fists on the ground. "I was supposed to be a bride by now! Living in a new home! But he's DEAD! Damn it, DO YOU HEAR ME? Lukas is DEAD!" She searched the skies as if his form would drop from the scattered clouds. Exhausted by her ravings, the pain reminded her of more urgent matters: a busted ankle.

Hannah unlaced her boot to examine the damage, but within minutes, her ankle swelled twice its normal size. She grabbed her sack, rummaging for an extra pair of woolen hose. She pulled at the bottom of her cloak, making a bandaging strip. She removed her wet hose then bound her ankle, wrapping the strip in figure-eight motions from her heel to the ball of her foot. This was not the first time she'd sprained that ankle, nor, she feared would it be the last. She placed both hose leggings over the foot, placing the wet one last as a new boot.

She struggled to stand, straining to keep her weight off the injury. Placing her palms on the ground in front of her, she pulled her left knee between them, heaved her weight forward then straightened the leg. The bandage held the right foot in squared traction, so that Hannah could place a little weight on the heel. The pain ran like slivers of cut glass, shooting up her leg. A walking stick would be invaluable, otherwise she would resemble a wood snail laying its slimy track.

Her face grim, she threw her sack over her shoulder, grateful for its lightened load after her simple meals. She didn't limp far before she saw stout larch branches lying ahead, residue from recent storms. She tested several before finding one worthy, but was now able to continue with less pain. What I wouldn't give for some feverfew or wintergreen tea, she thought.

The blue sky turned to bloodless grey as clouds clumped into thick masses like floating islands. The temperature dropped throughout the day as Hannah slowly hobbled along. She used her walking stick to ford two more streams, successfully nearing the junction of the Glen Geldie pass and the road east to Braemar. The Caledonia pines now mingled with their elders, for the woods now were comprised of mature hazels, oaks, larches, and cedars.

She turned right, continuing past Blair Atholl village on the Old Blair road which ran along the banks of the Tilt River. From there she would take the main road south through Dunkeld then finish through the short cut, the farmer's track, into Perth. So, another day and half to Blair Atholl, then possibly catch a ride to Dunkeld. From there, it was a leisurely day's walk to Perth. Now she had a plan.

Despite the growing cold, she knew her ankle would mend faster if she soaked it awhile in the cool river. Hannah noticed an oak log fallen into the water's edge, so laying aside her possessions, she scooted towards the water. Leaning forwards, she splashed some cold water on her face, wiping it dry with her sleeve. Her leggings came off easily, but as she unwound the bandage strip, she was shocked at immediate bruises of blues, maroons, and deep purples bleeding from her toes throughout her entire foot. She dipped her foot in the cold water, grimaced at the numbing cold then plunged the ankle deeper. The water swirled around her ankle, frigid currents embracing the bruised foot. She stayed as long as she dared then withdrew, drying the ankle with her damp kirtle's hem. Shivering fingers pulled the stubborn hose up until Hannah accomplished her task. The empty boot dangled like a derelict off her sack. "Traitor," she said, scowling at the leather.

Her stride compromised, Hannah walked several more miles. Awkward imprints of two feet, the left deeper than the right, with an additional indentation outside the right foot, created her broken legacy. She tightened her cloak about her with shivers as her constant companion. She hoped to reach the Falls of Tarf before sundown, for she knew the woods there offered shelter, perhaps even a hunter's lean-to.

Drained by the struggle of each footstep, Hannah slowed her pace. She did not notice when her hood fell back, exposing her auburn crown to bitter winds as the light snow began to fall. She spoke aloud, as if conversing with a fellow traveler, though tracks revealed her to be alone. "After that, Mother wouldn't let me play with Maire Stewart for over a week. A week, I tell you! Unlucky, we was, to be found out. But it's my secret now," she said, waggling her finger at an invisible face, "and nothing you say will make me tell." She pulled her finger to her lips in a silencing motion. "But I'll show them. I'll slow them . . . I'll slew thom." She staggered a bit, her head bobbing left to right, but braced herself with the walking stick. "Need to sleep, just stop . . ." she slipped to her knees, the ankle's pain beyond her now. She fell sideways, landing in the long grasses with her cloak covering her body. She did not move.

She dreamed.

The cold water seduced her . . . deeper, deeper, deeper still. She saw Lukas swimming towards her, so she reached for him. She felt his fingertips graze hers, but then he faded into bubbles, and her arms were empty. She sank. Auburn hair swirled around her in graceful arcs while she moved her arms in elegant concentric swirls, resembling a mermaid now more than a highland lassie.

She could open her eyes without pain, and saw rippling hills of sapphire blues and topaz greens of the sea. Her breathing shallowed. Her pulse paused for long breaks between beats.

She knew she was dying.

The darkness of the ocean seeped into her body as if replacing the life once housed there. She could do nothing more to save herself. She resigned herself to the watery grave. All was blackness.

CHAPTER FOURTEEN

"Is she dead?"

"No, my lord, but she's froze through and through!" Neil noted the steady yet thin vaporous stream rising from Hannah's face. "There is but a bit of breath, so death may be near."

"Well, pick her up gently then lay her on one of the carts," said Lachlan Grant. "If we put her between these two fresh kills, their bodies are still warm enough to aid her. Now, hurry man, before this snow turns on us!" Grant, a nobleman from Kingussie, was visiting the Stewarts of Blair Castle. "And fetch that sack by her side, for it may be her only property."

The hunting party quickly dispersed and traversed the lower section of the Falls of Tarf followed by a narrow glen where the steep slopes of Beinn a' Ghlo were barely visible. They crossed the Tilt River quickly then made haste as snow continued to fall. After two more hours of dodging through larches and firs, the horses crossed the final Bridge onto the Blair Atholl estate.

Lachlan ordered Hannah, still unconscious, to be carried through the kitchen where several serving wenches were assisting Hilda, the head cook, with the evening meal. Hilda, short and stout befitting an excellent pastry chef's form, began to rant about the filth as the hunters stalked through her kitchen until she realized they were not carrying a carcass.

"Holy mother of God! What's this?" she asked, pulling back the blood-soaked tangles to reveal Hannah's pale grey face. "Where did you find her?"

"Little does that matter now, good woman," said Lachlan. "But I ask for your assistance. This young woman is in need of warming. After a bath, her wet clothes must be exchanged for dry if we are to save her. Death may be impatient."

"But this blood," started Hilda, examining Hannah's head for a gruesome wound.

"Only from the deer we killed this day, for she shared their cart," said Lachlan. "We found her all but frozen, fallen in the road."

Hilda took off her white cap and slapped it down on the wooden planked table before her. Why this night? The household was all a flitter with royal visitors! She ran her stubby fingers through her tight, grey curls as she looked about the kitchen, deciding which girl to use for such an errand. Mary was a bit flighty, being the youngest of the pair, while Jenny had proven solid during a crisis in previous household episodes. It was all too much. "Jenny, come here. Lead these men through the back hallway to the servants' quarters. There, remove her wet things, bathe her with warm water, and if she wakes, try to get some hot tea inside her. Now hurry, girl . . . and let little Mary help you."

Both girls had been silent as the unexpected visitors trampled into their domain with a bloodied body. Mary shied away, yet Jenny, once commanded by Hilda, wiped her floured hands on her white apron, set her cap straight (tucking in brown stragglers framing her face) and took a deep breath. She would not let her mistress down. "Mary, run downstairs and begin the bath while I assist these gentlemen with the young lady."

Mary, eyes wide and alert, nodded her head then practically flew down the stairs, her petite frame barely a wisp of vision as she darted around the winding turns. Jenny, an able girl of average height and weight, led Neil and Kyle downstairs.

Hilda sent word for a doctor then returned to her food prep while the girls returned to their duties.

Neil and Kyle followed Jenny into a small room, placing the frozen young highlander on the rug in front of the hearth. The men built a fire, relieved of their post by Jenny, then rejoined their company. As the small room warmed, Jenny and Mary filled a large basin with warm water. While undressing Hannah, Jenny discovered her injured ankle. She methodically unwrapped the foot, horrified by its ghastly discoloration and swollen state.

"What do you wonder happened to her?" asked Jenny, but all little Mary could do was cry.

The two worked together, lifting Hannah over the basin's rim into the soap-filled bath. Mary cradled Hannah's head, using a warm rag to clean away the deer blood from her face and hair. Jenny bathed arms, legs, and torso, careful not to rub too hard, for she'd dealt with this freezing sickness before. Slowly, the body needed to come back, very slowly.

173

"I'll be right back," said Jenny, leaving Mary with the naked girl. Hannah still had not revived. Minutes later, Jenny returned with lavender bathing salts and lemon oils.

"Where did you get those?" asked Mary. "Surely you didn't nick them from the missus?"

"Don't be daft," said Jenny. "These were a present to me from my aunt, you know, the wealthy one in Perth. I'll be thinking that this girl here needs them more than myself." She dumped the lavender into the water then doused her hands with the oils, gently rubbing them into Hannah's skin. "Here, cover her face with a cloth so no water gets in, and I'll wash that blood out of her hair."

Mary did as instructed. She felt like she was preparing a body for burial rather than resurrection. Still their charge did not move, so they allowed her to soak for about twenty minutes more till the water cooled. Mary turned down the bed then the two serving women once again hoisted Hannah over the side, laying her on the clean sheets. Mary dried the girl's pale white skin while Jenny placed a clean white sleeping shift over Hannah's broad shoulders. They combed out all the tangles from the day's arduous events then covered Hannah with layers of woolen blankets and cloth-covered bricks warmed by the hearth. Constant heat might yet save their frozen charge. Jenny sent Mary to inform Hilda of Hannah's injuries and ask for further instructions.

Hilda informed Lady Stewart of their ward and her circumstances, so the gentle Lady insisted that both girls tend to the poor girl until her health should return. After his examination of Hannah, the doctor gave instructions to deal with the hypothermia, the sprained ankle and the bronchial infection. The girls remained with their ward for the next three days, taking shifts between their usual household duties and nursing while the world of dreams held Hannah captive.

Not until the dawn of the fourth morning did Jenny, dozing in a chair by the bed, hear the name, "Lukas." She straightened, shook herself, then looked down at the bed. Hannah's eyes fluttered open then immediately closed. Her head rolled from side to side on the goose down pillow, her breathing regular and revitalized.

"Mary! Wake up, girl!" Jenny jumped up, shaking her assistant from a well-deserved reverie. "I think she's coming back!" The two now stared at Hannah, ethereal as the fey themselves, yet with a blush appearing on her cheeks. "Mary, run tell Mistress Hilda that we need some fresh tea!" Mary rushed from the room set on her mission.

Moments later Mary returned followed by Hilda, carrying a tray with a silver tea service, setting it on the stand next to the bed. Hilda sat in the chair by the bed and gently grasped Hannah's hand.

"Jenny," said Hilda, "lift her head, gently now girl, and let's see if we can get her to drink a bit of peppermint tea. I've even added a bit of angelica to warm those frozen feet." Jenny raised Hannah's shoulders while Mary propped two pillows behind, helping Hannah sit up.

Hannah looked around, not recognizing her surroundings. Like a roe deer in the hunter's sight, she stared into the three sets of eyes locked on her face. She backed into the bed frame, nearly knocking over the tea service.

Before she could speak, Hilda said, "Good morning to you, missus. You've given us quite a scare, you have. Now don't fret; we've been taking good care of you. The doctor even came to settle that nasty cough in your chest, so we've been brewin' up something special, just as he directed. But now it's your turn, so drink this tea."

Hannah took the cup in her trembling fingers, lifting the steamy drink to her lips. She sipped the tea, her eyes roving back and forth between the women surrounding her.

"We found these two tangled around your neck," said Hilda, handing the green ribbon bearing Lukas's ring to Hannah alongside Rosamond's abalone necklace. "I wondered that you might want to be putting them back on, seeing as I expect you hid them so no harm would come to you. A lady like yourself, I mean, traveling alone on the road. You never know who might be lurking about.'

Hannah looked at the ring dangling before her. Without hesitation, she tore the ring from the ribbon and placed it on her left hand, ring finger, announcing her widow status. "Thank you," said Hannah, then looped the abalone shell over her head where it nestled nicely just above her breasts.

"Just one more thing, miss. Not wanting to bother you or such, but we'd just like to know what to call you, if that's okay," said Hilda.

"Hannah. Hannah Mac . . ." she looked at the ring, "MacLaren," she stammered, unaccustomed to the flavor of this new identity.

"Well then, Miss Hannah, we'll just let you rest a bit more then try a bit of breakfast, now that you're awake," said Hilda, rising from her chair. She collected the tea service then facing Hannah said, "Try not to walk though, for I hear you've taken a nasty turn. We'll be back soon. Come along, girls." The younger women scurried out of the room leaving Hannah alone.

Hannah slept intermittently in the four poster bed while Hilda allowed Jenny and Mary to check on the patient every hour, plying her with steaming barley beef soups, slices of brown bread, and peppermint tea. As Hannah regained her strength, cheeses and dried fruits appeared. A set of crutches leaned in the corner, like a pair of soldiers on alert. Hushed voices could be heard throughout the house conjecturing the young woman's sudden appearance. Even Lachlan leaned his ear to hear of the girl's progress.

Hannah's first attempt to put weight on her injured ankle was heard throughout the house. Hilda gave the poor girl willow bark to chew for the pain, telling her to raise the foot on pillows until the swelling reduced. They wrapped it in warm compresses and were pleased to see the bruising change from dark purples to pale yellows and greens as the blood circulated more freely. Hannah rotated the ankle periodically as the swelling reduced.

By the week's end, Hannah could walk with minimal pain. She offered to help in the kitchen for repayment, but Hilda would have none of it. Many in Perthshire knew of the Stewart's hospitality and regular reports were sent to Lady Stewart, who was still tending to her regal guests.

Hannah was eager to move on. She knew Beltane was only a few days away, and she did not want to miss the market at Perth. Although she appreciated the borrowed clothing while hers were being mended, it felt right to be wearing her own boots and kirtle again. After lunch, she hobbled into the kitchen, using only one crutch now as she tested the ankle then plopped down on a stool next to the roasting spit. Hilda was turning a pig, already charred on the spit, when Hannah asked for extra victuals to send her on her way.

"What? You can't be thinking of walking all the way to Perth on that foot?" asked Hilda, churning the crank with massive effort. "What madness is it that drives you, girl?"

"I must find a man, in Perth. I've been gone much longer than I ever intended."

"Ah, I should have known all this stemmed from a man. Well, you can't leave without saying a word to her Ladyship. I'll see if she's available. With so many guests, she may not be able to see you, but she does enjoy an afternoon tea in the music room. Go and wait for her there a bit." After instructing Jenny to take Hannah to the music room, Hilda disappeared upstairs.

Jenny led Hannah down a dark hallway, past several drawing rooms then into the front entrance hall where an ornate mahogany staircase rose to the second floor. Jenny pointed upstairs: "That's where everyone sleeps. The family stays on the second floor with their visitors while we run up and down the stairs all day!"

As they made their way towards the music room, Hannah noticed that the castle seemed a bit unusual, like many houses joined together with twisting walkways at odd angles rather than one completed plan. She admired the richly colored tapestries and family flags of yellows and blues which hung in the Great Hall opposite an immense stone fireplace framed with a marble mantle.

Jenny turned one last corner, leading Hannah into the music room where an unusually large lute, a chittarone, was propped in the corner. Suddenly the servant's bell rang three times.

"Oh, I have to run to the kitchens, Hannah," said Jenny. "Have a look around. Her Ladyship should be here soon." Her white apron fairly flew about her like a goose taking flight as the young woman departed.

Hannah noticed smaller lutes, pipes, a pianoforte, and a host of musical scores scattered about the room. Although she'd never been taught to read music, she'd once seen Mr. Robertson at the kirk following the funny little black dots while playing the flute. She sat in a plush red velvet chair in the corner, resting her ankle on the ottoman for a moment. Absentmindedly, she ran her fingers across the strings of the chittarone propped beside her. She could not play, yet hearing even single notes again, after months of not singing, made her sigh. She missed the songs Lukas would sing to her beneath their rowan tree. Singing was like breathing to her, but the grief had stilled her voice. Yet now a melody murmured inside her head, bubbling to the surface of her sorrows, commanding to be sung. With her chest constricted by bronchial infection, she breathed lightly so as not to commence coughing then softly began.

> "It was early one morning
>
> young Willie arose
>
> And off to his comrade's
>
> bedchamber he goes
>
> 'Arise my dear comrade
>
> and let no one know
>
> 'Tis a fine sunny morning
>
> and a bathing we will go.'"

Her voice, like a thin silk thread, wove its way mellifluously around the room, trailing into the opened hallway behind her. She closed her eyes, wondering why this particular song, a lament about young man's drowning, had first come to mind. Her heart softened, receiving its tuneful master once more as the magic of music released her pain. She continued.

> "O Willie plunged in and
>
> he swam the lake round
>
> He swam to an island
>
> it was soft marshy ground
>
> 'O comrade, dear comrade
>
> do not venture in
>
> For there is deep and false water
>
> in the Lakes of Coolfin.' "

She did not see him enter. A stout man, squat in stature, stood in the hallway, wishing not to disturb the singer. It had been years since he had heard such clarity, even from his own students. Murdoch remained, keeping a silent vigil. The face of Muriel, Lukas's sister, darted across Hannah's mind as she started the third stanza.

> "It was early that morning
>
> Willie's sister arose

And up to her mother's

bedchamber she goes

'I dreamed a sad dream

about Willie last night,

He was dressed in a shroud,

in a shroud of snow white.'

She remembered how Muriel had given her a snippet of the winding sheet when Lukas was laid out. Her hands trembled, remembering his bloated visage in the pine box. Eglantyne MacLaren, in the weeks that followed, had been so kind to Hannah. The sorrow they shared seemed unparalleled to others in Feshiebridge. A silent knowing passed between them. Now the song persisted, so Hannah obeyed.

"It was early that morning

Willie's mother came in

She was wringing her hands

and tearing her hair

'O woe is the hour

young Willie plunged in

For there is deep and false water

in the Lakes of Coolfin.' "

She dared not sing the final verse. Tears begged to be released. Hannah tried not to yield, but the sadness deepened, overwhelming her. She lowered her head into her lap, her shoulders quaking beneath moans of "Lukas, oh Lukas."

But another voice, sonorous and deep, was present, and it startled her as the song's final verse draped over her like a mantle.

"And I saw a fair maid

standing by the shore

Her face it was pale

she was weeping full sore

In deep anguish she gazed

at where young Willie plunged in

Ah, there is deep and false waters

in the Lakes of Coolfin."

A gentle hand patted her shoulder as she looked through a watery veil into Murdoch's kind face.

"Give the grief its freedom, lass," he said, offering Hannah his cream linen handkerchief.

She wiped her face with his handkerchief then gripping it tightly, asked, "Who are you?" Hannah lowered her ankle to accommodate him, thinking he resembled a mushroom as he centered his portly frame upon the cushioned ottoman.

"My name is Murdoch," he answered, "and I hope you'll excuse me for imposing on such a delicate moment." Despite her gloomy appearance, he could not but help notice her gentle beauty.

Hannah, not wanting to discuss her tears with a stranger, said nothing.

Murdoch continued. "You see, dear, I am a Master Musician, here to serve the Blair Atholl Stewarts as instructor to their children in the finer points of music." He wafted his right hand high, flourishing it back to his waist in a grand gesture. "And who might you be?" He leaned forward a little too far, almost losing his precarious perch. He quickly righted himself then waited.

"Hannah, Hannah MacLaren," she replied.

"Well, Mistress MacLaren, pleased I am to make your acquaintance," he said, bowing ever so slightly. "You'll have to pardon me once more if I appear rude, but I have visited Blair Atholl many times and never seen you present. Are you a cousin perhaps, visiting the Stewarts?"

"Well, no," she answered bluntly. When Jenny had told Hannah how her body had been thrown on a cart of dead deer and hauled into the estate like carrion, she had cringed. In fact, she could not relay this part of her journey to anyone, for she knew little of the story herself. She opted for the truth. "I was traveling to Perth to visit relatives but fell ill along the way. The Stewarts have been more than kind. But as you see, I'm feeling a bit better now, so I'll be on my way tomorrow morning."

"And how are you traveling, may I ask? I noticed this crutch, you see. Surely you don't mean to walk. Have you a horse, my dear?" He smiled, seeming to enjoy her company.

"No sir, I dont. I think my stout walking stick will do me just fine."

He beckoned Hannah to lean closer. "Well," he whispered, "it just so happens that I myself will be traveling southerly tomorrow with my apprentice Colin. We have a wagon, you see, to protect the instruments, and we hope to reach Perth in two days' time. We will spend tomorrow evening in Dunkeld with my sister then proceed to Perth the next day. Why, it would be so delightful if you would accompany us!"

"But I hardly know you, sir. It would not be . . ." she stammered.

"What?" he said, rising in offense, "Young lady, you mistake me. I wish merely to aid a fellow singer. I could not help but hear your lovely voice, rich and full like a fine claret." He strode around the room, carelessly plucking random strings from the various lutes. "However, I do confess at hoping to convince you to perhaps perform with me at the Perth Festival. My singing partner is ill, so I am at a loss. I admit I was surprised to hear a highland lass singing so . . . so accomplished."

Hannah could not believe her luck; she could hasten reaching Perth by the market time, allowing her ankle additional healing time. His idea of her performing was absolutely preposterous, but a wagon! That was enticing! In case the ride hinged upon her acceptance to sing, she said, "Master Murdoch, I'm glad my singing pleases you, being a master and all, but it has been quite a while since I've set my heart to it. I will accept your kind offer to carry me to Perth; however, my mind is not yet made up about singing at any festival. But if you're willing to take me as I am, I will leave with you tomorrow."

"Splendid, my dear girl, absolutely splendid!" he cheered, extending his hand to seal the arrangement.

Hannah took his hand, surprised when Murdoch kissed it lightly. She'd never been treated with such manners, and leaned back into the chair.

"I see you are not acquainted with gentlemanly ways," said Murdoch. "No need. Just know that I will take great care of you, young Hannah, for I will be carrying precious goods having you along." He bowed deeply this time, taking one last look at the bewildered young woman before leaving. "What a treasure!" he said to himself in the hallway, "an absolute treasure!"

Hannah sighed. With her travel plans set now, an ease settled upon her. She still wondered at singing in public, but she would worry about that later. For now, her mission was renewed. She would find Michael and take him to her mother within the week!

CHAPTER FIFTEEN

Mary bustled quickly into the room spouting apologies from Lady Stewart, who was detained and not able to have tea with Hannah. So, not wanting to impose on Lady Stewart's generosity, Hannah decided to make herself useful in the kitchen. She heaved herself out of the chair and stood, swaying a bit, but the ankle held. She reached for the crutch, wanting to return it to the family, when she turned too quickly. Her ankle slipped out from under, causing her to fall.

Moments earlier, Murdoch's mutterings had been overheard by Lachlan Grant as he descended the master staircase, hoping for a walk in the woods before dinner. He had glanced into the music room to see a tall, slender woman walking tentatively toward a crutch. Fortunately for Hannah, Lachlan was entering the room as she began to fall. He reached for her, catching Hannah around her waist before she fell.

"Well now, if I'm right, I believe that's twice I've rescued you, young lady," he said, easing her back into the chair. "Let's have a look at that foot, now shall we?" Before Hannah could protest, he knelt down in front of her, unlaced the boot then began slowly turning it right then left, watching for reactions. "Does that hurt you, lass?"

"I'll thank you to put my foot back on the floor where you found it!" she said. The ankle still felt tender, but fortunately the fall had not compromised the healing.

"Begging your pardon, young woman," he said, rising quickly. "It's just that I have some experience with these things, being a man of the woods myself, and wanted to be sure you were all right."

He turned to leave when Hannah reconsidered. "Wait, please," she said, "I'm sorry, really I am." Her expression was so sincere that Lachlan stopped. My mother would roast me for sure acting so ungrateful. Here, let me at least make it up to you. My name is Hannah, Hannah MacLaren," she said, offering her hand.

"Lachlan Grant of Kingussie, at your service," he said, taking her hand and kissing it, mirroring Murdoch's gesture. He remained standing.

"Well, Lachlan Grant of Kingussie, I am in your debt. But explain to me something," she said, "didn't you say that you've rescued me twice?"

"Yes, indeed. Aren't you the lass recovering from that snowstorm several days ago?"

"I am."

"Then it was myself and my men, while out on the hunt that we discovered you lying in the road half-dead. We could tell the cold was seeping into your bones by the chill of your skin, so we warmed you the best we knew how by putting you between two fresh kills. It still took another two hours to reach the castle, but the women popped you in a warm bath to get your blood flowing properly again. I see you're looking much better now." He gave her a slight smile.

So this was the whole of it. The story she'd only gleaned fragments about from Jenny and Mary. "Half-dead, you say?" asked Hannah.

"Aye," he replied.

His sober response sent a chill throughout Hannah's body. "Then it seems I will never be able to repay such kindness. I cannot think what to say."

"Well," he said, "I was curious as to what a highland lass was doing out in the woods alone." He sat abruptly on the floor, disregarding the fine furnishings surrounding him.

Hannah liked his lack of reserve wrapped in genteel manners. His sable brown hair, tipped with premature grey, was pulled back in a leather thong, revealing his square jaw line. She felt as if she'd known him for years, a neighbor down the road perhaps. With the first sense of comfort in days, Hannah relayed her tale, simply and without fanfare. She'd slipped, sprained her ankle, soaked her clothing then woken up in Blair Castle. Now here they sat.

He listened, his brow furrowing at times. "And where are you from, Hannah?"

"I was born near Perth I believe, but I've lived most of my life with my mother in Feshiebridge. She's the local weaver." Hannah wondered how her mother fared with her daughter's sudden disappearance.

"I wonder if you're not Rosamond's daughter then," he said, smiling then slapping his knee. "Why, I've see you both for years at the market in Ruthven. In fact, I just bought my wife a new cloak from your mother a few weeks ago."

Hannah remembered now the couple at the Ruthven market, the one she'd commented about to her mother. She smiled, thinking him more of a friend now than a stranger.

"Hannah, I was about to take a short stroll on the grounds, for there are expansive gardens surrounded by enchanting woods on this estate, and it appears the other guests are still playing cards." He stood now, tall and straight with that highlander pride. "I would gladly give you my arm if you'd care to join me."

Without a second thought, she laced her arm through his, and limping slightly, walked out through the front hall into the pink-laced gloaming. Hannah, not having seen beyond the walls of the servant's quarters, marveled at the immensity of the estate. Lachlan told her it covered over 145,000 acres with highland cattle roaming its ridges, champion horses running in the fields, and fine Scottish white-faced sheep ready with wool. Both red deer and roe benefitted from the pines and pasture areas while serpentine footpaths wound throughout the estate grounds.

"Though I've visited here several times, I still seem to find new paths," he told her, guiding his charge carefully beneath the looming larches, fragrant cedars, and majestic rowans.

The cleared walkways allowed for pleasurable meanderings by the family and their guests. The late afternoon light suffused through the overhangs, creating patchwork patterns on both trunks and trail. A whiffling sound startled them as a black grouse left in search of more private spaces.

"Do you only hunt the deer?" she asked.

"I hunt whatever meat's to be found," answered Lachlan, "but mostly deer and wild birds. Why, I've seen even ptarmigans roosting in those hills," he said, pointing north. "I once spotted a golden eagle as well, even though I'd never eat one. Noble creatures, they are. Have you ever seen one up close?"

"That I have," smiled Hannah, well remembering her ledge encounter.

"Well, there are streams that run through here, too, with funny little creatures like otters, dippers, and wagtails all about," laughed Lachlan.

He seemed so comfortable with her. Yet conversing effortlessly with someone again, walking through the woods like this reminded Hannah of Lukas and her loss. The levity passed like a broken spell, replaced with restraint. "I don't mean to be rude, Master Grant," said Hannah, "but I believe I'd like to wander alone for a bit. My ankle seems fit, so if you don't mind . . ." her voice fading. She pulled her arm from his side, unable to look into his charming brown eyes.

Lachlan looked confused, but took the feigned rejection like a gentleman. "I can well understand, Mistress MacFey, at wanting to enjoy such a glorious afternoon in solitude. I''l alert your nurses that you're here, so they'll not be worried." He took her hand once more, kissed it lightly then retreated down the lane.

As she headed toward the bridge, Hannah rebuked herself for not considering Jenny and Mary, possibly worried when Hannah was no longer in the house. What a kind and considerate man, she thought, turning to see Lachlan once more, but his swift gait took him beyond her view.

She sat for a while, wondering at her good fortune of Murdoch's offer to take her to Perth the next morning. What other surprises awaited her on this journey?

The stone bridge arched over a small stream where amber water, rich in peat, ran steadily over the rocks below. Hannah listened to the rippling rhythms, pulsating in consistent beats. She closed her eyes, listening, realizing the beats mirrored her heart. She stared into the hypnotic stream, its dark swirls mesmerizing her until the stream blurred into a single flow with no beginning, no ending. She could fall, slip easily over the side of this low stone wall, by simply shifting her weight forward. She wore sorrow like a woolen shawl, containing her within the small world of despair. Her thoughts slid back to the dream on the road by the Tilt River . . . dark waters, sinking into their deep mysteries, Lukas swimming towards her.

Crying aloud, she said, "I can't stand it anymore! I love my mother, and want to see her well and content, but I want my Lukas back! All the times he held me, told me he loved me, and I didn't believe him."

She sank to the ground and whispered, "Why do I doubt others when they tell me I am loved?"

Here stood the true question. The air was silent, but inside her heart, the wall, separating her from the world since Lukas's death, shuddered. The uncertainty that anyone would ever really love her again matched the depths of her grief for Lukas.

She was about to venture up the small knoll leading to the church when a sudden movement in the woods stayed her. She knew the Stewarts' guests were probably in the house, so she turned, craning her neck to the left, searching for evidence of a wild animal in the larch underbrush. She was startled to see two tall red cedars, standing approximately ten feet apart, twitch. Their leaves quivered, but no wind blew. Then two faerie beings emerged from their trunks.

They were slim and tall, red-skinned like the cedar bark. Both sported green-dotted conical caps, sorrel tunics belted at the waist with ivy, and feathered boots. Each held a three-pronged spear, intersecting each other at defensive angles to halt entrance of enemies. Hannah didn't move.

"Let the mortal pass, you buffoons!" shouted the Faerie Queen. Hannah observed the tallest larch melt into a woman sitting on a simple wooden throne. "Can you not discern that the girl can see you?" Then motioning Hannah forward, she said softly, "Hannah, come here, child."

The faerie guards lifted their spears, bowed once to the Queen, then stepped back inside their respective trees. Hannah, being called by name, felt compelled to obey. This queen exuded a noble air through her upright bearing and stature common to Scottish royalty. A three-tiered wind chime with slivers of mauve, topaz, olive, and indigo delivered delicate notes, sending a myriad of prismatic rainbows dancing about the queen. She wore a golden diadem of agates, amethysts, garnets and lazurite with matching jeweled girdle around a gown of moonlight ivory. She bore no rings or bracelets, yet a simple silver four-pointed star, traced in looping knot work, hung elegantly about her neck.

Hannah curtsied to the queen but said nothing.

"I see you have come," said the Queen. "You may sit, as I fear your injury is not as well as you think."

Wondering at how the queen knew not only her name but also the state of her sprained ankle, Hannah lowered herself onto the ground, sitting with both legs extended to relieve pressure. Not wishing to be rude yet intrigued, Hannah asked, "Please ma'am, could you be telling me how you know who I am?"

The queen raised her chin, gazing through the laced boughs overhead, then replied, "I have several in my kingdom whom you have 'encountered,' shall we say? I did not expect you this far south, but there are few nowadays gifted such as yourself."

Unlike the other fey Hannah had spoken with, this queen apparently gained knowledge from many sources. Drawn to the necklace's design, Hannah ran her fingers across her covered shoulder where a similar design lay embedded in her skin. Could I be? she wondered. Could I really be one of them? Emboldened by her curiosity, she asked, "Excuse me, Queen, but I notice that you wear a necklace with the same design as my birthmark." Hannah pulled the white blouse just low enough to expose her right shoulder, revealing an identical print. "Here?"

The queen nodded in agreement.

"You see," continued Hannah, "Friends have always told me I have a bit of the faerie about me, but that was just talk, wasn't it?"

The queen considered this query for several moments before replying. "It is true, you bear the Mark of Faerie, as well as our name do you not, Hannah Mac*Fey*? Yet you are mortal, to be sure. You will live, and you will die, just as other mortals do in the cycles of nature. But you also have the ability to seek aid from us, to see into the hearts of men when they hide truths even from themselves. Moreover, you can calm their pains. This discernment can be of value."

"But how?"

The Faerie Queen leaned forward, looking straight into Hannah's eyes, "By living, child. Through meeting each day, one by one, with a willingness to be whatever is required of you. This you can do." She placed her hand upon Hannah's head, singing in low tones. Silver shivers shot through Hannah's body, laced with a warming sensation which lingered for several minutes. The image of the queen began to fade. "We may meet again, or we may not. But receive my blessing, child, and deny not your heritage." With that pronouncement, the queen vanished.

Hannah remained seated, absolutely lost in the wonder of it all. So the tales were true, indeed! The Fair Folk were not only alive and well, but looking out for her, like kinfolk. She marveled at how faerie blood could be coursing through her veins, a simple weaver's daughter with a fair singing voice. Yet the Faerie Queen would not deceive her, not about this. The birthmark provided evidence even if Hannah's heart did not believe.

The Faerie Queen also delineated gifts, qualities within Hannah to help herself and others. That explained her second sight, the visions, even her recent episode with Lukas as he left this earthly plane. She would no longer deny this part of her being, but rather activate it in her search for Michael and her father.

Her father! With the Faerie Queen's pronouncement of Hannah's faerie heritage, the identity of her mysterious father was beginning to clear. Surely not a local man, a farmer, for one of faerie descent would have been noticed, revealed. Maybe some man of the wood, The Green Man himself perhaps? What being, fey or mortal with fey ancestry, had beguiled her mother so? Hannah had to know; somehow, she needed to know the truth.

She tried breathing deeply several times, her chest lifting ever so slightly with a minor cough, then careful of her tender ankle rose slowly then proceeded across a small bridge in measured strides going back towards the castle. Tall firs and larches, heavily laden with new growth, lined the path from the stream towards the Stewart family cemetery and their private chapel. Hannah walked with care towards the church, thinking to take a moment for silent reflection in the comfort of its sanctity. She paused at the family plot, noticing the ornate grave slabs covered in Celtic designs. Even though Lukas had been given a proper Highland burial in the Feshiebridge parish, only a simple head stone with the lamb marked his grave. Although his body lay decaying in the ground, it was not where his soul dwelled now. Hannah sighed, remembering the last time he'd held her in the cottage and the feel of him as she began this journey.

A sharp bell resounded twice - dinner already?

As she took the footpath returning towards the castle, the trail led up a slight grade on her left where she saw a sign, "St. Bride's Kirk" next to a long rectangular stone building where a progression of additional gravestones, indicating Blair Atholl villagers, punctuated the hillside. She noticed the rowan to the left of the opened entranceway, but to her surprise, eating a red berry, sat a blackbird.

"So I see you travel as well, my friend," said Hannah, observing the tiny bird's blue-black wings offset by the gold ring surrounding his obsidian eye. His golden beak worked quickly, disseminating the berried treasure. Unlike the earlier grave-side visitation, it was now dusk, twilight, so observing this avian fellow wayfarer seemed less startling.

"But I must confess, that seeing you again now makes me wonder. I'm a believer in omens, just like many a highlander, so I'm thinkin' you're tellin' me to seek my heart." She knelt beneath the tree now, exhausted from more than her first outing. The sentiments of the faerie aid sparked a glimmer of hope once more in her heart, yet the shroud of grief blackened the light.

"But how can I even see my heart, for it aches with such agony as I never thought possible?" She gazed at the bird, who sat reverently as if listening, then Hannah whispered, "To love so deeply . . . then to lose him."

The blackbird having completed his meal, sang three doleful notes, then flew into the gloaming.

Hannah, needing to calm herself before returning to the house, entered the tiny stone chapel and walked down the single aisle leading to the front altar where hand-hewn beams crisscrossed the ceiling. Four windows directly behind the altar emitted a vestige of light through the stained glass designs, heavy in dark blues, rubied crimsons, and emerald greens; however, the single clear pane in the peak shone with a brilliance of late afternoon sunlight, beaming onto Hannah's head.

As Hannah knelt, the light haloed her bowed head, much like St. Brighid upon her baptism where flames of fire signaled her sainthood. Habits created by years of faithful kirk attendance now led Hannah, but it was her need to be loved again which broke through the resentments towards her Maker. She closed her eyes then prayed aloud, "O Holy One, forgive my selfish heart. Without my Lukas, I didn't want to carry on in this world. But I love Ma, and she would be lost without me. So help me find this man she loves. I have to find him, for it's a promise I made to her. And in the midst of this journey, lead me to my true father. Guide me, Saint Brighid, by the power and light of your flame." She whispered a closing prayer of thanksgiving to St. Brighid then rose to leave.

She paused, looking up at the pastoral scenes in the stained glass. For the first time in weeks, she felt at peace. She stood up, released a slow sigh, and left. Striding towards the castle, she smiled, knowing she would be on her way to Perth at first light.

She had not seen the man on the back row, seated quietly in the corner. Having overheard her pleas from the back of the kirk, Lachlan Grant rose, silent as a shadow. He sighed then pacing himself behind her, followed Hannah back to the castle.

CHAPTER SIXTEEN

"COLIN! For God's sake, boy, be careful with that lute!" cried Murdoch, placing the finishing touches on the wagon. "There now, lad, I believe that will do," he said, patting the red-headed young man on the shoulder. Colin, a stocky, sturdy lad of fourteen and accustomed to the Master Musician's temperament, accepted the light praise then jumped into his place next to the baggage. Hannah's pack, secured with the rest, looked shabby compared to the fine trappings of Murdoch and his apprentice.

As Hannah walked through the kitchen to say her good-byes, Hilda pressed a sack of breads and baked pies into Hannah's hand, saying, "You look a sight better than when we first laid eyes on you, that's for sure. You be careful with yourself, now."

"You come back when you can, miss," said Jenny, shifting uneasily from one foot to the other. Tears trickled down her cheeks as Jenny suddenly reached for Hannah, hugging her fiercely, "I will miss seeing you, I will." She sniffled, shuffling back into her position alongside Mary and the other kitchen staff.

"Thank you, Jenny," said Hannah, limping slightly. She approached the front entrance way to meet Murdoch. Lady Stewart stood in the castle doorway, conversing with Murdoch as Hannah drew near.

"Will you return to us next year, same time?" asked Lady Stewart, shifting her elegant stance to a more solid position. The lavender satin dress trimmed in deep purple lace accentuated her statuesque height. Her husband, along with the other guests (including Lachlan Grant) had not yet risen.

"Aye, that I will ma'am, that I will," responded Murdoch. He knelt on the stone steps, kissing her extended hand in courtesy.

"And this must be our patient," exclaimed Lady Stewart, nodding to Hannah.

"Yes ma'am," replied Hannah. "Rare it is to find such charity." She knew enough to curtsy, yet she feared her ankle would buckle again, so she simply bowed her head. This fine woman had opened her home to Hannah, so the young highlander was not surprised to see only gracious generosity radiating from the Lady of the House.

"Well, child, Lachlan couldn't leave you out in the cold to die, now could he?" said Lady Stewart. Her gaze scanned Hannah from head to foot, "especially such a lovely creature as yourself. My kitchen staff tells me you're a kind-hearted soul, so your appreciation is accepted." Lady Stewart retired into the house for her morning tea.

With some assistance from Colin, Hannah situated herself onto the slatted wooden seat, settling in for the ride while awaiting Murdoch to take his place as the driver.

"Let us be off!" he said, brandishing the air with a farewell flourish as he heaved his plump frame onto the seat next to Hannah. He snapped the reins, and in the twinkling of a bell, they were gone.

The morning air, commanding notice, blew in wild fits as they left Blair Atholl village, heading south. Their destination for that evening, the small village of Dunkeld, hailed a full thirty-five miles away, a full day of travel. Hannah discovered Murdoch's penchant for chatter, possessing many ideas, all of which he shared unreservedly with his two young companions while riding through the Pass of Killiecrankie. Colin said little, jostling with the sudden pitch of the wagon over deep ruts from the recent snows. Soon the road smoothed, and Colin drifted into a young man's fantasies. Hannah felt jealous, desiring some solitude of her own. However, Murdoch was a jolly fellow, and after several hours, she began to enjoy his company.

"So tell me, Mistress MacLaren, or may I call you Hannah?" he asked, treating her like one of his chorister students.

Hannah nodded in agreement.

"So, Hannah, we will be staying with my sister Moira as I have let three students use my home while I travel. But tell me, once you find your relatives in Perth, what next?" He smiled broadly at his new charge.

"I'm not at all certain, sir, for I'm a bit on my own right now," she said. But then, remembering Murdoch's connections with other renowned musicians, she wondered if he knew Michael. She hesitated, but then boldly asked, "Sir, do you happen to know a harper by the name of Michael, one who frequents the festival at Perth?"

Murdoch frowned, deep in thought, then threw back his head in laughter. "Why, of course there was a fellow, Michael. Oh, what was his last name, now? Anyway, he was a pupil of mine-many years ago - became quite an accomplished harper himself if it's the same fellow. He never spoke much about his family though, so I'm not certain of his surname. Now that you mention it, he did perform in Perth, along with several other venues, but he dropped off the circuit about five or six years ago. A bit of mystery there. Why do you ask?"

"He was a friend of my mother's, and she's needing to see him," said Hannah with a reserved air, not alerting Murdoch to the passionate nature of her search.

"Well, I wish you luck then, little miss. Sorry not to be of more help," said Murdoch. "But I was wondering, what does life hold for such a lovely young lass, who happens to possess such a fine singing voice, one of perfect pitch? Have you ever considered singing for a fee?"

For just a moment, she imagined herself singing, in the grand ballrooms for lords and ladies, just as her earlier dreams had prescribed. But those were childhood fancies, and now too much had happened. That light-hearted young girl had disappeared. "I have considered such, but I believe that I will be taking up my mother's craft as village weaver," said Hannah.

But Murdoch noted a hint of remorse, so seizing this opportunity, he dangled the possibilities before her. "Why, you could travel the countryside and sing with me, my girl," said Murdoch. "The lodgings are above average, the pay is acceptable, and why the company, stupendous! I'm sure I could find a suitable teaching position for you at the sang skule in Dunkeld during the off-season. I'm wagering you have an extensive song repertoire. For you see, although I am usually found in Dunkeld, teaching at the music school or giving private instruction, such as I did at Blair Atholl, in the spring the school allows me to travel to various castles and private homes for competitions and performances. It is on such a journey that I am making now, and we could have such fun!" He leaned over to her and whispered, "And I so miss my vocalist."

Hannah regarded the man's carefree air, wishing for such an ease with life as well, yet her face remained pensive.

"I can see that you have much on your mind at present, young woman," said Murdoch, jostling the carriage as he barely missed a deep hole in the road. "But I know quality when I see it, and you, dear girl, have indeed such a natural talent that I'd be remiss not to engage you in my services. So, when you've completed your visit in Perth, you are welcome to join Colin and myself as we continue westward. You see, there is a harping competition on the Isle of Skye later in May, hosted by Clan Donald at their estate, and having never won it myself, I wish to try. It's quite the honor, a prestigious prize to be sure, and even though I've won many awards for my other musical achievements, this could be my crowning glory!"

Hannah noticed a school-boy gleam in the Master Musician's eye, and found herself wondering what it would be like to attend such a musical event. "I will think on your gracious offer, Master Murdoch." She tightened the scarf about her neck, not wanting the cough to return, its voracious tenacity only evident in the early morn.

"'Tis all that I ask, all that I ask."

The wagon rocked over stones and gullies, mile after mile. They skirted both Pitlochry and Ballinluig to avoid unnecessary delays since Murdoch wanted to arrive at his sister's home before dark.

The road paralleled the dark waters of the River Tay. Rowan trees bordered its banks while firs and Scots pines filled the ridges. Small stone crofter cottages with red slated roofs, prominent amidst the vibrant greens, sporadically marked the countryside while puffs of white sheep freckled the landscape. When they reached Dowally, Murdoch stopped by the roadside for lunch, sharing a basket of beef pies, black pudding, and fresh fruit prepared by Hilda for the travelers. The three walked around a bit, stretching their stiff limbs. Hannah, careful not to overexert her ankle, rotated it slowly, still finding it tender at times. She whispered a prayer of gratitude to St. Brighid for supplying such timely transportation. She had to find Michael before the festivities of the Beltane market concluded.

A little more than an hour later, Murdoch turned the wagon onto a smaller track leading off to the right. A large hedge of stone and evergreen shrubbery trimmed the track on the right as more crofter cottages became visible. Soon the threesome arrived on the outskirts of Dunkeld where Murdoch's sister Moira, round-faced and cheery, met them at the door. Her boys, ages four, six, eight, and ten respectively, came howling through the door of the small cottage like a pack of wild dogs, jumping in circles around their uncle, pawing his pockets for concealed candies.

"Now hold on, lads, I've not forgotten you," he said, reaching into his money bag and pulling out four colored candies. "There's one of each of you, so just hold still." He held the treats above their heads where they leapt like hounds.

Colin pulled out their clothing sacks while Hannah carefully climbed down from her wooden perch, shy about accepting hospitality again from strangers. After the horse was stabled, they all went inside where a steamy vegetable broth, chunks of bright orange cheese, and brown ale awaited them.

Like twin magpies, brother and sister regaled each other with all the gossip since their last meeting. Colin, locating his usual spot by the fire, curled up on the hearth then went to sleep. Fraser, Moira's husband, put the boys to bed in a small room open to the center of the cottage. Hannah listened to giggles and shrieks as Fraser told his lads their favorite nighttime tales. Although Rosamond was always quick with a tune, Hannah rarely remembered instances of bedtime stories. Perhaps her father might have told them to her, as Fraser was doing now. Instinctively, she placed her palm over her heart, a pattern she observed Rosamond enact during times of sadness.

The embers flickered like hidden jewels in a dark cavern as Fraser smoored the fire then disappeared behind the sleeping curtain. Moira had prepared a pallet by the fire for Murdoch, but seeing Hannah, offered it to her, making room for her brother in the boys' room. Hannah, so worn from the traveling, opted to dismiss changing into her sleeping shift and simply fell into bed. She pulled a yellow blanket over her shoulders, punched the small pillow into shape then flopped back on the bed. She slept without dreams.

The boys rose early, pouncing on their visitors. Hot tea revived the wearied travelers while hearty oat brose and bannocks covered in slides of butter and jam filled their empty bellies. Eager to reach Perth, Hannah replaced the clothing packs in the wagon, carefully padding the parting box within her own belongings, in hopes of aiding a speedy departure. After pleasantries of "Thank you" and "We appreciate your hospitality," Colin scurried into his spot while Hannah regained her position. Fraser hitched the horse to the wagon.

Murdoch stood in the doorway saying good-bye to Moira while the boys finished their breakfast inside. "Dear sister," began Murdoch, "a most delightful visit, to be sure. I shall be in Perth for at least a week at the Market Place Inn near St. John's Kirk in the center of town. Surely you know it, so don't be a stranger!" He kissed her cheek then after a warm embrace, Murdoch took his seat at the helm. With a snap of the reins, the wagon creaked down the lane towards the center of town.

Dunkeld, a small village seated along the River Tay, boasted of a lovely cathedral near the center of town. They had not gone but a mile or two when the whitewashed houses of town appeared where window boxes gleamed with early blooms, quite a welcoming sight. The town roads merged in the center, like the spokes of a wagon wheel.

Murdoch turned right down a cobbled path leading towards the cathedral where the road ended at the gardens surrounding the kirk. "Hannah, do you know about the famous cathedral here in Dunkeld, home of our esteemed sang skule?"

Hannah shook her head.

"Well, let me tell you then. It's quite illustrious. The monks first established this monastery in 1325 in honor of St. Columba, the man from the Isle of Iona. It's said that sacred relics of this blessed saint reside within those walls. None may look upon them save the priests. Still, very impressive!"

Hannah, less intrigued with the history lesson, found her attention drawn to the blue-black waters of the River Tay to the left of the massive white and grey stone structure.

Murdoch lashed the horse under a larch growing on the riverbanks while the three strolled about the kirk grounds. Colin gasped at the grandeur of the numerous stone columns then in a child-like response, began running, like a wild hare, dashing in and out of the grey archways. Murdoch just laughed then offered to show Hannah the teaching quarters, where he still hoped to employ her someday. No students were visible yet since classes did not begin for several hours. Instead, the abbots were conducting morning matins rather than instructing musical chants, calligraphy, and Biblical studies.

Inside the doorway, Hannah viewed the praying brethren. Her spiritual devotion during the home kirk services led by Father Logan had always revolved around expected rituals and faithful recitations while parishioners presented themselves as contrite yet humble. This style of worship often felt foreign to Hannah. For her truest spirit flew towards the natural world, hovering around the purple heathers and rebounding against the highland hills where she connected with the One who had created such pleasures. It was His hand she now sought, no longer as the petulant child who lacked vision or understanding, but as the young woman who knew wisdom lay beyond herself.

They moved into the sanctuary, stepping lightly on its jacquard floor so as not to disturb the brothers in prayer. As she continued down the stone aisle, Hannah could not help but stare at the stained glass window above the altar where rays of indigo, burgundy, and emerald shimmered on the wooden railings and altar, speckling the cloth vestments honoring St. Columba and his teachings. A pastoral scene of Christ giving the Sermon on the Mount occupied the lower five windows, topped by five smaller windows of shepherds in the fields listening to the Savior. Images of angelic choruses peered down at the rustics from the top of each arch. Likenesses depicting a knight and king centered the uppermost points, offset by crests for God and country denoting nobility and service. Delicate wooden scroll work, like lace curtains, veiled the sacrificial tables of the inner sanctum just beneath the arched window. She had never seen anything so marvelous.

Murdoch waited by the side door, allowing his young singer a moment of solitude. Hannah sank into one of the red cushioned pews, facing this magnificent view. How she wished Lukas were here to see such a glorious sight! But with that singular thought, sorrow washed over her once more. The Faerie Queen's words had lightened her load a bit, yet she still missed him. How could others go about daily affairs when most mornings she viewed the world through this depressing haze? Her persistent cough struck so deep like a morning assailant that it pierced her heart, mirroring the loss. As of late, her belly kicked into nervous spasms, making Hannah nauseous. Her body was obviously rebelling at the stress load she maintained. This journey needed to end soon.

Her thoughts returned to Rosamond, so she whispered supplications for her mother's healing then silently pleaded to Saint Brighid for aid in accomplishing this task before her. She must first find Michael for her mother then resolve the issue of her father's identity for herself.

Murdoch offered his hand as she left the oak pew then walked her through the offices and rooms used for class instruction. He rattled on about lodging options, the amenities of Dunkeld, and the advantage of its proximity to both the Highlands, the Lowlands, and the Isle of Skye. Soon they were outside once more where Colin sat in the wagon, awaiting his companions.

Hannah wandered down the banks of the River Tay then stood a moment, breathing in the swiftness of the river, the grounding of the larches, and the holiness of this cathedral. Without a word, she mounted the wagon, nodding to her companions that she was ready to move on.

Isle of Iona, Caledonia

Michael's trip was delayed due to the impending death of his traveling companion's mother. The Campbells, Brother Aidan's family, lived on the northern tip of Mull, so he took the first ferry to the mainland. Michael was to join Brother Aidan after the funeral three days later. This leg of the trip would be easily maneuvered by Michael alone, for it took only two day's journey after the crossing. When news of Mrs. Campbell's death arrived, Michael made ready for his departure.

The morning began with a light drizzle, a silvery mist veiling the island. Michael awoke early, having slept very little. He packed his sleeping shirt and robe, wearing the trousers and shirt he'd used for gardening, topped with his cloak. He possessed only a few personal belongings, secured by the monks when they found him injured on the road that dreadful night. He felt the curves of the triad necklace against his bare chest. Did Rosamond still wear hers, he wondered. Michael commissioned the pair, a keepsake, during the months they were apart, and had given it to her on their last meeting.

Once again, doubts swatted his thoughts like unwanted gnats. Playing for the brothers in the safety of the Abbey was comfortable, but could he perform in public again? Would the traveling lifestyle of a harper fit his transformation after remaining for years on this blessed isle? Yet Father Callum's unswerving faith in him, shown graciously through the gift of transportation (Molly, the horse), companionship (Brother Aidan), and means (the parish collection), left Michael speechless. He would do his best to make himself a believer now. He took one last look around his cell, said a quick prayer of thanksgiving for the generosity of these brethren then descended the stairs one last time, passing through the Cloister into the Abbey's front grounds.

Molly arrived early. Several brothers were petting her, tempting her with sweet carrots. To further support Michael on this journey, several villagers stood by with additional clothing needed for life outside the Abbey walls to replace the coarse brown habits Michael had worn for the last five years: thigh-high boots, leggings, tunics, trousers, sweaters, sleeping shirts, belts, and an extra cloak. They bundled the clothing quickly, placing it onto Molly's back. Michael turned towards the Abbey Choir door to retrieve his harp, but two brothers slipped through the massive oak doors carrying a gangly burden. They grinned at each other then placed it at Michael's feet.

"What's this?" he asked.

Father Callum stepped up. "Michael, we know you've played the Abbey's harp for us these five years, seeing as your own was destroyed. But the brothers wanted to give you something, a remembrance if you will, of your time here, for you've meant a great deal to us."

Michael didn't know what to say.

"Well, open it, man," said Father Callum. "Take a look."

Michael unwrapped the instrument. The brothers had wrapped the harp in heavy russet for protection then placed it in a large leather-strapped sack, easy to attach to the horse's trappings. He smiled broadly as he saw not the lowland harp with gut strings so mellow for psalms, but a true highland clarsech, a harp with wire strings bringing about a rich, ancient sound. "But how?" Michael began.

But Father Callum just nodded, saying, "God supplies our needs. And I believe, dear friend, that this will suit yours well." He clasped Michael on the shoulders then gave him a farewell embrace. "Just one more thing, Michael. I've also made inquiries, to assist you in returning to the world of music, and entered you in the harping competition at Clan Donald's estate on Skye later in May. Such an enticement may prove just the goal you need to raise your confidence, for I've been told you've won this prize in years past. So you'll need to start practicing, man, and make us proud!"

Michael was overwhelmed by the gracious gift, the thoughtful support, and their confident belief in him.

Once all was made ready, the two brothers heaved Michael onto Molly's back, slightly swayed after years behind the plough. It was time.

The monks paraded Michael from the Abbey through the town to the ferry dock. The stone walls lining the lane directed the flow as villagers joined the group. As the ferry approached, Father Callum raised his hand in parting with a traditional Celtic blessing:

"May the blessing of light be on you,

light without and light within.

May the blessed sunlight shine

upon you and warm your heart

till it glows like a great fire

and strangers may warm themselves

as well as friends.

Bless to us, O God,

the earth beneath our feet.

Bless to us, O God,

the path whereon we go.

Bless to us, O God,

the people whom we meet. Amen."

Amens echoed throughout the throng followed by hails of "Safe Journey" and "We'll miss you!"

Michael rode Molly over the small ramp where a ferryman took her lead. Michael slipped off his mount, facing the smiling group. I meant something to them, he thought. My time here has not been in vain. He waved good-bye as the boat rocked gently in the low breeze. He hoped to return . . . someday.

The sunlight glinted off the waves while the peaks of Iona descended directly into the darkened waters. A double rainbow filtered through the mist. God's promise, Michael remembered from the Old Testament teachings. Would God stay with him now? Michael turned from his monastic home to face an uncertain future. He rested against Molly, seeking muscle relief for his aching right side. He took solace in the strength of such a solid comrade. He spotted several grey herons along the oncoming shore, perched in their singular space with spear-like beaks at the ready to pierce unsuspecting fish. Eiders and mergansers plunged the depths in search of food, diving from their empyrean glides amongst the clouds to projectile force into the waters below.

Michael did not see the solitary seal in the ferry's wake.

Within minutes, the shoreline of Mull loomed ahead. The ferryman lowered the plank on the simple dock and escorted Molly and Michael to land. The Isle of Mull - he was here - once again. The sky rumbled as Michael's feet touched the sandy shoreline of Fionnphort.

There was a single track road dividing the island from tip to tip. It ran in a northerly direction dividing the mountainous peaks on either side, threading along Loch Scridain on its left till midway through the island. Next, it crossed through Glen Moore to follow the southern shores of Loch Spelve. It was after passing through the small village of Lochdonnead that the land narrowed to a point at Castle Duart. Michael well remembered the ferry crossing of the Sound of Mull from the vast port of Oban on Caledonia's mainland to this tip. Castle Duart - the wedding. He would not dwell on that now. He would find Aidan's family just north of the docks in Cragnure.

As Molly plodded along, Michael concerned himself with the countryside. Prior to the performance at Duart Castle, he had never been on the island. He recalled little of this portion of the journey, having passed in and out of consciousness while the monks transported him in a wagon. Now, green hillsides sloped in gentle angles away from the road, reaching stone-capped elevations. Heavy mosses with spring foliage covered the ground amidst burgeoning waterfalls. Michael pulled up his cloak's hood as the rain plopped in generous spurts.

"Molly, it looks like a long ride," said Michael, patting the horse affectionately on her neck. "But I thank you for the service."

Molly walked steadily for several hours, accustomed to carrying heavier loads than Michael. Horse and rider passed in silence through small fishing villages along the loch. Michael kept his hood close to his face, concealing his scar, sensing it blazed upon his cheek like a brand for all to see as villagers stared at the pair. How could he ever consider playing for audiences when he felt embarrassed as curious villagers stared on?

After crossing a small stream beyond Pennyghael, Michael stopped, allowing Molly fresh water while he munched on brown bread and a spiced apple tart. They rested for a short while then moved on. The mountains towered over them as the pair strode through the valley in Glen Moore. The rain hardened, pelting both horse and rider. With no shelter, Michael resigned himself to being soaked. He continued to the small fishing village of Strathcoil where he discovered room at a local inn which also provided a stable for Molly. Raucous laughter welcomed him inside as he carried his harp and personal belongings to the single room, ensuring their safety.

CHAPTER SEVENTEEN

The wagon swayed back and forth along the southerly rutted road. Recent rains created muddy craters not easily maneuvered by the splintered wooden wheels. The trip was brief, bringing Hannah and her fellow travelers into Perth, the Fair City, across the Queen's Bridge dividing the two large public areas known as the North and South Inch. The main street bustled with sounds of the upcoming festival: sparkling tunes from wandering pipers, lilting harp octaves in practice scales, and dancing reels from fiddlers fast enough to exhaust even the faeries. Throngs of vendors shouted commands to their assistants at the erection of booths and tents. Murdoch brightened at the barrage of music, feeling entirely at home.

They passed St. John's Kirk then turned right down an alley bursting with artist guild stalls. Weavers displayed their woven goods next to the litsters with their dyed skeins of every color imaginable. Fletchers aligned their arrows with goose-feathered shafts, pointed away from potential customers. Wood turners with bowls of birch and beech stacked them in precarious piles, tempting mischievous children to knock them down. Further down were the leather goods. Those needing new shoes purchased them from the cordwainer while those needing shoe repairs sought the cobbler. The food booths ended the alley, reminding Hannah of the smells from the Ruthven market.

"Ah yes, there it is!" said Murdoch, pointing to the far left where a sign for the inn protruded from a smaller alley where the performers were to stay. He turned the wagon off the hurried street, following the paving stones to a stable next to the inn. "Colin, go inside and tell the proprietor that Murdoch, the Master Musician, has arrived! Discover our room then begin unloading the instruments. I shall tend to the horse this time."

Hannah dismounted, realizing that in his excitement Murdoch had completely forgotten her presence. She grabbed her sack and walking stick from the rear then tapped him on the shoulder.

He whirled about to see who was accosting him. He smiled at her, saying, "Ah, sweet Hannah, forgive me child. You will be seeking out your relatives no doubt, but I put to you that if you should ever consider a public career in singing, I would be disheartened not to be the first to hear of it!"

"Yes sir, you shall indeed," said Hannah.

"So remember, from here we travel west to Drummond Castle near Comrie, where we'll stay a week then continue northerly through Glen Coe to Ballachulish, on the sunlit shores of Loch Linnhe. We'll be following the loch towards Invergarry where we'll turn west, taking us through the inviting countryside prior to reaching Skye. Once we've taken the ferry to Skye, we take the first left southward to Armadale where the coveted harping competition will take place at Armadale Castle, end of May at Clan Donald's estate."

Hannah frowned, attempting to remember all these names, but failed miserably.

"Oh, my dear girl, whatever am I thinking? Colin, fetch my itinerary. I know it by heart and shall be in no need of it."

Colin searched the bag filled with his master's important papers, but being unable to read, could not discern one page from the other.

"I must be out of my mind today with all the excitement of this festival," said Murdoch, "here, give the bag to me." He quickly ascertained the correct sheet, then handing it to Hannah, asked, "Can you read?" He offered her the handwritten copy.

"Yes, sir," said Hannah, stuffing the page with her own belongings.

"Very well, then. Here are the dates, overnight lodgings, and performance locations. If you can't tell, I'm eager to add you to my musical array. Now, to matters at hand. If, by chance, you should require lodgings during your stay, go to the Stray Away Inn, three streets down, and tell Maggie the innkeeper I sent you. All charges are to be sent to me."

"But Master Murdoch, you've already been so kind by bringing me here. I simply couldn't expect you to pay . . ."

"Nonsense, child. You've been a lovely surprise to my world, and I hope this will not be the last I see of you." He leaned over and kissed her on the cheek. "Now, I must be about finding the Master of the Revels, so we must part company. Good luck with your quest!" He turned to deal with a surly stable hand leading Murdoch's horse inside.

Hannah walked down the alley, knowing her mother must have traveled this very path. Hannah must succeed. And the first step was finding Rosamond's cousin.

But where to begin?

Hannah knew little about her mother's cousin. He had married distant relatives in Kingussie then moved to Perth, or so the story went. Perhaps the local priest could assist Hannah. Murdoch had passed St. John's Kirk only a block or two away, on the way to the inn, so, slinging her pack over her left shoulder, Hannah plodded over the cobbled pavers towards the church.

The parish priest, a lanky man with bristly eyebrows and a furrowed brow, appeared to be taking a respite from his duties when Hannah spied him leaning against the arched alcove. He seemed fascinated with the traveling troupe of actors setting up their stage across the street. The caravan opened to colorful sidings, decorative curtains, and an odd assortment of props which were being strategically placed for the onset of the play. Many thespians still performed the older religious-based stories such as "The Second Shepherd's Play" or "Noah and the Ark," so he watched with interest to discern if he could recommend this troupe to his parishioners. Hannah sidled up the brick steps then stood beside him. The priest, so entranced in the troupe, did not notice his new companion.

"Father, excuse me," started Hannah.

The priest jumped. "OH! Good gracious young lady, why you gave me such a start! Please forgive me. What can I do for you?"

Hannah, not wanting to delay this trip further, came straight to the point. "My name is Hannah, Hannah MacLaren, (still unaccustomed to the name but determined to use it), and I'm looking for family, a cousin named MacFey. I wondered if perhaps you knew him?"

"What's his common name?" asked the priest, "for there are a few families in my parish with that name."

"I don't rightly know, Father," answered Hannah. "He's a cousin to my mother, Rosamond MacFey from Feshiebridge, in the Highlands.

"So, a cousin whose name you do not know." He scratched his chin. "Yes, well, distance does cut down on knowing one's own kin, does it not?"

"Yes, Father," replied Hannah.

He stood up, glancing one last time at the actors draping elaborate costumes over the props. After noticing several shepherd's cloaks, he nodded to Hannah saying, "It appears they will perform a play from the Wakefield cycle, so I am inclined to recommend them. But never mind, come inside where we may check my parishioner listings. I may be able to assist you." He offered his hand to Hannah who followed him inside.

They strode down the sanctuary aisle, passing the altar, where the priest motioned Hannah towards the open office door.

"Please be seated," said the priest, offering her the slat-backed wooden chair facing his simple oak desk. On the wall directly behind the desk stood three bookshelves, filled from top to bottom with leather-bound volumes. He browsed through those in the mid-section, on the shelf labeled "PARISHIONERS" until he spied the spine marked "M." The priest placed the book on his desk, licking his index finger then pealing back the parchment from the top right-hand corner of each page as Hannah watched his facial expressions change from speculation to consternation,. "Ah ha," he said, scrolling down a list of names, "here we are. There are only two MacFey families now residing in Perth. One lives across the river on Dundee Road, and the other lives only a few blocks from here on Tay Street." He gave Hannah the particulars of each household then wished her well, saying, "God's speed to you, young woman." He ushered her back to South Street, the main thoroughfare, and closed the door behind her.

Hannah's search proved uneventful. Neither of the women in these families knew Rosamond, much less any other MacFeys from the Highlands. One wife suggested that since Rosamond always visited during festival and feast days, being a weaving vendor, that Hannah might question some of the other market vendors. The other reminded Hannah that the local kirk kept records of all marriages, births, and deaths.

The inquiries had taken up the better part of the day, so it was late afternoon when Hannah followed the River Tay back to the center of town. Its waters were as nefarious here as in Dunkeld. Since Hannah couldn't locate the cousin, maybe there was evidence of her mother's presence in Perth as suggested. Considering marital documentation a solid lead now, she quickly returned to the kirk.

She passed through the sanctuary then knocked on the office door.

"Come in," answered a friendly voice. As Hannah entered, the priest glanced up from his studies. "Ah, young Hannah. Back with good news, I hope?"

"Not exactly, Father," said Hannah. "Neither family knew my mother, but I was wondering about the marriage records. You see, my mother and father were married here in Perth by a priest from this parish."

"Really?" exclaimed the priest, reaching now for a tall black binder. "We certainly do keep meticulous accounts of all births, deaths, and marriages. Forgive me, child, for not thinking of looking in those books during your earlier visit. When would that have been, Hannah?"

"I'm seventeen, and I believe they were married not too long before I was born."

The priest flipped back pages in the Births, Deaths, and Marriages sections to those from seventeen years earlier. He scowled as he perused the names of couples, not locating a Rosamond MacFey amongst them. "Are you sure it was in this parish?"

"Yes," replied Hannah. "Mother even told me about the flower boxes along the river. It had to be here."

"Well, I'm sorry to disappoint you again, but there is no record of a Rosamond MacFey marrying anybody here seventeen years ago. Let me look through those marriages occurring afterwards as well." He took several minutes, running his index finger up and down columns of black scribblings. "No, there is no Rosamond MacFey married in this parish at all. It could be an oversight, but I declare it would be a rare one." He sat down in his seat once more, looking befuddled.

Hannah offered a quick appreciation then left, needing time to think. Something was dreadfully wrong.

After passing by the trade guild tables, Hannah made her way to the food vendors where she bought a finely sugar-glazed pastry and a small shepherd's pie. She sat on the stoop of a nearby residence, wondering where to go next. Remembering the suggestion about asking vendors, Hannah finished her meal then ambled down the aisle of goods, querying each stall owner. She was met with vacant stares and more questions such as "Who d'ya say?" or "Have I heard of who?" However, one woman proved helpful when she told Hannah to ask the weavers.

Cursing under her breath for not thinking of this herself, Hannah marked a straight path to the weaver stalls. There were three, yet only one of the women seemed to know Hannah's mother.

"Why, I've known Rosamond for over twenty years, girl," said the dark-haired woman. "Why she and me, we'd visit in between customers, watch each other's goods when one of us got hungry. But who did you say you were?" She leaned close to Hannah's face, scrutinizing every inch.

"I'm her daughter, Hannah. Mother taught me the weaving trade as well." Hannah took two steps back, smelling a recent drought of ale on the woman's breath.

"Her daughter? Why it can't be the same woman then, for the Rosamond I knew never said nothing about having no daughter, especially one she's training in the craft."

"But it must be her," pleaded Hannah, trying to salvage the Madonna image of her mother that now seemed to be dissolving with every passing moment. "She brings her woven goods down twice a year, at Beltane Festival and Lammas Fairs, stays about two weeks, then comes home. She's from Feshiebridge, in the Highlands, tall like me but with long brown hair."

"Aye," said the woman thoughtfully, "now that do sound like her. Pretty thing. Used to be in the company of that harper who used to perform here, but ain't seen him for some time. Now what was his name?" She leaned away from Hannah, craning her neck towards the fletcher. " 'Ey Wally, what's the name of that harper who always stuck so close to Rosamond MacFey, you know, the weaver?"

Wally, impatient to finish a sale, yelled back, "Michael. Arrogant sot." He turned back to the customer, resuming his business.

"Ah, Michael, that's it," said the weaver, sighing as she pronounced his name slowly, letting his name linger on her lips. "Now he was a handsome one, that he was. Lovely hair, like waves of sunlight. Similar to yours, now that I look at you. But mind me words, many's a woman tried to gain his affections after he met the weaver, but he'd have nobody but his highland lass."

"Is he here?" asked Hannah.

"Ah, no. There's the mystery of it, you see. Nobody's seen nor heard from him in several years." Just then a stout woman, apparently not lacking in finances, approached the table. The weaver cut her conversation with Hannah short, attending to the customer.

Hannah rounded the corner down a small alley, threw her pack on the ground then plopped down beside it. She needed to scream - loud and long.

Nothing but lies - through Rosamond's omission and shame of having a daughter - compounded with more lies: no cousin, no marriage. The only truth seemed to be the existence of the handsome harper, Michael, with whom Rosamond had cavorted for over twenty years.

So, was her father dead after all? Who as he, anyway? Could he even be this harper, Michael? And if so, had Rosamond finally told him of his daughter, only to have him disappear from both their lives? Either way, Nell was right - Hannah was a bastard.

Betrayal consumed Hannah, confirming her heart wounds of never being good enough, unworthy of anyone's affections. Her mother had always hidden part of her heart, and now Hannah knew why.

Since the elusive Michael was not to be found here, Hannah realized she'd come to the end of her task. She would return to Feshiebridge, tell her mother of Michael's apparent disappearance, and then decide which direction her life would take.

With so many conflicting emotions battling within, she knew she needed rest before undertaking the long journey home. She located the Stray Away Inn where the red-headed Maggie, once hearing Murdoch's instructions, shot Hannah a wry smile then led her to a room. Hannah washed herself with cold water from the blue porcelain basin then shed her travel clothing, replacing them with her sleeping shift.

She removed Rosamond's abalone necklace, placing it along with her mother's treasures in the small wooden box. She fingered the ribbons, allowing them to cascade through her fingertips. Imagining Rosamond's hair, all fancied up with such fineries when she came to Perth, playing the role of lover while leaving the role of mother behind in the highland heathers. It was all so contemptible. Hannah actually felt ill with waves of nausea rolling through her belly. She sipped some tea then while closing the box lid, tried flipping the farthing like she'd observed street players. But it simply rolled on the floor. The abalone necklace covered the amethyst torque, but the pearl-laden caul for encasing long hair, now there was something worth noting. Perhaps someday she would wear it, to spite her mother. Now it was time for rest.

But it proved to be a fretful night.

Despite the comfortable bedding of the Stray Away Inn, sleep hid its drowsy face from Hannah. By morning, her long hair twisted about her neck like a knotted scarf while the bed sheets spilled over the sides in a tangled heap. After splashing her face with cold water, she tore her sleeping shift as she took it off, fidgeting after a long, restless night.

"By St. Brighid's flames!" she grumbled, kicking her pack against the wall. Suddenly her stomach heaved. Hannah lurched forward, barely making it to the chamber pot. She fell to her knees, groaning as two more waves of nausea overcame her. The stench was overpowering. It caused her to retch once more, spraying her naked belly. When her stomach eased, she slumped against the wooden wall beside her bed, cradling herself. She hated being sick, stomach sick most of all. Rosamond always made her feel better by plying her with chamomile tea and brown bread till the illness passed.

In this child-like neediness, just thinking of Rosamond roused her anger which rivaled the bitter taste now in her mouth. She stood up, placing most of her weight on the good ankle, then stumbled to the basin. She poured water from the blue glazed pitcher into the bowl, slurping and spitting water into the chamber pot. The cold water revived her soiled skin. She dressed quickly, tearing the hem of her sleeping shift into a strip for binding her ankle. Hannah stowed the ornate wooden box in the bottom once more, picked up her pack then left the room.

Maggie, noticing Hannah's whitened face, said, "Now, you look like a woman who's been ill, sure enough. I'll not have you leaving here looking so pale. Come to my room, and I'll make you a cup of mint tea. Cures everything!" She shuttled Hannah to the back, sat her down on the bed then proceeded to fill her with two cups of steaming tea. Hannah felt a bit revived, and noticing this, Maggie offered Hannah two small oat cakes as well. Hannah ate one and saved the other for later, not knowing when her next meal would appear.

Hannah picked up her pack and followed Maggie to the front door. "Thank you, Maggie," said Hannah, "you're a kind woman. I can see why Murdoch favors you."

Maggie opened the door then blushed, turning her head to the side like a shy schoolgirl. She patted Hannah on the back, saying, "Well, take care of yourself, now, and come back anytime." She watched Hannah move slowly down the alley out to South Street then returned to the business of the day.

CHAPTER EIGHTEEN

Pinks and oranges crested the horizon as the morning sun beaconed its rays. The healing properties of Maggie's mint tea soothed Hannah's aching belly, enough so that within the hour she felt ready for a good day's walk. She picked up her pace a bit, watching the ankle. Her plan was to take the main road back by Blair Atholl then follow the Drover's Pass north through Glenfeshie Forest again, returning home within possibly four to five days, depending on the weather. Thus far, the warm breezes were unseasonably early, but she did not complain.

Her highland temper fueled her pace, for an angry woman walks fast. After two hours, Hannah was just passing Bankfoot when she heard the steady rhythm of hoof beats. She had passed travelers heading south to the festival, but none heading north. She stepped into the grass to allow easy passage for the horse to maneuver the upcoming turn when she heard a familiar voice hail her.

"Good morning, Hannah," said Lachlan Grant, halting his steed by her side. He remained in his seat but extended his hand in welcome.

"Good morning to you, Lachlan," said Hannah, returning the informality of his greeting by shaking his hand. His calming demeanor completely disarmed her.

He did not release his hold. He looked down at her, saying, "I see the ankle must be healing. Are you returning home now?"

"Yes," she said simply, answering both questions then pulling her hand free. Her emotions seemed so raw this morning that she feared saying something insulting.

"I've an idea," he said, jumping down beside her. "I am returning home myself after completing business in Perth. It would take you at least three more days on foot to reach even Blair Atholl.

I realize I haven't a proper seat, like a carriage for you, but I would be happy to offer my horse as an alternative to walking."

Hannah considered this for a moment. "You mean, ride, up there, with you? But you're a married man."

"That I am, but my wife would scold me heartily if I allowed an injured young lady to walk further," laughed Lachlan. "So, if you don't mind sitting behind me, I think Raney and I would welcome your company."

"I could get home much sooner, couldn't I?" she pondered aloud. "I mean, you could take me to Kingussie then I could finish on the path just south of home." Raney appeared a fine horse, fit for two riders without discomfort. "I know you to be kind man, Lachlan, and not an old sort by any means. So I accept your offer, for I'm in terrible need of reaching home as fast as possible." She handed her pack and walking stick to Lachlan who secured them beneath his belongings.

He leapt onto the horse, gathering the reins. "Up you go, young miss," he said, lowering his arm.

Hannah snaked her arm up to his shoulder, hopped on her good ankle then pulled herself onto Raney's back. She wrapped her arms around Lachlan's middle, setting her thighs firmly about the horse. With a snap of the cords, the horse sped over rutted tracks as if racing at the Lammas Fair.

They talked very little, which suited Hannah since her moods seem to rise and fall like the road. She focused on the hills, mounting higher and higher as the pair continued north. Raney galloped steadily, arriving at Blair Atholl village by midday. Lachlan treated Hannah to a filling lunch at the local inn, telling her about his family and farm over barley soup and beef pies. She could not keep from smiling when he talked about falling in the muck during a rescue attempt of one of his sheep. She could imagine him falling, like a tower tumbling down into the earthy browns.

He seemed to be fed by her attentions, so they lingered, finishing the meal with sweet cakes. Hannah's nausea did not return. Her spirits lifted, and she realized she liked Lachlan. She wondered if she might see him again, perhaps at the Ruthven Market with his wife. He spoke so lovingly of her that Hannah would be pleased to meet this sweet woman. It was refreshing to be so at ease in the company of a relative stranger, affording her a respite from her own life.

The afternoon brought heavy rains as they rode through Glen Garry. Trying to offer protection, Lachlan produced his tartan from one of his packs, slid Hannah in front then wrapped themselves in the woolen shield. The high winds flapped the sides like a mad goose, but it kept them from becoming completely drenched. They slowed through the Pass of Drumochter, not wanting Raney to misstep in the deepening mud. Deafening thunderclaps startled the horse, yet Raney persevered.

Yelling through the rain, Lachlan said, "I think we should stay overnight in Dalwhinnie. We'll never reach Kingussie in this storm." He looked down into Hannah's face so close to his own. She nodded in agreement, raising the tartan to shield her face from splattering rains. They rode for one more hour when Lachlan saw lights of the small village of Dalwhinnie. He recalled a small inn, The Gryphon's Claw, located in the center of town where he and his wife had often stayed after visiting her relatives in Fort William. He steered Raney towards the only stable in the village, sidling through the open doors to the surprise of the sleeping stable hand. Lachlan shook the rain-soaked plaid, showering the golden hay.

"Let me help you down, Hannah," said Lachlan, slipping down Raney's wet flank.

His large hands gripped her waist tightly, securing her descent. He quickly made arrangements for Raney, lifted their packs onto his shoulders, and walked Hannah two doors down to the inn.

A bright red fire emanated from the hearth encircled by several planked tables and benches. The smoke lay thick over the back corner where peat aromas mingled with pipe rings.

An elderly balding innkeeper waved Lachlan and Hannah over to the counter where he conducted business. "And what will ye being needing on this dark and stormy night?" he asked, leering a bit towards the sodden Hannah whose kirtle and shift clung to her body.

Lachlan noticed this at once, shoving her behind him. "We'll be needing lodging for the night." His commanding tone ruffled the innkeeper's pride.

"Aye, well, there's only the one room left to let," he said, hoisting his trousers over his ale stuffed belly. "But I'm bettin' that won't be a problem, eh?" He winked at Lachlan.

"Sir, as we have no other options, we will take the room," he said gruffly. "But I will ask you to place a second mattress on the floor."

Hannah marveled at Lachlan's commanding tone, immediately deflating the innkeeper's lascivious thoughts. The innkeeper led them two floors up a winding wooden staircase to a small attic space. The bed rested below two windows that peaked in the roof line. The innkeeper lit a small fire in the common chimney then left the room. With the storm over, a glimmer of evening light suffused through the dingy glass panes. The wearied travelers made a silent pact: dry clothes before a meal.

Lachlan pulled out a dry shirt and pair of brown trousers, best suited for riding. "I'll turn my back to give you a bit of privacy, Hannah, but you'll catch your death if you don't get out of those wet things." He faced a dark corner and changed clothes while Hannah rummaged through her few belongings in search of something dry. To her surprise, there was a green dress stuffed in the base of the sack. She pulled it out, recognizing it at once.

"That Jenny!" she exclaimed, smiling in remembrance of the dear girl who spent days telling Hannah stories while the ankle healed and the wink she offered at Hannah's departure. Hannah stripped off her saturated layers, dried off with a towel located at the foot of the bed then slid into the gown. The open-necked bodice was trimmed with purple knot work embroidery. A slender waistline cut offset Hannah's trim figure. The fabric felt softer than wool yet slick like butter. The folds of deep green reminded Hannah of her wedding gown, one that she had never worn, but she remembered Jenny showing her this dress, commenting on the care her mother had taken in making something so special for her daughter. I will take it back someday, thought Hannah, but for now, I will enjoy it. With an extra ribbon she discovered in the lacings, Hannah braided her hair then pulling out her mother's pearl caul, looped the hair into the netting which looked wild after the storm then adorning her neck with the amethyst torque. The abalone shells remained packed in its heart-shaped protector, unburdening Hannah of her mixed emotions surrounding Rosamond.

"Ready," she said, with a trembling smile.

As Lachlan turned around, he gasped. The bedraggled girl he'd pulled off the road weeks ago had transformed into a faerie queen. "Why Hannah, I'm amazed at your charming beauty, lass. It's a wonder you've not been taken up by one of those young Feshiebridge farmers.' Then he noticed the ring. "Ah, so one has spoken for you. That's fine, girl, just fine."

Hannah fought the sadness, not wanting to venture into Lukas's death tonight. She determined to remain good company for the evening, for Lachlan's sake, to repay his kindness. She moved the single three-legged chair by the fire, draping their wet belongings over it in hopes of dry fare for the next day's ride.

Lachlan extended his arm, as to a lady, "Might I escort you to dinner?"

"Kind sir, I'd be pleased to share a meal with you tonight," she said in an unusually melodic voice. She grinned at such foppish airs, but nevertheless, took his arm.

They chose seats nearest the fire, for despite the dry clothes, Hannah still felt chilled. Thick slices of bread topped with melted cheese soon appeared alongside two steaming bowls of vegetable barley soup. Room temperature ale in bottomless tankards warmed Hannah's belly, quiet after the morning episode. Lachlan spoke of his childhood days, his two brothers, and the migration of the family. His parents, clamoring for city social life, left the rural holdings to Lachlan, being the eldest. One brother had become a clergyman while his youngest brother remained in Kingussie, working alongside his older brother.

Hannah found Lachlan's company soothing, his stories interesting. She considered his kind face, and observed that despite his graying temples, he was barely cresting thirty years of age. She closed her mind to a world filled with so many uncertainties and fell into his tales, just for a while. She found herself relaxing in the wake of the peat fire, the strong ale, and road weariness. She tried to stifle a yawn, but Lachlan saw it.

"Hannah, I'm feeling a bit worn from the trip, and need some sleep. I hope you don't think me rude, but I believe we should retire."

"Not a bit," she said, standing up slowly.

"I'll settle up for the meal then make sure the innkeeper has placed the extra mattress in the room," he said, steadying Hannah on her feet. She wobbled slightly. "Or maybe I'll just take you to the room first." He guided her up the stairs to the aerie, pleased to see the second mattress in the corner. Hannah gave a gaping yawn then stretched out full length on the bed. "You best change into a sleeping shift for a good night's sleep. We'll break at first light tomorrow," he said, then left, returning to the main floor to complete his transactions.

Hannah's eyes refused to open fully as she undressed, flopping the dress over the wooden chair then replacing the jewelry in the parting box. Her sleeping shift was damp, but the excess blankets in the room would keep her warm. By the time Lachlan returned, she was snoring heavily.

The next morning, Hannah rose before Lachlan, quickly changing into her dry traveling clothes. Her thick hair remained damp, so she wore the caul once more to keep stragglers out of her face. The pair would arrive early in Kingussie then she could easily maneuver the last bit home. Home. This daughter, determining Rosamond's full recovery from the pox, required answers now from her mother.

Lachlan awoke as Hannah finalized her packing, placing the green dress securely inside. The faerie guise disappeared, leaving a simple highland lass.

Enjoying a light breakfast of bannocks and tea, the two reunited with Raney and headed north, with Hannah riding behind Lachlan. The peaks of Glen Truim paralleled the valley track below. Lulled by Raney's smooth and steady gait, Hannah sighed and rested her head on Lachlan's shoulder, encircling his waist once more. A slight mist clung to the pair as they rode through the early morning quiet.

She felt close to this man, relieved to know she could be herself with another man. For weeks after Lukas's death, she'd doubted if she would be fit company for anyone, ever. Yet now, this gentle man had proven her wrong. For this, she would always be indebted. Instinctively, she hugged him.

The rocking of Raney's pace paired with the occasional coo-rooing of the blackcock cocooned the pair in nature's serenity. "Hannah, I wonder if I could ask you a question?" whispered Lachlan, his tone so soft that Hannah barely heard him.

"You may, but I reserve the right not to answer," she said plainly, sitting up.

"Fair enough," replied Lachlan. "I know you must be a determined woman, setting on such a journey when you did. And I'm not asking you to share your business with me if you do not wish to do so. But I am concerned with the sadness I see about you, always clinging like a wraith. It lifts for a moment, but returns with such a vengeance. I just wondered . . ."

The request came without guile, so she told him everything. She began with Lukas, their love and his death. Tears trickled, but she did not stop. By not facing him, it was easier to tell these sad truths. Next came Rosamond's illness which led to searching for the mysterious Michael. She spoke fast, the anger escalating as she felt the betrayal of her mother's lies again. Confusion mingled with confession.

Lachlan urged Raney on, affording Hannah privacy by continuing. He released her hold, grasping her hand as she spoke. His silent consolations strengthened her, comforted her. The grief exposed, Hannah sat upright, looking at the surrounding peaks and feeling very small. There was nothing more to say.

Within two hours they reached the outskirts of Kingussie. The grassy crossroad along the River Spey connecting to the Drover's Pass bore to the right while the Grant farm lay further north. Lachlan stopped by the water's edge, permitting Raney some refreshment. He lifted Hannah from the steed's back, holding her just a moment longer than necessary once her feet reached the ground. He loosened her pack and walking stick from Raney's load.

"Sorry I am to see you go, Hannah," said Lachlan, handing Hannah her things, "for I've enjoyed your company tremendously and grown quite fond of you. Know that the Grant farm will always be open to you, for I speak for my wife as well as myself in saying we always welcome friends. And we are friends, aren't we, girl?" he asked with a wink.

Hannah smiled, a half smile, but a smile nonetheless. "Yes," she answered softly, "and I will try to come, or perhaps we will meet again at Ruthven, for I will be weaving more with my mother now."

"Yes, so this need not be farewell, but merely until the next time, agreed?"

"Agreed."

With their pledge in place, the two embraced then parted company. As Hannah waved good-bye to Raney and his rider, a sense of loss reappeared in response to Lachlan's departure. She would miss him, miss the old Hannah that seemed at ease with him. But now she had other more serious demands drawing her focus, questions that needed answers.

The highly traveled road to Kingussie was less than busy that afternoon. Hannah would bear off to the right a few miles up for the short cut to Feshiebridge. Although Hannah had been grateful to Lachlan for Raney's ride, the continual bouncing agitated her ankle, leaving it somewhat tender now as she walked slowly down the road, limping slightly. As two women, heavily laden with parcels, passed Hannah, she overheard part of their ongoing conversation.

"It's such a pity, it is," said the first, a stout woman who simultaneously strove to maintain her speech and match her companion's brisk gait, but her puffing pink cheeks betrayed her.

"Aye," said the second, a tall thin woman wearing a green cloak.

"Why, I bought exquisite shawls at the Ruthven Market this very year from the dear woman. And now, well, I'm just wonderin' who will take over? Most of the best weavers are either north in Inverness or south in Perth, with little concern for the likes of us simple farming folk who has needs just like them city folk."

"Aye," said the second.

"Poor thing, dying that way, and all alone they say," said the first, shaking her head.

"Aye," agreed the second.

"Where did you think her girl ran off to, in such a rush, leaving a dying mother behind like that? Poor Rosamond. The local highlanders will suffer the loss of MacFey woolens. 'Tis a pity that's for sure," said the first woman.

The words hung over Hannah like a guillotine's blade – "dying that way, all alone." Once more her body passed into shock, unable to move as the two women disappeared down the lane.

She would have questioned them further, had she the presence of mind, but her thoughts swirled with the incredulity of it all. She dropped her pack as her knees buckled, causing her to fall hard to the ground. She lay there, curling herself around the pack as if holding Rosamond once more while a watershed of tears spilled onto her cloak.

Rosamond was dead?

Mistress Stewart's healing arts must have failed. For Hannah, the grave now proved her mother's confidant, taking old secrets into its cold, dark womb.

Hannah whimpered, like a simpering dog lost in the cold - desperate, hopeless, alone. She curled inward, like a babe in its mother's belly, squeezing the pack beneath her head as she lay in the new grasses by the road. A warm breeze, initializing May's sweet breath, grazed her cheek, like a mother's kiss. Instantly Hannah's fingers caressed the spot, remembering the many times from early childhood when Rosamond had kissed that very place each evening as she sang Hannah to sleep.

Suddenly, reminiscent of her morning at the Stray Away Inn, Hannah's stomach lurched with urgency, expelling the oat bannocks from breakfast. She cursed the sky for its brilliant blue then ravaged the newly-bloomed bluebells, carpeting the grasses with indigo petals. How could nature continue when life, for her, was over?

She attempted to sit upright, but her muscles ached, so leaning to one side, she opened her sack, fumbled for a handkerchief then wiped her mouth. Grateful now for the flask of water Lachlan gave to her just prior to his departure, Hannah rinsed out her mouth then spat the foul residue on the ground.

Death tasted bitter.

She laid back down then closed her eyes, barely breathing, trying to visualize their home now without Rosamond. The bleak images caused Hannah to shudder: the unattended hearth, its embers cold, housing a single black cauldron suspended on the iron loop filled with stale water, unfinished threads hung in limbo upon the loom while dishes, left askew on the kitchen table, waited for tender cleansing care. Her mother's bedclothes would be strewn in chaotic swirls amidst her blankets, never to feel human heat again. The rafters, once the blessed roost for constant laughter and song, would forever remain empty- only wood, supporting a simple roof.

There would be no home for Hannah, ever again. Not there.

From the depths of her sorrow roared the unanswered questions, especially those dealing with her father. How would she ever know the truth?

There was one who might know, one man who had held her mother's heart all these years. She had to find Michael.

With a new resolve, she picked herself up, snatched her bag then remembered the tokens in the parting box, gifts of love from his travels. She knew that now. She rummaged through her meager things and whipped out the box, prying open the lid. Clues, clues to his previous adventures could lead to current venues. She flipped through the colorful ribbons, recognizing they could have been purchased at any market, so she lay them aside.

The morning sun bounced off the opalescent abalone shell necklace, catching Hannah's eye. By wearing the necklace, she had felt close to Rosamond. In tearing it from her neck, she expelled the anger and frustration at all the lies and deceit. But now it simply lay among her mother's treasures, another symbol of Michael's love for her. Perhaps it could lead Hannah to him, so she slipped the necklace over her head till it lay cradled over her heart.

She replaced the pearl caul back in the box, marveling at its beauty. She considered the crafting of the jewelry was most likely purchased near larger towns, but she imagined the pearl caul and abalone shell necklace fashioned in ports or towns with access to sea-fed lochs.

Ballachulish could be such a port, one of Murdoch's stops before crossing to Skye which lay southerly from Kingussie on Loch Linnhe. Perhaps someone there knew of Michael, or possibly would recognize the caul or necklace. Additionally, she considered that if Michael were still harping, he might be drawn to the competition at Armadale, so by accepting Murdoch's insistence that she accompany him, she opted for Ballachulish. She would start there.

With grim determination, she braided her hair and rose, facing south once more. It was time. No more lies. She had to know the truth.

CHAPTER NINETEEN
Isle of Mull, Caledonia

Early the next morning, stiff from the abused horsehair pallet which served as a bed, Michael chose to walk a bit, pulling out his walking stick. After paying for her feed, he loaded Molly with expert ease, stretched his leg muscles a bit then ambled along the muddy track. A cool breeze blew in from the north while the sea sported turquoise and midnight blues, weaving in and out of the waves. He did not see the dark-headed, whiskered face bobbing in the water, eyes intently watching the shoreline.

As he walked along the road, a slight trembling began in his belly. He tried to ignore it, but then it tightened like a snake coiling around its prey. He did not recognize this stretch of road, but knew he was passing Lochdonhead, the small village which housed the Conger Eel Inn where he should have leisurely spent the night five years ago.

The light of the morning sun obscured in mental blackness as the memories drenched his soul. Michael's head reeled from side to side. He faltered like a drunkard then hit the ground, causing Molly to halt. His cane fell, covered in splatters of blood-red muck from the road where Michael lay on the ground, writhing as if the being beaten by invisible assailants.

Only one being, rocking in the sea, heard his screams.

The tormented soul reached out to the ground of its birthing, remembering the cruelty it suffered on this very spot. The body recoiled, recalling it all, blow by blow. The scene played itself to its gruesome conclusion. Michael lay exhausted, his tears melting into mud.

"NO MORE!" he shouted, "I won't carry this any longer, you hear!" raising his fists to the heavens. "O God, rip these horrors from me. How am I to live with such infernal enemies within me?" He wept openly now, not caring if anyone did see.

A silent visitor stood vigil.

"Michael" came a soft voice.

The sound of his name echoed through his reality.

"Michael, I'm here. Let me help you." Strong arms reached under Michael's shoulders, lifting him up to lean against Molly. His cane was placed in his right hand. "Can you stand?" asked Ronan, moving the packs aside.

Michael leaned heavily on the wizard-faced cane, staring through watery eyes at the dark man beside him. After so many years gone from the world of men, could anyone even recognize this harper now? Yet this man seemed familiar.

"I know of a place nearby where you can rest. Let me ride behind you. You've fallen enough today. Come," said Ronan as he lifted Michael onto Molly's back, securing the cane under the harp. Ronan hoisted himself up, straddling Michael; with one arm around his friend and the other on the reins, they rode north.

Michael rested his head on Ronan's shoulder, still woozy from the episode. After smelling the heavy scent of sea about his rescuer, he whispered, "Ronan?" then fell into a deep sleep.

They rode only a few more miles on the main road then followed a smaller track off to the right. Molly's gentle gait lulled Michael, allowing him to rest comfortably. After about three more miles, a rectangular stone fortress built by the Macleans, a three-leveled keep facing the sea, came into view. Ronan's strength never faltered, bringing Molly and Michael safely into the courtyard.

"Master Ronan," said one of the stable lads, running to see him, "so good to see you again, sir."

"And you as well, Gregory," said Ronan, smiling down at the lad. "Can you fetch Jock? I need to stable this horse. Be quick, now boy."

The tow-headed lad ran quickly into the stables then returned with matched haste, accompanied by a stout man, Jock

MacHenry, Groom Master for the Maclean horses. Jock eased Michael off the horse, supporting his shoulders while Ronan descended on the other side. Michael's head lolled from side to side as he gazed about the white-speckled stone courtyard.

"I've known your lord's kindness," said Ronan to Jock, "I wish only a few night's lodging. My friend is ill and needs rest."

"Well, I canna spake for the Master," said Jock, his rural upbringing betraying him, "but I'll send the lad up to the house. I'm sure we can find a patch of soft hay, if he's not got a problem sleeping with the foals." Jock motioned for Gregory to take a message to the house then, after settling Michael on the closest bench, walked Molly into a clean stable. He supplied her with clean water and fresh feed while unloading her goods. The harp was placed in the corner while Ronan rifled through the sack, pulling out Michael's Abbey robe.

"Thank you," replied Ronan, "I will stay with him. We wish to be no burden on Lord Maclean." Ronan placed a wool horse blanket over tufts of sweet hay then folding Michael's robe into a pillow, laid Michael in the makeshift bedding.

"Ronan, how can you be here?" asked the bewildered man, regarding his rescuer.

"I followed you," replied the selkie, "now rest. I'll return with food."

Ronan disappeared towards the kitchens. In his human form, he'd come to know this family well, though none suspected his secret identity. He had even been at the wedding of young Isobel five years earlier, but he did not recognize Michael upon their meetings at Iona as the harper from that night. He remembered the boldness of the musician in offering condolences to the bride when congratulations were customary. He, like everyone else, was completely unaware of the cruel dealings in the dark later that night. Now, watching Michael five years later and hearing his torments, Ronan surmised the impact of that dreadful event, for he remembered too the harper was quite handsome by the ladies' attentions. But this man was barely recognizable as that confident singer.

Ronan was greeted with warm embraces as he entered the main quarters of the house. The current lord of the Maclean clan was known by those around as good, brave, and kind. The youngest daughter Isobel first met Ronan when only ten, insisting that he join her family for dinner one evening. Her innocence reigned him in, so child-like yet assertive as befitting aristocracy. During the years that followed, many enjoyable evenings were shared.

Mistress Maclean, upon hearing of Ronan's arrival and the circumstances, insisted that he bring his friend into the house where they would place him in a guest bedroom, leaving a servant to wait on him. Ronan and Gregory roused Michael, aiding him into the house then up the stairs to a guest bedroom. The four-poster cedar bed stood in the center of the room, filled with cream-colored pillows atop a rose coverlet. A pitcher of water with cut glass tumblers sat on a matching oval bed stand.

Sarah, the maidservant, first pulled down the sheets then fluffed the pillows. She drew the damask rose draperies over the two windows. "Will that be all, sir?" she asked.

"Yes," replied Ronan, "and please send my thanks to your mistress."

"As you wish, sir," said Sarah. After flourishing with a lop-sided curtsy, she left, followed by Gregory, allowing the men their privacy.

Ronan stripped Michael of his traveling clothes, replacing them with a sleeping shirt. Michael remained docile, like a boy whose nanny was preparing him for bed. He settled into the goose-down pillows then took the water offered him by Ronan. Sipping it slowly, Michael tried to take in what was happening, but his vision blurred, creating grotesque shadings to the lovely surroundings. He swooned, surrendering to the heaviness in his head. The fine linen sheets cocooned Michael, providing a safe haven for his wearied spirit.

Michael slept fitfully for three days while Ronan never left his side. He placed cooling cloths on Michael's forehead, straightened the twisted sheets after Michael's wrestling with fevered bouts, and plied him with light brothy soups and water during periods of lucidity. Slowly, the haze enveloping the harper's mind began to clear. Michael sat in bed, wondering at the rich furnishings and his presence here. When Ronan mentioned his relationship with the Macleans, Michael bolted upright, shooting two pillows to the floor.

"Macleans, you say?" asked Michael.

"I did," responded Ronan, replacing the stranded pillows.

"Don't tell me, man, you've brought me to Duart Castle?" Michael's eyes were suddenly clear.

"Indeed I have, Michael," said Ronan.

The harper wailed aloud and began flailing about the bedclothes.

"For God's sake, Ronan, do you not know they are the reason for my suffering?"

"I was uncertain before, but I know this family is not to blame. What happened to you?" Ronan sat on the edge of the bed, waiting on the harper's timing.

"Oh, you know about the wedding, then do you?" Michael leaned back into the pillows, his arms crossed over his chest.

"I was there," said Ronan. "I've known Isobel for many years."

"So that's her name is it? Isobel?"

"Yes."

"Well, it's for her sake, knowing she wed without love, that I handed her a rose when I'd finished my playing. I'd heard the stories on the ferry from a few of the guests. They said the groom himself carried on in brutish ways, despite his wealthy upbringing. Many pitied her, 'Such a sweet thing' they'd said. Then when I played, I saw such a sadness in her eyes that I could not restrain my strings. I played for her that night, and her alone."

"But how did it result in such violence?" asked Ronan.

"Those ruffians came at me from behind," said Michael, his voice graveled with disdain, "the cowards. At first, they punched me repeatedly, nearly knocked me senseless. The painful burning across my cheek kept me in this world. Then I heard the splintering of my harp as one of the bastards stomped on my leg. The groom threatened me, just so I'd know it was he who'd done this dirty deed." He paused. "They laughed, Ronan. I heard them laughing as they left me there, alone in the dark." He shuddered as a chill ran the length of his body.

Ronan observed this but said nothing. He knew Michael's attacker by name.

"I lay in the dark then," continued Michael, much softer than before. "Alone. Broken. Unable to move. I knew I was going to die." A stillness settled like a haunt upon his shoulders.

"But you didn't die, Michael,"said Ronan, probing for resolution.

"Aye, for some reason I was spared, left to live my life in this broken shell," said Michael, passing his fingers before his torn face.

"But Michael, you are whole."

"What the devil do you mean?" asked Michael, anger from years of containment now surfacing. "Can you not see me, man? I've got this damned scar that still blazes my cheek, and my bones never mended properly in the leg, so I'll always limp. Even my face still sags a bit to one side like a puppet gone awry with my slackened jaw. I even tried growing a beard to cover the mess, but all that grows is stubble. How the devil can you call me whole?"

Ronan shifted from his seat, leaning in closer, "I will ask you again, as upon our first meeting. If the body changes its form, does the soul change as well?"

Michael grimaced, remembering his answer.

"You said it retained its natural qualities, regardless of the shape."

"I did," said Michael, conceding to the truth.

"Can you not see then that your spirit is still whole, bruised by the hurting of the body but able to heal?" His soft tones parried with Michael's anger.

Ronan asked with such gentleness that Michael had to consider this. He'd always viewed himself as a broken man since that night, never having the chance at a suitable life again. Yet his very words, mirrored through Ronan, rang true.

"I see your meaning, Ronan, but I don't believe it because of these damned visions. How can I stop them?"

"Those fears lie deep. You must release them, as they arise. It may not come all at once, but allow them to wash over you, like the sea. Ride the wave, into its belly, then rise on the swell. You thought you died that day. That belief will triumph if you accept it."

Michael reflected on these truths silently, but remained uncertain of their reality.

"Michael, you did survive, but you will be different. Are you willing to pick up your path again?" The selkie's dark eyes bore down on Michael.

"I'm scared," he whispered.

"Then you will learn to use courage once more," replied Ronan.

Michael sat up in bed and ran his fingers through his wavy hair, the tonsure barely visible as the locks crested his ears. "You speak of courage. Ah man, there is one love that outweighs all my fears, and it's her heart that I'm needing to be close to now. I've stayed away from her, fearing rejection, but if you say that I am whole now, even in this altered form, then I will go to her, pledge my love to her. After all, perhaps I may still have something to offer her."

"You offer her what no other man can, Michael," said Ronan.

"And what is that?"

"The love of a man her soul desires." The selkie smiled at his friend.

Michael knew better than to question how Ronan might know such a thing. Once again, he heard the truth resound in his own heart. His love for this woman had never ceased, even when he'd been traveling. Yet for too long his pride and vanity kept his longings for notoriety as a court harper more important than the simple love of this good woman. His arrogance had been his downfall, but it would not separate them any longer. "I'm going to find her, tell her everything. And if she's not already promised, then I will ask her to marry me. I fear children may not come easily to a woman her age now, but if she wishes, I'll give her all the children she wants!"

Ronan laughed aloud. "I see joy coming into your life once more, my friend."

"Yes, thinking of spending my life with Rosamond does bring me joy. How is it that it has taken me so long to understand that?"

"You passed through the darkness before the light could return."

Ronan placed his hand on Michael's head and began murmuring a soft, lulling tune, a selkie tune. A calming sensation like warm molasses ran throughout Michael's body, replacing his agitations and fears. As he leaned back into the supportive pillows, Michael sighing deeply.

"I will leave soon, for I'm needed in Loch Linnhe," said Ronan, "but rest for now. Be well, my friend."

Sarah brought Michael's meals three times daily and checked his progress between. She reported his progress to Mistress Maclean, who trusted Ronan to let her know of this stranger's progress should further arrangements be necessary. After three more days, Michael felt well enough to travel. He requested that Molly be made ready with his few belongings early the next morning, for his delay could cause Brother Aidan to worry. Ronan and Michael agreed to keep the harper's identity from the family, fearing it would cause them grief to hear of his sufferings. Ronan did disclose that Isobel remained married still, living with the groom's family on the Isle of Skye, but happiness seemed not to dwell within that marriage. There were no children.

On the morning of Michael's departure, Sarah helped Michael to the stable.

No fanfare like after the wedding. No applause. Nothing but snoring stable boys met him, for even Ronan had disappeared. Michael turned toward Castle Duart and said aloud, "I leave those nightmares here. No longer will I carry them, but should they rise again, I'll let them roll over me, ride their horrendous swells until they dissolve like foam on the shore. For I am a harper, and will not be robbed of life any longer."

He breathed deeply, releasing the hold of his tragedy, and set his feet to a new path, one leading to his true north.

CHAPTER TWENTY

The southern carriage from Aviemore, on its normal weekly route, appeared within an hour's time of Hannah's collapse, and in her weakened state, she gave thanks for the aid. Since Murdoch had generously paid for her Perth lodgings, her traveling funds could best serve her now. After two days by carriage, the forty miles to Ballachulish, a tiny village perched on Loch Linnhe, passed quickly as the wooden iron-shod wheels creaked over jarring ruts and navigating muddy holes.

By her calculations, Murdoch should be arriving at the Bristlewaith Manor in two days, allowing her time to rest then locate the estate. After paying the carriage driver, she threw her pack over her shoulder in search of an inn. The Barking Seal, a quaint cottage facing the sea, let rooms at a reasonable rate, so she reserved two nights' stay then ambled down the village lane, paralleling the sea wall, in search of dinner.

Street vendors from earlier Beltane celebrations still tended their booths as Hannah regarded floral head circlets, Green Man masks, and ribboned May boughs comprised of primroses, cowslips, buttercups, and marsh marigolds. Vestiges of leafy boughs lined the street from the Mummer's parade held on May first, welcoming spring, thus bringing good fortune to the village. She opened her cloak as the warming sea winds caressed her, revealing her mother's abalone necklace which shimmered in remembrance of its briny birth.

An elderly man with a mop of gray sprouting from beneath his navy seaman's cap accosted Hannah, saying, "Ah, now there, a handsome young lady like yourself wandering the streets with no fella on her arm? Don't seem right, it don't." He rose from his seat, sifted through his goods, then held out a rose silk shawl. "Why not buy a little something just to please yourself?" Glimmering strands of golden mylar thread, randomly interwoven throughout the shawl, gleamed and sparkled like the early evening stars.

She was tempted - truth be known. The shawl struck Hannah as more than lovely, but regarding her meager money pouch, she declined.

Before continuing her stroll, the old man noticed Hannah's necklace then laughed aloud. "Why bless my soul, if it ain't one of me own creations walking down the street. Here you go, lassie, let's have a closer look at that shell."

Suspicious, Hannah intended to walk on, but realizing this fortunate opportunity as a clue about Michael, she hesitated. "Do you really know this necklace?" she asked, lifting the large creamy shell with its loops of variegated browns and golds swirling into a delicate spiral.

The vendor scrutinized the shell, then fondled the smaller three-beaded strands of browns and whites. He knew many makers could form such a piece, but the unique clasp was of his own design. "Aye, miss, this be mine for certain. See this here locking chain on the back? Why I'm the only soul in these parts to make such linking."

Hannah's hopes rose, for if he was the maker, certainly he was the seller as well. "And do you recall who you sold this necklace to? A harper, perhaps?"

Squinting skyward, as if trailing back through history, he beamed. "You know, I believe I did, but now that's been many years back. He were a chatty fellow when he wanted to be. I wouldn't have remembered it so clearly if he'd not made such a fuss over the thing."

The old man's knee wobbled slightly, so he regained his seat then continued his story. "I'd seen the harper here before, playing and singing for the All Soul's night, at Samhain. A jolly fellow, by my recollection. Had the eye of nearly every woman in town, he did! But he'd smile politely, offer a grand flourishing of his hand then head back to the inn alone. Used to stay just up the street, at The Barking Seal. Said he never tired of watching the sun setting over the loch cause'n it reminded him of his boyhood days, watching by the sea." He pulled out his pipe, filled it, lit it then puffed peacefully.

Hannah's theories about the parting box were now confirmed. "But did he say anything about the lady he was buying it for, or perhaps where he lived?"

"I don't know much about his whereabouts, but seems he did say that the browns of the necklace would match his lady's hair. But he couldn't have meant you, now could he?" He leaned towards her, eying her autumnal waves. "So how did you come by it?"

"He gave it to my mother," stated Hannah simply, "and I'm trying to find him. He's been gone for several years, but I wonder if you haven't seen him lately, maybe last Samhain?"

"Nah, he didn't show. But now that you mention it, been some years since he's passed through these parts. Bought that necklace from me, oh, had to be at least seven or eight years ago now. See, my eyes started going, so I had to give up the trade of making them little lovelies. Now I just sell what others make." He leaned back, taking a few large puffs while circles of smoke wreathed his head.

Hannah thanked the man then continued down the street where she located a pub filled with smells of local foods: meat pies, haggis, cheese bridies, and colcannon. She drank apple beer and ordered the colcannon, a hearty stew made from cabbage, turnips, and carrots. A young couple in the corner clearly had eyes only for each other, their meal cooling without being touched. Hannah sighed, missing the intimate times she'd had with Lukas back home in such public surroundings, neither caring what fodder they were providing for the town gossips. The meal settled her roiling stomach, so she rested a bit before venturing into the night air.

She replayed her conversation with the old man in her mind, sifting through his stories for pertinent details that might help her locate Michael. She knew he had preferred Rosamond over other women, so for that, she was grateful. Her mother's love had not been taken for granted. Also, he took pleasure in seaside sunsets, reminding him of his childhood, so he must have been raised in a coastal village. But Caledonia was bounded by water in the east, north, and west, so that fact did nothing to narrow the field of villages. However, he traveled for a living, performing in venues that ranged from high-brow estates to local street fairs. So, to make money, he would need to avoid the less remote areas, perhaps sprinkling shows in between annual commitments.

So here, in the first week of May, he would have finished Beltane celebrations and if still harping, be heading towards the Isle of Skye for the Armadale competition. Would she find him there? She must find Murdoch as soon as he arrived to guarantee her arrival at Clan Donald's estate.

With a full belly, Hannah strayed along the sea wall, gazing at the blue-green waves rising then cascading into gentle ripples against the grey boulders lining the shore. She fingered the necklace, lamenting that she had no memory of it gracing Rosamond's neck. She imagined the colors of its sea swirls bringing out the highlights of her mother's hair prior to the grays that began peeking their way through the mass of late. She sensed the joy that must have risen in Rosamond's heart as she wore it, a feeling all women share when given a gift of love.

Her heart raced back to Rowan Hill when Lukas placed the amethyst ring on her finger. The softness of his eyes, the tenderness of his touch afterwards . . . she sighed.

She slowly rotated the ring around her finger, the amethyst purples glistening in the setting oranges and mauves of twilight. She bowed her head, as if in prayer, but no words of comfort stroked her heart. Her breathing became labored as she held the grief in reserve while surges of her persistent cough expelled her pain.

"Are you all right?" asked a soft voice behind her.

Hannah took a deep breath, willing the coughing to cease, then looked up into a kind face framed by long black curls. She thought his blue eyes matched the sea, for they seem to change from one shade to the next like undulating waves. "I will be fine," she replied. "I just need to sit here for a moment."

"May I join you?" asked Ronan.

Her intuitive leanings sensed his gentle nature, so feeling safe, nodded. Ronan carefully sat down, placing a small burlap pouch beside him. He noticed her wedding ring and asked, "Where is your husband?"

"The waters took him," said Hannah, staring across the dark waves of Loch Linnhe. "Not these here, but waters nonetheless."

"It was too soon, his death?"

"Yes," said Hannah, her words barely above a breath. Her wall of reserve felt pressure, unsure of its stability. "The night before we were to be wed. But we exchanged vows, sealed our love, though not before any priest or witnesses."

Ronan, considering this last statement a moment, asked, "What need is there for either when two souls commit? Their love seals the union, not the law."

"But I am widow now before ever becoming a wife," said Hannah, her eyes flush with tears as her shoulders trembled at the realization of a lifetime of loss looming before her. The highland heart so well-versed in loving would remain behind closed doors.

She placed her arms about herself, willing the shaking to stop, but her thoughts betrayed her. No daughter would ever ride on Lukas's shoulders; they would never sing the old songs on those long, cold winter nights. And without Rosamond, too, all that remained now was to survive.

Ronan regarded Hannah's protective form, yet even as she sat, cradling her arms about her, he saw the truth. "You may not be Wife, but he has made you Mother."

Hannah gasped. "What? That's impossible." Yet even as she said the words, pregnant with truth, a deeper knowing took hold. Grief over Lukas's death followed by concern for Rosamond had caused her to dismiss the lack of monthly courses. She recalled now the waves of nausea at the inn, and her tightening belly, believing these symptoms hailed from anxiety. "But how could you know?"

"A woman appears . . . different, when carrying a life inside her." A ghost of a smile lingered on his lips then he gazed at the sky clouding with stars.

Hannah rubbed her belly then stared at her ring - their lovemaking on Rowan Hill from four months ago now resulted in this life burgeoning inside her. She sighed, remembering her hopes for a daughter, but now wishing to see Lukas's face once more, began praying for a son. But how could she go through this rite of passage without her mother? The grief and loneliness absorbed her once more as the sadness masked her hidden joy.

"I must leave now. Shall you sit a while longer?" asked Ronan, standing to leave as he picked up his satchel.

"Yes, I believe I will," said, Hannah, gazing across the illuminated waters. A stillness glazed the surface, as if all life had stopped for a single moment to join her in this revelation. Earlier seductive calls to surrender beneath the waves faded as Hannah embraced this new purpose in her journey.

Mother.

Hope reigned once more within her heart.

Ronan stepped away quietly, walking towards The Barking Seal where his friend, the innkeeper, awaited this seasonal arrival.

Oban, Caledonia

Michael met Brother Aidan at his family's home on the northern tip of Mull, and after a brief visit, the pair departed for the ferry where they were to cross the Firth of Lorn to Oban, the busiest Caledonia port on the west coast. Brother Aidan's subdued manner, contrary to his everyday demeanor, gave Michael pause. It distressed him to see grief so close to this brother.

The open boat slid effortlessly through the gentle waves as sea gulls hovered, seeking food. Their squawking heralded a new day as the morning breeze gently lifted Michael's hair, its growth quickened since his decision to leave the island as if his body were aligning itself for life in the world. He lifted his head in remembrance.

The two sat in the prow of the boat in silence with Molly secured in the middle until Michael queried, "Do you have Father Callum's letter for the monastery?"

Brother Aidan reached inside his robes, producing a folded parchment which he handed to Michael. "I believe they will want us to stay for at least two days, communing and worshiping with their monks. They have no harper, and with Father Callum singing your praises, I'm sure they'll be expecting some tunes for the prayers."

"Well, that I can do well enough," said Michael. His deeper worry was the expectations that may fall at Armadale. How he wished Father Callum had not made application for that contest. It was too much pressure, not to have played the old tunes in over five years, and for such an auspicious gathering! Practice lay in the hours and days ahead, for they had less than two weeks before arriving on the Isle of Skye.

After paying the ferryman, they left the seaside; Brother Aidan eased Michael onto Molly's back, loaded their packs then headed north of Oban to Ardchattan Priory, the Benedictine monastery recommended by their priest.

After two hours of travel, Michael spied the one-lane path bearing off to the right which led to the monastery. He'd heard the Iona brethren speak of these monks, fervent in their rituals of conservatism and discipline who followed the Rule of St. Benedict without faltering. St. Benedict believed in healthy living, commending the monks to live without distractions, so meals consisted of meat with two additional dishes supplied three times daily. Each monk was given ample bedding such as a horsehair mattress, a wool blanket, a russet coverlet, and a goose-down pillow to secure sufficient rest. Their habits were worn to suit the climate, neither too warm nor too cold. However, these were considered their only luxuries. How different from life at Iona Abbey. But change was on the wind, so Michael took a deep breath in readiness.

The weary pair wound their way along the grassy path leading to the main quarters. The priory, a small group of large-stoned buildings, was located on Loch Etive with enticing gardens already blooming along the water's edge. The doves in the dove-coterie near the stable ruffled their downy plumage at the strangers' arrival as Molly was handed over for care. Michael and Brother Aidan were greeted warmly by a small group of brethren then taken to the head abbot's quarters. Father Callum's letter of reference ensured fine treatment, so the Ionians joined the others for a simple meal before evening prayers.

After dinner, Michael strolled through the gardens, side-stepping the elaborate grave slabs in the private cemetery. Several large stone crosses encircled with a traditional ring around the crossbars denoted a respect for ancestry. A large rowan tree on the south corner, its branches spreading over the graves like a protective cloak, appeared to be guarding these departed souls.

He still felt a little wearied from his ordeal near Duart Castle, but he was determined to say nothing of it to Brother Aidan, nor to anyone else. Some things are better left in the silences of the heart, thought Michael. He would try to live according to his own proclamation of healing. He roved among the new blossoms of bluebells, yarrows, and roses toward the low stone wall separating the loch from the priory. This ocean-fed loch smelled of briny mysteries, too many to be imagined.

The evening starlight flickered as Michael hoisted himself over the wall, pulling his leg over with minor difficulty. His thoughts turned to Rosamond. Before the Duart Castle incident, he'd been ready to give up his wanderlust and traveling career to marry her, yet she never knew. She had longed for a child, his child. She'd seemed content though, and he had accepted her complacency. Michael could not fault her for finding another man when not even news of her harper could be heard on the wind.

But I must know, thought Michael.

He noticed candlelight emanating from the priory, so remembering that he was to play, he carved his path carefully through the blooming herbs and floral array to the main house.

After locating Brother Aidan, who appeared with Michael's new harp, the two joined the brothers for evening prayers. The notes from the harp resonated throughout the rafters, and gentle sighs could be heard throughout the sanctuary. Michael played simple liturgical pieces, but to these listeners it seemed as if the angels themselves undergirded their prayers.

Once dismissed, the brothers heartily thanked Michael for sharing his gift from God, and wished him every blessing on his travels. Brother Aidan smiled, a respite from his sadness, grateful for the musical solace.

The two found their quarters, and within moments Brother Aidan fell sound asleep, so Michael quietly disrobed, slipped underneath the blanket, but sleep would not come. In a few day's time, they would be on the Isle of Skye. Fifteen years had passed since his father's heated words were spoken which led to Michael's hurried departure, from both the island and his family.

Michael closed his eyes, hearing that searing conversation once more in his mind.

"I'll not have any son of mine traveling about like some gypsy, sleeping in taverns with wild women," screamed Lord MacLeod. He paced the gallery where portraits of his ancestors hung, distinguished in their lives and honored in their deaths. "You're my first born, for God's sake! I've given you everything, yet you dismiss this life as if it were rubbish. Michael, what the devil can ye be thinking?" He stared at his favorite son, but not

with loving paternal care as was his nature, but rather complete disdain and bewilderment.

"But, Father, surely you must see how I've been gifted with music," stammered Michael, holding his own ground. The two were matched in height, but there the similarities ended. "I mean no disrespect. Why, you are more than fit, with no need of my taking over for many years to come. Can I not try this, if just for a little while?" Michael was barely twenty, but his longing for adventure drove him beyond the shores of Dunvegan.

His mother sat weeping in the corner, draped in elegant fineries yet sitting in fear of this conversation's outcome.

Lord MacLeod wheeled on his son, standing inches from the lad's face, "If you leave, don't bother ever returning. I shall pass this legacy onto your brother who appreciates his heritage." The elder spat on the floor. "I am done," he said, stomping down the hallway.

"NO!" sobbed Lady MacLeod, covering her face with her palms, but it was too late.

Michael knelt on the floor beside her, trying to console this woman he loved more than anyone else in the world.

But as she laid her hands in her lap, a cold resolve spread across her features. Her loyalties lay with her husband, first and foremost, despite the love she held for her son. "You must go now," she said. "I'll have the servants prepare some food for you, and I will give you money to begin your travels. I've heard there is excellent training for harpers at the sang skule in Dunkeld, just north of Perth, so if you wish to make a living, you should apprentice yourself."

Shocked by this turn of events, Michael laid a gentle kiss upon his mother's cheek, quickly packed some belongings, and with his mother's provisions, headed east towards Dunkeld.

Michael had missed them both over the years, wanting to return, but knowing his father's pride all too well, forgiveness seemed impossible. Finally he drifted to sleep into watery dreams.

Awakened early, Michael and Brother Aidan attended morning matins, followed by a simple breakfast of oat bannocks and tea. Molly, already fed, seemed rested and ready for another day's work. The Benedictine brothers were kindly solicitous, extending their hospitality to future meetings if necessary, so not wishing to delay their new friends' journey, bid them farewell. By mid-morning, Michael and Brother Aidan reached the main track, turned right, and continued their journey north.

The road paralleled Loch Linnhe the first day, providing Michael and Brother Aidan with breathtaking views. By nightfall, the evening sky cleared, so they slept outside near Ballachulish. From there, they followed the loch to Fort William then veered directly west through the lush valley of Glen Finnan. Each night they found lodging without problems and reasonable fares for their meals. Michael practiced the old tunes on breaks, chatting about grand homes where he'd performed, dukes and ladies who had danced to his tunes. Brother Aidan's grief over his mother's death soon dissolved as he made peace with her passing, so choosing life once more, he delighted in hearing Michael's tales: expressing shock, surprise, and amazement at timely intervals which encouraged more outrageous tellings.

Michael even confessed that in spite of all that grandeur and fame, loneliness had been a constant companion. Following the competition, he would set things right, if Rosamond would still have him. He must take the risk.

Braithwait Manor

Laughter bounced off the portraited halls then outside as the nursery maid chased her young charges into the May morning where a familiar young woman strode towards Master Murdoch, dodging the children through the floral maze.

"Why Hannah," said Murdoch, sipping hot tea between mouthfuls of fried eggs, broiled tomatoes, and toast, "I must confess I am surprised to see you." He preferred breakfast in the cool morning air, so the family offered their favorite music instructor a private meal in the gardens each day. "I hope that your presence here portends good fortune for us both," said Murdoch, beaming at Hannah. His assistant Colin sat in the grass, munching on a cranberry muffin.

"I don't rightly know about being a good omen, sir," replied Hannah, laying her traveling bag on the ground as she sat in the iron chair opposite the Master. She breathed deeply, the delicate scent of early roses refreshing her, for her nights at the Barking Seal Inn had been less than restful. Grief visited her still in the dark silences of the night, resulting in lackluster slumber; nevertheless, she plunged forward in her quest. "Sir, I've a favor to ask."

"Anything, my dear girl," he said, giving her such an impish wink that she had to smile.

"I know that you wish for me to sing with you, so, here I am, if you still want me," said Hannah.

"A favor? To want you to sing with me? Why, of course, I do, dear child. It will be a delight, for your voice is sheer perfection," said Murdoch, clapping his hands. "You shall perform with me at Armadale then we'll venture back to Dunkeld where the school can provide you lodgings as you teach young choristers. But it would be helpful for me to know more of your repertoire, so we shall practice in the afternoons while the children here learn their academic lessons. Ah, I have it! I will also ask the Braithwaits if we might not set up a small evening affair, give you a proper audience."

Hannah grimaced, wondering if she'd made the right decision. In years past, her shy nature prevailed, refusing to sing publicly, but she set aside those earlier fears and said with confidence, "Thank you. That would be just fine."

"Now, we only have three more days here in Ballachulish, so I will inquire about a room for you here then attend to the children's morning harpsichord lessons. Please feel free to wander the grounds, for the gardens are just now showing their wealth!" He tapped his linen napkin against his lips three times then taking her hand, said, "Ah, Hannah, you'll not be sorry lass. 'Tis a fine adventure we begin!" He practically skipped back to the manor, leaving Hannah to explore the grounds.

The next two days passed without incident. Each day progressed with Hannah observing the Master and his teaching techniques in the mornings to singing every song Rosamond taught her in the afternoons. She even regaled Murdoch with some of the Gaelic lullabies, a nostalgic salve to her wounded heart. As he listened, the Music Master gained respect for both Hannah and the mother who had passed on this singing tradition. Murdoch deduced that these songs represented the whole of Caledonia, not simply tunes heard by highland farmers. On the eve of the small gathering of local gentry, neighbors of the Braithwaits, Murdoch questioned the young highlander about her song list.

"Hannah, tell me how your mother learned so many variations in her style of songs," he said, packing up his harpsichord scores. Colin scuttled about the room looking for strays, and finding one beneath a song stand, retrieved it and returned it to his master.

"She learned many from her mother, a native of the highlands, but she also brought back songs after her market fair travels to Perth," said Hannah.

"I see, so she heard them performed by traveling singers, regulars at such venues?"

"She might have, but I also know that the musician I once mentioned to you, Michael, was a singer as well as harper. I believe he was close to my mother."

"Yes, that would make sense then," said Murdoch, placing the final papers in his leather satchel. "What matters most is my good fortune that you are so well versed! The school Masters will be more than pleased that I bring them such a rare find." Murdoch took Hannah's hand and kissed it gently. "Now, what shall you sing tonight?"

Until now, singing for Murdoch was like singing at home while doing chores. She simply breathed, in and out, reaching for notes with ease, yet they lacked the luster she knew they often had cast in happier days.

It's difficult to sing anything well but laments when a singer's heart is broken.

However, not wanting to embarrass Murdoch before the Braithwait family by breaking into tears, she said, "Perhaps something the merchants can relate to, like 'The Barnyards of Delgaty' then a simple pastoral tune, such as 'Wild Mountain Thyme'."

"Excellent choices, my dear," said Murdoch. "Every singer must learn how to gauge the audience then select songs to match, or at the very least be appreciated. Begin with 'Wild Mountain Thyme,' lulling them into a serene state then leave them laughing with the barters of the Delgaty market. I shall play the harpsichord prior to your songs then close the program with a few harp selections."

It was settled.

The night arrived much too soon for Hannah's liking, her shoulders drawn up with nervous strain. She paced, attempting to draw out her bodily tension, but to no avail. She wore the green dress given to her at Blair Atholl with her hair up, braiding then twining the twist around her crown. She took out the pearl caul from her mother's wooden box, encasing her hair. For this debut, she wanted to look the part of a real singer, even if she felt like an actor playing a role in some dramatist's fancy.

Gone were the well-laid plans of wife on the MacLaren farm. Gone were the fairs to sell her woven goods. Without Lukas and Rosamond, those dreams twisted into unrecognizable shapes.

She must create a new life for herself and her child. With Murdoch's generous offer, she had seized the opportunity. So firmly placing herself on this new path, Hannah ventured into the dining room.

Tonight. It begins tonight.

She ate very little at dinner, chatting primarily with the children. It seemed easier to listen to their stories of garden faeries or rambunctious antics intended to raise the cook's terrible temper rather than answer probing adult questions. The guests seemed amiable enough, happy for an evening out. The meal proved a success, but the best was still to come.

The music room, lit by candle wall sconces, accommodated one harpsichord, a rectangular psaltery, one four-foot harp, and several music stands centralized for tonight's affair. A semi-circle of chairs had been created where listeners eagerly awaited the after-dinner entertainment. Master Murdoch introduced both himself and his protégée as Colin sat to his right, ready to turn the pages. He played several rollicking tunes to begin the evening on a cheery note then moved into more sophisticated scores. The audience applauded as the Master bowed after the final note.

"And now, it is with great pleasure that I introduce to you a new singer, Mistress Hannah MacLaren!" He waved his palm to her, ushering her to stand before the harpsichord. He reseated himself, ready to accompany at her signal.

Steadying herself before the nameless faces, she took a deep breath then said, "I will begin with a song which brings to mind the rolling hills of my home in Feshiebridge, 'Wild Mountain Thyme'." She breathed deeply and nodded to Murdoch who played introductory rolling triads. Hannah began to sing.

"Oh the summer time is coming

And the trees are sweetly blooming

And the wild mountain thyme

Grows around the blooming heather.

Will you go, lassie go?"

As she rounded into the familiar chorus, the room swelled as listeners and players alike sang together. She held her pain in reserve as the second verse began.

"I will build my love a bower

By yon clear, crystal fountain

And all around the bower

I'll pile flowers of the mountain.

Will you go, lassie, go?"

Her voice emanated with such clarity throughout the household that even the kitchen staff huddled by the doors to listen. Once more the chorus filled the room. She realized her mistake now in choosing this song, for the third spoke about taking a new lover. But she persevered, and closed with only a slight tremble in her voice. She bowed at their applause, grateful for the break in her concentration.

She glanced over at Murdoch, who smiled and nodded in pleasure. She quickly moved into the market song, singing unaccompanied, which told of a farmer who was sold an unfit pair of horses, yet the ruse remained undiscovered until the farmer reached his home. Though a familiar tune, the audience laughed in all the right places, as if hearing it for the first time. Once more Hannah bowed then regained her seat. Sighs of relief melted within - she had done it.

Murdoch played a sweet melody on the harp to close the evening, and all were more than complimentary to both musician and singer as they filed out the door to their respective homes. The Braithwaits were thrilled to have offered such quality performances to their guests, hoping news of this triumphant evening would travel quickly throughout their community.

As for Hannah, Murdoch informed her they would depart for Armadale Castle the next morning after breakfast. He congratulated himself again and again for having spotted her talent then profusely thanked her for joining his retinue before retiring.

She lay huddled beneath the soft woolen blanket, wondering at the incredulity of it all. How quickly life transforms itself, she thought, when one is simply willing to allow it.

Armadale Castle - would he be there?

With motherhood now a reality, Hannah's own desire to know the truth of her parentage, her heritage, intensified. She determined that night never to lie to her daughter, regardless of the cost. Rosamond had not trusted Hannah to hold the truth, and now it might be too late.

CHAPTER TWENTY-ONE

Armadale Castle

The entrance way to the grey stone castle revealed delicate bluebell lavenders and spotted orchids in purples and fuchsias dotting the purple moor grasses. Atop the three-storied fortress walls, the tooth-like pattern of alternating merlons and crenels offered a defensive stance rather than the more sculpted turret peaks announcing the seat of elegance and high society. However, despite its overbearing facade, the light-hearted musicians, having traveled from all over Caledonia for this musical competition, filled the air with festivity.

As Murdoch's wagon plodded along beneath the stone archway heavily laden with May ivy, Hannah surveyed the open courtyard. She was immediately reminded of the sounds and smells of the Perth market place where stalls lined the inner perimeter. After goods were unloaded, both horses and wagons were escorted towards the stables, just south of the main estate. Heavy serge coverings in russets and browns covered what appeared to be harps as their masters conversed like magpies, delighted at this reunion with old friends. Murdoch himself was regaled with welcomes upon his entrance, waving in response and smiling broadly at his contemporaries. Hannah knew she could have found no better mentor, and offered a silent prayer of thanksgiving to St. Brigid for this bit of good fortune.

After securing their personal bags and instruments, Colin took charge of the wagon while Murdoch introduced Hannah into her new life. Never before had her hand been kissed so frequently nor her handshake pumped with such vigor as player after player invited her into this kindred of performers. With her immediate family gone, save her unborn child, this open reception filled her with some anticipation of their expectations regarding her talents. Subtle fears began to rise once more, sneering, "Who do you think you are, anyway? Some grand singer like these folks? You sing well enough, but do you have what it takes to be a performer?" Instead of greeting this new group with an open heart, she found herself shying away from their gracious acceptances. How could she belong to any family when she still didn't know her own heritage?

She had to talk to Michael.

"Master Murdoch," said Hannah, "can you point me in the direction of where we'll be sleeping? After I put my bag away, I thought I'd wander the grounds a bit, maybe practice a few songs."

"Of course, dear," said Murdoch. He looked about the crowd then said, "See that woman in the yellow frock? That's Sally. She lodges the women. Tell her you're with me, and she'll take great care of you. I'll meet you here later for the evening meal - oh it's such a grand occasion the night before the contest! Now, as for a walk, there are some lovely sculptured gardens along the sea wall if you fancy a bit of privacy. Good place for singing to the sea." He hugged her fiercely, like that of a long-lost father reconciled with his devoted daughter, full of pride and joy. Then he assimilated into the motley crowd amongst his fellow musicians.

Sally took Hannah to the second floor to a large room where extra cots lined the sturdy stone walls. She motioned the young singer towards a bed beneath colorful tapestries of unicorn hunts and wild stags which hung from the high ceiling to the tip of her bed-coverings then quietly slipped downstairs. Similar tapestries draped the walls while finely carved wooden chairs, with plump red and orange embroidered seat cushions, sat at conversing angles in the corners. Iron sconces with large cream candles hung at regular intervals, illuminating the fineries. Hannah took in these new surroundings - she had never seen such elegance and grandeur! She closed her eyes and breathed deeply, marveling at how Fate continued to twist her life.

Were it not for the sadness that still weighted her heart, she would have been exceeding her dreams. Gravity grounded her.

Not wanting to disappoint Master Murdoch, Hannah decided to practice then allow the Master to choose those songs best suited for the competition. Following his advice, she found her way past the main entranceway through the wild-flowered lawn to the trails leading through the formal gardens. A large, solitary monk leading a riderless, grey farm horse passed through the main gates, unnoticed by the young singer.

Tall verdant hedges created labyrinthine trails, while stony-eyed rabbits, frozen in their creator's gaze, peeped through the vegetation. Additional statues of grazing deer remained steadfast in winding corners while thinly-clad goddesses allowed gentle flowing fountains to pour from their palms. The plentitude of stone works reminded Hannah that she was in the presence of wealth.

Needing to feel closer to her highland roots, she meandered through this maze to the forest which edged the estate. The salty island air replaced the fresh Caledonia pine scents of her home while the oceanic woods calmed her spirit as she walked slowly beneath its leafy canopy.

Being in the woods brought her mother's voice to mind, so in Rosamond's honor Hannah warmed up her voice by singing "The Song of the Seal," a childhood favorite. Neither she nor her mother had ever seen the ocean, yet through the song they could feel its promise of mystery. Since none of the highlanders knew the tune, Hannah wondered where Rosamond had learned it. The rowan and white beam leaves trembled above her as the tune was released:

"The seal maid sings on yonder reef

The spell-bound seals draw near

A lilt that lures beyond belief

Mortals enchanted hear."

The vocabell chorus, used for maintaining the rhythmic flow, floated through the air as easily as never-ceasing waves upon the sea:

"Coir an oir an oir an eer o,

Coir an oir an oir an eer o.

Coir an oir an oir an ee lalyran

Coir an oir an eer o."

She breathed deeply, supporting the higher octaves with a subtle strength. As she remembered how Rosamond loved to hear her daughter sing, Hannah's voice trembled with the memory. She wondered if singing such a tune in public would arouse too much emotion now. She would wait for Master Murdoch's leading.

Hannah moved into the next verse, her favorite because it blended sea and field, ocean and farm.

"The wandering ploughman

halts his plough

The maid her milking stays

And sheep on hillside, bird on bough

Pause and listen in amaze."

When she'd sung halfway through the chorus, she stopped, as a male harmony came threading through the wood, in perfect accompaniment. She turned to see a man, dressed in traveling attire, sitting on a stone outcrop. He sang full throated, matching Hannah's clarity.

He smiled as she approached. "Please don't stop on my account," he said, "I didn't mean to intrude. It's just that I've not heard that tune in many's a year, and it felt good to fill myself with it again. The mystery of the selkie lies in the last verse. Do you know it?"

Hannah, looking bemused and bewildered, confessed that she did not.

"Then I'll finish, if I may." He rose, and singing with a voice rich and full, made his presence known throughout the wood.

"Was it a dream? Were all asleep?

Of did she cease her lay?

For the seals with a splash

dive into the deep,

And the world goes on again."

Hannah rejoined him in the chorus, their tones blending like mated songbirds.

Michael nodded his head, as in days of old, and discovered a deep satisfaction, feeling his soul revitalized. He looked at Hannah saying, "Well, miss, you've a fine voice, especially for one so young. Have you had any training?"

"Well, not exactly," she replied, "my mother taught me that song, along with many others besides the more popular Gaelic songs traditionally sung in the Highlands. For training, she showed me how to listen to the birds, to mimic their tunes."

"Ah, a smart woman, for I learned that way myself before my music apprenticeship," said Michael. "But if you come from the Highlands, however did she learn that particular tune, for it's not widely known. Did she travel much?"

"Aye, to Perth for market twice a year," replied Hannah. The young woman's defenses, pliable due to her earlier singing, gave this stranger entrance for his ways were gentle. She felt compelled to answer his professional curiosity about her musical background, not observing the trickle into her personal life. "She knew a harper who taught his songs to her, then she passed them on to me."

Michael studied her closely, examining the earnest face before him. "And where exactly is your home?"

"A small village along the River Feshie."

Michael now wondered if perhaps this young woman had news of his beloved, so he ventured on. "Perhaps you've met a friend of mine, who lives in Feshiebridge itself. She's a local weaver, named Rosamond MacFey. Do you know her?"

Hannah laughed for the first time in many moons. "Know her? I should say so. For she's the woman I've been telling you about. I'm her daughter Hannah, Hannah MacFey."

Michael grappled with his wizard-faced cane, standing up abruptly. "What the devil do you mean, her daughter?" He gasped aloud as he now recognized the face of his beloved in this young singer's visage, framed not with brown hair but a burnished russet, much like his own.

Hannah was shaken by the man's contorted expression, noting now an ugly scar racing down his face. But then she saw it - a small harp leaning against the stone. "I am Rosamond's daughter, her only daughter, but I'm guessing by that harp at your side that you be Michael. Am I right?"

"I am."

"Her lover from the Perth Market, all those years ago?"

Michael stood amazed at this young woman's effrontery, yet the accusation held truth, so he could not deny it. "I'm the man who has loved her for more years than I reckon you've been alive, lassie."

Unwilling to make any mistake, Hannah plunged her hand beneath her traveling cloak and pulled the abalone necklace into Michael's view. "Did you give this to her?"

Michael eyed the love token he'd not seen for many years. He smiled in remembrance of the lovemaking after the reception of his gift. "Aye, that I did. It was the last time I saw her, a little over five years ago."

The harper before her looked nothing like the handsome man her mother had described, yet here he stood, with all the right answers. But did he hold the crucial answer?

Anger over years of watching her mother's heartbreak spilled over Hannah's lips, "How could you leave her if you loved her so much? Don't you know that loving you, all this time, has done nothing but break her heart? She never loved anyone other than you. She even lied to me about my father, saying he died when I was a baby. But it has to be you, it just has to be . . . you." Her shoulders tremored as shock waves rippled down her spine.

"Hold on, a moment, girl." Michael stood inches from her face now. "Are you saying that I'm your father?"

"Yes."

"Well that's a bold faced lie." He turned now, regaining his seat on the stone.

Hannah expected his denial, for after all, Hannah believed Michael had rejected Rosamond five years ago when she finally told him of Hannah's existence. But this arrogance unnerved her. "Don't you dare deny it, you bastard!" she screamed, her calm speaking voice rising in decibels with each pronouncement. "She must have had her reasons for not telling you at my birth, but you left her, five years ago with no word, nothing in all this time. She must have told you then. How could you reject her like that?" Tears began, wetting her long black lashes over the feral green eyes.

"Leave her? Leave the only woman I've truly loved? Why, I was planning on marrying her, the following Lammas Fair, but . . ." his voice faltered.

Hannah paced circles in the long grasses, almost stumbling as they entangled her feet. This was not how she had imagined this conversation, not at all. "But nothing. I wonder if she knows what a coward you've become. You are nothing like the handsome harper she has fancied her thoughts with all these years. If you'd had any decency at all, you'd have made her an honorable woman instead of making us live with the shame and gossiping villager tongues."

Her words spat on his deformity, and they burned.

"Hannah, sit down for a moment."

"I won't be told . . . ,"

"I said sit down, lass. There's some straightening out to be done here, and I swear I cannot do it with you whirling about like that. Now sit!"

His commanding voice so surprised Hannah that like a child hearing her father's voice, she obeyed. She looked up at him, unwilling to show weakness by crying, yet the tears leaked out the corners creating tiny streaks down her cheeks.

"Now, first of all, I am the harper that met your mother, twice a year, in Perth. If I'd had my way I'd have seen her much more, but my harping life took me all over Caledonia, so in the early stages we decided to not speak of our lives apart from one another, but to simply enjoy the time together. There were no constraints on loving another, yet as years passed, it became clear that we each had hearts only meant for one another."

Hannah listened intently, remembering those earlier days when her mother returned from the fairs so full of life and sheer happiness. The cause of that joy now sat in front of her.

Michael continued. "Five years ago I decided to give up my traveling ways, for I ached to be with Rosamond. I thought I could marry her, even teach locally perhaps. I planned on asking her to marry me that Beltane, but I took a wedding on the Isle of Mull just before the fair." Here he stopped, his finger grazing his cheek as was his habit when recalling that night. "I was badly beaten afterwards by an angry groom and left by the roadside to die. Some of the brethren from the Isle of Iona discovered me, lying in my blood-soaked cloak, and took me to their abbey. I've been on that island ever since, transcribing scripture and playing the harp for services."

"But why didn't you send word? She all but died from grief after that first year, and nobody in Perth knew a thing."

"I was too ashamed for her to see me. You've said it yourself – I'm not the man she loved. And so for years I've hidden myself away, unable to face her rejection, for it would crush my will to live."

Hannah breathed deeply, letting the story take hold in her mind. She tried to see how his disfigurement could stop him from coming back to her mother, but what about her, his daughter? "But what about me? Didn't she ever tell you about me?"

"Darlin' girl, I would have passed through tempest seas to reach Feshiebridge and make Rosamond my wife if I'd known I was a father. And since she never told me, I can only assume that it was someone else, and not me." He stared at her thoughtfully, half wishing that he were her father, for he saw the spirit and strength of this girl, and knew he could love her.

Hannah rose, a bit unsteadily, a cold myth laying hold of her, saying, "Then the villagers have been right all along. I am the child of some bastard who either didn't have the nerve to come forward or," she cocked her head to one side, "didn't really belong in this world. Either way, I'll never know now." She stared beyond Michael into the forest, its mysteries as deep as her own.

"But why not simply ask your mother? Surely, with you now practically a woman yourself, she'd be willing to tell you the truth."

"It's too late."

"Ah, it is never too late. Why, in fact, I've finally plucked up enough courage to make her my wife, if she'll still have me. I plan on going to her just as soon as the competition is over."

Hannah turned, the tears now steadily falling, "No, you don't understand. It's too late, for both of us. My mother is dead."

That final sentence reverberated throughout Michael's entire being, with the word "dead" bouncing off the walls of his now empty heart. "But you're mistaken, surely, I mean, it cannot be," as his voice trailed off. "But how?"

"Small pox. She healed from the worst of the pox itself before I left, but the illness had ravaged her body, leaving her with little strength remaining. I heard the news while traveling home as two women passed me. I could hardly believe it myself. So I came here, looking for you, hoping you could tell me the truth about being my father. You see, my love died the night before we were to be wed, so now without Lukas and my mother, I am alone." Her right hand gently grazed her belly, reassuring the unborn child within that it would never feel alone.

Michael understood sorrow, and felt anguish that one so young should have to shoulder it so early in life. He still had not completely taken in his own loss, but he knew what must be done now. "Hannah, even though I'm not you're real father, would you be willing to accept the protection of a man who dearly loved your mother? As long as I have breath, I will not have Rosamond's only daughter live as a cast away on this earth."

His offered surprised both Hannah and himself, yet Michael felt compelled to make amends for his beloved, and if that meant caring for her daughter then so be it.

"I find that a very generous offer," said Hannah, kneeling before him. "I'm not certain if I can accept, but I will not say no."

He took her hands in his, placing a gentle kiss upon them. " 'Tis much to be considered. Let us get through this bloody competition tomorrow then travel together to Feshiebridge, if for nothing more than to pay respects. After that, we'll see."

"Agreed," said Hannah. She rose slowly, but as she began walking towards the house she turned, and beheld Michael, head down in his lap as his shoulders shook. At least now this pain was shared.

She whipped her traveling cloak about her shoulders, despite the warming breeze off the sea. Attempting to regain the path, she made a wrong turn in the garden and found herself lost in the greenery of Armadale Castle. Bewildered yet unconcerned at being lost, she sat down on a wooden bench and simply sobbed.

Thoughts ran like swirling wraiths inside her head, her temples throbbing. The secret of her father's identity now truly laid in the grave with her mother's bones, never to see the light of revelation. She suddenly felt dirty and unloved. Would any man ever want her like this, the product a lusty, ritual rutting? Or perhaps her mother was taken against her will, and that the lie obscured the horrific event? Possibilities of her conception grew darker with each option until Hannah could stand it no longer.

She held her belly, her tears staining her shift as she cried out, "I will never make you feel unwanted. You were made out of purest love, no matter what anybody says! I will protect you from the evil tongues that have made my life a living hell. We will move away, far away where we can start anew. I swear to you, I will make things right."

A sudden movement on the path behind her startled Hannah, but thinking it only a small animal, she dismissed it. Imagine the surprise when Lachlan Grant surfaced around the bend to behold his friend Hannah, sitting on a bench, in absolute despair.

"Hannah, sweet girl, can it be you?" he asked, sitting down beside her now. He took out a handkerchief and gently began wiping her cheeks, easing away the pain.

"Oh, Lachlan," she said, then without hesitation, buried her head in his chest as he opened his arms to her. He cradled her while the tears flowed freely, for there were no words - too much had happened.

He waited, holding her while he stroked her hair in a rhythmic, cooing fashion.

For several moments they sat in silence until Hannah lifted her head, the anguish, for now, spent.

She looked at his face, and through her daze saw that he looked even older than before. But how could that be when they had only parted a few weeks prior? "Lachlan, why are you here?" she asked, straightening herself. She ran her fingers through her hair as if to shed the emotional tide.

"Odd, I might say, to find you here as well, Hannah," said Lachlan.

"I am in the competition tomorrow, for singers, in the company of Master Murdoch."

"But you were going back to Feshiebridge when last we parted. What caused you to change your mind?"

At this, Hannah told him everything. Rosamond's death. Discovering Michael. Her questionable identity. The stories of these devastating events tumbled headlong like a roaring waterfall after a heavy spring thaw.

Lachlan listened to every word, sensing their significance in this young woman's life.

"And I'm pregnant, with Lukas's child," said Hannah. "That is the only light in this abysmal thing I call a life. Master Murdoch has offered me a position teaching songs in Dunkeld at the sang skule, and I'm thinking it could be a way for me to make a suitable living, for me and my child. I don't wish to return to Feshiebridge with a baby and no father, like my mother did so many years ago. I'll not have this child brought up in such a shadow of shame."

Lachlan took her hands in his. At her touch, his own unspoken grief surfaced, but he held it in reserve. He would tell Hannah soon enough. "I admire you, Hannah, for wanting only the best for your child. Know this now," he said, lifting her face to match his gaze, "if there is anything that I can do for you, my dear friend, please do not hesitate, for even in our brief times together, you have become important to me. Do you believe me?"

She looked into his eyes, and saw the truth of his words. "Yes," she whispered.

"I don't know how, but it will all work out. Now, let's get some food in you, for I fear you've worn yourself out with sorrow. This child of yours needs tending now." He stood up, offering his hand to Hannah, who then rose slowly by his side. He twined her arm through his as he easily maneuvered the vegetative maze.

"You seem to know this path," said Hannah. "Have you been here before, Lachlan?"

"Aye, lass, many times. You see, the Clan Donald is my wife's family. That is why I am here," he said.

"So you've brought her with you? I will be honored to meet her."

"That will not be possible."

"But why ever not?" She began to question his vow so recently stated. She attempted to pull herself away, but he clung to her tightly.

"The reason I am here is to return some of my wife's personal items to her family. For you see, she died on the night of my return." He was staring straight ahead as he spoke, as if looking through a veil of grey mist.

"Your wife is dead? But how, Lachlan?"

"My dearest always had a delicate nature, but her heart was never strong. It seems that while I was away she contracted a deep cold in her chest. A fevered chill took her to the grave."

Hannah stopped, knowing she had mistaken sorrow for his aged appearance. "Lachlan, I am so sorry," she said, and clung both hands to his now as they continued through the garden.

As they reached the lawn, bouncing notes of lively jigs and reels met them for the feast was about to begin. The solemn pair strode beneath the arches into the open courtyard where tables were laden with platters of Hotch-Potch beef stew, oysters, sliced venison, and spicy ham dips intermingled with cheese bridies, sausage rolls, and meat pies. Bread bowls overflowed with creamy cheese soups while wooden bowls held bright lemon yellows and citrus oranges. Mulled wine overflowed the earthen mugs, along with spiced ales and cider. The celebration had begun!

Lachlan and Hannah sat in an isolated corner, both with too much on their minds to converse any longer. The future was so uncertain, yet tomorrow would come.

CHAPTER TWENTY-TWO

The common seal barked relief after concluding a lengthy swim, pulling itself onto the rocky shoreline paralleling Armadale Castle. Dusk settled on the sleek grey pelt, casting a murky shadow in the gloaming. Strong human arms pushed through the fur coat, replacing clawed flippers with firm, finger-nailed hands. The hood slipped back, revealing long strands of black curls in wet spirals falling onto Ronan's broad shoulders. He rose, a man once more.

His route had been long, but a natural choice of other Scottish seals in the early summer months, spanning the western coastline of Caledonia from south of Iona to the far northern reaches of the Isle of Lewis. He knew these waters well, both as man and seal, for it was here, on the Isle of Skye, that he had been fostered to the MacDonald relations, raised as a son, and dearly loved in spite of his complex selkie inheritance. Their love healed the broken spaces of his heart where his own family had abandoned him.

His early childhood days were often spent playing tag with his cousin Eleanor through the mazed gardens or in later years, boating with her brothers - Coll, Bruce, and Eoghan. The children wondered at the mystery surrounding their cousin when he would gaze out to sea as if hypnotized, but only Laird and Lady MacDonald possessed knowledge of Ronan's secret, hiding the child's need to transform. Since the age of ten, Ronan had played in a protected cove as a seal among the rocks fortifying the sea wall with his uncle as guardian, never staying long but satisfying his undeniable desire for the sea, for a season. It was only when he gained manhood that he learned how to control his novel nature.

Ronan navigated the white stone boulders leading to the sea wall, stopping at a small stack of five rocks topped with moss. After years of being both man and selkie, Ronan had created similar caches along the Scottish seaboard where clothes were kept in watertight sacks, ready for his trek with humanity. He quickly uncovered the bag, emptying its contents on the sand and replacing them with his own seal skin. He dressed himself, then hoisting the sack over his shoulder, made his way down through the tree-lined path to the open grounds in front of his family home. His secret had remained well hidden, even after all these years, for his aunt and uncle told others that Ronan was a sailor, at sea for months at a time, returning whenever he was able. He often arrived at the end of May, so Mary, the cook, was delighted yet unsurprised as she saw the young master entering the kitchen through the private servant's entrance.

"Well, iff'n it ain't Master Ronan!" said Mary, slipping her doughy arms about his neck. "I'm always happy to feed a lad with such a hearty appetite."

"Good to see you, too, Mary," said Ronan, returning the embrace. He noticed a few more straggling greys peeping underneath her cap's rim. She had been with the family long before his arrival some twenty-five years back, shouldering the responsibilities of the kitchen alone but allowing younger bodies now to do the work. Her apron could not conceal the short, stout cook's love for pastries, a small pleasure she afforded herself in her elder years.

"Now, I'd love to sit a spell, and hear your wonderful stories, but you may have noticed we've quite a crowd to feed tonight with all these music folk about. Will you be stayin' long?"

"A bit, Mary, long enough to fill you with new tales," said Ronan, leaning against the wooden counter and slipping a cheese bridie into his mouth.

"That's my little Ronie! No matter how old you get, you still remember how old Cook loves those stories about the sea. Bless you," she said, and after placing a wet kiss on his cheek, she returned to shouting out commands like a naval commander upon the sea.

Ronan picked up his sack, slipped up the back stairs to his bedroom on the second floor then tucked himself into the downy goodness of his bed for a much needed rest. He was sure the family would know of his return, thanks to the wagging tongues of the kitchen staff. He was anxious to see Coll, the eldest MacDonald, Ronan's truest friend in all the world. For though they were cousins, Coll treated him like a brother. But tomorrow would come soon enough, along with the competition and all its wonderful songs and tunes.

Down the hall from Ronan's bedchamber, Hannah slept little that night, flipping like a bannock on a hot griddle, with no nighttime reprieve due to the external choir of snores from the other women performers as they slogged into bed at all hours of the night. She was grieved that Lachlan's wife had died, for as the evening progressed he'd shared with Hannah more of his life in Kingussie, particularly his love for Eleanor. Now they shared the deep anguish that resides with the living when such tragedy occurs.

But add to this sorrow her confusion over the meeting with Michael, for she was certain not only that he was indeed her father, but that he had known so for years, and in that knowledge had rejected both Hannah and Rosamond. Yet the apparent truth disclosed that her preconceived notions were nothing more than pure myth - falsehoods born out of necessity. Hannah simply never wanted to believe that her birth had been a mistake, but rather a deliberate act of love.

The infernal, internal refrain of Nell Robertson's voice rang clear - - Bastard!

By morning, Hannah wore a melancholic mask: wearied swollen eyelids crusted with spent tears. Her despondency remained private as she appeared unnoticed by the other performers who were slowly rising from a long night of revelries, their sluggish limbs scraping slowly across the hard, wooden floors. Fortunately, the competitions did not begin until noon.

Now, what should she wear? Hannah would have chosen the green dress gifted to her at Blair Atholl, but her belly was now too swollen for such a fitted garment. She pulled out her golden kirtle with the purple embroidery, noting the fresh appearance despite the crumpled lines of fabric. Its fashionable bodice could be loosely laced at the base without disclosing Hannah's pregnancy. She opened the wooden treasure box and withdrew the pearl caul, holding it up to the morning light. The opalescence quality of each pearl shimmered, as if by magic. Hannah twisted her hair behind her head, securing the caul with extra hair pins. "For you, Ma," she whispered.

She met with Murdoch after breakfast, who, noting her haggard appearance, stared at his new singer with alarm. "I trust you slept well," he lied, but believing the weariness was due to something more than a night of merrymaking, he focused on the business at hand - choosing the two most dynamic songs in Hannah's repertoire. Murdoch knew that many singers were just now being allowed into the musical competitions, once held for instruments only, so the judges would expect popular folk tunes rather than elevated styles of melody. He opted to surprise them with this young highlander's offerings by having her lure them into a vocal lair - one folk tune and one Gaelic lament. The first, accompanied by Murdoch on the clavichord, would prove her perfect pitch through the simplicity of the symphonic melody, a pairing of two octaves. However, the lament, sung a cappella, could follow higher ranges, allowing the emotions to layer the melody with ornamentations of trills and grace notes. Hannah possessed a skilled voice, yet how she came by such complex patterns remained a mystery to the music master, and he counted on this very secret to impress the judges.

The two pieces chosen were the folk song "The Wark O' the Weavers," in honor of Rosamond, and "Gradh Geal Mo Chridh" ["Fair Love of my Heart"] for the lament portraying a young woman determined to wed her beloved. Hannah knew both pieces would be emotionally charged for her, and tried to dissuade the Master, but he would not hear of it.

"You will need to learn how to take those emotions, raw though they may be, and use them to your advantage," said Master Murdoch, sifting through his own scores of harp music. "Let the notes carry your sadness, lingering in the air as the stilled heartbeats of a broken lover, but do not give yourself entirely over to it, for if you do, the tears will fall too readily."

"I am in your hands, Master," she said, sighing heavily at this new road she had chosen.

All morning one could hear various scales resounding through the courtyard by flutes, recorders, drons (bagpipes) and quhissels (whistles). The highland clarsech, strung with metal strings, overran its gentler opponent, the Lowland harp with gut strings while the other stringed instruments, such as the psaltery and dulcimer, supplied lengthening tones mixed with short, skipping notes. In the background percussive beats of the kettledrum, cymbals, and bells pounded out the excitement of the day. Soon the hand bells tolled - noon had arrived - the competitions could begin!

The grand hall, decorated with festive ribbons trailing the walled sconces, floral arrangements bedecking tall iron stands, and greenery boughs over each window arch, suggested good will to all the participants. At one end stood an elevated wooden stage with several music stands crowded at the back along with a clavichord and organ. To the left of this performance dais sat a long, clothed table for the reigning MacDonalds, paralleling the judges table on the stage's right where three elderly men sat. The performers were huddled in groups, holding their instruments, while local gentry were seated in a semicircle before the stage, playing the role of the listening audience.

Hannah's eyes roved over the wealthy family members: Laird and Lady MacDonald, their sons, Coll, Eoghan, and Bruce, and a lovely young woman she supposed was the latter's wife. At the end of the line, Hannah was startled to see a familiar face seated next to Lachlan, who seemed still engrossed in his own mourning. She recognized the dark-headed man from the sea wall in Ballachulish, the one who told Hannah she was with child. She did not recall his name, but thought it peculiar that he should be here. She discovered herself staring at him, unintentionally, when he suddenly turned in her direction under that scrutinizing gaze, smiled then nodded in acknowledgment.

She had not seen Michael all morning, and wondered if perhaps the news of Rosamond's death proved lethal to his playing. She had mentioned him to Master Murdoch who seemed pleased that his previous pupil should be here once more, remembering when Michael's harping had been unparalleled. Yet underlying his desire to see Michael was a thread of jealousy, for if anyone could steal this coveted harping prize from Murdoch's talented grasp it would be that man.

The Master of Revels, dressed in motley silks, unrolled the long scrolled parchment filled with the day's players, arranged by instrumental groupings and specialties. "My lords and ladies, the MacDonald Annual Music Competition will now officially begin! We wish to extend all courtesies and thanks to the MacDonald family for their generous hospitality in hosting such a prestigious event, one that thrills the heart of any Scottish musician. Within each musical grouping, players will be asked to share two works. Applause should be held until the conclusion of the second tune. Judges will take notes on each performer but reserve final judgments until the entire group has finished. Winning pronouncements will be made at the conclusion of the last group with the awarding of prizes. So, let us now begin!"

The first group to play was the bowed instruments: the fiddle and the viol. Names were called as each performer took the stage. Jigs and reels abounded while a few slow airs altered the pace. Next came the woodwinds whose fast-paced melodies set every toe to tapping. The percussive instruments accompanied various players throughout the day, leaving the singers and harpers last.

The harpers were the most plentiful, taking almost two hours to complete their presentations. Most played on lowland harps, gentle airs whose soft strains floated like butterflies over the crowd. Master Murdoch had chosen two sophisticated pieces, played upon his clarsech with nimble dexterity as rills and triplets in glissando style graced the audience. He bowed with a flourish at his conclusion, feeling confidant of his win.

"Next, Michael, from Iona," shouted the Master of Revels.

Michael eased his way through the crowd while Brother Aidan carried the clarsech bestowed by the brethren of Iona. Vanity overcame Michael's sense of practicality, having left his cane with his belongings. He would not be pitied, so he walked slowly, deliberately placing each footfall with precision on the solid wooden flooring. Brother Aidan placed the harp in the center of the stage as Michael ascended, slow intakes of breath shot through the pain of each step. He sat, harp between his legs at the ready. He bowed his head toward the lead table of MacDonalds then grinned ever so slightly at his dear friend, Ronan.

The selkie mouthed, "Good luck!"

Hannah, standing next to Murdoch, raised her hand, smiling at him and filling him with confidence.

The time was here to reclaim his musical birthright which had lain dormant these last five years. His fears of ever performing in public again now lay, as dust, at his feet. Regardless of the physical changes, the spirit of a performer still reigned within his heart. The simple prayer tunes had been nothing but practice for such a skilled player as Michael, keeping his fingers limber for the day when he would once again return to the stage.

Now was the time.

He closed his eyes, reviewing the two tunes briefly in his head. He repressed the sorrowful thoughts about his beloved highland lass, put fingertips to strings, and played. The first air created a magic all its own: gentle rolling notes filled with poetry of fresh fields, birdsong, and gleaming sunshine. A hush fell over the room as each listener became transported into idyllic meadows amongst meandering hillsides.

Master Murdoch wrung his hands together, shaking his head from side to side in defeat.

Hannah found herself longing for home.

Despite the Master of Revel's ruling, applause rippled through the audience, reverie guiding each hand. Rather than stand, Michael simply bowed his head in appreciation then continued with his second piece. He had chosen a lovely highland folk piece, to honor his dearest love, having practiced more complex patterns than normally played with such a popular tune. His fingers darted over the strings like mating bees in flight, revealing an expertise not yet experienced by this audience. He allowed the music to carry him, back to the green hills of Feshiebridge where his sweet Rosamond had lived. He swayed, his eyes closed while in his imagination he saw only the sights and sounds brought to him by the music: the delicate lines of her smile, the sparkle in her deep brown eyes, the silken strands that framed her beauty.

Those features now lay deep within the earth's womb, never to bask in the sunshine of his love again. A darkness came over Michael, and without realizing it, he changed tunes. His fingers never stopped, but the discord was more than evident as a melancholic melody pervaded the hall. Ironically, it was the same tune that he had played at Duart Castle those many years ago which had been his undoing.

He stopped - abruptly. Heavy silence met his ceasing, as the confused listeners sat motionless. A single clapping, emanating from Ronan, stirred the crowd into polite applause. Brother Aidan took the harp and escorted Michael off the stage.

He was no longer broken, as he had been these past few years, for his first playing had now proven that. But he honored his Rosamond's memory by grieving, and would let this pain play its course. If he had learned anything these past few months, it was that by holding onto the pain, he had given it power over his life. By releasing it, giving into the fullness of the emotion, he would eventually heal his battered heart.

As he followed Brother Aidan towards the back of the room, Michael passed the MacDonald family. A young woman reached across the table to congratulate him, shaking his hand and saying

"Thank you" so softly he barely heard it. But as he looked into her eyes, he saw the lovely Isobel from the fated wedding. Recognition told him the man beside her was his attacker, her husband Bruce MacDonald. Bruce cared nothing about this contest, bored by his perfunctory family duty, but this scene between his wife and a harper brought back memories. His jealousy noted her kindness, and he found himself looking into the face of the harper he had beaten years ago.

Bruce grabbed Michael's hand from his wife's grasp, holding it tightly and pulling Michael across the table so sharply that his elbow dug into the table.

Ronan rose quickly, ready to restrain his cousin while Bruce leaned in, his head close beside Michael's ear and whispered, "Ah, harper, we meet again, do we? I see I've made a lasting impression on you," then with his free hand, attempted to graze Michael's facial scar.

A swift movement stayed the bully as Michael defended himself, grabbing Bruce's hand then slamming their joined fists onto the table with a loud crack.

The crowd seemed oblivious to this exchange, partaking in private conversations, but Hannah and Murdoch both turned toward the sound and were shocked to see Michael in such a tortured fray.

"Stay, child. Let the men settle this," said Murdoch.

Hannah took the Master's advice.

The jarring motion, paired with a resounding wooden smack, startled the rest of the MacDonald family, all turning in Bruce's direction. Knowing his son's quick temper, Laird MacDonald had leapt to his feet, attempting to avoid any scandal at such an auspicious public occasion. He pulled backwards on his son's broad shoulders while with Ronan's assistance, they wrenched the two men apart.

"You'll never touch me again, MacDonald," hissed Michael, spitting out contemptuous words. "No more, do you hear? I said no more!" He backed away, slamming the table once more then strode confidently through a stunned crowd, despite the pain in his leg, leaving Laird MacDonald to deal with his son.

"A moment, Uncle?" asked Ronan, pulling the large redheaded man aside. In hushed whispers Ronan revealed the reason for this volatile encounter. Laird MacDonald's face changed from queried to disgust then finally to anger as he snatched his son off his feet and escorted him from the room.

Brother Aidan, busy with securing Michael's harp, had not seen the brief fracas. He waited for his friend at their spot near the back of the great hall when Michael joined him. The tender monk was appalled as he saw his friend's face, a contortion of anger and resolution. As he began to question the harper, Michael stopped him saying, "I saw him, my attacker. It is finally over. Let it be."

As Michael sat down, Brother Aidan patted Michael's shoulder then remained at his friend's side, steadfast, as a devoted companion. Beneath the monk's tunic his muscles rippled in a quiet rage, understanding this was Michael's battle alone. Yet the protector within demanded justice.

Wanting to return the focus to the competition at hand, the Master of Revels said, "Now that concludes our harping competitors. On to the singers!"

There were few singers, due to the novelty of this occasion, but Hannah found herself ranked among four other women and three men. The men began, each singing familiar tunes heard around Beltane fires or in smoke-filled pubs. Their lusty voices and boisterous renditions received heavy applauds.

When the Master of Revels announced it was now time for the ladies, the female vocalists, a hush fell over the crowd as an elegant woman of about fifty years of age took the platform. A lovely midnight blue caul snooded the singer's auburn hair, allowing several curls streaked with grey to escape around the edges and blend with her grey velvet gown. With head uplifted, she opened her mouth and sang, unaccompanied. Hannah immediately knew she was in the presence of a well-trained singer. The voice filled the wooden rafters and bounced off the stone walls, reverberating in every listener's ear with perfection. At the conclusion of her second piece, the applause was deafening. Hannah glanced at the judges, each beaming and nodding at each other with great enthusiasm.

Nudging her mentor, she asked, "Who is she?"

"That, my dear, is Shelagh of Skye, who performs regularly at Scone Palace and in Perth," said Master Murdoch. "She is one of the most celebrated royal singers in all of Caledonia. She's won this competition for many years, but there are new singers each year, and one year a rival shall appear." He smiled at Hannah, "Perhaps even this year."

Hannah breathed deeply, not wanting to discourage his belief in her, yet doubts filled her second by second. She winced when her name was called, finding herself shushed up the stairs with Murdoch close behind. He seated himself at the claviclord, ready for the first song while Hannah centered herself on the stage. She looked at Lachlan, who had slowly risen from his melancholy during the afternoon's proceedings and now smiled encouragements toward her. She scanned the audience for Michael and discovered him in the far back corner, barely discernible to the crowd, with a towering monk by his side. His face was hidden by the shadows.

How she wished Rosamond were here, to see the labor of all those nights teaching songs to Hannah by the fire, rolling colorful wools into balls for the weaving work. How appropriate then to begin with a song that elevated her mother's trade above all others. She nodded to Murdoch, who played a gentle rolling underscore then she made it through the first verse. The familiar chorus echoed in the hall:

"If it wasna for the weavers,

what would they do?

They wadna have cloth

made oot' 'oor wool'

They wadna have a coat

neither black nor blue

If it wasna for the wark o' the weavers."

The next four verses compared the weavers to all other trades, with the last lines commenting:

"So let us a' be merry

over a bicker o' good ale,

An' drink tae the health o' the weavers."

She turned to see Murdoch lit up like a lamppost while Lachlan's gentle smile now brightened his doleful appearance.

Michael rose from his seat, clearly visible now to Hannah. Their eyes met, both feeling Rosamond's presence between them. He placed his hand, palm down over his heart then extended it towards Hannah mouthing, "Thank you."

She bowed, a brief but gently lowing, in reply.

To feel Rosamond so close, so palpable, was almost unbearable. And now for her to sing a lament for a missing lover - could she do it? Her thoughts rarely strayed from Lukas for long, but lately the immediacy of her meeting with Michael, Lachlan's grief, Murdoch's expectations - thoughts swirled in chaotic spirals. But now, to sing honestly, she must open her heart once more to those secret places in her soul where love was once twinned. To Lukas.

She began with the vocabell chorus, running for three lines, then ending with her highland Gaelic strain singing, "Smi fobhron's tu gam dhith" [I am sad without thee]. The verses ebbed and flowed with an intensity Hannah never revealed in public, yet the song, describing the young woman's will to marry her beloved regardless of the cost, mirrored Hannah's own situation so clearly that images of Lukas from the past year flew before her imagination: dancing in the MacFey cottage, asking her hand in marriage, lovemaking on Rowan Hill. Instead of bringing forth pain, the bittersweet memories caused her voice to tremble with emotion; but she breathed deeply, willing herself to continue. She slowed the pace for the last chorus, each note saturated with her love for Lukas.

"Bheir mi o hu o

Bheir mi o hu o hi

Bheir mi o hu o ho

Smi fobhron's tu gam dhith."

At last, it was finished, and her final note was met not with thunderous applause but rather impeccable silence.

Hannah stood still, baffled at such a response. Feeling she had disappointed Master Murdoch, she remembered protocol to curtsy towards their hosts prior to exiting the stage. Lachlan's eyes were filled with tears for the loss of his own beloved, but he nodded at Hannah.

Suddenly, the crowd awoke from their reverie, lulled by her delicate voice into their own love misadventures. The applause reached her in waves as the crowd roared its approval. Hannah bowed, humbled by the gracious response then was accompanied offstage by Master Murdoch. She followed her mentor through the crowd to where Colin waited for them, eager to hear the Master of Revels report the winners.

"My lords and ladies, we will take a brief respite while the judges confer on their final evaluations. Please enjoy the lovely spread at the side tables provided by our benevolent hosts, the MacDonald family. And for all our players today, a round of applause, please!"

The crowd responded with roars of "Hurrah!" as Laird MacDonald reclaimed his seat. Bruce remained absent.

In a little less than an hour, hand bells were rung to silence the group as the three judges took the stage. The Master of Revels called out each category, matching their performance order, then named first and second place winner. Both winners received a pouch of gold coins in addition to a leather thong with Clan MacDonald's family crest emblazoned on a silver disc. The first place winner also now assumed the title of Grand Master of the Isles in their division, along with a list of possible patrons securing their next year's work. The winners were to remain on the stage until all groups had been announced.

"In the harping category," continued the Master of Revels, "we heard excellent players today, making it a difficult decision for the judges. But discerning ears have deemed the following: in second place, and glad we are to have him back in our midst, goes to Michael from Iona!"

Brother Aidan assisted Michael through the crowd and up the stairs, who seemed shocked to have been chosen this year after his doleful playing. He bowed his head as the family crest rested on his chest, similar to the bronze disc he'd won years ago at a competition at the Castle Eilean Donan. He took the pouch then stood aside as the Master of Revels continued.

"And in first place, a well-renown player and teacher, Master Murdoch from Dunkeld's own sang skule!"

Loud clapping and cheers followed the pronouncement as Murdoch closed his eyes, breathed deeply, and gave a silent prayer of gratitude to St. Brighid.

Hannah hugged her mentor fiercely then watched him, bowing from side to side at the crowd with singular steps to the platform. He lifted his head as the medallion was placed around his neck, pocketed the pouch of gold, then with a grand wafting of his right hand, bowed deeply to the judges then once more to the audience. He turned to stand beside Michael, who shook the talented hand of his old friend.

"Lastly, for our lovely group of singers, we continue to encourage more of you to venture into this new level of the competition. In second place, we are happy to have a new singer with us who delighted the judges with her passionate style. I give you Hannah MacLaren of the Highlands!"

A gentle rolling cheer accompanied Hannah up the stage steps where she received her prizes. She bowed to the audience then took her place between Master Murdoch and Michael, both well pleased at this achievement. Murdoch gave her a congratulatory hug while Michael whispered, "Well done."

"And first place is no surprise to our very own songbird, Shelagh of Skye!"

Exhibiting both grace and elegance, Shelagh received the prizes then bowed slowly from the waist at the judges, the MacDonalds, and the audience. She waved graciously at them all then lined up with the other winners.

"That now concludes the formalities of the competition, so let the festivities begin!" More cheers and applause met the Master of Revels's decree as this edict for frivolity and merriment was well known.

As the winners descended the steps, Ronan came forward to congratulate Michael while Lachlan squeezed through the well-wishers to embrace Hannah. Introductions were made all around as Coll came up behind the happy group and said, "Ronan, I've a brand new sailboat that needs some testing. It's quite a step up from the small open coracles we used for fishing. Why don't we take you and your friends for a sunset sail? There's plenty of room, and I've oars should the winds fail us. Come on, it'll be like old times!"

Ronan looked at the smiling faces, saying, "Well, Michael, are you up for a bit of sea salt in your hair?"

"I am if Hannah and Murdoch will join us."

"Good," said Coll, "it's settled. Lachlan, bring this group down to the boat landing next to the gardens in about half an hour. I'll have the sails readied. Ronan, why don't you check with Mary and have her pack a basket of her wonderful pastries for us. Some wine as well!"

"It shall be done," said Ronan, who disappeared towards his room first to retrieve his travel sack then down to the kitchen.

"Well, it seems we've a bit of fine luck this day, eh, Michael?" said Murdoch. "An evening sail to top off this momentous occasion. I hope you take no offense at my pleasure at beating you this year?"

"None taken," said Michael. "I am simply grateful to have the blasted event over."

So the three wove their way through the bustling crowd, following Lachlan's lead, into the afternoon's refreshing cool breeze, enjoying the fragrant gardens.

"A word, please sir," said Laird MacDonald, placing his hand on Michael's shoulder as the others sauntered into the gardens.

The request felt more like a command, so Michael waved his group on while he stayed behind. "Of course, my lord, what can I do for you?" asked Michael.

"Do for me? I feel you've done quite enough by sharing your talents with us all this day. But more to the point, I wish to discuss my son Bruce." The lord, formidable and firm, seemed uncomfortable in having this conversation but family honor required it.

Michael stiffened, "Aye, and what of your son?"

"I want you to know that we MacDonalds take pride in treating our fellow man fairly. And in saying so, I've just been told by Ronan how you've received less than fair treatment from my boy."

"Aye, that I have, sir," said Michael, considering such an understatement. He wondered where this discourse would lead, but since the Laird instigated it, Michael would listen.

"I will not have the name of MacDonald shamed by his mistake. The boy's always been a bit too arrogant. Know that his punishment for such a heinous deed will be just. It may be too late, but I wish to make amends, if they can be made. I know there can be no true compensation for the loss of the years of your life spent

282

in healing on Iona, but I wish to make some reparations on Bruce's behalf. Ronan told me that walking is often difficult for you since the . . ." he struggled for a word to describe his son's heinous deed.

"Beating, sir."

"Aye, beating," said Laird MacDonald, swallowing hard. "So, to assist you in your travels, you were supplied with a farm horse and companion?"

"That would be Molly and Brother Aidan, sir."

"Well, I would like to provide a more comfortable way of traveling for you both. A horse-drawn carriage, perhaps?"

Michael considered the benevolent offer, then said, "I thank you for making such a kind gesture, but I believe Brother Aidan would feel uncomfortable in so grand a ride. Perhaps something more practical, a wagon or large cart?"

"Of course, with an extra horse so that both may ride."

"Thank you, Laird MacDonald."

"But that's not all. I wish to pay you, for the five years you've not been able to work, and I'll take no humble naysaying about it. The monies come directly from Bruce's inheritance. Besides, it should provide some ease for you as you regain your harping stature. You've proven today, despite coming in second, that you're still the best harper in the land. I'm sure you will have no trouble in securing positions."

"Thank you again, sir. I accept your generosity," said Michael, knowing how difficult it was for this man to be party to such dealings. Anger served no one now.

"Then we have a bargain?" asked Laird MacDonald, extending his right hand.

"That we do," replied Michael, shaking the lord's hand with a firm grip.

"Then it's settled," said Laird MacDonald, releasing a sigh. "I'll have all at the ready for your departure. Have Brother Aidan see the master of the stables for the wagon and my house man for monies." He turned to walk away but then stopped, looking squarely at Michael, "There's no excuse for what the boy did. The boy's always had too much pride, but I'll not have a bully in this family. I am deeply sorry."

Michael nodded in acceptance then walked through the gardens to locate his group.

When Michael rejoined his friends, they did not notice the silvery grey clouds skirting across the northern sky.

CHAPTER TWENTY-THREE

The golden grain of the *Pearl*, a single-mast wooden boat, glistened in the late afternoon sun as its two sails, the large mainsail and the smaller jib, flapped in the wind. Ronan stood on the slatted landing to assist boarding guests, taking hold of their arms and gently guiding them over the boat's edge while Coll held the twenty-foot boat head line steady. Murdoch boarded first, sitting next to the rudder then Michael beside him, both seated on the port side to accommodate loading the rest of the company. Hannah underestimated her new pregnancy weight, so when she stepped forward, she lost her balance, despite Ronan's sturdy grasp, and fell headlong into Michael's lap.

"Hannah, are you all right?" asked Michael. As he grasped the young highlander's shoulders firmly to steady the lass, her kirtle and shift slipped a bit off her right shoulder. Michael thought he saw something dark on her skin, but dismissing it as simply a shadow, he readjusted her clothing as he lifted her upright then settled her next to him.

Hannah instinctively placed her hand upon her belly, knowing she had fallen directly on it. But sensing no pain or discomfort, concluded all was well. "I'm fine, Michael," said Hannah, "just a bit clumsy. I will take more care in the future." She glanced at Lachlan, who distressed at seeing her fall, remained quiet as a silent knowing passed between them. She would need to be more mindful of the child she carried.

Lachlan leapt aboard, followed by Ronan, who stashed his travel sack in the bow with Coll last, pulling the line in behind him. He secured two oars against the ship's hull should the winds die down.

"Ready the sail!" cried Coll, motioning for his passengers to duck as the boom switched sides, inflating the mainsail into a puffy fullness. They were off!

The Sound of Sleat, that narrow stretch of sea between the Isle of Skye and the mainland, held little traffic this late afternoon, so the boat easily maneuvered around the point, skimming across the glassy surface then north toward the Isle of Uist. They passed the small islands of Eigg and Rum, noting the tall fortressed walls of Kinloch Castle on Rum. They chatted quietly amongst themselves, though sometimes the beauty of the sea left them all speechless. Tall black peaks of the Cuillin mountains, resembling jagged giants' teeth, shot upward on their right as the boat sailed through the Cuillin Sound. The crew spotted solitary fishing boats finishing their day's catch. Coll's buoyant grin cast aside any worries today, enabling the riders to embrace this oceanic freedom.

After sailing for about an hour, Coll announced his intentions, "We'll sail north for just a bit more, toward Idrigill Point where we can best see the setting sun then return home." Ronan acted as first mate, ever happy to be at sea. Shouts of "Trim that mainsail" and "Duck, boom away!" kept everyone alert.

"Coll, see those clouds forming to the west?" asked Lachlan, "Don't you think perhaps we should turn around?"

Coll stood beside the mast, examining the low formation of pewter grey clouds, flat as if lying on the horizon. "I don't believe they'll hold any rain for us," he said. "Besides, they're moving north, faster than this sailboat, so we should miss them. We'll be fine." He smiled reassuringly at the small group, but began to wonder himself if maybe the trip should be shortened.

As if to argue the point, the sea gods blew a stiff wind directly into Coll's face, catching him off guard and causing him to stumble backwards into Murdoch, almost pushing him overboard. The portly musician grabbed hold of the tiller as Ronan clutched Murdoch's feet, landing Coll squarely in the center of the boat. He quickly returned to his post by the mast.

"My thanks to you, young man," said Murdoch, righting himself with much grunting as Ronan released his hold. "I'd hate to be washed over, for making music beneath the waves is not my calling!" He laughed, trying to make light of what could have been a dreadful situation. The others joined him, but now the possible dangers of this sunset sail seemed to lurk just beneath the waters.

As to the oncoming storm, Coll was mistaken.

The darkening clouds, now accompanied by strong winds and pelting rains, were moving south, not north, making a direct line for the small sailing craft. Suddenly, the storm lashed its fury on the sailors as waves rose high and lightning cracked above them in jagged lines, mirroring the Cuillin peaks.

Coll's face flashed white in the oncoming darkness as he desperately tried to devise a plan. "Everybody huddle in the middle of the boat," he yelled, "that should help balance the boat. Ronan, grab that main sheet line and rein in the sail. These winds are too strong, and will tear it to shreds. Lachlan, do the same with the jib, that smaller line there," he said, pointing towards the bow. "Murdoch, steady the tiller, so the rudder won't break."

Hannah screamed as the green-black waves engulfed the bow, pulling the tip downward.

"I've got you, Hannah," said Michael, wrapping his arms protectively around her. He pulled Hannah closer to the hull of the boat, shielding her face with his cloak as their bodies turned inward for protection.

She clung to him instinctively, for she must remain safe. She remembered how not so long ago she would have welcomed a watery grave, but not now. She must live.

The boat rocked hard on the water, slapping the ocean with fierce smacks. For over half an hour the rains slashed the sea-goers faces.

Then it happened.

A flash of brilliance sliced the sky, landing on the mast in burning, orange flames. The gale-force winds grasped the weakened wood and snapped the pole in half, crashing down in the center of the boat.

All was chaos.

Murdoch screamed as the heavy wooden timber's end landed on his right hand then he fainted from the pain. Ronan dropped his line as the mast hit the deck, causing the boom to swing at will. Lachlan lurched for Coll who yelped loudly when the weight of the mast wrenched his shoulder out of its socket, and the halyard chain popped him in the face. Coll's agony pierced the storm.

The broken mast end tumbled overboard, taking most of the shredded mainsail with it.

The boat leaned starboard with the shift in weight, jolting Hannah out of Michael's embrace. The boom whipped around again, hitting Hannah in the temple then knocking her overboard.

"Ronan, do something!" shouted Michael. Useless in the water with his impaired leg, Michael felt more than helpless as he watched Hannah's limp body drifting out to open sea. "For God's sake, man, you're the only one who can save her!"

Ronan knew that as man, he was a strong swimmer, but if the waves continued to drag Hannah further out to sea, his best chance would be to glide beneath her, supporting her - as a seal. He grabbed his sack, still tucked up in the bow, tore it open and retrieved his grey skin. Without a moment's hesitation, he stripped off his clothing, placed the hood over his head, slid his hands into the short flippers then dove into the water.

Michael was too fearful for Hannah's safety to be unnerved by the selkie's transformation, but Coll witnessed it, and his eyes widened in disbelief as he called out, "Ronan!"

Hannah floated, unconscious, with her head flopping from side to side like a dead fish as the briny waves washed over her face. She was only in the water for a few moments when a dark shadow bumped underneath her, its grey fur cushioning her as it lifted her up, just cresting the foam-flecked waves so as not to ingest the water.

Relentless walls of water pounded the small craft, almost sinking her, but the *Pearl* remained intact, all but the mast and mainsail. After a dreadful hour, the winds and rains soon abated as the sky grew calm once more, turning from bleakest black to misty rose.

The seal bore Hannah's body through the waves back to the *Pearl*. Michael grabbed Hannah underneath her shoulders as Lachlan grasped Michael's waist. The two struggled to lift her body into the center of the boat as her legs plopped over the side with a heavy thud.

"Is she alive?" asked Lachlan.

Michael cradled her, supporting her head, then felt along her throat for a pulse. "Yes, her pulse is weak, but she's knocked out cold. We've got to get her to a physician as soon as we land." He smoothed the wet hair from her face then he saw it clearly, cresting her shoulder as it did his own - the MacLeod four-pointed star. "Holy St. Brighid!" He exclaimed, knowing with certainty that the young woman in his arms was indeed his daughter.

"I just pray the babe will make it as well," said Lachlan. Haggard lines crossing his face betrayed his worry. Too much had happened.

Michael, distracted by this paternal confirmation, looked up saying, "What? She's with child?"

"Aye, from the lad she was to marry. He died the night before their wedding."

"Quite a load for a young lass on her own," said Michael. He held her close now.

"Aye, 'tis for sure," agreed Lachlan.

By this time, Murdoch revived from his swoon and holding his broken fingers to his chest cried aloud, "Oh dear God, look at my hand! My fingers are broken into so many pieces that I'll never play the harp again! Oh what will I do?" he wailed, moaning into the winds like a banshee at the injustice. He looked at the survivors, but realized someone was missing. "But where's Ronan?"

Michael answered quickly, "He was thrown overboard, along with the mast, but I know him to be an excellent swimmer, and I believe I saw a small fishing boat trying to beat that squall as well. If Ronan paces himself, he'll reach that craft. I can't believe we've seen the last of him."

Coll, thinking his cousin lost at sea, in addition to being shaken by the entire ordeal, knew he must save the others. He asked Lachlan to lash his shoulder to his chest using a broken line and to wrap Murdoch's hand with strips from the torn sail. Both men, even with only one useful arm, would be needed if they were to reach land safely. After the injured were tended, Coll assessed the damages. "We've been blown off course, much farther north. Murdoch, I'll need you to hold Hannah while Michael and Lachlan each take an oar. Judging by the land, I believe we've passed Neist Point which means the next closest holding would be Dunvegan Castle. I know the MacLeods, and feel certain they will assist us in every way possible. Let's get to it, men, or we'll be out here all night."

Michael shuddered at those words, "Dunvegan Castle," but sensed there was no other choice. He was going home, and bringing a daughter in tow.

The storm, rapidly spun itself out of power, leaving no traces behind but a small sailboat heading north with five passengers and one seal in its wake.

It took several hours, for the oars were slow-going, as early slivers of moonlight guided the weary passengers of the *Pearl* towards the whiskey-gold peat banks of Dunvegan Castle perched atop its impenetrable rock base. Darkness cloaked the upper reaches of the castle while a solitary light at the base of the sea wall stairs beaconed. Michael stared at the three-storied battlement, its fortress buttresses with decorative spiraled layers adorning each corner. How often as a boy he had stood within those curved walls, peering out through the slim window arches with a bow knocked, an arrow at the ready for invisible foes. Having been away now for almost twenty years, he was uncertain as to his reception at this sudden homecoming.

Lachlan jumped ashore first, pulling the line and securing it around a boulder. He offered his arm to Michael for balance who was carrying Ronan's sack with his clothing inside. It felt good to set his feet on the familiar soil. Murdoch slid Hannah's silent form across the bow where Lachlan gathered her in his arms. Then Coll, ashamed at his arrogance, sat on the *Pearl's* edge and hoisted himself ashore.

Nobody noticed the grey seal head bobbing in the moonlit waters.

Michael and Coll finished securing the boat then led the travelers up the solitary stone steps to the sea gate entranceway, an iron gate of woven bands which could only be opened from within.

"How the hell are we to get inside?" asked Coll.

Michael knew ascending the stairs, an intricate narrow tunnel of passageways leading to the open courtyard, would be no easy feat, especially for wounded. But these were desperate times, and someone in the household needed to be awakened. He looked around for a large stone, then finding one, began clanging on the gate with all his might. Within a few minutes, a streak of glimmer bounced off the dense walls as Michael heard heavy footfalls paired with mutterings.

"Who the devil's there? Do you have any idea how late it is?" asked a gravely male voice.

Coll was about to answer, but recognizing the voice, Michael spoke first, "Daniel, it's me, Michael. Now open up the bloody gate, for we've got folks here that need tending." He stood close to the gate, allowing the lamp to shed light on the situation.

"Master Michael, is it you? Oh, Holy mother, please forgive me." He held the lantern high enough to see the scar creasing the harper's face. "I didn't recognize you, after all these years. Why, you've certainly changed since you've been away."

"Truer words were never said, Daniel. Now be on with it - open the gate!"

The middle-aged man hurriedly plucked the keys from his pocket, opened the gate, then stood aside as the four men entered, Hannah cradled in Lachlan's arms.

"Daniel, all will be told later. Right now, we're in need of a physician, fresh bandages along with some food and drink, whiskey if you've got some for the pain. One more man may appear, and if he does, give him these," said Michael, handing the servant Ronan's sack. "We'll stay in the Fairy Tower. I will deal with the family tomorrow. Now, quickly man, dispatch someone to fetch a physician!"

Coll glanced at Michael, impressed by his commanding tone and decisive manner, and considered that there was more to this man than a simple harper.

Daniel scurried down the passage ahead of them as the four men, with Lachlan still carrying Hannah, walked single file through the maze of corridors before entering the courtyard. They walked to the freshwater well where Michael immediately retrieved some water by lowering a bucket, filled it then passed it around with a ladle. Lachlan wetted his handkerchief then cooled Hannah's face. She remained in her own silent world.

The group followed Michael, the true Dunvegan heir, inside the four-tiered spiral staircase of the Fairy Tower, each floor containing a single small room with a cot, chair, table and oil lamp.

"Murdoch, you and Coll take a room upstairs," said Michael, "for it will be morning before medical help arrives. I'll send Daniel up with food and whiskey."

The two men complied with Michael's instructions, allowing Lachlan to follow Michael to the first room where they would share a nighttime vigil over Hannah.

Daniel reappeared about half an hour later with cheeses, breads, and flasks of wine, and whiskey, enough to sustain the men till a hearty breakfast in the morning. He departed, but entered the main keep rather than returning to his room.

Hannah, her mind locked within her body, dreamed deeply.

She was in a cottage Lukas had built for them on the MacLaren farm, rocking a cradle with her foot as she spun woolen threads into balls. The wooden door opened as her beloved husband came through the door, wearied from a day of hard work on the farm.

"Look at our angel, how peacefully he sleeps," said Hannah.

Lukas bent forward and kissed Hannah then leaned over the cradle, placing a soft kiss upon his son's brow. "You know, there's no point in telling anybody that he's a MacFey, for he's the spittin' image of every man in the MacLaren clan!"

"I don't mind at all," said Hannah, "for that means he'll grow into a fine man someday."

"Aye, we can only hope," agreed Lukas.

He began ladling the soup, prepared earlier in the day by Hannah, into two pottery bowls. He slathered butter and honey on thick slices of brown bread, laying them in the wooden trenchers then poured two cups of wine.

"Wine, is it? Why, on so common a day?" asked Hannah.

"No day is common with my wife by my side and my son at my feet." Handing Hannah her clay chalice, he raised his own and toasted: "To the loves of my life!"

"I will never tire of loving you, Lukas," whispered Hannah. She laid the balls aside and reached for Lukas, but his body began dissolving. She cried out, "LUKAS! LUKAS!"

Her eyes moved rapidly back and forth under closed eyelids, followed by muscular twitches.

"Michael, she's coming back to us!" said Lachlan, standing over her bedside.

"Lukas!" she cried aloud as she tumbled into the real world once more. Her head rolled from side to side on the goose pillow.

"Hannah, are you all right?" asked Michael. He sat on the pallet beside her, patting her hand. "You've scared the life out of us, girl. Lachlan, fetch her some water."

The highlander bolted down the steps into the courtyard and returned with a fresh bucket of water. He cradled her head then lifted the ladle to Hannah's lips where she gingerly sipped.

"Darlin', can you sit up?" asked Michael.

Hannah tried, but the room seemed blurry, as if underwater, so she laid back down. She combed her fingers through her hair, confused by her surroundings, then felt the knot on the side of her head. "What's happened? Where are we?"

"All in good time, but just know that you're safe, child," said Michael, "and we're all doing fair, considering. We've landed at Dunvegan Castle, where I have relations." Not wanting to go into his family history at this time, he continued. "They have taken us in, and a physician should arrive by morning to look at you, along with patching up Coll's shoulder and Murdoch's hand." There would be time to reveal his own connection to her once she recovered. "You just rest, and all will be better come sunrise."

Footsteps could be heard ascending the first flight of the stone stairwell, so thinking it was Daniel, Michael opened the door wide. He was shocked to see a face much like his own, only with greying temples. It was Laird MacLeod, his father. Michael froze.

The elder raised his lantern high to clearly see the man before him. "I've come to see if Daniel is telling the truth or if he'd been dippin' into the spiced ale a bit. "Well boy," scrutinizing every inch of his son, "your hair's a bit longer, and I see you've been in some sort of scrap according to that scar on your face, although how any son of mine could fare the worst in such a situation is beyond me." Tears began to fill the old man's eyes, his judgments softening. "My God, Michael, I never meant for you to leave. You must forgive a man for wanting only the best for his family. Come here, son," and the father, putting his lantern on the floor, embraced his prodigal son, once lost to him but now returned.

Unaccustomed to physical affection from his father, Michael was unsure how to accept this gesture. But the elder MacLeod wrapped his strong arms about his son so tightly that Michael could do nothing more than reciprocate.

Laird MacLeod released his hold, conveying a congratulatory slap on his son's shoulder. "So, I know we've much to discuss, but let's leave all that till morning light. Let's talk about more pressing needs. Daniel tells me you've some injured, during a boating incident?"

"That's true, sir," said Michael, finally recovering his voice.

"Well, we've sent for the village physician. It must be midnight by now, but we'll send him over just as soon as he arrives. Is there any more we can do for you or your friends?" The old man glanced at Hannah lying on the bed, aware from her appearance that she, too, was ill.

"I believe the young lady will need to be examined. She was struck in the head and tossed overboard, but it appears she might have a concussion. She is also newly with child."

Laird MacLeod stared at Michael with raised eyebrows, and discerning his meaning, Michael quickly added, "She was to be wed several months ago to a young man who died the night before their wedding. The baby is his."

Laird MacLeod nodded then said, "All will be done. Michael, I believe this young man can look after the young lady, so if you will come with me, I know your mother is anxious to see you. She will not wait till morning."

After all that had occurred, Michael was uncertain if he had the strength for this reunion, but noting his father's generosity, he agreed.

The two crossed the courtyard where Michael now noted many lights emanating from inside the keep. His mother ran to him, her tears rolling down her cheeks and onto his cloak as she embraced him. His younger brother, Tormod, was all grins, having missed his brother greatly. The threesome made quite a lovely sight, hugging in the moonlight.

His mother placed her hand on his face, then noting the scar, took Michael by the hand and led him inside. "There will be time to tell all that needs to be told, but for now, let us simply enjoy the pleasure of your company once more, my son, my own Michael."

So the heir apparent remained inside the keep with his family for the rest of the night, and despite their ploys to wait, questions flew like magpies, so he answered them all. That is, almost all - he avoided those circling Hannah beyond her injuries.

Her parentage could wait.

He must tell her first.

Hannah awoke the next morning to the physician's poking and prodding, for she slept deeply throughout the night. The covers had been pulled back with her shift lifted over her hose to expose her bare belly.

"I believe the baby will be fine, miss," said the stout man, his pudgy face reminding Hannah of a puffy pillow. "But as for your head, I believe it may take a while for the fuzziness to go away. Take some feverfew, just in case, and I'll leave extra wintergreen for the headaches, which I'm certain you'll be plagued with for some time. Is there anything else?"

Hannah glanced about the room and discovered she was alone with the physician, probably for privacy sake. Her golden kirtle hung on a peg on the door. "Thank you," she said softly, "I believe that's all." She smoothed her shift down over her body, and feeling a slight chill, pulled up the cotton sheet and wool blankets to cocoon herself.

He stood, his form much like Master Murdoch's frame. "Well then, I'll just be looking after the men then. Seems a shoulder needs setting, along with splinting some broken fingers." He turned to leave, then commented, "You'll need to lie still for at least a day or two, three would be best. Only get up to relieve yourself. I'll ask that a chamber pot be brought in." With that, he exited, leaving Hannah relieved that both she and her child had survived.

The door did not remain closed for long as Michael entered, dressed in an elegant leather vest, ruffled white shirt, and sea-colored tartan. His hair was combed back and tied, having grown long again over his weeks of travel. He'd left his cane at Armadale Castle, but Hannah noticed he barely limped. He set a wooden tray with breakfast on the table then brought over the small wooden chair, and placing it next to the bed, sat quietly next to his daughter.

"How are you feeling?" he asked.

"Well, I'm not sure. I feel a bit achy all over, and my brain feels like a rolling marble in my head."

"You must keep still. It may take some time, but we've been assured the dizzy spells will eventually stop. Now Hannah, I'm sure you must have questions about the storm, so let me tell you first that everyone is all right."

"That's a relief," said Hannah.

Michael continued, "Coll has a damaged shoulder, along with a gash on his cheek, but he will be fine. Master Murdoch, however, received such a blow to his right hand that four of his fingers were broken in several places. The physician is in with him now, but I fear the man will never play the harp again. Lachlan remained close by your side all night, and is now at breakfast. Ronan," here Michael stopped. "Well, he was separated from us at sea, thrown into the water like yourself. But there were several small fishing boats in the area, and I'm certain they've picked him up. We'll see him again soon.   Now, I knew you might be hungry, so I've brought food for you."

He retrieved the wooden tray filled with oat bannocks, glistening butter melting in yellow rivers between them, along with slices of creamy cheeses and a steaming mug of cider.   Hannah sat up, finding herself ravenous, and began eating immediately.

Michael watched, relieved to see her with an appetite.   "You must eat well, for both yourself and the wee one," he said.

Hannah stopped chewing, her mouth full of the tasty bannocks.

"It's all right, lass. Lachlan explained it all.   You see, with the medic coming we needed to be sure all was well."

Hannah saw the sense in the revelation then continued her meal.

When she had finished, Michael propped up several more pillows, supporting her head, so she could rest comfortably.   "Now, lass, there is one more thing I need to tell you, rather show you." He pulled off his leather vest then pushed the frilled white shirt collar aside, revealing his four-pointed star.

Hannah gasped.

"It's the MacLeod birthmark, Hannah. Passed down through many generations but only seen on this island. During the storm, I noticed you bear the same mark, on your shoulder."

"I do," stammered Hannah, still not thinking clearly enough to make the connection. "But I was told that was the mark of the fey? How does your family come by it then?"

Seeing her confusion, Michael sat down on the chair beside the bed and told the tale outright. "Well, in our ancestry, there was a faerie lass who was Lady of this castle for a time, after bearing a child. Since then the MacLeod line has been linked, although somewhat faintly over the generations, with the Fair Folk. What does seem consistent though is the mark." He took her hand in his, then quietly stated, "So, what I'm telling you girl, is that this mark proves that I am your father. True enough."

Tears caused her green eyes to sparkle. Her lips trembled - so many unsaid words attempting to spill out at once that none were heard.

Michael opened his arms to her, and she gently moved into them. She laid her head on his shoulder as he cupped his hand over her the crown of her head, stroking her hair with his fingertips.

The sincerity of his words and truth in his face rang deep inside Hannah's heart. He was not running away from her, rather he was by her side, just as a father should be. The gossiping taunts from all those years, the tears spilled in response to Nell's lies no longer held her in their power. No more.

She knew that Rosamond and Michael's love for each other had been constant, cherished, and favored above all others. To be born out of such a connection now caused all those uncertainties about her own identity to melt away like well-spent clouds after a storm.

She closed her eyes, snuggling into the safety of Michael's arms, her father's embrace. She was home.

CHAPTER TWENTY-FOUR

Hannah remained in the Fairy Tower for three days while the rest of the group recovered from their oceanic ordeal. The MacLeods continued as gracious hosts to the traumatized group and sent word to Armadale Castle that Coll and his friends were safe, along with instructions for Colin and Brother Aidan to prepare the instruments and any other belongings for travel once Master Murdoch and Michael returned.

Hannah's room was never want for visitors, but severe headaches prevailed, causing her to sleep for hours at a time. Michael and Lachlan took turns keeping watch while both Coll and Master Murdoch nursed their injuries. Michael spent the remaining time with his family.

One morning, Ronan surprised everyone by turning up for breakfast. With a salty grin upon his face, he nodded at Michael who smiled broadly in thanksgiving, still marveling at the wonders that surrounded this man's life.

But Coll, shocked by Ronan's entrance, leapt from the table, almost knocking over the platter of oat cakes, then grabbed his cousin in a firm embrace. "My God, man, I thought you were dead!"

Ronan held his cousin close, then pulled back saying, "You know I've always been a strong swimmer."

Michael quickly interjected, "I told them all how I saw a small fishing boat nearby, and when you were washed overboard, I felt certain that you could swim to that craft. That's what happened, right?"

The lie stood.

"That's exactly it," replied Ronan, his arm draped over Coll's shoulder.

"But I saw you, you," Coll stammered, recalling the vivid memory.

"Let's go for a walk, shall we cousin?" And with that, Ronan whisked the perplexed man out into the courtyard before anymore could be said.

When they reached the well, Ronan leaned over, pulling up the bucket and ladling some water for Coll. "Here, you're going to need this," he said.

Coll drank a sip, but just stared at this man he'd known all his life, loved more than his own brothers. "Tell me."

"What did you see?"

"Well, it was difficult to make it all out, especially since I'd just had my shoulder ripped apart, and the rains were so thick. But it looked like you took something dark, like a cloak, out of your sack, then after quickly undressing, you placed it over your head then dove into the waters. But how could you not drown, or at least be ill after the deep cold of those waves?"

"It's true, those waves would stop any man's heart."

"So what happened?"

Coll appeared so distraught by recalling the incident that Ronan felt he had no choice but to finally relay the truth. "Cold waters soothe a seal's heart, not chill it. I'm a selkie."

"You're a what?"

"A selkie, one of the seal people."

"But how can that be? We're from the same family, and I've never heard of anyone claiming such outrageous birthright!" Coll stared at the surrounding sea, totally confused.

"You watched me transform. 'Twas the only way to save the young woman."

"So you, what, brought her to the boat?"

"Aye, buoyed on my back above the waves."

"I see," said Coll, not truly seeing at all. "But I still don't understand how you can transform like that, at will. All the stories I've heard about selkies say they only transform during a full moon."

Ronan laughed, "That's just a myth."

"A myth?" Coll looked at his cousin, and in view of the incredulity of the entire situation, they both laughed out loud. "All right then, so you've been able to shift from man to seal all this time?"

"Since childhood."

"So when my parents say you're 'out to sea' they really mean it?"

"Aye, they do. My own parents could not handle having such a bairn, thinking I'd been cursed somehow. That's why I came to live with you, my only other relatives," said Ronan. "But I had to keep my true identity a secret, for Uncle thought it might scare Eleanor, and you boys at the time."

"Well, I can understand that. But this is great news! Now I see where your marvelous stories of the sea were born. Ah, Ronan, I do believe I love you even more – you're a brave soul to take on such a life," and Coll hugged the selkie once more.

Ronan savored Coll's acceptance, for fear of losing this friendship had made him conceal the truth. The two men rejoined the others after making a pact to maintain the secret.

Inside the keep, Laird and Lady MacLeod, ecstatic to have their son in their midst once more, were both genuinely pleased to hear high praises from Master Murdoch concerning Michael's harping abilities. But despite the number of years away and having grown into a man, Michael discovered the role of parent to child never really lessens. They would still want to control his future, insisting that he give up his traveling ways and take on the family legacy. In Michael's absence, the younger brother Tormod had learned from his father how to manage the fortress. Michael did not wish to dishonor Tormod by simply taking over.

For Michael, new roles were emerging - with Hannah, a father. With her unborn child - a grandfather. Yet his most treasured role, that of husband to Rosamond, would remain an empty dream, leaving his future unclear, rudderless.

On the morning of their departure, over rashes of pork, scones, and potato cakes, Master Murdoch spoke in low tones with Michael concerning the school at Dunkeld. The man's hand was irreparable, and once the splints were removed, his fingers would remain straightened and stiff. He needed Michael's help.

"Think about it, man," said Murdoch. "I would stay on in an advisory capacity, as well as assisting with vocal and fundamental music classes. But there's no way I can ever instruct in harp again."

"Well, I'm just not sure," said Michael, hedging his options.

"There may be one enticement I can offer," said Murdoch, helping himself to a third scone.

"Aye, and what would that be?"

"I've observed how protective you seem to be concerning a certain young highland singer," said Murdoch, raising his eyebrows in a taunting fashion.

"She's my daughter, you old fool."

"Oh, goodness me, I had no idea!" said Murdoch, dropping the scone.

"Neither did we, but all is clear now."

"Well, then all the more reason to stay close to your kin, for she is also considering making Dunkeld her home, teaching songs at the school. I know life on the road holds little glamour for you now as it did in your younger years. You could still perform at fairs and estates throughout the summer months. I need you, man. Please?"

The musician was so earnest, and the idea of being close to Hannah, helping her raise this child, seemed exceptionally appealing. "I'll need to discuss it first with Hannah."

"Oh, by all means. For she was waiting till after the competition to confirm her position. I shall await your decision." He popped the scone remnant into his mouth, slurped down his staunch black tea then licking his lips like a satisfied customer, returned to his room.

Daniel approached, saying, "Master Michael, your parents are waiting in the Great Hall to speak with you. They request your presence as soon as possible."

"Thank you, Daniel. Tell them I'm going to check on Hannah then will be right in."

"As you say, sir. Also, the horses, along with two carriages are being readied for your departure," said Daniel, bowing then leaving the room.

Much to consider, thought Michael as he strode across the courtyard to the Fairy Tower.

Hannah sat on the edge of the bed, fully dressed. Lachlan sat opposite her, clearing away her breakfast tray. His constant friendship was becoming more dear to Hannah, although at times, when he wasn't looking, she saw a sadness creep over him. His sweet Eleanor - Hannah knew how much Lachlan missed her.

"Good morning, Michael," said Lachlan. "Our patient is ready for travel with a good breakfast in her belly."

"That's just fine. Thank you, Lachlan. Could I have a moment alone, please, before we leave?"

"Why, certainly," said Lachlan, "I'll just take this tray back to the kitchens and be sure the rest of the group is ready." He gathered up the breakfast trencher then made his way carefully down the spiral stairs.

Hannah attempted to stand, but the spinning in her head proved too much as she faltered back onto the bed.

"Steady, lass," said Michael, sitting beside her and holding her hand. "I'll take you down when it's time. I've something to talk over with you first." He explained Murdoch's offer to teach the harp at Dunkeld in addition to reminding Hannah of the Master's previous offer to herself. "In spite of my parents wanting me to remain here at Dunvegan, I wish to be near you, and this wee babe. With no husband by your side, it would please me to provide shelter, a home, for the two of you."

Hannah listened and weighed this option, thinking not only could the school at Dunkeld provide a stable community in which to raise her child, but by earning a living as a singing teacher, she would not be dependent on the charity of others.

"Murdoch is most insistent on a reply."

Hannah smiled, placing both hands in Michael's. "We will go to Dunkeld, all three of us. The Master has already told me there are living quarters available for the instructors, and I can think of no better place for me to raise my baby than one where both love and music fill each day."

"It's settled then," said Michael. "We shall pick up Brother Aidan at Armadale Castle, return to Feshiebridge as we agreed earlier, where you can collect any other personal belongings, then meet Murdoch in a month's time at Dunkeld." He breathed deeply, grounding their decision in his heart.

It was the right thing, and they both knew it.

Michael escorted Hannah slowly down the one flight of stairs, out into the morning sunshine where the others were waiting by the carriages, packing the traveling provisions for the long trip. As the pair approached the music Master, Michael smiled and nodded at Murdoch.

"Splendid!" said Murdoch, shaking Hannah's hand heartily. "Oh my, how the students will blossom under your tutelage. You won't regret this!"

Lachlan, Ronan, and Coll seated themselves in one carriage while Murdoch assisted Hannah up into the second.

"I'll be just a moment," said Michael, then hurried into the Great Hall to say good-bye to his parents. He disappeared into the keep for only a few minutes then rejoined the group.

"How did they take the news that you weren't staying?" asked Hannah.

"My mother cried, but I assured them both that I would make regular trips home every year."

"Did you tell them, about me?"

Michael shook his head. "They've had so much to take in these last few days. I thought that sometime after the baby is born, we could all return together."

"You know them best," said Hannah.

Michael eased himself into the carriage, and the company was off once more.

After several days travel, the two carriages approached Armadale Castle. With the music competitors having taken their leave, the servants had busied themselves collecting refuse, cleaning linens, and replenishing food stores. Both Colin and Brother Aidan kept a watchful eye on the castle's entranceway, so when they heard the clammering of iron-shod carriage wheels and rhythmic hoof beats, they ran to greet their friends.

Lachlan assisted Coll descend the carriage steps, his shoulder still causing great pain. The physician had popped the dislocated shoulder back into place, but bound the healing limb to insure its protection. Several stitches had been needed to mend the torn cheek, but the young MacDonald's spirit was well revived. His decision to make the *Pearl* a gift to the MacLeods for their hospitality was based more on regret than honor. He knew he could never sail her again.

Ronan grabbed his travel sack and aided Michael, who with so much riding found his knee to be stiff. But he stretched out the unused muscles, flexing his foot, and discovered the entire leg offering more stability than in years past. He found he still missed that old wizard's face atop his cane, a steady old friend. He should not have been surprised when Brother Aidan appeared to assist in his descent, handing his friend the beloved cane. They smiled, for no words were needed.

Colin was grief-stricken when he saw Master Murdoch's hand bandaged, but the musician hailed him away with his left hand, stating all would be well. Colin helped Hannah down, who still seemed a bit unsteady.

"I believe you should all take a day's break here," said Coll, "rest from our journey, before heading off to your own destinations, agreed?" They all breathed a communal "Yes," so each found their way back to their previous accommodations to follow Coll's advice.

Later that afternoon following a much needed nap, Hannah decided on a short stroll through the gardens. The bouts of deep sleep were slowly healing her woozy spells, so feeling refreshed, she slipped on a clean shift beneath her travel kirtle then walked, slowly and with determined footfalls, into the softening twilight, its rose and orange hues casting a spell over the blossoming petals.

She mused as she walked, reflecting on how quickly her life had transformed over the past several weeks. When she left her home in Feshiebridge, her heart was filled with deep sorrows over losing Lukas, paired with a grim determination to find her mother's lover. Then, after discovering Rosamond's lies and betrayals, she found herself becoming a mother, relating now to a woman's need to do anything to protect her child, even from unknown hurts. This revelation eased earlier anger and frustrations, replacing them with a soulful yearning to simply be held in her mother's loving arms once more. With a child on the way, she needed Rosamond's wisdom and advice. But at least now she had a father, one whom she was certain would love and support both she and this child.

She sat on the bench where she had talked with Lachlan only a little over a week ago, when she felt her world evaporating before her eyes. But blessings now filled those gaps, as she looked forward to a new life in Dunkeld. She bowed her head and gave a prayer of thanksgiving to St. Brighid, for watching over her and leading.

"May I sit?" asked a familiar voice.

Hannah looked up to see the tall, broad-shoulder Lachlan once more at her side. She beamed up at him, "Of course, silly. Since when do you need my permission?" Their friendship had deepened during his bedside conversations and nursing in the Fairy Tower.

Lachlan sat down next to the highlander, grinning at her genuine ease in his presence. "I guess you'll be taking off for Dunkeld with Master Murdoch tomorrow, eh?"

"Well, not exactly. You see, I'm going home to Feshiebridge first, to close up the cottage and gather a few things, then move to the school. Master Murdoch says they provide lodging for their teachers."

"I see," said Lachlan. "So, you'll be a teacher then?"

"Aye, of songs! Can you believe it? Master Murdoch thinks my own style of natural training will add to the book learning style they normally teach. I might even take a few classes myself!"

"Well, lass, it seems that things worked out quite well for you, and the wee one. But if you'll be traveling alone," he said, taking her hand in his, "I could shorten my stay here and take you home."

"That's very kind of you, Lachlan, but Michael is taking me."

"Oh," he said flatly, dropping her hand. "I see." He turned his head, looking at nothing particular.

Hannah, sensing his disappointment, quickly interjected, "Because Master Murdoch has offered him a teaching job as well. It seems he'll have a wagon and an extra horse, owing to the MacDonalds, so he'll have plenty of room."

"Fine."

Hannah, confused by this reaction, opted to tell him the whole truth. "Lachlan, look at me, please."

He angled his body towards her but made no attempts to touch her.

"You see," Hannah continued, "the truth of it is, Michael actually is my father."

"He's what?" asked Lachlan. "But how? When did you find out?"

"After the storm. It seems he saw a birthmark on my shoulder, a very particular birthmark running in the MacLeod family, matching the very one borne on his own shoulder."

"Well that explains his sudden devotion to you, then," said Lachlan, an easy smile spreading once more over his handsome features. He released a sigh, nodding his head.

"It does," replied Hannah, "and he wishes to be a part of my life, mine and the baby's as well."

Lachlan slapped his knee then laughed out loud. "Well, the saints be praised! Here I was worried about you, so young and alone with a babe to raise. I'll set my fears aside. I come to Perth at least once a month on business, and I can easily come back through Dunkeld, should you want some company." He leaned in close now, needing reassurance.

"Why, Lachlan, you'll always be welcomed in a MacFey cottage."

"MacFey, but I thought you said your name was MacLaren?"

"In truth, it would have been had Lukas and I wed. When I woke up in Blair Atholl, and saw his ring dangling before me, all I could think of was being his wife, so I took the name. Even after that, in all my searching for Michael, I wasn't sure who Hannah

MacFey really was anymore. I find MacLaren suits me, for now." She sat upright, holding her head high as she spoke.

Lachlan noticed a burgeoning strength enveloping his new friend, and knew that no matter what obstacles found their way to her path, Hannah MacLaren would be just fine.

The final evening was spent in much merriment, and on the following morn, the travelers said their farewells. Hannah embraced Lachlan, and whispered in his ear, "I will be in Dunkeld by June's end."

He nodded, then kissed her on the cheek.

Colin jumped onto the slatted wagon seat beside Master Murdoch, the musician now unable to drive. At the sound of snapping reins, they headed south along the sea wall road toward the Mallaig ferry with Murdoch waving at Hannah and Michael, "See you two in June!"

Brother Aidan, assisted by the stable master, packed both Michael and Hannah's belongings in the large two-seated cart, being drawn by a strong, chestnut mare. Molly would carry Brother Aidan alongside.

Ronan stood by the cart and hoisted both Hannah and Michael into the cart.

"So it's good-bye then, is it?" asked Michael.

"Let us just say farewell for now," said Ronan, "for the River Tay runs along the village of Dunkeld before sliding its ocean home. You never know what lurks beneath those waters." He smiled broadly at his friend, so glad for the kind fortune that now lay ahead.

Michael shook his head, laughing to himself at the selkie's sense of humor. "Let's be off!" So with salutes and fond farewells, the group headed toward the northern ferry.

CHAPTER TWENTY-FIVE

The single track lane curved through the forest, resembling a footpath rather than a well-traveled choice. The cart rocked from side to side, its passengers taking no notice of the woodcock and grouse harboring their spring eggs in low-lying nests. A badger popped its black and white-striped nose out his home as hoof beats reverberated through the soft earth.

It had taken them about a week to journey from Skye, crossing onto the mainland then down the main road at Loch Cluanie, where sunny yellows dotted the roadside and rippling mountain meadows resembled slumbering dragons. Inns were rare in such desolate areas, so the travelers often slept beneath a blanket of stars. In passing by Kingussie, Hannah considered her good fortune in meeting so kind a man as Lachlan Grant, and looked forward to seeing him again.

Brother Aidan's good humor kept conversation light. Michael and Hannah's recent familial discovery was no longer held in secret, so the monk was both surprised and pleased for the pair upon such good news. Father and daughter often sang to shorten the road, with Michael layering lovely harmonies in their wake.

The morning they arrived in Feshiebridge, a bittersweet solemnity mantled the jovial group, each lost in their own thoughts. The news of Rosamond's death grieved Brother Aidan not only for Michael, in losing his beloved, but also for Hannah, connecting with her grief due to the recent death of his own mother. Hannah dreaded closing up the cottage, but it must be done. For Michael, finally able to see Rosamond's home, he knew a certain emptiness would greet him. They all remained silent.

Knowing the house would lack any food, Hannah opted to go straight through the village rather than taking the short cut around the tip of the farm holdings. The day was waning, and a supper would be wanted by all three travelers. The primary lane along which Hannah had walked many times still bustled with activity as Hannah lead them to the grocer's for some fresh vegetables and cheeses.

While Brother Aidan stayed with the horses, Michael and Hannah dismounted, each careful of their infirmities. Suddenly the grocer's door flew open as a stream of white linen flounces and skirts ruffled toward them amongst hushed whispers and muffled giggles.

It was the spinster twins, Claire and Aulaire Sutherland. They were ecstatic over the latest gossip just discovered between the tomatoes and pickling cucumbers! Their two heads leaned close together as they conspired how best to share this juicy tidbit of village news that they did not see Hannah or Michael, and practically ran the pair down.

Hannah recovered quickly, taking Michael's arm in hers to steady them both.

"OH!" the women exclaimed simultaneously. Being proper ladies, they quickly recovered their decorum, tidying their dresses. Aulaire spoke first, "Why, Sister, it's the poor unfortunate child, Hannah MacFey." Swinging her head from side to side she muttered, "Tsk, Tsk, Tsk. Nothing but despair follows this young lady, sister."

"Why yes," agreed Claire, "such misery to lose one's fiancee and then one's mother. Almost too much for a body to bear."

"Must be, or else why would she leave town with her mother on her death bed?" continued Aulaire. She barely acknowledged Michael's presence but concentrated solely on Hannah.

Both women now leaned close, scrutinizing Hannah like geese craning their necks to devour their next meal. "So, how are you doing, girl?"

The effrontery of these two ladies at first set Hannah's anger ablaze. How dare they talk so casually about her life, her losses? For these two, and others like them, created a web of insecurity which cloaked Hannah's childhood, a constant shadow about her parentage. Well, no more. Hannah drew her shoulders back, took a deep breath, and with new confidence replied, "Ladies, as you can imagine, I am still grieving over the loss of Lukas MacLaren. My parting was to locate my mother's friend in hopes of reviving her spirits after the small pox illness." Here she paused, "I did not realize the sickness would take her life so quickly."

"So sad," said the twins.

"Yes," said Hannah, holding back the rush of tears.

"To be all alone in the world with none to truly love you," chided Aulaire, wringing her hands in false agitation.

"But as you see," Hannah said, patting Michael's arm, "I'm not alone after all." A brief smile calmed her tense features.

The ladies' eyes widened in scandalous surprise. "A new husband?" asked Aulaire.

At the mistaken connection, Hannah and Michael both laughed out loud. "Ladies, excuse me, but no. Not a husband. This is Michael MacLeod, a well-known harper throughout all of Caledonia. And my father."

"Your father," they gasped, stepping back a bit.

"Yes, and if you'll pardon us now, we're a bit hungry and in need of the grocer's help." With that, Hannah led Michael into the shop. She turned to watch the sisters waddle down the street, stopping to chat with neighbors. Well, she thought to herself, at least for once the rumors will be of my own making. With that settled, the goods were quickly chosen, paid for, and placed in the cart. Michael and Hannah walked towards the baker's shop for a fresh loaf of bread before moving on to the MacFey cottage.

Who should be leaving the pastry shop stuffing a berry muffin in her mouth but Nell Robertson, accompanied by her mother. When Nell saw Hannah, she choked, spluttering muffin crumbs all over the road. Nell's mother began smacking the girl between the shoulder blades, fluttering her with cooing sounds while Nell flailed her arms in protest.

"Mother, leave off. I'm fine," she said, straightening herself. The commanding tone left naught to misinterpret, so Mistress Robertson stopped hovering.

Hannah tightened her grip on Michael's arm. Sensing the tension between these two girls and hoping to spare his daughter further indignation, Michael stepped in saying, "Can I help?"

Nell ignored Michael. She glared at Hannah, pushed out her chin then in a tight, prim voice replied, "So Hannah, you've returned."

"Yes, Nell," said Hannah simply.

"Well, as you can see," began Nell, waving her left hand in the wind to be certain Hannah saw the wedding ring, "I am now happily married to quite a handsome lad from Ruthven. You may recall I was engaged before your sudden, and might I add mysterious, departure."

"I remember." Hannah relaxed her grip on Michael who remained by her side, a solid reinforcement.

Mistress Robertson interrupted, "Hannah, dear. I am so sorry about your mother's passing. She was well-loved in this community and will be sorely missed."

The kind sentiment broke through Hannah's defensive wall, causing Hannah to tremble. Michael, seeing her distress, once again came to her rescue. "Thank you for your condolences. As you can see, it still affects my daughter rather deeply."

Both Robertson women nodded politely, but then, almost like an earthquake's aftershock, one word drew their attention. "Did you say 'daughter'?" asked Nell.

"That I did," replied Michael. "Might I introduce myself to you? I am Michael MacLeod, and Rosamond would have been my wife, had she lived."

Nell's mouth gaped open wide.

Hannah, feeling recovered, opted for one last gibe to finish this battle with Nell. "Yes, Nell, my father, of the Dunvegan Castle nobility. Surely you and your family have heard of those MacLeods?" Hannah stood firm now, squaring her shoulders and breathing deeply.

Nell looked abashed, "Why yes, yes of course." She poked her mother in the ribs, "Haven't we, Mother?" She looked to her mother for support.

"Of course, dear," agreed Mistress Robertson.

"Well, you have a fine family then, Hannah. We will bid you good day," said Nell, shooing her mother down the street.

Michael looked at Hannah then said, "Dispersing old ghosts today, are we, lass?"

"Apparently," said Hannah. "Come on, let's get the bread. I'm suddenly very tired." So they bought two loaves of brown bread and six hearty oat rolls then joined Brother Aidan at the cart, heading toward the cottage.

The trio ambled through town as Hannah began to recognize farms and holdings. She spied the shortcut bearing left between twinned oaks, leading to her home. Home - how that image was changing. No longer would she sit by the fire and roll wool into balls while lulling tunes sung in Rosamond's vibrant voice filled the cottage. In preparing herself for living with Lukas, she had known the mother/daughter routines would change. But she had never considered this bleak reality.

She rubbed her belly, consoling the unborn child within that all would be well, trying to believe it herself.

"This one, Hannah?" asked Michael, pointing down a small lane covered with ferns.

"Aye, that be the one, takes you right to the front door."

The cart rounded the bend, bringing the small stone cottage into view. The geese waded near the pond while the sheep ate the fresh green shoots of spring in the pen. No chain of smoke rose from the chimney.

Rosamond was truly gone.

"I suppose Mistress Stewart asked someone to care for the animals, till I returned," said Hannah, as Michael slowed the cart near the barn. Brother Aidan dismounted, unhitched the chestnut mare, and stabled both horses in the barn.

Hannah leapt down, the dizziness returning. She took a moment to settle her nerves then said, "Well, this is it. The MacFey family homestead," waving her arm across their meager holding. "Let's go inside, shall we?"

Michael eased himself off the cart seat, grabbed his cane, and slowly walked up the flat stoned walkway. His thumb caressed the wizened cane's face, and he mused in memory of Rosamond's fanciful tales about the faeries and wizards. How he missed her!

The door, still stubborn to a visitor's touch, heaved as Hannah placed her hip upon its planks and shoved it open. The air inside was not stale, as she would have expected, being closed up for weeks now. Her journey had taken close to two months, for the first days of June now blew their warming breezes across the heathered hills. Both beds were made, the cloth partition hanging limp by the wall. All the weaving supplies appeared in order; in fact, they looked as if they were still in use with an unfinished piece waiting patiently on the back loom and partially-rolled balls of spring colors dripping off the edges. Hannah knew Mistress Stewart was to thank for this welcoming sight.

But the hearth was cold.

Hannah, holding her tears in reserve, sat in one of the chairs facing the dead fireplace as Michael surveyed the room. He crossed the threshold, gazing at the kitchen, the looms, the sleeping area. What a contrast to his family home at Dunvegan, yet after his years on Iona, he knew he preferred the simplicity of life embodied here.

He sat opposite Hannah, taking her hands his, sharing their loss.

"It feels as if she could come walking through that door at any minute," said Hannah, her voice trembling, "carrying some fresh flowers for the kitchen table or maybe a basket filled with roots for dyes. She was just so sick, and I left her, without saying goodbye, to find you." She looked into Michael's face, who seemed to have aged with grief since entering the cottage.

"Well I, for one, am grateful," said Michael, placing a sympathetic kiss on Hannah's hand.

Hannah squeezed his hands in reply. "There's really not much work to be done here. Sell the animals, pack up the weaving tools and looms. I could see if anyone would buy the cottage as I won't be having much need for it, moving to Dunkeld and all. I'll need only my travel bag, but I would like to take some of Ma's dresses, to remember her by. I believe it will all fit easily into the providan . . . I was going to . . . use that . . . for when I moved in with . . . Lukas." The thought of him, dancing with her in this cottage, asking for her hand in marriage, holding her in that last damp embrace - it was too much.

She wailed aloud as the heartache unleashed its full vengeance.

Michael tried to calm her, but she jumped from her chair, pacing restless circles around the tiny cottage until she stood at the doorway, looking to River Feshie and the fertile fields below. She loved it here, yet without her mother, without Lukas . . . Tears spilled down her cheeks, fast and furious.

Michael built the fire while Brother Aidan began preparing a light supper. Both men knew there was only one balm to comfort this level of pain.

They cocooned her with prayers.

Hannah knelt on the lintel, just like the night when Rosamond found her daughter crazed with grief during a maddening storm following a ghostly visitation from Lukas, declaring his undying love for her. The memories flooded her heart as she wrapped her arms about herself, closing her eyes. Like flickering shadows melting and merging from one shape to the next, the scenes of her life with both Rosamond and Lukas took on a new hue. The greys underscored her grief, yet now there were bursts of bright greens, soft yellows, and comforting blues.

Her highland heart opened itself to the possibilities of a new life before her while absorbing the love from her past. She sighed, and crumpled from exhaustion.

With the supper ready, Michael rose and gently led his daughter to the table spread with a simple repast of bread, fruits, cheese, and raspberry mint tea. Realizing her body was spent, Hannah rose slowly, still a bit wobbly as she accepted his aid. The trio spoke little, eating in quiet reflection.

They turned their attention after the evening meal was cleared away to sitting quietly by the fire, reminiscing about the music competition. As yawns became more pervasive, sleeping assignments were given with Michael in Rosamond's bed, Hannah on her own bed, and a makeshift pallet of bulky blankets next to the fire for Brother Aidan. Hannah instinctively pulled the heavy sleeping curtain to conceal her within the once comforting chamber of her childhood.

The next morning found the travelers a bit groggy as heavy knocks pounded the door. Michael stretched, both arms and legs over the side of the bed and slowly began redressing.

"I'll get it," said Hannah, pulling by the curtain and moving slowly to the door. She threw her shawl around her sleeping shift then noticed the smell of fresh oatcakes. She was surprised to see a rich, peat fire baking the belly of the black kettle, now ready for tea. Brother Aidan had risen earlier, folding his blankets and making sure his companions would be well nourished, not knowing what the day held for them.

The door creaked and groaned, once more scraping the stone floor until it suddenly flew open, having been pushed with excessive force from without. "Hannah!" cried Lally and Caitlin as both girls flew into the room like chattering magpies. They grabbed Hannah, almost crushing her within their friendly embrace. Still reeling from a sleepless night, Hannah leaned heavily into their arms and sighed.

"Oh Hannah!" cried Lally. "We didn't think. You must be exhausted from your travels. Here, sit by the fire. It's just, . . . just." Tears slowly cascaded down Lally's cheeks.

"We were so worried when you didn't return," finished Caitlin, giving Lally reassuring pats.

The two girls took up their customary places on the floor next to Hannah's chair. They seemed oblivious to the fact that two men were also in the cottage.

"Yes, and then when your mother died," continued Caitlin, "we had no way of contacting you. Mistress Stewart mentioned some long lost relatives in Perth, but that was all. So we've just been waiting."

The weaver's daughter took in the sight - her two dearest friends looked careworn despite their joy at her return. She tried to reassure them she was well. "I had some trouble on my journey, which I can tell you about later, but for now, let me say that I am so happy to be with you both again." She reached for their hands, and each girl offered hers, sealing the bond once more between them.

Michael moved to stand behind Hannah, placing his hands on her shoulders. "Ladies, I am pleased that Hannah has such endearing friends. But I believe introductions are in order. Hannah?"

"Yes, of course. Girls, that is Brother Aidan at the table, a monk from the Isle of Iona who is not only a good friend but also an excellent cook!"

Brother Aidan grinned and continued slicing fresh fruit for the oatcakes.

"And standing behind me is Michael, Michael MacLeod. He was my mother's . . ." Hannah faltered, not knowing exactly how much of this story to reveal.

Michael interjected quickly, "I knew Rosamond from our days in Perth, a woman who stole my heart nearly twenty years ago. It grieves me to hear of her passing with my absence over these last five years, but I have come to learn that in her stead I have been granted a daughter, in whom I am well pleased." He beamed, placing a tender kiss atop Hannah's head.

"Did you say 'daughter'?" asked Lally.

"That I did, lass," replied Michael.

"Oh, Hannah," cried Lally, "you've found your father at last!" Unable to contain her joy, Lally leapt from the floor and grabbed Michael in a hearty hug. "All these years, and now, well, it's just too wonderful, isn't it Caitlin?"

Caitlin seemed a bit more stunned, but nodded her head in agreement. Michael smiled then joined Brother Aidan in completing the breakfast plans.

Hannah breathed, letting old shadows disperse in the light of day and gladdened revelations. "But that's not all," she said, slowly rising. She opened her shawl, exposing her ripening belly which now protruded a bit through the thin sleeping shift. "I'm to have Lukas's baby!"

Lally and Caitlin screamed in delight then danced around the room, laughing and giggling like old times. It did Hannah's heart good to hear such ebullient merriment again. Then Caitlin nudged Lally, saying, "You may as well tell her your good news."

Lally shied a bit, but finally stammered, "Well, it seems a certain young man has taken a strong fancy to me in your absence, and last week asked for my hand in marriage. Can you believe it?"

"Well, who is it?" asked Hannah, scrolling through the list of likely candidates in her mind.

"You'll never guess, so I'll tell you. It's Rory MacLaren."

"Really, but how? He never said anything before?" asked Hannah.

Lally settled down then shared how during the search for Lukas and the weeks that followed she had visited regularly with the MacLaren family. "Then one day he took my hand in his, and well, it was like magic!" Lally smiled so broadly it almost slipped off her cheeks.

"I couldn't be happier," said Hannah, spotting the bloom of new love upon her best friend's face. "When is the happy day?"

"Well, we were thinking in about three weeks, the first of June," said Lally. "That will give me time to get things ready. You remember, Hannah, all those plans, flowers, packing," She caught herself and stopped, "Hannah, I'm so sorry."

The gaiety faltered, but only for a second. Hannah decided not to undermine Lally's happiness with past sorrows. So, taking Lally's hands once more, she said, "Now listen, I am fine. I want to help with the arrangements. You can't go jumping the chanty without me!"

"You're the best friend a girl could ever have," said Lally.

Brother Aidan clapped his hands, "Ladies, breakfast is served."

The three girls giggled like children and took seats on the wooden benches. The food was blessed then quickly devoured. Light conversation moved into future plans. Caitlin asked, "So Hannah, will you and the baby be staying here, taking up the weaving trade like your mother?"

"Oh no, not at all. In fact, I intend to sell the cottage, animals, the whole lot. On my journey, I met the Master of the sang skule in Dunkeld, and he's offered both me and Michael positions teaching there. Housing is provided for instructors, and honestly, to live here again, well, ..." Her voice trailed off.

"I totally understand,"said Caitlin, "so when do you leave?"

"Well, we were going in just a few days, but perhaps I can put off leaving till after the wedding?" Hannah looked at Michael for his take on this new plan.

"I believe that can be arranged," he said. "I will send Brother Aidan back with the cart, so pack up any belongings you've deemed to keep and be ready. Brother, will that suit you?"

"What, to take a lovely drive through the highlands in the peak of summer? Aye, that I'd be more than glad to do for you, miss." He smiled at Hannah, sealing this new itinerary.

"If that's the case then," said Lally, "I overheard Mr. MacLaren just last week wondering what you might be doing with the cottage if you chose not to live there any longer. With its close proximity to their farm, he thought it might make a nice wedding gift to Rory and me. What do you think Hannah?"

"I can think of no better couple to take up residence here," said Hannah. "It warms me to know that love will once more reside within these walls. I was going to visit the family later today, so I will confirm the details."

"Oh Hannah, you're the best!" cried Lally, hugging her best friend once more.

"Well," said Caitlin, surveying the room with a discerning glance, "we have to be going. I'm sure you have things to do, Hannah. We will see you later, all right?"

"Yes," she said, hugging each girl as they proceeded out the door.

Once the girls were gone, Michael sat on Rosamond's bed, slowly running his hand over the sheets that once covered his sweet highland lass. He allowed the pain room to maneuver throughout this house, these walls, this space where she lived without him for so many years. The ache of regret overcame him. His shoulders shook like tremors yet tears remained at bay. With a heavy sigh, he stood up to face his companions, trying to think about his new future. "So it's all settled then," said Michael. "Hannah, Brother Aidan and I will leave in a few days to begin setting up our new home in Dunkeld while you remain here till after the wedding. Are you sure you want to stay, lass, alone here for a few weeks?"

Hannah considered her options, but knew she would never forgive herself for missing Lally's wedding. "I will manage. It will give me some time to settle out the animals, rest a bit, and assist with the wedding plans. So let's consider today, shall we? How about we finish dressing then walk over to the MacLaren's house? Although I was never legally their daughter, and not certain that I would have been had his mother held the reins, they were kind to me. The boys and Muriel were more than happy to have me as an extra sister in the family. So I'd like you to meet them. We might even go by the graveyard behind the church later in the day, maybe pick some fresh flowers, if you want to go."

"I'm in full agreement wherever you lead, miss," said Brother Aidan.

Michael placed his arm around Hannah's shoulders, "Yes, lass, that all sounds fine. As for the church, it is time to say our farewells."

CHAPTER TWENTY-SIX

The morning light filtered through the Caledonia pines as the trio tramped through forested woodlands of Feshiebridge. Gentle echoes of bird songs by Crested Tits and the Capercailles wove through the tall branches. Hannah felt most like herself in these woods. She wanted Michael to see firsthand the land which grounded his daughter. Tufts of red deer fur shed from winter coats hung like wooly caterpillars on the jagged bark of the oaks. Periwinkle Bluebells, white Wood Anemones, and yellow saxifrage raised their petalled heads amongst the many shrubs and bulky mosses. Befitting the reverence due this ancient wood, Brother Aidan hummed lilting tunes Michael recognized as psalms he used to play on Iona.

Before long, they ascended a long slope opening to the peak of Rowan Hill. Having a father, and truly learning to love him meant Hannah must be willing to share herself with him in return. So, despite the bittersweet respite this spot now offered, it remained a sacred space in her personal landscape.

She led the men over to the rowan tree, its bright green foliage absorbing the summer sun. She straightened her shoulders, and with a heavy sigh began, "I wanted to bring you here for a reason, a particular reason. This is where Lukas and I, well," she stammered a bit, not wanting to expose the intimacy shared beneath these boughs.

Michael, having made love many times in the great outdoors, took her meaning. "Is this where Lukas told you he loved you?" asked her father, wanting to temper the situation from its possible sense of indelicacy.

"Yes," said Hannah. "We both did; in fact, this is where he gave me the wonderful wedding ring during an informal handfasting ceremony the day before we were to wed. It was so lovely, just the two of us," she said.

"And it was the next day when you discovered he was lost in the storm?" asked Brother Aidan, clarifying the bits and pieces he'd pick up during their travels together.

"Yes," affirmed Hannah. "His body was not found for several days later after endless searching of glens and caves, but I was given a lead about searching the river from," she paused. Standing beneath the home itself she felt at ease talking about its unusual inhabitant, yet not wanting to share this fey ability yet, she backtracked. "That is to say, I just wondered if Jed, the horse Lukas was searching for, could have gotten turned around in all that snow, so I suggested looking in the river. They found his body lodged between the rocks and a fallen tree." She shivered, remembering his blue distorted features.

"Well, it was a good thought you had, too, lass," said Michael. "The worry itself of not knowing can do a body more harm than would be believed."

"Aye, that it can," said Hannah. "It was not exactly relief once we knew he was dead, but finding him offered a way forward." She looked now down the hill - the unbidden sorrows returning full force. "There is the MacLarens' farm," she said. "Do you see it?"

Both men nodded.

"Perhaps if you could begin down the slope, I can join you in just a few moments." The unspoken plea was "Please, just let me be alone, here. For one last time."

"That will be fine, lass," said Michael. "My leg is beginning to feel a bit stiff after our morning jaunt, so Brother Aidan, if you will join me?"

"But, of course," said Brother Aidan, and the two men quietly left.

Hannah leaned carefully against the trunk then slowly slid down to the roots, allowing them to cradle her once more. She closed her eyes, traveling back to those delicious times of sweet lovemaking. She fondly rubbed her belly, whispering, "This is where we called you into being, Little One. You will always know that you were born from love, true love. And you will know your father, for I will tell you more stories than a travel chest can hold of his goodness, his laughter, his lines of poetry. Yes, you will learn to love him, through me, precious child." She sighed, marveling at the wonder of all that had happened.

"I see you found your man," a faint voice whispered, as Oonagh slipped through the bark to sit beside Hannah, her pastel sheath covering her golden green limbs.

"I would say I'm startled to see you, but in truth, I am not. And yes, you were right about the waters - that is where his body was found."

"And yet today you come with other men?"

"I do - friends. More than friends actually since one is my father," said Hannah.

"Then you will not be alone in raising the child within you. That is good," said Oonagh.

"I will be leaving this place soon," said Hannah, "and uncertain of my return. But I had hoped to see you once more before I left. I wanted to thank you."

"But you have no need, little heart," said Oonagh. "We are part of the same, the world of the fey, yet different. That connection will remain wherever you go." She rose, stretching her arms wide then tilting her head as if in reverie said, "I confess, I will miss your trysts, for I did so enjoy the lines of love your man often spoke to you. I wish you more than good fortune." And like winter snow on soft embers, she melted into the tree once again.

"Still, thank you," whispered Hannah. She braced herself against the trunk once more then made her descent towards the MacLarens' farm.

Before she reached the front door to the MacLarens' home, Muriel came dashing out the front door, yelling, "Hannah! You're back, oh you're back!"

Hannah opened her arms wide for this girl who loved her, clutching her close, for she had been the favorite of Lukas among all his siblings. "And how are you since I've been away? Why, it looks like you've grown into a lovely young lady, you have," she said.

Muriel released herself gently from the embrace, clutched the hem of her dress and bowed graciously, saying, "Why I thank you, I do. Now, tell me where you've been and who is that monk inside talking to Mother?"

Hannah realized her visitors preceded her, not realizing her visit with Oonagh had taken quite so long. "Well, let's go find out, shall we?" She laced her arm through Muriel's as the two walked through the open door then into the parlor, for the MacLarens' holdings were expansive, as evidenced by their two-storied home. She found both Brother Aidan and Michael seated opposite Mistress MacLaren in casual conversation. Muriel took her seat on the floor next to her mother on a large, overstuffed pillow.

"Oh Hannah, my dear, " said Mistress MacLaren, rising to offer a genuine embrace. "But it is good see you safely returned from your travels. And I see you have brought company with you. We were just about to make our introductions as you came in, so please?" She waved her arm in the men's direction, clearly wanting Hannah to begin.

"Well, Mistress MacLaren, this gentleman with the broad smile is Brother Aidan from the Isle of Iona. A trusted friend and companion of Michael, Michael MacLeod, of Dunvegan Castle and famous Scottish harper."

Both men stood then bowed as their names were called then took their seats again.

"Well, I see you have chosen interesting company for your journey. And how is it that you've come to make their acquaintance?" Her piercing stare could bore holes into wood.

"Actually," began Hannah, "I was looking for Michael who is an old friend of my mother's from their time in Perth. When the worst of the pox symptoms had passed, I thought having him near might strengthen her spirit to speed along her recovery. I never realized that death was already dealing with her. Had I known, I would never have left."

"Yes, well, that was a bit of mystery to us as to why you left so suddenly when Rosamond appeared to be on her death bed. But it sounds as if your intentions were well crafted, despite the tragic conclusion." She now turned to her daughter, "Muriel, check on Cook to see if the tea is ready. Thank you, dear."

The dutiful daughter left the room only to return a few minutes later with a tea tray, china tea cups and saucers, along with thick slices of cinnamon raisin fruit cake. She served everyone then regained her seat by her mother.

Despite the polite air, Mistress MacLaren did seem pleased to welcome Hannah. However, Hannah wondered how she could tell this woman that she would soon be a grandmother. How does one slip that into a conversation full of social niceties? She would begin with family. "So, I also learned that not only did Michael know my mother well, but that they had been in love for almost twenty years. In fact, he was hoping to propose to her upon our return."

"Ah, twenty years was not enough time, Mr. MacLeod? Terrible waste that, I believe, for two people to be so, shall we say, 'de-parted,' from one another?"

Michael took her meaning, yet quietly answered, "Yes, a decision I will always regret."

Now it was Hannah's turn to rescue him. She was still a bit intimidated by this stately woman, so her nerves betrayed her as she blurted out a bit too fast, "But there is good news, for you see, Michael is my father, and we intend to work and live in Dunkeld at the sang skule, having both been offered permanent positions."

"That does sound fine indeed," said Mistress MacLaren, "Why, I believe the boys are returning, so they can meet our guests." She looked toward the door as she heard the familiar voices in mingled conversations. Gerald MacLaren came in first followed by Malcolm and Rory. Each took off their cap when they saw the visitors and were introduced. After bringing in two more chairs, all were seated with Rory on the floor next to Muriel.

Mr. MacLaren spoke first. "So Hannah girl, good it is to see you well and home. We've missed you, girl." His smile warmed the room, and Hannah caught a vision of the man Lukas might have become. "But have you heard our good news? This youngster here (pointing to Rory) has taken quite a fancy to that friend of yours, Lally MacPherson. Seems there is to be wedding in a few weeks."

"I saw Lally this morning, and she told me," said Hannah. "I could''t be more pleased."

Rory just grinned and pulled out a small knife and piece of wood, whittling his life away.

"So what are your plans, darlin'? Will you be weaving like Rosamond?"

"Oh no, dear, you just missed that exciting news," started Mistress MacLaren. "Hannah and Michael, and I assume Brother Aidan . . .?"

He nodded in agreement.

"Yes, and Brother Aidan will be living in Dunkeld, teaching music. Singing and harping and such. Won't that be nice, dear?"

"I must say I'm surprised, and I'm sure there's quite a tale about how all this has come about, but if you're happy, Hannah, then well done!" He lifted his tea in congratulations.

But before Hannah could respond, Mistress MacLaren continued. "Oh, but there's more, Gerald. You see, Mr. MacLeod is Hannah's rightful father, so she will be with family after all. Isn't that true, Hannah?" Mistress MacLaren's prim tone was not lost on anyone present.

"Yes, m'am," said Hannah. She exchanged glances with Michael, uncertain of how best to proceed.

Rory jumped in, saying, "Why, Hannah, I think that's great. Lukas told me once how much you missed not knowing your father, so at least now you'll have one man in your life if you can't have . . . two." Lukas - gone, dead. Even after several months, the grief of his brother's death caught Rory off guard. "Excuse me, please," he said as he bounded up the wooden staircase to his room.

Michael had learned on Iona to confront your demons, and even though these were not traumatic forces, he recognized a battle when he saw one. Best to be the aggressor than put on the defensive. "Mistress MacLaren, Mr. MacLaren, you should be told the full truth of things between my daughter and your son. Hannah, if I may?"

Surprised by his gracious offer, she nodded.

"You see," said Michael, "the night before they were to wed, these two held their own ceremony, a handfasting, where they made their pledges of love to one another."

The MacLarens looked at each other, not surprised by this news. "I always knew the lad to be a romantic," said Gerald. Mistress MacLaren remained silent.

"Yes, well, they sealed their love, if you take my meaning."

It took only seconds before the lady of the house was on her feet, "Hannah, MacFey, do you mean to sit there and tell me you're are pregnant with my son's child?"

"Yes, I am," she replied. "We knew it would all be made legal the next day, but I don't believe either of us considered that a child would come to us so soon."

"Then tell me, if you would be so kind, how you know for certain that the child is his?"

This verbal slap left a cruel mark upon Hannah's cheeks. A blistering bile of indignation swelled in her throat, commanding release. So this is how her mother must have felt, all those times folk spoke in disparaging tones about an unwed mother. The fury on Hannah's face was not be denied as she shot out of her chair, facing Eglantyne MacLaren. "I will not have my child raised a bastard, as I was. This baby will know Lukas through me. If you choose to be a part of this baby's life, the decision is yours. I would prefer that, for I know that would be what Lukas wanted. But if I am to be too troublesome for your gentry ways, too embarrassing to have the weaver's daughter as mother to your grandchild, then I will leave this village and never return!"

The explosion of emotion caused Muriel to run crying from the room while the men just sat there, stunned. As if waking from a nightmare, Mr. MacLaren interrupted the ladies. "Wait, now Hannah, girl. Nobody is saying anything of the sort. You don't need to be running away from us just because your dander is up, heated and fired, but up nonetheless. Sit down, now, and let's think about this."

His calm voice of reason was the perfect balm to soothe Hannah's wounds brought about by years of rebukes. She knew the second she released the tirade that the true abusers lived throughout the village, not in this house. The MacLarens had never been anything but polite and kind to her. Although she still did not fully appreciate Mistress MacLaren's wedding plans for Lukas remaining in the gentry ranks when true love was in his heart, she knew the woman didn't hold anything against her personally.

"I am sorry," she whispered.

"As am I," said Mistress MacLaren. She stood, regal, and approaching Hannah, took the young highlander's hands in her own, forcing Hannah to look her in the face. "I put too much stock in my own foolish pride, forcing my boy into a loveless match when he had you, a strong woman with a fierce love for him. Please forgive me for not seeing the truth."

"I do," said Hannah, slowly rising into the open arms offered to her. The two held each other, the loss of Lukas, the loss of a son, a husband, all wrapped into one embrace. A few tears were shed as the women parted and regained their seats.

"Women!" whispered Michael to Brother Aidan.

"Right, well , I have an idea," said Gerald. "And if Father Logan is in agreement, I believe we have some quick work ahead of us." He turned to Hannah, "Dear Hannah, what would you say to a wedding, a legal binding of yourself to this family, eh?"

"To be honest," said Hannah, "during my travels I went by 'Hannah MacLaren' feeling more like his widow than his wife. I believe the name suits me, and I would be more than grateful to pass this name along to the child. But how?"

Gerald stood up and began pacing about the room. Phrases like "Malcolm could stand in" and "they were practically married anyway with the handfasting" and "need to make it legal."

Malcolm was the first to see the full picture, "Da, you're a genius! I would be honored to stand in for Lukas. We'll do it at the church, keep it small with just family."

"A wedding?" exclaimed Hannah, "a real wedding? I would have to invite Caitlin and Lally, but beyond them, and of course my father and Brother Aidan, that would suffice for my side." The weight of this afternoon's revelations dispelled like a fine mist. "Can we really do this?"

"Aye, that we can. I will head over to the church now and let you know this evening what Father Logan says. If he says yes, we'll not delay. We'll do it in two days' time!"

Rory, followed by Muriel rejoined the group when they heard shouts and laughter coming from the parlor. "What's going on?" asked Rory.

Mistress MacLaren took his hands and wheeled him about the room, "We're going to have a wedding!"

"I know, but that's not for a few weeks off."

"No, silly, not yours. Not yet. For Lukas and Hannah." Seeing the confusion on her son's face, she said, "Oh, run outside and go with your father. He'll explain everything." Then she turned to Muriel, who was beaming once more with the truth of innocence. "Now, my dear, we have some plans to make. Hannah, let's sit

down in the kitchen and see how you'd like to do the ceremony."
The women left the room as words like "flowers" and "cakes"
followed them.

"Well, gentleman," said Malcolm, "since my family has
apparently abandoned all good manners by leaving guests
unattended, shall I take you for a stroll around the farm? We've
some lovely views of the village. And I fear the ladies will be
making plans for quite some time." He grinned, a grander host was
never seen.

"We would be delighted," said Michael. Then looking at
Brother Aidan, he asked, "Shall we?" The monk simply rose,
taking his place once more by Michael's side as the three strode out
into the day.

Two hours later, the basic plans were laid to everyone's
satisfaction. Now all they needed was the pastor's approval. As
Hannah and her group were walking out the front door after fond
good-byes, Rory came running into the yard. "He said, yes,
Hannah! Father Logan said yes! It's all set for two days from now,
eleven o'clock in the morning."

She could hardly believe her ears, for such an occasion had
never been attempted in their fair village. He could easily have said
it did not follow the proper laws or procedures, yet here was her
miracle. She hugged Rory then Michael then Brother Aidan then
Rory again. There was too much joy for her body to contain, so she
had to spread it around. Rory ran inside to tell his family the good
news.

The threesome began their walk towards the church to visit
the cemetery when they came upon Gerald MacLaren. Having
completed a few errands after the meeting with Father Logan, he
was happy to run into the merry travelers.

"So, I see Rory told you the good news. Well, that's just
fine!" he said, a big smile crossing his gentle face. "I did have one
other thing to discuss you, Hannah, if you've a moment now."

"Certainly," she said.

"Since you are not going to remain in Feshiebridge, have you any thoughts to your cottage?"

In all the excitement about the wedding, Hannah clean forgot about offering this sale to the MacLarens. "Please forgive me," she said. "Lally mentioned this morning that you might consider buying it from me as a wedding gift to she and Rory. I can think of no better couple I would rather have living there, housing love there."

"Excellent! I was hoping you would say that. I have just come from the land agent's office, and we are comparing your farm, all out buildings, the animals, and the cottage to others in the area to determine a fair price. Since you will be staying a few more weeks till Rory's wedding, we can firm up the details later. Look at the money as a possible dowry for the child as well as a nest egg should you need one."

"You are too generous, sir," she said, and kissed him on the cheek.

"I will see you all soon, I am sure. Till then," he said and continued down the path.

As they reached the small stone rectory, Hannah guided Michael and Brother Aidan around to the left, past the blooming rose bushes and through a small, black iron gate. A low, stone wall encircled the cemetery while birch and hazel trees offered shade to its guests. Hannah wove her way among the headstones until she came to the one with a lamb below the name, the name of "Lukas MacLaren." She had plucked a few wildflowers as they walked here and now laid them on the ground in front of the stone. Michael and Brother Aidan stood silently behind her.

"Lukas," said Hannah, "I know your spirit is not here, but I wanted to tell you that I miss you, love, more than any words you could ever write. So we are to be wed after all, and the child will bear your name. I could only be happier if you were standing by my side. But do not worry for me now, for all will be well." She sighed, breathing in slowly and releasing the tension of her loss.

She gazed across the stones then cocked her head upward through the hazel branches when who should be watching her but a small blackbird. She was not surprised to see this feathered visitor. "You are here, I see. You have done right by me, watching over me at times when I needed clarity. Reminding me that life is meant to be lived, fully, placing my feet on the spiritual path by loving others. I know you can traverse realms, at least according to legend, so if you see my Lukas, you tell him I will be fine."

The bird trilled three times, nodded its head at Hannah then flew into the cerulean blue sky.

"Another friend?" asked Michael.

"You could say so," responded Hannah. "Now as to my mother's grave, I have no idea as to where it might be. Usually folks are buried near family, but since it was just she and myself, well I'm just not sure. Let's look around a bit."

They did not have to look long before they saw a new stone, underneath a white birch sapling. The stone was laid flat on the ground with her name boldly printed in capital letters: "ROSAMOND MACFEY." Underneath in small script were the words "Beloved mother and friend to all." Hannah suspected that only Mistress Stewart could be responsible for this kindness, making the funeral and burial arrangements, so she decided to reimburse the widow from the proceeds of the cottage sale.

The three stood before the stone, each lost in their own thoughts. Brother Aidan found himself drifting back to the Isle of Mull, to the recent funeral of his own mother and quietly bowed his head. Michael, for the first time in his life, had no words. Hannah could no longer hold back the tears. She wept openly as Michael placed his arm around her shoulders, each needing the other.

As a gentle soughing of wind blew through the leaves, they left in silence.

CHAPTER TWENTY-SEVEN

The next two days flew by in a flurry of baking, packing, and arranging. The baking included a new wedding cake, which Mistress MacLaren insisted on creating, along with a few other pastry delicacies for a simple reception at their home following the ceremony. The arranging included the flowers: the bride's bouquet, smaller ones for the two bridesmaids, Caitlin and Lally, then single blossoms for the groomsmen, now expanded from Malcolm and Rory to include Patrick as well. Caitlin refreshed the original ones, created last winter from dried flowers, with June blossoms. Seamus offered to play his fiddle for the musical accompaniment.

While the others continued with wedding plans, Hannah focused on packing up the house, assisted by Michael. Brother Aidan could be found outside shepherding the animals. Hannah opted to leave the larger household goods such as the table, chairs, and bedding for the newlyweds. As she considered the looms and all the weaving paraphernalia, she contacted the local guild, asking them to disperse these goods to other highland weavers. Hannah kept a small table loom and a bag of her favorite dyed wools for small projects. The packing for Hannah was stressful as she sorted through Rosamond's belongings, keeping a few of the dresses which fit both women and a few personal trinkets.

The new plan included Michael taking Hannah's providan, loom, and a few boxes with him to set up their new lodgings at the sang skule while Hannah kept enough clothing to get her through the next three weeks until Lally's wedding. The MacDonalds, Caitlin's family, offered their extra room to Hannah. It would not be necessary for her to remain alone in the cottage with painful memories still so close at hand. Besides, Rory asked if he could begin making any repairs needed to the cottage prior to his wedding, so the house would be ready when he crossed the threshold with his new bride, Lally.

The night before the wedding, Hannah slept fitfully. The recurring nightmare of being lost in the maze of the Perth Market began as always, with the colorful sights and enticing smells which pulls the child Hannah's attention away from her mother. Once lost, the child runs in a panic in search of her mother.

But then she saw the familiar braid, swinging down the aisle once more. "Ma!" she cried. "Ma, I'm here!"

But this time, things changed. No deadly scarves attempting to scare her, strangle her.

The scarves remained luscious, like floating birds on the winds. The woman with the long brown braid turned around, smiled, and opened her arms saying, "Hannah, come here, girl." She wrapped the child in a cocoon of love only a mother could offer, whispering sweet assurances which melted into the child's heart. "I will always be with you," she said then walked down the lane, carrying the small bundle of love she called her daughter.

Hannah lay exhausted on the sleeping pallet, her cheeks wet with tears. "I need you here today, Ma," she whispered. "I'm getting married, and I so need your strength." She willed herself out of bed, no longer surprised to smell breakfast cooking due to Brother Aidan's courteous nature. She found herself enjoying the added layer of protection to her life by this wondrous monk, whom Hannah determined had bound himself willingly, apparently for life, to Michael. The pact now would include Hannah and her child. She smiled, considering the good fortune that now surrounded her when only weeks ago she felt more than alone in this world. How life changes!

She had laid out her wedding dress the night before, hanging it from a low rafter. She bathed quickly behind the curtain, layered herself in bridal glory then taking a deep breath, drew the sleeping curtain aside to meet the day.

"Ah, there she is, the bride to be!" exclaimed Michael, opening his arms to her. She accepted his paternal embrace then found herself being flung into a ceilidh dance twirl. "Let's see you, then," he said, examining the wave of white folds topped with a green bodice which matched the forest hues of her hazel eyes while the light blue ribbons acted as if their floating arms would carry Hannah straight into the heavens. "I could not be more proud," he said, smiling.

She ended her twirl in a curtsy, saying, "Well, I thank you."

The trio feasted on oat bannocks with melted butter and honey along with fresh hot black tea. By 10:30, the bride was on her way to the church with Michael and Brother Aidan by her side. As they entered the small stone chapel, Brother Aidan drifted to the left side and up the aisle to the front row, so Michael could escort Hannah to the altar where the group was already assembled. Caitlin and Lally stood on the left side holding their flowers while Malcolm stood in the groom's position. He was flanked by Rory and Patrick while Seamus was seated in the choir section playing a soft, lilting air. The MacLarens and Muriel remained on the front row on the right, the groom's side.

Michael laid aside his cane then took Hannah's arm. "Here we go, darlin,' " he whispered. Hannah draped her arm through Michael's while holding her lovely bridal bouquet of yellows, purples, and white in the other.

She looked down the aisle to the expectant faces of the crowd waiting for her, each one ready to support her on this new path. The strangeness of the binding, to a man by her side that looked somewhat like her beloved but not Lukas, suddenly struck her. Yet by going through with this, she would be taking on not only his name but his entire family, in full acceptance of herself and their unborn child. Their open hearts had created this magical opportunity, and she knew she would be forever grateful.

"Ready," she replied. The two slowly walked forward and stood beside Malcolm at the altar.

"Shall we begin?" asked Father Logan.

Hannah nodded.

"Dearly Beloved, we are gathered together this day in the sight of God with true believers at witnesses to join this man, standing in for his brother Lukas MacLaren, and this woman,

Hannah MacFey, in holy matrimony. Affirming this is a legal and binding agreement, they do not enter in lightly. If there be any impediment as to why these two may not be joined, let it be brought forth at this time." He paused a moment while all took in the silence.

"Who gives this woman to this man?"

Michael looked at Hannah, whose eyes were now glistening in the bittersweet joy of the moment, "Her mother Rosamond MacFey and I myself, her father, Michael MacLeod." He kissed her on the cheek then joined Brother Aidan seated on the bride's side.

Hannah and Malcolm now turned toward the priest as he walked them through the vows. When it came time to exchange rings, Hannah lifted her hand while Malcolm placed the amethyst ring his brother had purchased on her finger.

"And now, if you two will hold hands while I give you a traditional blessing." Malcolm took Hannah's hand, giving her trembling fingers a conspiratorial squeeze.

> "The love and affection of the angel
>
> be to you,
>
> The love and affection of the saints
>
> be to you,
>
> The love and affection of heaven
>
> be to you,
>
> To guard you and to cherish you.
>
> May God shield you on every step,
>
> May Christ aid you on every path,
>
> May Spirit fill you on every slope,
>
> On hill and on plain,
>
> Each day and night of your lives.

Amen."

A soft "Amen" echoed off the stone walls.

"So by the power given to me by God and this parish, I now declare that Lukas and Hannah are married. What God has joined together, may no man put asunder. You may, uh " and here Father Logan paused, "hug your new sister-in-law," he concluded.

Gentle laughter rippled through the wooden beams overhead as Hannah and Malcolm embraced. Warm hugs and sentiments of gladness welcomed Hannah into the family. Rory and Lally could not keep their eyes, and often hands, off each other while Hannah noticed that the elder MacLaren lad kept glancing at Caitlin with a newly found respect. Seamus played a rollicking jig to keep up the jubilation of the occasion should any hints of sorrow tempt their way into this gathering. Michael and Hannah both offered thanks to Father Logan for accepting this extraordinary event. They signed the church records, along with Malcolm, who placed his signature below that of his brother's on the groom's line. Now it was done.

"Let's go eat!" shouted Rory, grabbing Lally by the hand and the leading the entire group toward the MacLaren farm. Muriel trotted after her parents and brothers while Caitlin seemed engrossed in a conversation with Malcolm. Patrick and Seamus seemed a bit subdued to Hannah as they left the church, each still mantled by the loss of their dear friend.

She kissed Michael on the cheek saying, "You and Brother Aidan walk on ahead. I think I'd like just a moment alone, please."

"As you wish, lass," said Michael, nodding to his trusted friend.

The harper and the monk caught up with the wedding party while Hannah took a long look across the fields toward the River Feshie. She breathed in the fresh highland pine scent, filling her soul with its ever deepening peace. She closed her eyes, envisioning their new life in Dunkeld, draped in love while surrounded by song. She placed her hand on her belly, then rubbing it slowly in a spiral pattern, she whispered, "I will name you Lukas, after your father."

Then it happened - that tingling of quicksilver running through her veins whenever Lukas was near. A soft breeze grazed her cheek. She lifted her hand to the spot, and with a grateful heart, said aloud, "I love you, too."

THE END

BALLADS

Seen in text as narrative, storytelling (in poetic stanzas) or song excerpts

Chapter One

"Riddles Wisely Expounded"

"Lord Thomas and Fair Annet"

Chapter Two

"Tam Lin" (narrative storytelling)

Chapter Three

"Come By the Hills"

"Lord Thomas and Fair Annet"

Chapter Five

"The Seeds of Love"

"Raglan Road"

"A Lover's Reflection"

Chapter Six

"The Farmer's Curst Wife"

"Our Goodman"

Chapter Seven

"A Lover's Reflection"

"Clohinne Winds"

Chapter Eight

"Seothin, Seo ho"

"Deep in Love"

Chapter Nine

"The Twa Sisters" or "Binnorie" (narrative storytelling)

Chapter Ten

"How Cormac Mac Art Went to Faerie"

"The Great Silkie of Sule Skerry"

 "Lament for Red-Haired John."

Chapter Fourteen

"The Lakes of Coolfin"

Chapter Twenty

"The Barnyards of Delgaty"

"Wild Mountain Thyme"

Chapter Twenty-One

"The Song of the Seal"

Chapter Twenty-Two

"The Wark O' the Weavers"

"Gradh Geal Mo Chridh"

ABOUT THE AUTHOR

My goal is not only to entertain audiences of all ages through written stories and performance, but also to provide a way for individuals to recapture their imaginations. The realms of fantasy and reality are parted by a thin veil. The timeless truths woven into folk and fairy tales give me this opportunity.

I find great importance in sharing the impact of writing on the human soul. The gentle power of the word heals the wounded heart and uplifts our spirits.

In "The Songweavers' Chronicles," not only are affairs of the heart considered, but I also explore the impact of songs in daily living. Ballads played an important role in ancient Celtic and British societies where balladeers sang of love, country life, hardships, supernatural encounters, court splendors, and folly. Discover their magic!

After reading , please help me spread the word by clicking on the link below where you can **LIKE** and **SHARE** my page with your friends.

www.facebook.com/songweaverhighlandheart

Check out options below for the next exciting tale of

"The Songweavers' Chronicles"

Hannah uncovers remarkable gifts and joy in the midst of great uncertainty.

RELEASE DATE:

June 2017

Celtic New Year

To purchase, visit

www.bobbiepell.com/store.html

Other books available on Amazon
by Bobbie Pell

When a woman plans her life, she never includes tragedy.

"Words on a page are powerful." A healing memoir.

Celtic settings, magic, mystery - rue love shines in realms of Faery!

Made in the USA
Columbia, SC
14 September 2022

66748749R00192